the
matrimonial
flirtations
of
emma
kaulfield

the
matrimonial
flirtations
of
emma
kaulfield

a novel

ANNA FISHBEYN

Arcade Publishing • New York

Arcade Publishing books may be purchased in bulk at special discounts for sales promotion, corporate gifts, fund-raising, or educational purposes. Special editions can also be created to specifications. For details, contact the Special Sales Department, Arcade Publishing, 307 West 36th Street, 11th Floor, New York, NY 10018 or arcade@skyhorsepublishing.com.

Arcade Publishing® is a registered trademark of Skyhorse Publishing, Inc.®, a Delaware corporation.

Visit our website at www.arcadepub.com.

10 9 8 7 6 5 4 3 2 1

Library of Congress Cataloging-in-Publication Data is available on file.

Cover design by Erin Seaward-Hiatt
Cover photo credit Nikki Harrison

Print ISBN: 978-1-62872-758-6
Ebook ISBN: 978-1-62872-760-9

Printed in the United States

Prologue

One is never too young to receive unhelpful advice on marriage. I was barely over the hill of my fifth birthday when my grandmother told me that marriage is not for the feeble-minded masses who so readily and pathetically jump into it as if they're chewing gum. "Make sure you don't pick a *shmata*, a hysteric, or a philanderer," she warned. When Grandmother read *Cinderella* to me, she went off on tangents about injustice in general and unjust marriages in particular, and how she and Cinderella were practically the same person: "I too worked five jobs, fought in the war, cleaned and cooked for every aunt and cousin this side of the Baltic, and suffered from ulcers and insomnia. But when I went to the ball, I put a cheery face on for the crowd and pranced on the dance floor in imported Italian leather pumps three times smaller than my size, like every woman I knew. Your grandfather came up to me and said, 'Do you have a smoke, gorgeous?' and I said, 'You should quit.' It was love at first insult."

"Was he a prince?" I asked. Grandmother laughed and said, "A prince with empty pockets and a few gold teeth!" Still, Grandmother didn't want to snuff out all my childish optimism. In her awkward way, she tried to assure me that there were glorious men out there, but they were hidden—and it was my task in life to find them. Only my older, blonder sister, Bella, thought that a prince with an impish sense of humor and our father's brilliant brain (male looks were considered irrelevant in our family) was prowling the streets in search of her, and that all she had to do was appear magically on our balcony, arch her back, fling her hair, and *poof*—she would be a happily married woman. But as far as I could tell, marriage was just the beginning of suffering, some black void of happiness that human beings fell into and then were never heard of again. I believed this not only because I was born in Russia, nourished on Pushkin, Tolstoy, Dostoyevksy, fatalistic grandmothers, Communist propaganda, bronze sculptures of Lenin, and a scarcity of toilet paper, but because every marriage I knew, including the one that produced me, was a volatile volcano bordering on adultery and divorce.

That is why, at the age of five, I told Bella that I would never get married, even if Perfection Personified waltzed through our front door, and by that I certainly did not mean some insipid prince. "What about your suitors," she countered, "don't you want to marry them?" Mitya and Andre were my first potential husbands, and since all such husbands tend to be accidents of convenience, they lived next door. Andre lived below us and was decisively handsome, which in kindergarten amounted to dark locks and a natural tan, but he had little to offer in the way of intellect and barely understood the concept of a joke. I had to resort to slapping him to get him to run after me and pull on my hair—a popular Russian expression of love in extremely shy or extremely bellicose men. Mitya, on the other hand, resembled an undernourished piglet with wispy blond hair and wide curious eyes, but he was a kind-hearted boy who bought me presents with his parents' money and was the first to propose. Andre soon followed suit and the two of them fought for my hand, quite literally, by pulling on my arms and screaming: "Lenochka is mine!" "No, she's mine!" Already a closet feminist, I pounced on them: "I am no one's, no one's, you hear!"

At home I posed a hypothetical question to my mother: "Why can't women have more than one husband?"

"Because women prefer to have lovers on the side," she replied bluntly, for my mother was a blunt woman, with a rebellious fire in her bright turquoise eyes and the sort of wide evocative forehead that belonged to uniquely independent minds. She believed that children, namely myself and my sister, were far wiser than adults in the ways of the human heart and should be consulted in all matters of love, regardless of their age.

"What's a lover?" I asked.

"A man who isn't your father but who makes your mother happy."

"Do you have one?"

"No, but I should," my mother said wistfully, and then Grandmother came in. These types of conversations did not sit well with my grandmother, who, in addition to being the self-anointed Cinderella, was the moral force of the family, the Yiddish-speaking Virgin Incarnate, the Jewish Mother Theresa, the superhuman female who held it all together and then some.

"Mitya and Andre want to marry me," I told Grandmother. "They almost tore my arms out."

"That's how they always are in the beginning—men!" Grandmother moaned. "Prostrating themselves like pathetic dogs, but once you give them your heart, they'll step on it and then cheat on you to let you know they really care." She said this not only because my grandfather was a notorious philanderer—his list of women stretched all the way to Latvia and Odessa—but because Grandmother was too righteous to cheat back.

Then my mother turned to me with a serious gaze. "Remember, Lenochka, in the tricky business of predicting fidelity, age is an irrelevant factor, as are a man's looks." At which point my mother and grandmother leapt to discuss their theory of Russian men, which they felt perfectly captured the ordeal of being a Russian woman. It held that men who are uglier and shorter are more likely to cheat, since they are more insecure and too often suffer from the taxing Napoleon complex. Although they tend to have serious expertise in bed, it doesn't make up for their constant need to be buttered up and flattered by their mistresses. Due to their physical inadequacies, they tend to develop an oversized brain because they know a Russian woman goes limp in the knees when a man can recite all of *Evgeni Onegin*. The handsome ones, however, are always being pawed by adoring women and have to fight off superhuman temptations, which is an unrealistic goal. Their beauty makes them feel overly content with their brains, and as a result, not only do they have feeble memories, but they are usually selfish and uneventful lovers.

Although this theory was liberally applied to other women's husbands, my own handsome father was never subjected to its rigid laws. Grandmother believed that my mother lucked out with my father. First there were the essentials: he did *not* beat her, cheat on her, deal on the black market, drink enormous quantities of vodka, or refuse to take showers like some men they knew. "You're never gonna find a man as good as your Semeyon, *tfu, tfu, tfu,*" she would exclaim and knock on wood whenever my mother complained about my father. "Besides, no man is perfect," Grandmother would offer as an afterthought.

My mother would discover how true this particular afterthought was after that mysterious day in September of 1975 when Lana Rubin, our neighbor upstairs, burst into our apartment on Usiyevicha Street breathless with news.

"Jews are being let out!" she exclaimed, her face red and sweaty from the excitement. "My cousin and his wife are already applying for their exit visas."

"Are you sure we won't get arrested?" my mother asked.

"I don't know, but we can leave Russia! Can you imagine that?" No one could imagine that.

But a few months later, Lana's news was confirmed by Yakov, my father's older brother: a man who cheated on his wife, dealt on the black market, drank liberal amounts of vodka, and possessed few redeeming features on his pudgy perpetually red face. My mother and grandmother had long ago consigned Yakov to that category of men who lack the essentials. Against the backdrop of my father, Yakov appeared like an amusing mutation of all the wrong genes. Yet his bold move to start the application process early, to imagine a happier future in America when everyone else became morbidly pale from this very thought, impressed my mother. "He's got guts!" my mother announced. To which my father responded with an avalanche of criticisms: Yakov was a heartless letch, a materialist, the depraved son willing to abandon his mother for a wealthier life in America. "What does he want with more money?" my father threw out indignantly. "He already has enough here." "It's not about the money," my mother held, "it's about freedom." "The freedom to speculate?" my father roared. "Anything would be better than this, this"—here my mother pointed to her throat and squeezed it—"they suffocate you here." "I'm never leaving my mother," my father declared, "and that's the end of the discussion." But with each passing month, as others began to gather documents and whisper of a life beyond Soviet borders, Yakov became in my mother's eye a man of courage and vision, a prince in the garb of a frog. When a year later Yakov received permission to leave the Soviet Union with his wife, Katya, and his son from a previous marriage, Valeryi, my mother had a revelation: *we too* could leave. At their going-away party, dancing wildly on Yakov's parquet floors, her head buzzing with champagne and foreign music, my mother began to dream of her own going-away party, while my father dreamed of a life without Yakov.

When my parents returned from the airport after watching Yakov, Katya, and Valeryi board the plane to Vienna, the first stopover on their long journey to the United States, they were no longer on speaking terms. According to Grandmother, it was my mother's fault, as she indelicately told my father that he was a smelly *mudila* (my mother's endearing take on that succinct Russian swear word *mudak* that captured all the negative sides of a man's personality: idiot, asshole, imbecile, liar, and nag). My father retaliated by ordering my mother to shove herself up her own ass, and go marry Yakov. But when, in self-defense, my mother accused him of uttering an illogical syllogism, my father could only inhale gasoline reeking from a Russian cab and push waves of nausea back down his throat (as he was a very sensitive individual), which in turn led to self-pity and paralysis of the tongue. My mother continued to berate him, but after all, she was only human, and as my father said nothing, she lost interest in him.

She looked out the window and imagined a more valiant husband for herself, floating somewhere above the buildings bedecked in placards of Stalin and Lenin.

For the next several years, talk of emigrating would consume the Jews of Moscow, eating away at their daily routines, their Saturday night festivities, their thoughts before going to sleep and upon waking up. Their abstracted gazes followed them to their jobs, to the lavish Moscow subway adorned in mosaics and bronze heads of Lenin, and to long lines of waiting for meat, bread, and Italian leather boots. Recent updates on who was going, who was thinking of going, and who would never go became the focus of every hushed conversation. There was the couple downstairs who had been arrested at the last minute, the husband who had been a physicist for the military and would surely be denied permission to leave, and strange unexplained cases of many others who had been refused for no apparent reason—families with packed suitcases, sold furniture, and lost jobs.

Then there was Lana Rubin, who, after much haggling with her husband, had finally put her application documents in the mail exactly two years after our own Yakov left. "This business is not for the weak," she told my mother. "You have to contact a 'relative' in Israel, get them to 'invite' you, get an exit visa from the KGB, get yourself out of the Communist Party, sell all your furniture to pay 'taxes' in order to be able to actually leave—" Her voice faltered. "They hold meetings, call people, pass out flyers, and seat you on a stool in front of hundreds of die-hard patriots, including your own co-workers. Everyone starts yelling at you all at once—profanities, you know, 'you fucking *blyat*,' they say, 'you traitor of the motherland! Russia fed you, bathed you, educated you and now you're abandoning it for money, for fat capitalists! We're your friends, you treacherous Yid!' They cry out as though you're stabbing them with a knife. 'Decided to become a Zionist, did you? You dirty *Zhid*, you think Russia isn't good enough for you anymore!' Oh, the humiliation of it all! I had to do it, but Osik didn't—he's still working, staying under the radar. He says, 'What are we going to live on?'" Her face fell into her hands.

Through stilted breaths, she muttered, "No one knows anything! Who knows if we'll ever get out, and I don't have a job now—Oh, *Bozhenka* help us!"

Only when we were in America did I find out that as soon as our applications were received in OVIR, the Bureau of Immigration Affairs, we were branded traitors to the motherland and our citizenship was altered to a new status: people "*v podache*"—those waiting to get out. Banned from the Communist Party, my parents could no longer hold onto their jobs—an unthinkable concept under the theoretical tenets of Communism. "If you don't work, you don't eat bread," the slogans read. We became *tuniyadtzyi*—in the language of our favorite Politburo writers, parasites gnawing on the efficiency and beneficence of our great Soviet State, subject to arrest and a vague prison term.

In those years, no one knew why Jews were being allowed to leave the Soviet Union, while no other ethnicity—not the Georgians, the Ukrainians, the Lithuanians, the Belarusians, not even the native Russians could step beyond its iron borders. Beneath their dutiful Communist veneers, there were those who thirsted for the forbidden West, and envy fanned their centuries-old anti-Semitism. False reports of murders committed by people with Jewish last names began flooding newspapers and evening news. Bank robberies and small petty crimes that never took place were unequivocally committed by Jews, so that in addition to having to state our nationality as Jew on the fifth line of our passports, we could barely finish saying our last name before the comments started pouring in. Sometimes there would be an "Oh," or an "Aha," but most of the time people were very sympathetic, especially face to face. As soon as I said "Lena Kabelmacher," people wanted to give me the benefit of the doubt: "Are you sure you're an authentic Jew, or did your mother sin with a Slav?" Ludmilla Nicholayevna, my third grade teacher, complimented me by saying that even though I was a Jew, I didn't act or look like one, and that was why I was so well liked by my classmates. To carry such honor upon my young shoulders brought me enormous happiness indeed! We certainly weren't your stereotypical Jews, or so the Russians said, "because you have light hair and small straight noses, and because you're clean and good looking and because you're not petty and dirty and don't steal other people's money." Although we didn't know any truly stereotypical Jews, we believed that somewhere out there lurking in the corners of our building, hiding in the alleyways, stealthily creeping up our water pipes, were those real Jews, the dark-haired, crooked-nosed thieves who made us all suffer and accept this hatred as due justice for *their* sins. And we looked for vestiges of them in our friends, our relatives, ourselves. That's too Jewish, we'd say, or what a Yid she is, about someone who was ill-mannered or ungenerous.

From the moment we heard about the first wave of Jews leaving Russia, beginning in the early 1970s, not a week went by that my parents did not argue over the imaginary pros and cons of living in America. Since almost nothing was known about the West, these pros and cons were direct quotes from Yakov's letters. It was three years since he settled in Chicago, a city famous in Moscow for gangsters and high crime rates. But in his letters Yakov painted a picture of paradise on earth. One such letter took a particularly vicious hold of my mind and grew, as it were, into my own odd fantasy of a capitalist empire:

Dear Sonya and Semeyon,

Forgive me for such a long absence, but America is a very busy country. It is a sad business indeed that I have no time for our venerable Pushkin. My Russian has deteriorated and I can't make a frog's legs out of English. Americans treat us like we're mentally impaired or possibly deaf. They're always screaming at us, but no matter how loud they are, we still don't understand them. Katya takes classes at the local community college, but they don't help. I tell her she needs an American lover to immerse herself in this barbarian language, but she doesn't laugh at my jokes anymore. Only our Valerichka has become fluent and is now socializing with real-life Americans. Katya and I have turned into his children. We depend on him for everything—grocery shopping, bills, and ordering food in restaurants, and so now he's embarrassed of us. What's the world coming to?

But these gripes aside and the recent shooting on our block, America is an extraordinary place, full of happy surprises. Just the other day we found a blue satin couch in perfect condition right behind our building in what the Americans call their garbage dump. This garbage dump is full of wonders, and we are constantly examining it in case someone might have thrown out a valuable chest as we're drowning in old shit from Russia that Katya refuses to throw out. She suffers from the nostalgia disease that afflicts all the other sentimental immigrants we drink tea with, and whose nonsense I have to endure because Katya says we've become misanthropes. Nostalgia has not afflicted me in the least. All I need to do, if I'm feeling slightly nostalgic, is visit a place called the supermarket—an enormous store that has no analogue with anything we had in Moscow. You can buy meat and vegetables and toilet paper and a toothbrush, and whatever else your heart desires. It is so enormous one could only compare it to a Soviet hockey stadium, only with aisles. There is so much of everything you want to tear your hair out, and bow your head to the Capitalist devils!

Katya wants to buy everything, but we just don't have the money. Of course, like all women, she refuses to hear any logic and is always foisting new American customs on me, which usually translates into spending more money. She says that Americans use three or four different kinds of shampoos on their hair, and has forced me to do the same. Garik, our neighbor, says Americans take showers very seriously, and if your armpits have a natural odor, you could get fired from your job. One cannot account for all their mishugas, but I have Katya smell me before I leave for work every morning, just in case. Katya says we are getting too fat and dull, that we don't look like ourselves anymore. I blame it on a spectacular place called McDonalds. The potatoes are to die for, and they serve their katletta with cheese melted on top.

The best news of all is that I just got a job as an accountant for 19 thousand dollars a year! All the other Russians are going *into computers, but I'm shooting for the stars. Speaking of stars, I hear through the grapevine that dentists make millions here. Can you believe it, Semeyon, I used to make 1300 rubles a year as a dentist? I can't imagine what people do with all that money.*

"There is black tar," my mother whispered, "over the next five lines."

"Lana says her letters are practically blacked out. They're censoring everyone these days," Grandmother said.

"They're not censoring enough!" my father spat.

"What's at the end?" I asked, trying to stave off another parental scuffle.

We send all our love, and two pairs of jeans for the girls,
We kiss you, Yakov, Katya, and Valeryi.

My mother re-read this letter to the family like a religious chant to convince us that our future lay elsewhere—in this strange magical world we had been programmed from youth to hate. But the letter did not weaken my father's resistance; it only fortified it. "What did I tell you," he'd yell, "all he writes about is money." Staring accusingly at my mother, he'd say, "And where is there any mention of your precious freedom?"

But in 1978, after I had returned from the Camp for Intellectuals, I took to bed. An illness overtook me whose only symptoms were fatigue, a loss of appetite, and an inexplicable apathy to schoolwork. I, the straight-A high achiever, activities enthusiast, winner of numerous poetry and art awards, and the chief star in the school's theatrical production of *Pioneers Take Over the World*, complained of a headache so severe that it ruined my concentration and humiliated me in front of Lenin, our omniscient, red-headed God. After highly regarded doctors prescribed the infallible treatment of tea with honey, vitamin C powders, and raw eggs taken three times a day, and still there was no improvement, my mother was forced to consider the one diagnosis that had no name in Mother Russia: depression.

My father bought a sketchpad for me, a gift from the black market with small letters engraved at the top. It said DLYA HUDOZHNIKA, For the Artist. "You have an excellent eye for human faces," my father told me. "Perhaps if you draw your thoughts, you'll feel better." With a single black pen, I began to draw the faces, faces jutting from black shadows, monsters lit against the sun, eyes alive, untethered, floating, from normalcy to chaos, from black chaos into calm.

My mother knew enough about the monsters in the white birch forest to realize that the Camp for Intellectuals had become my nightmare, my indelible Russian scar. But what I told her and Grandmother and Father and Bella that day, when they demanded with typical Soviet zeal to know "everything," would become my mother's scar as well. There had been other incidents before this one—some troubling, others mere manifestations of the everyday fare of being a Jew in Russia—but none invaded my mother's soul as pervasively as the one that marked the summer of 1978 at that camp. The final disaster, as we came to call it in the family, convinced my mother that to remain in Russia would be an act of great cowardice and inhumanity to her children. She never spoke of it again, perhaps because it was unbearable to repeat it, but when my mother uttered the word "anti-Semitism," I knew she was referring specifically to what happened to me.

I was afraid of my mother during those years. She was not a particularly tall or heavy woman, but there was so much air and power in her gait that one had to step aside to give her room to pass. When she smiled, it was at once a moment of relief and pleasure, as though you had been doused in warm, perfumed water. She worked at one of Moscow's prestigious literary establishments as an editor, censoring poetry and novels, while secretly typing an anti-Soviet manuscript—part poem, part manifesto— she kept hidden in my room. And while her face had the large, thin, aristocratic features long associated with writers, she was wonderfully voluptuous and her skin melted under your fingers like smooth white velvet: the "perfect woman," many men had said. Yet when she became angry, walls and carpets and parquet floors seemed to grow angry, too, and I often wondered as a child whether the sky itself, with its darkening clouds and elusive sun, reflected my mother's moods. Her fury was indignant and pure, a typhoon rising up her neck into her nostrils and unfurling at the top of her lustrous, russet-colored head. One inevitably felt that she was right.

When my father still appeared to be in the throes of indecision about whether or not to apply for an exit visa, my mother called him a festering glob of mucus without balls and my father, for his part, demoted her to a yelping bitch doomed to wag her tail in fantasy all her life. These two insults captured the gist of all their protracted, foul-mouthed, foot-stomping, document-throwing fights. My parents' quarrels became more vitriolic and physically demanding with each passing month that saw my father gather application documents and then hide them from my mother. They blamed each other for my suffering, and broke two porcelain plates, three gold-rimmed shot glasses, and one Chinese vase along the way. My mother battled paralyzing migraines, and my father complained of numbness in the right side of his face and pain in his lower back. Yet despite these ominous symptoms or perhaps because of them, my father finally caved in under the great force that was my mother, the sort of force an ordinary man like him could not have withstood, and the question itself—whether to apply—ended on May 15, 1980, when my father put all the required documents in the mailbox. On that day, we entered the official state of limbo, and the interminable wait began. By then, Russia was at war with Afghanistan, America had boycotted the Russian Olympics, and the iron door had practically slammed shut. Every day Jews were receiving rejections, acquiring a new status known as "refuseniks," people forced to remain in Russia as official traitors, people with packed suitcases and sold furniture and no jobs and lost hope. We weren't them yet, but we were late bloomers, truants playing high-stakes *durak* with our lives.

My father was a professor of mathematics at Moscow State University, a position so difficult for a Jew to obtain and keep that he felt at thirty-eight he had reached the pinnacle of his career, and that from this point on he could only slide downward. He had published extensively, was lovingly dubbed "Jew-genius" among his colleagues, and even had visits from government officials for consultations. Although he protested against America on the grounds that he did not want to abandon his mother in Kiev, everyone in the family suspected that my father was equally loath to leave his illustrious career. The university atmosphere was so saturated with recruits from the KGB that once the documents had been mailed, my father had no choice but to announce his resignation.

That same day he plunged into an abysmal depression. He moped around the apartment, pretended to study English, and played cards with my grandfather, downing vodka like a goy. Eventually, to make money, he began tutoring children in math as an underground operation—the underground being the bedroom he shared with my mother. Private practice was illegal, and the fear of being discovered caused my father to develop a slight tremor in his right leg, one that he would carry with him to America as a kind of strange memento.

My father was a mild-mannered thinker who suffered from too much contemplation and had a quiet, snorting laugh. When he did get angry, he also shook but with a nervous twitch that made you suspect he was hiding something. Rather than fearing him, we usually felt sorry for him and wished for his outburst to subside and leave him in peace, primarily because he was blessed with a calm, handsome face and his wrath invariably contorted his otherwise perfect features. Although some people considered their cumulative beauty to be proof that good looks bring one success in life, for my mother and father it ended up being a curse.

My father's forlorn brown eyes, strong aquiline nose, and high contemplative forehead attracted swarms of women. They advanced on my father like royal knights about to attack, their tits in metal armor pressing into his tender flesh in my mother's presence. One was at once entertained and disgusted by their roaming hands, their veiled sexual laughter and cleverly constructed compliments—the sort one's wife could never in good conscience make. With one touch, one lick of a lip, one inviting glance, they made adultery meaningless and yet somehow full of suffering and soul. They were the beacons of tradition, the torchbearers of Russia's romanticization of adultery. And since the sexual consummation of adultery was not nearly as important as the act of stealing a spouse from his or her nest, married couples were always in high demand. Married men and women were almost unanimously disillusioned, hungry for any crumb of romance, determined to recreate their youthful ambition of loving passionately, wildly, and unreservedly the way aristocrats loved in the time of Pushkin and Tolstoy; they too were destined to be Anna Kareninas and Vronskys (without, of course, the ensuing suicide).

So it often happened that one of my mother's married girlfriends would settle in my father's lap, squeeze his temples, and play joyously with his curly yellow hair. Although my father had two thinning spots on his head that shone brightly under lamps, women never minded. Looks were not a requirement for men in the easy business of committing adultery, and my father had more looks to offer than most men. But like most men, my father could never send the women away—I can think of at least three that pressed their breasts into his nose in my very presence—because he suffered from a perverse politeness, even though he could see, through the back of his skull, blood igniting my mother's pale face. He could anticipate within milliseconds of the offending woman's departure when the screaming would begin. His only defense would be a mild-voiced murmur: "What was I supposed to do— beat her till she got off my lap?" "My dearest *mudila*," my mother would begin, "there are so many polite approaches at your disposal, like asking the woman where her husband is, or declaring that you adore your wife and your wife—your *wife*—is the most gorgeous woman in the room!" "That's for you women to squabble over," my father would chuckle maliciously. "Oh, I see! Then might I suggest popping her forehead!" At which point my mother would press her thumb and middle finger together and make a loud snap against my father's head. "You ungrateful coward—you perfidious traitor!" she'd rail. But my father felt helpless in the face of these straying women. Or perhaps he harbored hidden pleasures at the attention he received. For if you considered the matter closely, you would see how deeply my father enjoyed goading my mother. My mother's anger and jealousy calmed his nerves, lifted him into the echelons of power, gave him an exaggerated sense of his own virility and value as a man. Her jealousy was the one thing he held over her. Her jealousy was the one moment between them when he did not have to feel stifled by the righteous wind in her lungs.

But at Lana Rubin's going-away party, at the height of his mind-compressing depression, my father latched on to one woman with particularly large breasts, a pudgy upturned nose, and badly colored blonde hair. She laughed at all his jokes, even when he wasn't making any, stroked his head in that soft manner women adopt when they envision themselves as mistresses, and pressed her oversized breasts into his nose to help him orient himself in the world. But worst of all, she was married to one of our relatives, on my mother's side, which gave this situation a most unsavory flavor, the sort that always ruins a good yarn about infidelity. To have bleached frizzy hair and be related, to wear so much cheap perfume that we could taste it on our tongues and be related, to have pockmarks on her cheeks that were badly concealed by Russia's defective powders and be related, *that* riled my mother more than the actual concept of her husband having an affair. The very image of the two fornicating nauseated my mother, and at night, we could hear her vomiting in our toilet. But my grandmother pointed out that my father needed a woman inferior to himself, that it was Djenna's inferiority that made her so sweetly appealing and drove my poor father into her bulbous arms, that *man's insecurity* was the principal cause of adultery, which in turn convinced the man that he was blameless and that it was his wife's fault, after all, that he was fucking her third cousin-in-law.

My mother responded to this smirch on her dignity by taking herself a lover. This lover happened to be a student of my father's from the university, one of the few loyal souls who still admired my father and was a frequent guest at our dinner parties. He was a decade younger than my mother, and while my father was finely sculpted in face and thin in body, the lover was bulky and coarse, a round-faced, pink-cheeked young man with a loud, infectious laugh and dazzling green eyes. A *chazar*, Grandmother called him, a goy—my mother's adolescent rebellion. But unlike my father, my mother fell deeply, irrevocably in love. She became chirpy, frighteningly energetic, and visibly shinier, as though love was the very cause of grease in your T-zone. Her skin glistened in the sun or under a warm lamp, heightening the perfection of her features, and at the same time making one want to dab her with a handkerchief. Her expressions acquired a new vibrancy and impatience with the world, as though she were flying off somewhere and people took too long to finish their sentences. The anger receded into some imperceptible corner of her mouth that would twitch and then not be seen again. At the same time, she took up smoking, started drinking more, and her hands trembled from an escalating nervousness that forced her to put glasses or plates down until she could regain her composure. For a while Bella and I supposed it was the stress of having to wait for the government's permission slip, but eventually through eavesdropping we learned the truth.

Bella and I were always spying on the adults. Their lives seemed to us full of glamor and decadence: parties that lasted into the morning hours, rows of vodka and champagne bottles, plates overflowing with caviar and herring and *vobla*, lovers lurking in darkened corners, talented fingers of some engineer or physicist strumming on a guitar, operatic voices of perfectly sculpted women who dreamed of being on stage, dancing that erupted after midnight and shook our parquet floors until the sun settled in the sky. It was this incessant humming, the constant pulse of a world that never slept—a world we could not yet inhabit but only observe from doorways perched on our father's shoulders—that kept us awake at night and gave our imaginations undue freedom. Between the two of us, we knew almost everything, collecting in our large bag of adult secrets their fights, their jealousies, their sins. What Bella missed because she was taller, older, and more visible than me, I seized with my small eyes and ears. With the double affair in our house, it was impossible not to feel tension coiling round our necks like Stalin's phantom hand waiting to suffocate us all. But when our parents passed each other in the hallway, their heads cocked in affected disgust, they remained civil and orderly, never daring to confront one another in the open. This heroism was quietly commended by all their friends: Look at the Kabelmachers, they would say, they have problems but they wisely keep them to themselves. It was distinctly Russian wisdom.

My mother and grandmother spoke of my mother's affair in strained voices, whispers broken by shrieks, percolating our narrow halls with a current of nervous desperation. One morning on my way to breakfast, I heard Grandmother Zinayida say, "You have to end it! I don't care what it costs you—I'm sick and tired of your feelings!"

My mother, who rarely let out a tear, was weeping.

"Do you want to stay here?" Grandmother yelled, her face turning mauve. "Leave your children in this country after what Lenochka went through—"

"You have to understand, Mother, I never intended it, never!"

"Oh, you intended it all right," Grandmother said, "but now it seems like you've forgotten who you are, what your purpose in life is! I can understand a few months, a few nights, but this has gone on for over a year, and you're starting to scare me, Sonichka. Are you getting serious with him? He's a student, a green-faced child—what can he offer you?"

"He's so smart and ambitious—he'll have a brilliant career in the States—"

"You're going to ask for a *divorce*?" Grandmother lowered her voice as though someone was about to be arrested. "Have you lost your mind—have you forgotten that you have children?"

"The children will come with me—with, with *us*, and you'll come with us," my mother whimpered, looking beseechingly at my grandmother.

"No," my grandmother shot back, her glare like a spear glistened between them. "If you do that, Semeyon will stay here in

Russia and ask for his old job back. And don't think he won't try to keep the children here, with him, with his mother—it's too much of a risk—besides, he's a good father, despite everything."

"He started all this," my mother snapped.

"All men are the same in this respect," Grandmother noted reassuringly, "but he'll leave her—she hasn't made a dent on him. He needs her now because you've been too hard on him—you've always been too much! But look at what this has done to you—you're a wreck!"

"Lenochka," my mother cried out upon seeing me behind the kitchen door. "What are you doing there?"

"Nothing." I played innocent. "Just wanted some caviar—why are you crying?"

My mother scooped me up in her arms and murmured, "When you fall in love, Lenochka, make sure it's pure, untainted by other considerations, search your soul to figure out if it's truly love—"

"Why are you feeding her idealistic nonsense from romance novels? Reality—you have to make your children face reality at an early age! There's no love out there, no Prince Charmings—only tireless cheaters and accidental ones," Grandmother assured me.

"Are you fighting with Daddy?" I asked, but only to convince Grandmother that I didn't understand anything. Bella and I knew that our mother wasn't in love with our father anymore, and that our father's loquacious student who played *durak* with us after midnight was my mother's secret friend—a suitor not unlike the suitors who proposed marriage to Bella and me.

"No, of course not," my mother said, instinctively denying everything. "I'm just worried about the exit visas—they're not here and time is—time is passing—"

"We *are* going to America," my grandmother announced, as if this too were an unalterable reality.

"Will I have to be friends with capitalists?" I asked.

"That's just propaganda," my mother said. "The government wants you to believe that capitalists are evil, but they're not any different from us—we're all human beings, aren't we?" She glanced at Grandmother in search of a crutch to lean on, her face slack from loss of confidence. But Grandmother wouldn't budge, crushing my mother with her silence.

"I know, I know, propaganda is a bunch of bureaucratic lies," I announced.

"Who told you that?"

"Bella!"

"Well, don't speak of this to anyone at school. Nothing that is said in this house must go out that door," my mother said, pointing at the kitchen door. "Nothing, nothing!"

"You have to be smart, Lenochka," Grandmother finally said, her eyes resting on my mother. "We all have to be smart."

Grandmother's face grew hard and pale, and rigid lines sank into her skin. She extracted four eggs from the refrigerator and smashed them against the table counter. The sound of the whisk against the bowl seemed to end this conversation in the affirmative and announce the imposition of a new silence.

Ten days later, on March 8, 1982, the government's answer came in a simple white envelope with the words THE BUREAU OF IMMIGRATION AFFAIRS printed on top. Inside, we found the words PERMISSION GRANTED in black bold-faced letters, officially stamped and signed by the KGB, and detailed instructions on how to leave Russia. We had exactly two months to sell all our belongings, collect two thousand rubles to pay off the KGB, and pack one suitcase per person, excluding all items that might be deemed treasures of Mother Russia. The definition of a "treasure" was vague, and as we soon found out, anything could be deemed a property of the Soviet Union: Grandmother's emerald earrings that she inherited from her great-great-grandmother, my mother's black shawl embroidered in silk flowers, my father's gold medals for math competitions awarded to him by the university, and of course, our prized collection of Pushkin's poetry that took my parents fifteen years on the waiting list to get.

We made a family pact that same month, as the permission slip sat grimly on my father's desk, that no matter who we loved or confided in, which teacher was most attached to me and Bella, which of our friends would be most devastated by our departure, we would never tell anyone that we were leaving: we would pretend to eat, drink, live, love in "normalcy," in a stew of lies, our new shroud of protection against the ever-watchful eye of the KGB. Our impending departure was always a conjecture, a hope, never a fait accompli. The KGB worked randomly but consciously, each family surveilled, the permission slip always under the threat of being revoked. In secret, without ever speaking out loud, we said our goodbyes to the things and people we loved, to Moscow, to the past, to our own selves. Both of my parents mourned the lovers they'd have to abandon; fifteen-year-old Bella abandoned her virginity one night to a man twice her age at a drunken ball; I had my suitors to excise from my consciousness; and Grandmother had to leave a circle of close-knit gossipers and a dead husband. My grandfather was beaten by the KGB and died of a heart attack a few short months before we received our permission to leave, so we understood the importance of silence. Bella and I continued to go to school and music lessons, Grandmother stood in line at the meat market and gossiped with the old ladies on benches, Father continued to teach underground inside our apartment, and my mother sold our furniture and China and Persian rugs to relatives and friends to raise enough money to pay off the KGB to ensure the "legitimacy" of our exit visas and the "verification" of our passports.

Within the privacy of our homes we were turning into ghosts, wandering in and out of stores, roaming the streets, haunting our parks, absenting conversations for our minds were elsewhere, spinning from fear and uncertainty, breathing in the thrill of the unknown. Each day carried us toward some imperceptible end, each day was a ritual of death: our clothes were packed, our furniture sold off, our apartment emptied of our belongings, pictures, memories, our bodies followed weekly by the KGB. Yet I maintained my straight-A record, continued with the violin and piano and drawing lessons, scheduled a violin recital in June when I'd be long gone, painted a portrait of my grandmother I'd never take with me or see hung as a lasting memorial in my school's hallway.

To Andrei and Mitya I pretended to deliberate marriage as before, citing my youthful age of nine and a love for them both as reasons for my perpetual indecisiveness. But in my mind I was already being chased by English-speaking ruffians, and alone in my room, I would invoke mangled Russian words and guttural sounds to create a foreign language, the language of my future love affairs. On June 2, 1982, my parents woke me up at five in the morning and we stole away in a taxi with all our belongings squeezed between our knees, and my two suitors remained, wondering for years how all the Kabelmachers could so suddenly, so inexplicably, disappear.

PART I

15 Years Later . . .

The Extraordinary Powers of Raw Garlic

My grandmother thinks that with my looks and figure I should have been married four times by now. When I remind her that I'm only twenty-four, a mere infant by American standards, Grandmother assures me that Americans have very low standards, and American women are currently drowning in the putrid waters of spinsterhood. "When are you going to have children?" she moans, "in your thirties, God forbid?" These discussions have no actual point except to prove to me that while we may physically be living in America, mentally we are still stuck in Russia.

Grandmother chose a groom for me during my senior year in college while I was dating someone else. In theory he was my perfect mate: a Russian Jew like me, with a BA from the University of Chicago, my alma mater, and a future in internal medicine to cure me of all my real and imagined illnesses. In reality he was a mule, who redoubled his wooing efforts when he found out that my boyfriend was undecided about his major. I received mass deliveries of red gardenias, regular invitations to dinner at Château Le Tiff (or Miff) and such delicate assurances as "I just want to be friends," which could easily have meant "Let's have friendly sex." It took an emergency intervention by Grandmother to keep his family from ruining my family's good name after I told him in plain Russian to fuck off. When I raised these facts against him,

Grandmother nodded her head in approval and said, "Now there's a real man." By which she meant that my boyfriend was not.

To define a real man is a very difficult business indeed, but my grandmother is an expert in this field. I shall attempt to capture the highlights here.

1. A real man can withstand a woman's emotional outburst without having one himself.
2. A real man has to rise above the debasing insults of a marital squabble and, regardless of whether he is right (no one but Grandmother was right all the time), apologize for everything.
3. A real man always wakes up early in the morning. Waking up at noon or in the taboo hours of a late afternoon can get him instantly demoted to a sloth, which, in real-man speak, is akin to a pussy.
4. A real man will not complain about his current job even if in the motherland he was once a prodigy violinist, pianist, or a philandering conductor; an engineer, chemical or otherwise, who also by the way wrote poetry in his spare time; a mathematician, physicist, chemist, or any other scientific subfield with unscientific hobbies; a dentist, surgeon, obstetrician, or a KGB-employed psychiatrist; a black market specialist; a director of an X factory or rising star in a fledgling computer industry. He has to endure his new humiliations with the courage and willpower of a war hero, and try not to focus too much on the fact that he's now a cab driver, a driving instructor, a fixer of broken typewriters, a hotel janitor, an uncertified masseuse, a mover of boxes, a liquor store cashier, or, saddest of all, an unemployed intellectual.
5. A real man is always a cauldron of ambition, striving to rise, to transcend his current mess, to look at his English not as a done deal, but as a trajectory leading to self-improvement, and finally never feel offended when his wife

corrects his pronunciation, because a real man has bound-
less reserves of confidence.

6. Finally (or not so finally), a real man, under no circumstances, would major in the humanities, which oddly
enough included philosophy, literature, and drama, but
not history. History majors sat on the borderline of real
manhood, in that they were still technically real but so boring that they failed to inspire the passions of a real woman.

I knew very early in life that I would never find myself a "real" man,
nor did I want to. Unlike many women I knew, I did not suffer
from the panic of no longer being a virgin and remaining unmarried. Although my sister was not one of these women (she felt that
the whole point of emigrating to America was to free ourselves
from Soviet idolatry of virgins), she was still deeply affected by
Grandmother's lectures on the pitfalls of slutdom, and believed,
possibly in tandem with Grandmother, that a prolonged single life
led to social retardation and acne. Under such pressures, Bella
married the most persistent of her suitors at twenty-five, a certain Igor Rabinsky, and a year later bore us a beautiful daughter
named Sirofima. Having achieved the state of desired normalcy,
Bella was now free to be tragically unhappy and blame everyone
for having given up her dream of becoming a Broadway actress.

Against the backdrop of my sister's *tragediya*, I refused to date
Russian men. Deeply obsessed with reaching the highest state
of Americanization, I jumped into long-term relationships with
upstanding American men: a whining intellectual on the verge of
self-discovery and in the throes of a dissertation on Brezhnev's
Five-Year Economic Plan, and a self-absorbed, intellectually
vapid, pompously moralistic, romantically minded gynecologist.
They were my most persistent suitors, with whom I stayed longer
than my nerves could bear, in part because they were both Jewish
and therefore Grandmother would be tepidly satisfied, and in
part because of their creative marriage proposals. The intellectual, a dabbler in many arts, painted a rose with a diamond ring

hanging on one of its thorns and presented it to me at the History Department annual spring picnic. Needless to say, there was celebratory boohooing, whistling, and smacking of lips, which made it impossible for me to say "no" once I realized that this was a proposal—the intellectual did not actually articulate the words, "Will you marry me?" but rather stared smugly at my face. The gynecologist was more conventional in style—he took me to a fancy restaurant where he spoke about the indeterminate color of my eyes, my soft skin and hot body, and how he was also good looking, which led to the unexpected topic of our future children and a scrumptious blueberry mousse cake, which I was forced to lick off the plate without swallowing and thus uncover an enormous diamond ring, shrouded in blue mousse, which therefore did not shine but did scrape my sensitive tongue.

An artist's journal, the gift from my father, became my refuge in those early years. Without language, I sketched, drew, painted to express myself, expressions that filled more journals and sketchbooks and soon needed canvases to capture them all. Although my parents complained about the messes I made and the money they were spending on art supplies, they never denied me: they purchased the best oil pastels and oil paints and acrylics and a panoply of watercolors and top-of-the-line sable brushes and fancy stretched canvases intended only for real artists. "We are in America," my father would say, carrying an enormous sketchpad under his arm. "We sacrifice ourselves for our children!" My mother acknowledged that I had "talent," but no one in the family was certain if it was "real," as they required, like most people from Eastern Europe, confirmation from above—from those invisible authority figures who decreed what is and what isn't, what is talent and what is mere facade. The idea that art might be *my* career was unfathomable. But in college, I began to hear people throw around a wildly shocking, original, thoroughly innovative concept that I had never encountered before: "do what you want!" Here people spoke of "talent," broadly defined, as a matter of hard work and determination and subjectivity, not simply a black-and-white preordained God-given gift. It was here that I first tasted a tentative longing to paint full time. Friends encouraged me to enter my work into contests and, to my great surprise, I won the first prize in a citywide College Surrealism Competition. The *Chicago Herald* published tiny images of my paintings and award next to an article, entitled "Young Chicago Artists at Work," and I brought home this incontrovertible evidence to prove to my mother and grandmother and father that I was in possession of "raw God-given" talent. But they scoffed at the idea: "You're just a university student," my mother pointed out, "you haven't competed in the 'real' world, with 'real' artists." For Grandmother, the world was simpler: "Over *my dead* body," she said, "we didn't bring you to America so that you could waste your life, your brains, your University of Chicago education, making doodles and googly eyes all day long." My father was manly and resourceful: "Why don't you try your hand at mathematics like me or Computer Sciences like your third cousin Yulya. She's now programming at CitiBank and to think that not so long ago she wanted to be an actress!"

It was inevitable, I suppose, the obligatory fate of our young immigrant generation: children with suppressed dreams and Herculean stamina for enduring careers that made us want to slit our wrists. And among them, indeed, sat I. I juggled three nightmares in my head—physics, computers, and mathematics. My competence in all three fields was in the sub-zero region. Gradewise, I was mustering B-minuses because the university had a propensity for grade inflation and because my father was working overtime, doing my homework for me, calling me "stupid" out of desperation. One day, my father's boss recommended that I should look into becoming an actuary. "A wonderful field with numerous job prospects," the man assured my father. Although I had failed my first statistics exam and loathed every graph and probability equation with the passion of an axe-murderer, my father gave me positive reinforcements: "You're Russian," Father said, "and Russians do not give up!" I chose statistics as my major, with a minor in feminist theory and gender studies, which became known in my family as my little immigrant rebellion, my American *mishugas*. During my senior year, I applied and was accepted to a program called Statistics Probability and Survey Modeling, nicknamed SPASM, at NYU's prestigious school of Arts and Sciences. In the Russian community of Chicago's wealthy suburbs, my new program was viewed as my parents' grand achievement and unanimously hailed as an ideal career for a woman: I could become an actuary, a professor, a wife, a mother, and a money-making entity by analyzing, constructing, and concocting surveys that explained Americans' way of life. What glorious conversations Grandmother was now having with grandmothers and mothers of daughters who went to mediocre colleges and ended up hygienists, accountants, optometrists, and careerless wives: "Well, our Lenochka is studying Matimatiku at New York University, the Center for Matimatika, studying to be a professor, our Lenochka, or she can be a CEO if that's where her heart leads!"

After I moved to New York City to pursue SPASM, I became the perfect immigrant child. I avowed to my mom and grandma that my "silly" dream of becoming a painter had now been fully submerged under my "serious" dream of becoming an actuary.

To bring matters to a state of almost hysterical bliss, I was at long last dating the man of Grandmother's dreams, a *real man*: a certain Alexei Bagdanovich, a Princeton graduate with the manners and looks of a White Russian aristocrat, and the blood of a pure Jew.

But as all perfect immigrant children know, I wasn't without my scintillating little secrets. My apartment in the West Village, which I affectionately dubbed "the dungeon," was one of the most hideous dwelling places I had ever chanced upon in my short life. The kitchen boasted a healthy population of cockroaches; the toilet required manual pumping with a plunger to properly flush; a four-foot-long blue pet iguana resided in the living room; and a roommate named Natasha, originally Nancy—a self-proclaimed Russophile—hung tiny snapshots of her asshole and vagina examined from a variety of perspectives on the hallway walls. This exposé, Natasha was quick to elucidate, marked her short stint as a "model" during her "early years" in New York.

After spending a studious, will-defying, brain-numbing, hands-wringing, depression-inducing, face-contorting year studying a field I had no aptitude for or interest in, and receiving a C+ for Survey Analysis, a D– for Advanced Statistics Level 400, and an F for Probability and Stochastic Modeling, I threw myself into researching the key ingredients of successful suicide attempts. But again, I had to remind myself of this execrable fact—we are Russian, after all, and Russians don't give up . . . they lie.

Fall was upon me, a new semester was in full swing, and I was now auditing a secret art class, which was run by the tyrannically and openly philandering Professor Grayhart. Though Grayhart—an attractive old letch, if you don't mind sagging skin and a smoker's rasp—became obsessed with trying to recruit me to model in the nude (after class, that is), I adored him for all the right reasons: his incisive critiques of my disproportionate figures and his insistence that painting can be a career, a concept so taboo in my family that you might as well major in cannibalism.

Finally, there was the microscopic fact that despite my heavy commitment to Alex, I was now eyeing other men. Let me broadly define "eyeing": flipping one's hair in a come-hither fashion; staring lustily while pretending not to stare; mouthing pleasantries like "Oh you didn't have to, but thank you for that blueberry muffin," or "I guess a cup of Starbucks coffee never hurt anyone," or that well-known death to all fidelity: "Hah, hah, hah, that's so funny!" When these small infractions started happening, I attributed them to general youthful malaise and restlessness—my joie de vivre, my last cough against society's deification of monogamy. Once Alex and I were married, I reassured myself, these strange virulent longings would subside, these flirtations would level off into a kind of humdrum marital nod to past transgressions, and I would be an exemplary wife. As I nestled in his arms, discussing our favorite English translation of Anna Karenina, I'd swear that I would never stray again, that upon smelling another man, I'd handcuff myself to the nearest pole and imagine that I was Odysseus on the open sea being seduced by the Sirens. But a few weeks later, while perusing my beloved feminist theorists at Barnes & Noble, I found myself etching my phone number into some guy's palm. While attending a lecture on Simone de Beauvoir's tortured affair with Sartre, I found myself discussing the quest for a perfect feminist orgasm with a continental philosopher in a dusty hallway corner (a kind of virtual simulation of sex, if you ask me). I consoled myself with only one recurring thought—thank God for my Silver and Bronze Rules, respectively: (1) Official Dates Are Not To Be Tolerated Under Any Pretenses; (2) No Slippery Foreign Tongue Inside Mouth, No Foreign Fingers Upon Breasts, No Foreign Penis Entity In Vagina; in a word, NO SEX, NO SEX, NO SEX Under Any Circumstances (not even in an overheated discotheque with writhing bodies swaying to that fatally sexual song, "Like A Virgin!"). Thus my guilt remained at tolerable levels, that is, my allergies were kept at bay, except for a few barely noteworthy incidents where my eyes began to itch uncontrollably, my throat stung, my esophagus convulsed, and my mucus flowed so generously from my nose that I had to tell people I had the flu. I called Mom and Grandma with the sincerest hope that they could cure me.

"*Mamochka, Babulya, dorogiye moyi,*" I murmured in my sweetest Russian voice, "I've been thinking—I mean Alex is great, really great, but what if I'm not ready—I mean would it make sense to date around a bit more, take a little tiny mini-break from Alex, and then, then go back to him later?"

"Are you speaking in Mongolian?" Grandmother cried.

"What do you mean 'go back to Alex'—go back from what? What's going on?" my mom, with her KGB-trained brain, asked.

"All these men ask me out—what I mean is that just the other day a nice Jewish boy wanted to take me to a movie—" (He was a graduate student in film studies and although he had no biological affiliation to Jews, he had a splendid knowledge of Holocaust movies.)

"You mean like that 'nice Jewish boy' you dated in college who told you he was adopted but whose parents turned out to be *Efiscofallicaans* and his last name turned out to be McNuel?"

"I've barely dated," I said, trying a different tack. "I've always been engaged."

"And whose fault was that?" Grandmother yelled. "The point of life is to marry, not date senselessly and idiotically! Listen to me, Alex is the best thing that ever happened to you. Look at your history, whenever you've chosen for yourself it's been a disaster! Like that *mudila* who believed in Communist fairy tales, or that imbecilic *ginecolog* who chewed with his mouth open and didn't say a word to me."

"That's because you don't speak a word of English, *babushka*!" I shot back.

"An educated brute is what he was—didn't even look me in the eye. Oh, why argue over your silly history—these were mistakes you made in your past, and now you're a success. Now you're doing smart things in your career, practical things with a future on the horizon, not like that Feeeeminist drivel you almost majored in—"

"*Feminist, feminist,*" I cried, "that was my minor—I minored in feminist studies."

"Or, God forbid, *Art!*" my mother added with a laugh. "Grandmother would never sleep again and therefore, neither would we!"

"Most importantly, you're now with Alexei," Grandmother assured me in a conciliatory voice. "Can you think of any other Russian Jew who doesn't make any grammatical mistakes in Russian and doesn't stick English into every godforsaken sentence?"

"And yet he's so wonderfully Americanized, just like you," my mother effused.

"And he's so handsome," Grandmother muttered breathlessly.

"He's practically Tom Cruise with a Jewish brain," my mother said.

"Better looking than Tom Cruise," Grandmother effused, "*Apollon!* And a genius in quantum physics."

"He's interviewing at banks, *Babushka*, he's going into business—"

"Details," she shot back. "You should wear that mauve velvet dress your mother bought you at Marshall Field's—it brings out your eyes—when he comes next weekend."

"Lenochka, we don't want to push you or make this important decision for you"—my mother was embracing her infamous manipulation strategy—"but you've always been blind when it comes to men, and now once again you don't see what is so patently clear to everyone else—that the right person for you, for *you*, my love, is Alex."

"I know, I know, I'm sure you're right; all I'm saying is that it's hard to have a long-distance relationship. There are all these temptations."

"Ah, well that's a different topic. Your mother and I are experts in this field," Grandmother boasted. "When a woman is beautiful it's hard to say 'no' to men; beauty as you well know is a disease. The only answer is the law of repulsion. Eat four cloves of garlic a day and you'll stink so bad no man will want to touch you—you'll even stink down there—"

"Garlic is wonderful," my mother burst out. "Did you know, Lenochka, that in Russia we used to stuff garlic up our assholes to get rid of parasites? But I've never heard of this nonsense—which aunt told you this ancient fairytale, *maman*?"

"Nonsense? Well this nonsense has kept numerous marriages together, plus warded off colds!"

"Thank you, Grandma, thank you, you're brilliant—I'll do that—I'll do exactly that!" I muttered happily and hung up.

That very weekend I purchased several wreaths of garlic and stuffed salted cloves into black bread. With my eyes watering and my tongue drawing fire, I devoured it like I did as a child in wintertime, like my grandmother did to survive the freezing winter and the Nazis of the war.

Meet Tom Cruise with a Jewish Brain

Let me backtrack for you, patient reader. About a year ago, Grandmother stepped up the perennial marriage nudge as my single status was giving her "*kolbasa*-heartburn" and "Stalinist insomnia." After two disastrous engagements that Grandmother strove to zap from the start, after months of dogged resistance and lackluster flings, I caved under Grandmother's nagathon. After all, she was Queen Guildenshtein, the reigning force behind most of the actions and inactions of my mother, father, sister Bella, and me, and her insistence that I needed a serious boyfriend (as opposed to the unserious ones who were neither fully Jewish nor mathematically inclined) was akin to a royal command. Alex Bagen (or, more precisely, Alexei Ifimovich Bagdanovich) was the fourth man Grandma sent to New York to marry me. After several unsuccessful matches—one was a bald-headed pharmacist, the second a tall engineer without social skills, and the third a computer genius suffering from an overproduction of saliva (he slobbered on my foot in preparation for a kiss)—Grandmother stumbled upon Mrs. Bagdanovich at the Three Sisters Delicatessen on Devon Avenue, a hobnob for nostalgic Russian immigrants. It was she—Alex's discerning mother—who saw me dancing with Bella in Moscow Nights (a Russian discotheque that also poses as a restaurant) and approached Grandmother about a possible merger. Mrs. Bagdanovich wanted me specifically, because she thought Bella was too "Russian looking" for her Americanized Alex. Bella's beauty evoked Botticelli's Venus, with her voluptuous figure, flowing blonde hair, and serene blue eyes, and Mrs. Bagdanovich was in search of something a little less intimidating and more modern for her son. Besides, Bella was already married, while I was the perfect postmodern beauty—a slouching skinny red-haired mess with pouty lips and eyes so dark no one could tell what color they were, except the woman who bore me and swore they were Byzantine green. Jeans were my preferred mode of existence, unless I was on a date with a Russian, and my language of choice was always English.

Alex arrived in New York like a prince on an alabaster unicorn—the unicorn being a white Mercedes where he offered me air cleansed of New York's diesel fumes and Corona beer, which neither of us drank. He resembled a Greek god perched on the Italian leather of the limo's interior—a dark-haired Zeus with philosophical brown eyes that assailed you with a mixture of disapproval and desire. He was the sort of handsome that made your tongue so moist it salivated clichés: "Do you come here often?" you wanted to say, or "You look familiar," even though he didn't. I imagined women drawn to him like refrigerator magnets, clinging to his chest, women Alex could never get rid of without the help of his mother.

For our first date, Alex wooed me with front-row seats to Broadway's *Beauty and the Beast* to satiate our musical souls, Tavern on the Green to impress our never-satisfied palates, and the Russian Tea Room to awaken our nostalgia through vodka and cheap caviar. He was also eager to demonstrate that he was not averse to spending his parents' money. We immediately seized on our mutual grueling years of trying to fit in and become egregiously American, and shared a secret sense of superiority over the other Russians.

"Why should I feel embarrassed at looking American?" Alex asked rhetorically, sipping his vodka cautiously as if it was poison. "Is it such a crime that I work out?" Alex ran in place on treadmills like all the other hardworking Americans, *not* in freezing winter storms along Lake Michigan like his nostalgic father. "It's not that I wanted so desperately to assimilate," Alex held forth when he explained why he changed his name. "I was just so sick of people asking: 'Where are you from?' or 'Isn't it freezing in Moscow?' I was the fucking valedictorian, for Christ's sake, I could take their English on any day, and these ignoramuses were asking me if I knew what *supercilious* meant?" During his second year at Princeton, he truncated his long name and reemerged as a new man in the quicker and less cumbersome form of Alex Bagen, which ironically led people to mistake his last name for "Bagel."

"I know exactly what you mean," I told Alex. "I'm not Lena Kabelmacher anymore."

"Mother didn't tell me you also changed your name!" He perked up with excitement.

"My grandmother keeps it a secret," I said. "Besides, she can't pronounce my new name—Emma Kaulfield."

"Emma Kaulfield—what an excellent appellation!"

"I know it doesn't sound too much like my name, but I figured I might as well go all the way . . ." My story came to me with a blend of pride and revulsion.

It wasn't that I was dissatisfied with Elena Kabelmacher; it had a certain exotic ring to it. In Russia, I was branded as the Jew, and in America, I was confused with a German, which accounted for such unsightly misspelled mutilations as Kabelhuffer and Habbermuffer. I was tired of being asked, "So what nationality are you?"—tired of being seen as the foreigner, tired of myself playing the part. And in my search for a new name, I wanted no chopping of consonants, no half-baked contortions that take pleasant names like Bayakovksy or Feldshtein and squeeze them into a legless Bayak or an insipid Feld. I chose an aesthetic overhaul: I would become Emma Kaulfield, a literary invention with a few key letters to pay homage to my past and a lilting musicality to signal my future. I alerted my family to my new name when we were standing before a judge with hundreds of other immigrants, renouncing our allegiance to the Soviet Union in order to become passport-waving, anthem-belting, fully-pledged American citizens. "I'm changing my name," I told my mother, arguing that I would have a better chance of getting into Harvard if I got rid of Kabelmacher, my father's ancestral calling (whose roots apparently reached all the way back to the Jewish Vikings). She in turn calmed my grandmother, saying, "She needs to do this for her career," and my father, like a soldier beaten in battle, nodded obsequiously. Only Bella bristled with indignation: "Traitor. It's like you're embarrassed of us."

"She got to me," I confessed to Alex. "I still feel like a traitor, especially when I date American men—it's like, like—"

"Like it's all part of our elaborate conspiracy to escape them, or something—"

"Exactly," I cried, full of gratitude. "It's like no matter what choice you make they think you're saying, 'I'm embarrassed to be seen with you!'"

"At least yours thought you were embarrassed of *them*," Alex noted ruefully. "My mother blushes every time she hears anyone call me Mr. Bagen."

"I hate vodka," I said suddenly.

"Me too," he murmured with passion and we leaned into each other simultaneously for a very public kiss against the plush crimson booth of the Russian Tea Room. Excitement gurgled in my stomach, brimming with the possibility of potential love, making me want to whisper: "You're so unbelievably gorgeous—it's a wonder, a miracle, really, that you also have a brain!" But I refrained. If he were an American, I would've spat it out without pause, but Russian men required serious circumspection.

I admired so much about him: his regular assaults on the Republicans and Democrats alike; his feverish adherence to notions of libertarianism and social hedonism; and the polite, gentle, non-judgmental way he denounced our parents (though never to their faces) for being so unflappably Republican. I revered him for being a Princeton man, and the only Russian Jew to have been accepted to an Ivy League institution without using his immigrant woes to beef up his application essay. In college, Alex could have done anything, but he majored in physics to prove to his parents that he was devoted to them. Despite constant praise from his mother, Alex experienced a loss of confidence upon graduation. Desire for travel, feelings of monetary inadequacies, and demanding girlfriends made him lose faith in his *priyemuschestva*—his great advantage. After highlighting his hair (an act dubbed by his father as "gay") and dabbling in everything from advertising to computer programming to freelance writing, Alex experienced a typical post-college, I-am-almost-American-without-a-career meltdown. But he did not wallow in self-pity for long and, gathering himself in his arms, as the Russian saying went, sent his resume to every bank and consulting firm in New York, causing his mother considerable discomfort at having to tell people that her son was now interested in "biziness." (To console his mother, he promised to apply to physics graduate programs at Harvard, MIT, and Cal Tech in December). Fantasies of rolling in wealth, traveling to Japan and China, and perhaps making a stopover in Mother Russia whirred in his brain and recalibrated his *priyemuschestva* in a new, dazzling light.

Alex and I saw each other as rebels, as rare immigrant speci-
mens that didn't obey their parents' commands. We argued vocif-
erously, criticizing other people with abandon, and boasted without applying to ourselves the American restraint of humility. Our
long-distance relationship of twelve months together amounted
to nine dates and fifty-six hours of phone conversations, canvass-
ing the hard terrain of Russian history. We spoke about pogroms,
Lenin's bald head and Trotsky's hubris, Stalin's mustache and his
bosom torturer, Beria, Brezhnev's bushy eyebrows and his abysmal articulation, and the grotesque absurdities of the KGB. Yet
somehow we eluded our personal histories, the miseries our families endured at the hands of those we mocked, the scars Russia
carved upon us all; it made us feel good about ourselves to know
that we had so much in common without having to expose our
skeletons and to feel that beneath all our sophisticated blather we
were dating the old-fashioned way—sans sex.

Grandmother warned me against having sex with him. "The
whole Russian community will find you out—wait till he proposes,"
she admonished. But I felt antiquated and buffoonish; after all, I
was twenty-four, almost at my sexual peak, which I imagined as
a state of unremitting horniness. I didn't consider myself a nym-
phomaniac or, in Grandmother's grand words, "an eternal slut,"
but I knew that sex mattered, the way food and water matter, the
way global warming matters. Yet after all those dates—during his
sporadic New York visits—after simpering innuendos in smelly
cabs, after feeling each other up and down (though not nearly up
nor down enough—how could we in the hotel lobby), Alex had
yet to invite me to his room. He bid me goodbye with *"arrive-
derci"* and a very unenthusiastic tongue, which barely grazed my
gums before sheepishly retreating to its own mouth. Alex fancied
himself a gentleman, a paragon of the self-restrained male, a relic
from the Victorian Age. The ass, the ass, I wanted to scream, I
want you to squeeze my ass. But his hands, those ticklish caterpil-
lars, stayed stubbornly on my lower back.

Still, one has to give me credit for my peerless restraint.
I stayed in my room and spoke to no one and kept my nose in

sexually neutered texts. I ate dinner alone. I was every man's fantasy of a long-distance girlfriend. I likened myself in my head to an existential stoic, a Russian monk, Nietzsche's ascetic ideal. Until, until, that is, November, when a cruel winter breeze began terrorizing the city and hot currents suddenly coursed through my veins, thawing my body for the advent of spring. I would sit next to a good-looking man in the library, gulp maniacally from a water bottle, and try not to think about ripping his shirt off together with his chest hair.

Against my better judgment, I suggested to Alex that we might consider taking our pawing to the next level. "What level might that be?" he inquired like an innocent lad of twelve. "The level of sex—of your room or my room or anywhere, let's just do it, do it!" Yes, I said those exact words in my usual straightforward uninhibited style. And in the face of my extraordinary courage and my obvious, mauve-hued embarrassment, he remained as unperturbed as ever, a cocoon of virtue and reserve, explaining himself as a "devout Romantic—some people believe in God, I believe in Love." I had no recourse but to wonder: (a) Do I have noxious oily fish breath? (b) Is he a Catholic priest masquerading as a Russian Jew? (c) Is he a repressed homosexual pretending to be a homophobic—bordering on chauvinistic—intellectual of the Russian variety? or (d) Is he the real article—a man of truly chivalrous convictions? Still, my pride wailed: how could any man not want me, *me*? And so I raged against him as if I were raging against racism, sexism, anti-Semitism, as if sex itself had become the great equalizer, an emblem of American democracy, and we either had to have it or die!

But Alex stopped my diatribe with a sumptuous, *almost* ardent kiss and this: "'Here I dwell, for heaven is in these lips / And all is dross that is not Helena.'"

So I replied: "'Some say the world will end in fire / Some say in ice / From what I've tasted of desire / I hold with those who favor fire.'"

"'Shall I compare thee to a summer's day?'"

"Please *don't!*" I cried and together, he and I burst into laughter. For only two immigrants with English-inferiority complexes and healthy self-esteems could suddenly, without blushing, quote Marlowe, Frost, and Shakespeare to recuperate from a fight.

The Bathroom Incident that Launched a Thousand Guilt Trips

So there I was, stuffing garlic cloves in my bras and under my pillows, impatiently awaiting Alex's return for his *tfu, tfu, tfu* interviews at New York banks, and my sex. My behavior was exemplary, my devotion pitch perfect, especially in my Probability and Stochastic Modeling class where I (being the only female) valiantly rebuffed the amorous attentions of two mathematically endowed men. When, alas, Alex called from the airport to announce, "I've arrived, expect the unexpected!" my heart pounded and my hands masterfully scrubbed my body to rid it of garlic odor—to prepare it for a full-scale physical seduction of the reluctant gentleman. Optimistically embracing the love-to-sex concept, I donned knee-length black leather boots, a leather miniskirt, and a leather jacket—the look of a slick badass or, worse, an Ivy League whore. Upon seeing me, Alex murmured, "Superb as ever!" and apologized for failing to secure reservations at Le Bernardin. Would I be terribly disappointed with the inferior La Cote Basque? No, I would not. Then he placed an airy peck on my puckered lips while I panted like an overheated dog in leather.

The dining room had the air of an old duchess, puffing with regal mannerisms and haughty remarks, and yet fully aware of her own decline and antediluvian views of the world. Stern rectangular white tables were met by plush blue sofas spiraling along the walls and gilded chandeliers, reminiscent of great Parisian ballrooms, offered only the illusion of light, enveloping each face in a gray glow. The restaurant appeared to be an enclave for the elderly with mink coats and cigars, and I instantly felt the need to pull my skirt down.

"I sal tell vou about ze speciales," our waiter said with a vague foreign accent, and Alex lifted his head abruptly to stare at him.

"*Qu'avez-vous pensé?*" Alex exclaimed in French to the waiter, for it turned out that Alex also spoke fluent or, as I liked to think of it, Russian-inflected French.

The waiter appeared not to hear him and then, politely lowering his head, said, "I vill be right back—give vou foo minute to make decision."

"He's clearly French," Alex announced. "I can spot the French anywhere. Did you see how polite he was?"

"How was he polite?" I asked.

"He didn't want to speak French to me out of respect for you."

"He looks Italian to me," I said.

The waiter returned with the bottle of red wine Alex had ordered and a shy smile on his face, again directed exclusively at me. He now visibly ignored Alex's appeals to him in French. I cringed, then grinned seductively at the waiter in an attempt to counteract Alex's faux pas.

"Are you making eyes at the waiter?" he asked angrily after we ordered our appetizers.

"What else am I supposed to do when you won't leave him alone?" I snapped.

"Are you still sore about the sex?"

"I'm not sure you can handle a modern woman," I said. "You are clearly put off by *my* desires."

"It's not that. You never gave me a chance to explain. I just like us the way we are—you reeling me in but not giving me what I want, and me running after you like your faithful dog servant." He paused as if to twirl the words on his tongue and rephrased the concept: "I want to keep feeling the way I'm feeling—ravenous but not yet satiated!"

"Do you have any idea how ridiculous that sounds?"

"I'm a gambling man," he said, smiling.

"And I'm a hard-core feminist," I flung back. "Are you aware that I wrote my bachelor's thesis on Judith Butler—the same Judith Butler who claimed that gender is performative, that we're not born male or female, but made so by our culture, a culture that stuffs these definitions down our throats! And did I tell you that my title was 'Burgeoning Feminism in Chauvinistic Immigrant Communities: A Cross-cultural Analysis of Judith Butler—'"

"On numerous occasions," Alex replied with a laugh. "Anyhow, I thought you were a statistician now?"

"I am—of course I am a statistician, but only because of them! If it hadn't been for them—" I thought with regret of that day in December when I carried two sets of application essays to the post office. I called my mom and said, "Mom, I don't know if statistics is for me—what I really want to do is study art and feminism, and there's a program at Irvine, California where I could do exactly that—I could become a professor—and I'd—" What I wanted to say was: paint, paint women's faces, their suffering, paint within a postmodern feminist tradition, paint to breathe. But instead I raised the fact that within our family and other Russian families the man still resides upon a throne: he is served, fed, clothed, and fanned with ridiculous compliments, and that women's rights, her rights, Grandmother's rights are brushed under the proverbial tablecloth. "We need a new language," I told her, "to cleanse our palate, and your core beliefs are in fact aligned with mine." But my mother's brilliant manipulative mind enveloped me at once: "Yes, of course I agree with you, Lenochka! So then imagine what you'll contribute to women's rights, to feminism itself, if you'll specialize in statistics—a lone woman in a male-dominated field. It's such a gift that you're sooooo good at this!" My ego swelled and got stuck in my throat, and at once, I dropped the folder containing the feminist theory and gender studies application to University of California at Irvine into the nearest garbage bin.

"For them—you mean your parents?" Alex asked.

"Yes, if it hadn't been for them, I'd be painting, and doing my PhD on Judith Butler or Luce Irigaray at Irvine—I had a good shot at getting in, too." I paused. "I'd be happy."

"And you would have been the butt of every joke among our relatives and friends—"

"Are you mocking me?" I asked with a murderous grin.

"Not at all! I simply disagree with you: Judith Butler, Simone de Beauvoir, Virginia Woolf in her own room, a naked pregnant Demi Moore—what's the difference? Their feathers might be of different colors, but under all that pomposity all these women want is the same thing: a good man. If you're honest with yourself, you'd see that feminism is just not realistic, not natural. Look at the way men and women interact. Look at real life, no matter what women say, a woman relinquishes control when she has sex and a man gains it. Women just cannot treat sex nonchalantly."

"I don't see why you have these absurd, antiquated Russian notions—" I protested loudly.

"You have an excellent vocabulary," he observed, then added, "Just because American men claim they're feminists in public doesn't mean they don't think like Russian men privately. They just hide better behind all that politically correct bullshit."

I wanted to paddle back to Judith Butler, but instead I said, "If you were American, we would have done it by now. I don't see what you were afraid of, unless you're—"

"I'm very, very potent," he protested, "in fact, so virile that women, once they sleep with me, can never leave me."

"You're not serious?" I laughed.

"Are you doubting my manhood?"

"No, I'm merely affecting shock at your purported sluttiness! Does your mother know?"

Through laughter, he replied, "No, she erroneously believes I'm averse to sexual pleasure."

"Why?"

"Because until you, no woman has yet given my heart cause to melt!" His beautiful dark brown eyes peered at me with confidence. "All jokes and metaphors aside, why don't you marry me, Elena?"

"Marry you?"

"I love the way you are, so full of desire and spunk," he continued in the same glowing tone, mistaking my response for a display of feminine insecurity. "I am utterly serious—my dearest Lenochka."

He reached across the table and laid a small velvet box next to my appetizer. Ah, the dreaded ring. When my eyes feasted on the magnificent emerald stone perched upon a skinny gold band, I swallowed the duck *foie gras* in its entirety and felt the grease coagulate in the back of my throat. Marriage rose before me like the parted jaws of a shark, and on its back sat Alex, murmuring: "I'll be a magnificent lover; I'm very well versed in the literature of sexual arousal."

He burst into a self-effacing chuckle and I laughed with relief. He pried my fingers open (both hands were apparently locked in tight fists) and, placing the ring in my palm, gravely declared, "This is no ordinary ring, Elena—my uncle Yossel smuggled it in his lower intestines. The KGB missed it—with their laser technology—those pompous fools! Yossel stuck it in caramel and swallowed it whole. He kept it in till he reached our apartment on Pratt Street eighteen years ago. This ring has been in my family for centuries—a survivor of Ivan the Terrible, Lenin, Stalin, the pogroms, World War II, the Cold War, The Reagan administration, and Yossel's bowels."

"Oh, Alex, thank you," I groaned. "It's beautiful, really, I feel honored, really—this is so unexpected—"

"Unexpected—my dear Elena, why, I wanted to propose on our first date—"

I smiled: to think that he wanted to marry me on the first date at the behest of his mother and my grandmother was at once endearing and nauseating.

"You know I'm crazy about you, Sashenka," I said, "but have we really had enough time? This is a colossal step."

"Yet you think that's a sufficient timetable for sex—" he countered with a laugh. "Look, my father proposed to my mother on the third date."

"So did my father to my mother—on the first date, on the first because she was so beautiful! But that was Russia—in America we can take our time and make sure we're not making a mistake."

"Oh, I know I'm not making a mistake," he said. "You're exactly what I want—what I need—feisty, opinioned and you will always call me on my bullshit."

I grabbed his hand and kissed it, "You're such a wonderful person, Sashenka, really, even with all your silly views of women—"

"Which you'll undoubtedly fix in no time!" He laughed good-naturedly, and I smiled. Smiled and trembled and held the table for support, and fought an urgent sensation in my bladder to deluge the entire marble entrails of La Cote Basque. I rose from my chair and announced, "I must go to the bathroom!"

"I understand: you want to torture me a little, give me a taste of purgatory—I'm willing to wait!" he sang after me. "I'm used to waiting." I heard him as I hurried away.

I stepped behind the purple mantle that separated the bathroom area from the dining room, and the sensation in my bladder miraculously receded. In the stilted, dusty confines of the waiting area, a man stood in an arrogant pose.

"Are you all right?" he asked.

"I think so," I muttered, feeling faint.

"You look pale," he said in a kind voice.

"I'm fine, thank you." I smiled at him and wiped my forehead. We stood looking at one another for a second, then directed our gaze to the two wooden bathroom doors.

"You can use the men's room if you want," the stranger offered, pointing in the direction of a flinging door.

"I'm not in a hurry," I sighed, shaking my head. "I'm just very warm."

"Yes, it's very warm in here," he whispered and, swinging his arm to lean against the wall, gently brushed my hair.

He cut a tall sharp figure in the dimness, with light eyes, the color of which I couldn't make out, and long muscular fingers, which periodically swept over his forehead to remove beads of sweat. He arched over me like a black amorphous shadow, his features blurring, his mouth a cave emitting strange soothing sounds.

"Life's just so confusing." I was apparently talking again, despite myself.

"Isn't it," he took me up. "If you ask me, he isn't for you."

"How did you conclude that?"

"Oh, that's easy—he lacks guts," he said.

"And you, I suppose, have them in spades?"

"If I weren't a feminist already, I'd convert. If I were a virgin, I'd beg for your mercy. And if *you* begged to sleep with *me*—well you can guess what I'd say—" He laughed warmly, somehow neutralizing this perverse intrusiveness with his coiling lips, and added, "You were very loud."

"That's not very nice."

"Who said I was nice?" He turned on me with brows raised in a triangle above his eyes, lips parted as if waiting still to speak, but offering only silence. Only the sentence—"Who said I was nice?"—rose into view like an opened gate, letting a stream of intimacy run between us.

The women's room opened up but we didn't move.

"Are you going in?" A lady was standing behind me.

"You go ahead," I said to her, remaining still, and perked my nose to inhale the stranger's breath. It smelled of wine and goat cheese and rushed into my lungs in hot puffs of air. I noticed after a while that we had breached each other's space. We kept up pretenses at first, as though our natural camaraderie was just a social fluke, an innocent exchange of pleasantries, but with each sentence and each person stealing our turns, our stillness grew and truncated our speech. I thought of breaking out, and quietly mouthed, "Well, it was nice to meet you. I better go." But in silence he kept at me, with eyes that fixed me to the wall—what was this strangeness we had bred between us? I turned to go, made two steps forward, but then my arm, as though of its own accord, leapt out at him. Our palms locked midair and we stayed tethered to the ground like two statues waiting to be moved. I felt his other hand across my back, his fingers on my red silk shirt, drawing imaginary lines round my shoulder blades, along my spine, delineating cloth from flesh, penetrating both. I shut my eyes, imbibing each sensation without consciousness or thought—existing only in the breathing of my body. I opened up my eyes in time to see that we had made our way into the men's room.

When we emerged, the man and I went our separate ways, without much spoken in between. I shook as I sashayed across the restaurant floor, my leather miniskirt chafing at my skin, my leather boots utterly inappropriate.

When I returned to the table, Alex was speaking to the waiter in broken French. I sat down at my chair and wiped my forehead with a soiled napkin. I felt my lungs constrict, breath becoming rapid. Please, dear Lord, do not let me have an allergic reaction right now—Benadryl was tucked away in my dungeon.

Allergies to dust, Lysol, ragweed, pollen, cats, chlorine, flowery detergents, or simply bad armpit odor were my constant companions, never failing to alert me to the unstable seesaw between life and death.

There was still the chunk of porterhouse I had not touched, and it lay there across my gold-rimmed plate with its blood seeping out, roiling my stomach with sudden nausea. My blood, I thought grimly, let it be my blood! I tried to concentrate on Alex's moving mouth, but the interlude in the bathroom danced in my head. And I saw his face again under the dim pink lighting, casting his features in a lurid glow. An aroma of lavender and thyme filled the air, and the oval mirror reflected my hand on his buttocks. "I've never done this before," I murmured into his ear, an old, female-honored platitude. "Yum, your hair smells like garlic bread," he murmured in return, as if this were a popular celebrity perfume. And then his hands, disregarding these peculiar discrepancies of language and odors, worked boldly over my body, rubbing my ribs and squeezing my leather-wrapped ass. I was hyperventilating, bordering on an orgasm of ancient Greek proportions—from what—from practically nothing if we consider the exhaustive literature on sex, and yet was it nothing when his fingers, like a horde of thieves, snuck over the border of my lacy red bra. (Yes, I wore red lace, out of that subterranean hope for an adventure.) Dear Aphrodite, then there were those lips: neither too wet nor too dry, neither too fat nor too slim, the perfect soft bowtie swirling over my breasts without touching them, then landing expertly on my nipples and pulling away, as though here was the god of foreplay in the flesh taunting me until I couldn't bear it any longer—until I burned to tear off my clothes and scream MUTINY ON BOARD! But I had Grandmother to consider and my ideal husband waiting for me in the main dining room; I was a feminist with numerous responsibilities, with several heads on top of my head. Responsibilities that obviously could wait—I kissed his cheeks, neck, fingers that seemed like extensions of my own limbs, but our mouths never met. We were at once too familiar and too estranged to kiss, our tongues reserved only for each other's skin. At some point he held me, for my knees caved, ankles bent to the floor. "Will I see you again?" he asked. "I want you," I whimpered pathetically, but in my mind, I was far more eloquent: *I'm fainting from pleasure— flying, somersaulting, whirling right up to the bathroom ventilator. I'm literally decomposing from the impossibility of what I'm doing, from the way you smell and grab me, from the muscles under your blue shirt, and yes, most of all, from the anonymity of your face.* He murmured something I couldn't understand, then lifted me into the air, my skirt riding up my waist—

"Well, my dearest Elena," Alex broke into my thoughts, "have you made your decision?"

"Yes, yes, *merci*, I'll marry you!" I cried because it was suddenly clear to me that if I didn't pledge my love to wonderful, loyal, brilliant Alex, to my Alexei Ifimovich Bagdanovich (what glorious features my children would have, what phenomenal brains and warm hearts), I'd be doomed, doomed to endless family squabbles and regrets and bathroom flings, to my grotesque desires, to my own dazzling reflection in the mirror: a scarlet-winged butterfly wanting every dandelion and pansy and sunflower in her path, masking sexual perversity in a feminist's cry.

"Glorious, glorious," Alex exclaimed, "You've made me a very happy man!" He opened his palm, which had grown moist from sweat and nerves, and gingerly tried to push the ring down my third finger. He failed at the second knuckle.

"Well, I guess I'll have to get the ring reset," Alex said, frowning from this unexpected hurdle. Within seconds he threw his jacket over his shoulders and stuffed a generous wad of cash into the reluctant hands of the assaulted waiter, who it turned out was not French after all, but Portuguese. Alex did not know any Portuguese but thought it was a fascinating culture.

I scanned the restaurant, miserably wanting to locate the stranger. The place swarmed with silver-haired men with wide luminous smiles and after-dinner drinks in their veiny hands, and I wondered if my stranger was not a few decades older than me. But as I stood up and swiveled my head, I caught his eyes settling on my behind, disrobing it. There was a blonde woman at his side and two handsomely dressed men seated at a large round table. They appeared animated, in some discussion about Microsoft stock. I heard one of the men say, "We shouldn't have been bankers—we should have been computer geeks." "Yeah, but then we'd have to wait till our IPO quadrupled to get the women," the stranger said, and the table, including the blonde, burst into a communal chuckle.

The stranger looked young, perhaps younger than his years. He had an easy contagious smile and eyes that shone in clear blue slivers out of a tan square face. He appeared at this range genial and pleasant, and despite wide shoulders and a solid thick body, he seemed light, almost weightless against the backdrop of Alex's perfectly sculpted solemn face.

"Ready, my love—are you ready to go?" Alex said in a buttery voice, pushing me along with stealth impatience. But I stood still, staring at the stranger.

"Goodbye," I said out loud, and then I heard an echo, a mantra whirring in my head: *goodbye all things fleeting and pleasurable and reckless and insane . . .*

His table quieted down and everyone turned to look at me.

"Goodbye," the stranger returned, his eyes latching onto my figure like two splendid cerulean doves, following me out of the restaurant as I held onto Alex for support.

Alex didn't seem to notice our exchange. In the cab, he was concerned about his blunder with the waiter. "I shouldn't have assumed he was French, just because the restaurant was French. I know better than that," he berated himself, and broke into a quiet laugh. We stepped out in front of my building and entered a narrow, dilapidated foyer with leaking walls and the stench of piss emanating from a cracked linoleum floor. I invited Alex to my apartment but he hesitated, initially seeming to be daunted by the prospect of climbing a broken staircase all the way up to the fifth floor. And when his mouth met mine with an erect tongue, when he pinned me against the besmirched mustard-colored wall of my foyer, I welcomed him, thinking, yes, I've been a miserable girlfriend, but I'll be an exemplary fiancée; I even tried to summon that ferocious desire, those notes of anonymity and truncated breaths, whispering to myself: *pretend you don't know his name.* But Alex slid his hands inside my bra and, patting my breasts, whispered, "my gorgeous perfectly contoured fiancée—till next time!" And with that, he sprang out the door, hailed a cab, and dove in like a man trying to outrun a fire.

The Men Who Take Us to Art Galleries

Two months into my engagement, I was wrapped in garlic from head to foot. Alex was in Chicago, living at his mother's house, taking a hiatus after having proposed to me. I didn't know whether he was afraid of sex or running out of his parents' frequent flier miles. Whatever his reasons, I learned to eat garlic straight up and raw, without any bread or condiments, just a self-executed human torture for my ballooning guilt. The incident in the bathroom had left me bedazzled and scared. The shadowy stranger awakened in me such a flurry of primitive desires that I locked myself in my room and swore I would never emerge, not even to pee, lest I bump into one of Natasha's lovers on the way to the malfunctioning toilet and grab his or her buttocks on a lusty whim. I had become aware of every tic in my body, every pang of perverse hunger, every murmur of the vagina apparatus—an intimacy I must say I never thought possible. So, in solitude and excellent humor, I did what any self-respecting, garlic-clad monk would do: I began a vigilant masturbation routine, preferably right before sleep, imagining the men's room of La Cote Basque as if it were a major research center for human sexuality. On the streets, I spied men everywhere, burgeoning out of desks and sidewalks and corners, their phone numbers pasted to their foreheads, approaching me with no regard for my garlic aroma. (Apparently, most men have no sense of smell whatsoever.)

At long last, in an anguished phone call, Alex admitted that he couldn't face me. His first round of interviews at New York banks had ended in excruciating failure.

But like all good immigrants, Alex was not one to give up easily. After enduring advice from condescending relatives and friends, he concurred that his job history was simply ill-matched for the narrow focus of an investment banker. So he sought out the Russian resume guru, Lenny Berman, who like the driver's license guru, Felix Luzhinsky, and the tax guru, Rita Gruffman, were loyal and wise servants of the Chicago Russian community, facilitating our smooth transition into the complex *mishugas* of American bureaucracies. For immigrants did not think the way Americans did: that one's life was a culmination of what one *actually* did, that it was bound by some unspoken honor code to be *truthful* and *accurate* about every event in one's life, and that a resume, while it certainly could be polished, could not be fundamentally changed. For an immigrant's life was a kaleidoscope of dreams, a reality so thoroughly interspersed with the surreal and fantastical that one's experiences, foibles, and even memories could easily be smudged, if not entirely written over, in one's struggle to catch that elusive American prize: success!

The banks responded in the affirmative to the fabricated resume, and now Alex was facing the staggering prospect of nine interviews. His trip would be paid for, and he arrived on Friday at my building, glowing with ethereal joy. It was the first time that he climbed the broken staircase and, panting heavily, stepped inside my apartment, where Natasha's nude photos greeted him in the hallway. I took him inside my room and spread my arms helplessly in a vague circle to indicate my life's passion: my paintings. But he didn't seem to see them. He said, "I can't believe it, nine interviews, nine! And one of them is with Norton Bank! They turned me down two months ago and they don't even remember! Amazing country, this America!" Squeezing my buttocks with his long, aristocratic fingers, he burrowed his tongue deeper inside my mouth than I had hoped. (Though it did indicate progress.) Then he checked himself, fixed his sweater, and within minutes started to lecture me on Degas.

"No, no—he wasn't really an impressionist—he was a realist," Alex said. The arts had taken a particularly vicious hold of him since he learned that I secretly wanted to be an artist.

"You look beautiful, my darling fiancée," he murmured, "like that effervescent dancer in *L'etoile*. Have you ever seen it? It's at the Musée d'Orsay?" I glanced at my own body in a tiny cracked hallway mirror, and felt his flattery seep into my veins like a disorienting barbiturate. I wanted him to comment on my work but instead I was suddenly struck with my self: I wore chocolate-hued suede boots, a beige suede skirt that clung to my thighs and buttocks and tapered off right above my knees, and a ribbed, cream-colored turtleneck that demarcated my breasts, which were loosely contained in a transparent silk bra. The overall effect of my outfit was one of a strange wintry transparency—of a figure so tightly bound in its thin wool fabrics that I appeared more exposed than if I were wearing a bikini. The only thing concealing me from the world was a striped brown jacket, which I threw on after Alex had a chance to absorb me in my original state. We could do it right now, I thought blissfully, but Alex asked, "Where are we going?" quite possibly to deflect my feeble attempts to seduce him again.

"Nebu, it's a gallery in Soho," I said in my offended voice.

"We should really be exploring the Met—they have an excellent Degas collection. Besides, you need to study from the masters—your attempts are infantile at best," he announced, pointing to a sketch of two suffering ballet dancers he glimpsed on my bed.

"I wish you wouldn't always say what's on your mind."

"If anyone can take it, it's you," he shot back, and at once I forgave him.

"How was your interview at Norton Bank?" I asked as we walked down Prince Street.

Alex furrowed his brows in disapproval at the question: "You know how I hate talking about this before I know anything for sure." Like my grandmother, he abided by all the Russian superstitions and I adored this about him. He saw a block of wood hanging from a run-down building, and knocked on it three times, murmuring the mandatory *tfu, tfu, tfu* under his breath. Then, with a relaxed smile, he said, "I think it actually went really well. The guy who interviewed me knew what he was doing, and we got along famously. This is the most prestigious bank in the city and the money—"

"That's nice," I interrupted without enthusiasm.

"It would really be something if they took me—I mean the money in this city—you can't imagine."

"I can imagine," I said even though I was never very good at imagining money. Although I had specifically matriculated in SPASM with a vague hope for a practical career, I could not understand what money was, or what I, for instance, would have to do to make it. I couldn't bring myself to imagine a cubicle, a desk, a name tag, a corporate ladder which *I* might climb. Nor did it occur to me that what Gloria Steinem and numerous other feminists wrote about and fought for—"equal pay for equal work"—could apply to *me*, could liberate *me*! Despite my protestations at the cultural inequity between the sexes, at the grotesque social burden placed on women to lose weight, look superb and wrinkle-free, and add dubious plastic matter to their breasts ("Why aren't men adding plastic matter to their penises?" "When are women going to start asking, 'is this *shlong* real?'"), I could not translate my feminist rage into practice. Like all women who've been inculcated for centuries with the Sleeping Beauty myth of a man rescuing, awakening, jump-starting a woman, I too longed for Alex to jump-start me. Perhaps in the back of my mind there lingered a secret egotistical wish: if I married Alex, I wouldn't have to pursue statistics—I could paint all day and night, paint until I conceived of myself

as a true artist. Then I wouldn't mind Alex's antiquated exposi-
tions on women or his derivative lectures on Degas. After all,
he lectured like all Russian men (or perhaps all men) lectured,
the way Igor misquoted Tolstoy, my father paraphrased *The
Economist*, and my ex-fiancé recited Marx—with the urgency of
an ego in need of constant watering like fussy hydrangea plants.
Ah, marriage, how akin you are to gardening!

By the time we got to the gallery, I was so exhausted, in such
urgent need of food and drink, that I was ready to marry Alex on
the spot. The doors were made of heavy glass, and as they closed
behind me, I found myself in the immaculate space of another
world. The paintings, covering almost the entirety of each wall,
were speckled in luminous orange and yellow flames that created an orgy of naked red bodies—men and women heaped one
top of the other, their legs and arms intertwining like thickly
woven ropes. The colors, although bright and sloppily protruding
from the canvas, filled one with grating melancholy. Some faces
appeared suspended in a spasm of pain while others curled with
joy, and one almost necessarily had to wonder if they were dying
or fucking.

"The artist has an unusually astute understanding of color,"
Alex exclaimed and whipped out a note pad to jot down the artist's name. The artist's name was Michael Cobb, and I found myself
imagining a buttery corn on the cob; I dabbed my mouth to guard
against the very real possibility of drooling. "It's obvious that the
color indicates the perverse pleasures of an orgy," Alex pontifi-
cated as I faded in and out of consciousness. I was gripped at once
with hunger and a gnawing sense of inadequacy before these sev-
en-foot-long pieces. My own paintings were small and modest,
attempts at capturing a singular face disconnected from its body:
a ballerina suspended in space, a woman merging into a man. I
could manage one, two figures at most, but to capture a throng of
people, to master so much human space—that I couldn't do.

Alex and I waltzed from painting to painting in a daze until we
ended up in the last room of the gallery. There, covering an entire
wall, was the artist's latest creation: grayish-blue, emaciated bodies

interlocked at the bottom of the canvas. Arms were reaching toward the sky, legs smashing against other people's breasts and abdomens. They too were naked, struggling in the blue light to reach some center that resided between them. Their fingers scratched and clawed each other's backs, and blood trickled from their bluish-gray skins. Under the painting, it said, THE ABYSS. I froze inside it. "What do you think it is?" I asked Alex after catching my breath.

"Exasperating! I detest postmodern art," he said with a loud sigh. "There's no attempt to reach higher ideals. This is horror, plain and simple—modern kitsch. This isn't art; this is the grotesque."

"I think it's about death," I said, unable to take my gaze off the blue center.

"This is so moving," I heard a voice behind me say. I could see from the corner of my eye an elegant thin blonde in a black jacket and a red scarf.

"Yes," the man next to her said, "very interesting."

"What do you think it means?" the woman went on.

"If I had to guess"—he paused and cleared his throat—"I'd say it's a Biblical story, an end to the human race. Perhaps they are sinners trying to claw their way out of death. I believe, but don't quote me on this: it's a scene right out of Jonah—"

"You read the title?"

"No, but if you look closely there is a whale behind the blue bodies—they're reaching toward it, and there's a tiny man inside the whale's mouth looking up at the sky. The painting is transparent—"

"I can't believe you saw that," the woman exclaimed. "That's so impressive!"

"That *is* impressive," I said, apparently out loud, and immediately noticed an enormous black mass in the shape of some underwater monstrosity. Behind the blue bodies, a brightly lit figure was suspended in the center with its face directed at them, so that it appeared as though the man and the human race were facing one another in some agonizing exchange.

The man and the woman had edged toward me, I imagined with horror, to reprimand me for interrupting their conversation.

"Sorry, I didn't mean to listen in, but I just saw that myself—" I muttered nervously, then my mouth went numb: the man looked painfully familiar. I felt those words, "dirty," "slutty," "easy"—words I taught myself no feminist should feel—burn fire into my skin, but couldn't figure out why.

"I know you from somewhere," he said. "I'm sure of it."

"Yes, so do I but I just can't recall where—" I kept it up with escalating enthusiasm when Alex exclaimed, "Ignatius Beltrafio—what a small world!"

"Hello, Alex," the man said, "but please call me Eddie, everyone calls me Eddie."

"Emma, this is Ignatius, I mean Eddie," Alex gushed, "the man who interviewed me this morning—what a coincidence!"

I stretched out my hand, and the man smiled awkwardly at me. He had magnificent blue eyes. I knew him and in that instant I knew where and how.

"Emma, Alex, this is Sylvia, my colleague at the bank," the man said, and gently drew the blonde at his side into our circle. She smiled but there were rigid lines round her mouth, signs of irritation surfacing on her neatly powdered face.

"Nice to meet you," I said to her, then turned to the stranger. "Ignatius—is that Catholic?"

"Yes," he said, hanging his head and blushing. "My mother named me after a saint and I still haven't gotten around to living up to her expectations." He winked at all of us, but I imagined it was somehow at me. "I should officially change my name to Edward, shouldn't I?"

"No, of course not, then how will you ever disappoint your mother's expectations?" I countered.

"You must be Catholic."

"No," I said, smiling, "but my closest friends are Catholic—the natural evolution of being Jewish."

"Right, me too." The stranger broke into a laugh. "But God, you do seem so familiar—perhaps you just have one of those great faces—"

"It will come to you," the blonde snapped in a petulant voice. "Let's get going, Eddie, I'm hungry."

"What are you two doing after this?" he asked Alex. "Sylvia and I were planning to grab a bite to eat—do you want to join us?"

I couldn't breathe.

"That's a great idea," Alex exclaimed.

"There's an excellent place around the corner—are you hungry?" the stranger addressed only me.

"Starving," I said. "I think this art has wiped me out."

We walked out of the gallery into the crisp winter air that stank of car exhaust and neglected trash. There was something inexplicably romantic in the mayhem of constantly jerking yellow cabs and impatient pedestrians and bare trees lining the sidewalks. Light snow drizzled from the sky and turned gray streets to white. I smiled at the ground and as my boots cut a path between my fiancé and this new strange man, I felt a sharp, electrifying thrill. Perhaps it was the thrill of being wanted from two sides, or the thrill of wanting two men at the same time, or simply wanting—wanting as the *raison d'être* for living.

I took note, however, of the polished blonde. Her hair was long and straight, harnessed by hairspray into submission, each tress conforming to the general flat shape of her head. She wore a heavy black coat over a heavy black suit that had been ironed and steamed, and kept her rigid in its frame. Only the red scarf looming around her neck murmured of repressed passions.

Alex started eyeing the blonde while the stranger and I gravitated toward each other.

"Do you go to galleries often?" he asked as we slowed down behind the other two.

"I don't get out much," I said, laughing, "Do you?"

"I try to make time for culture, otherwise I'll drown."

"In work?"

"In the process—of living only for work."

"Is it *a* process?"

"More like—an addiction—"

"To making money?"

"Is that how you see investment bankers?"

"Are you asking me what my perspective is on investment bankers in general or you in particular?"

He laughed casually.

"Are you always this direct?" he asked.

"Are you always this coquettish?" I returned.

"Me—coquettish?"

"Is that word a problem for you—because you're a man?"

"If I weren't a feminist already, I'd be confused right now. But as it happens, I'm a huge fan of Judith Butler."

"Now that's a first!" I laughed and he laughed in return, and that inexplicable ease erupted between us, and I knew at once that he recognized me, that he and I were playing the same game.

"Lena, Emma," Alex shouted, "this is Mercer Kitchen—the restaurant I just told you about with that famous chef I read about in the *New Yorker.*" He winked at Sylvia.

A staircase led into a pitch-black underground where only candlelight brought focus to our faces. There were black ceilings, black tables, black umbrellas hanging from black walls, and fashionable young people crowding the bar: men in sleek suits and stylish jackets, women in backless gowns and glittering halter tops, merciless eyes skipping over one another in search of greater perfection. Our table supposedly seated four, but it might as well have seated one person. The four of us had to suffer in unwanted intimacy. Our knees collapsed into each other under the table and fingers grazed elbows and forearms. Sylvia immediately took off her jacket to reveal her thin muscular frame and full round breasts. She glided her fingers along Ignatius's arm, and traced his back. He shifted with visible discomfort in his chair to edge away from her to me. I felt our knees rub, my skirt against his pants; then my knees smashed into hers.

Ignatius looked at me and said, "So, Emma, I know what Alex wants to do with his life—what do you want?"

I stared blankly at the menu, then met his gaze. "What do you mean—what do I want?"

"I meant in life—what do you do?"

"Oh, Emma is a statistician!" Alex answered for me proudly.

"Actually, I mean I am—but I'm also an artist on the side."

"She dabbles in it—it's a hobby."

"I see," the Ignatius returned with circumspection. "Do you see it as a hobby, Emma?"

"I—I—well, a very involved hobby—a hobby I work on—pretty much all the time."

"Emma is just saying that because she wants to impress you, Eddie, but she's going to be a statistician. She's extraordinary: the only woman in her department! Emma is a woman of many talents." Alex paused for an instant, reconsidered, and launched into this: "But I don't believe in this 'artist on the side' business. Either you're an artist like Van Gogh and you struggle and starve and live as a pauper and cut off your own ear, or you choose the sensible life and you work like everyone else and you call your artistic endeavors what they are: a hobby, a diversion. Like reading a good book."

"Well, I agree with you, Alex," Ignatius said, laughing. "I think Emma should definitely not cut off her ears!"

"I only meant that—"

"I know what you meant—a kind of metaphorical vision of self-sacrifice! I loved it, Alex, really! But the reality in this city is that people do all kinds of things to survive—for art."

"You speak like someone who knows from experience," I said.

He actually blushed. "At one point a while back I wanted to do photography."

"Oh, well, it's a good thing you didn't," Sylvia trilled. "Eddie is amazing—he's headed for the top. Everyone says so—Grant calls you his star!"

"I think you exaggerate, Sylvia, but thank you."

"Well the practical world is very seductive: I understand that," I said quietly.

"You shouldn't give up your art, Emma—if it's what you deeply want," he said.

"It's the way I breathe, Ignatius, I mean Eddie. If I didn't paint, I think I'd stop breathing."

The moment—with its visceral image, with its intonation of death and longing and wanting, with the memory of the bathroom—brought us together and in one swoop dispersed our anonymity. Like two winged compatriots in flight, we found ourselves suspended above, leaving Alex and Sylvia in the dark fog of the underground restaurant.

"Oh, Emma likes to be really melodramatic about these things." Alex broke through with his inveterate pragmatism. "But people get over this stuff. Life arrives—marriage, children, the need for survival. Especially for women."

"My program is called Statistics, Probability, and Survey Modeling—SPASM for short," I said.

"That's impressive," Sylvia said, "and you're the only woman in the program?"

"Yes, the other four who started with me have dropped out."

"And you're sticking with it, I suppose?" she remarked.

"That's a good question. Some days I'm sticking with it, other days I imagine myself impoverished and earless."

Eddie laughed uproariously.

The waitress came around and poured everyone a glass of wine, letting Eddie taste it first.

"Excellent," he said, looking at me, then he lifted his glass. "We must drink! To our fortuitous acquaintance!"

We clinked glasses, the four of us, and Alex exclaimed, "Yes, what luck, what luck to have bumped into you, Eddie!"

"Well, Alex, I really hope you join Norton. Eddie and I are on this *insaaaane* project together, and when Alex joins the firm, which I'm sure you will"—Sylvia smiled encouragingly at Alex—"he'll also be doing all-nighters with us. Isn't that right, Eddie?"

"You're gonna get the real truth here," Eddie said, and then, as if he were offering Alex a relaxing massage, he added, "By the time we get through with dessert, you won't want to work for Norton Bank."

"How does it look?" Alex still wanted to know. "I mean, about my prospects?"

"It looks good for you, my friend," Eddie replied, then turned abruptly to me. "How did you and Alex meet?"

"We were set up," I said, breaking into a laugh, squeezing Alex's frozen shoulder, "of all people, by my grandmother, but in our world, it's common practice."

I knew at once, without having to look at his expression, that Alex had intended to hide his Russian self. But *I* felt free, riding high on my vanity, wanting desperately to win, to reel this stranger into my world.

"Alex and I are Russian," I announced boldly.

"Oh, how interesting," Sylvia observed. "Isn't there a large Russian community in Brighton Beach?"

"We're not recent arrivals—Emma and I have been here forever," Alex explained in a tense voice.

"*Forever*," I echoed. "I, for one, have been in this country for fifteen years."

"You immigrated?" Eddie asked.

"My family and I—we were political refugees—we fled Russia."

"How did you get out?" he asked, drawing his hands under his chin, like a child preparing for a fairy tale.

"It's actually a fascinating story," I burst out, bubbling with excitement. "Russian Jews were traded for grain. In 1974 two senators helped create the Jackson-Vanik Amendment—an agreement with the Soviet Union that would allow Jews to leave Russia, and in exchange, Russia would receive grain from the United States. And since it was the Cold War, America wanted the world to know about the oppression in Russia—"

"That's unbelievable," Eddie interrupted. "I never knew that."

"I had no idea we were in for a history lesson," Sylvia put in casually.

"A Jew for a loaf of bread," I added in a peppy shrill, as though this meant nothing to me, as though I had come across these tidbits on a graffiti wall or in some antiquated encyclopedia and gleefully recited them at cocktail parties to seduce ignorant American men. When, in fact, I was obsessed. During my second year at the University of Chicago, while taking a class on Russian Civilization, I came across a strange red book that told the story of sixteen dissidents who attempt to hijack a Soviet airplane on June 15, 1970. Knowing the KGB were closely monitoring them, the dissidents proceeded with their plan undaunted, only to be arrested at the Swedish border before they could approach the plane—to be arrested, the little red book argued, with such a thud and ceremony, with so much death and publicity cloying the air as to awaken the entire world to the plight of Soviet Jews. As I memorized their names, their prison terms, their fates, I felt my own life quaking with a silent mutiny against its current uselessness; the simple rituals of going to class, speaking on the phone to my family, musing over dinner, flirting, dating, chasing love—all stank of ordinariness and meaninglessness. And I longed for it again—the loud explosion of anti-Semitism to sear my flesh, to re-ignite my childhood pain. When I learned that hundreds of other dissidents from Moscow to Kiev to Kazakhstan who had signed petitions and worked underground to free Soviet Jews were arrested at the same time under charges of espionage, I suddenly wished that *my* parents had been the dissidents, two of the sixteen, two of the hundred, that *they* had the vision to imagine in the sixties that the Soviet monolith could be moved, and risked their lives—my life—for this freedom which I now held so carelessly in my hands. I wanted to breathe and rot and die in their war. Had I, had we suffered at all in comparison to them? They seemed like gods whose capacity for enduring humiliation and torture was infinite, sacrificing themselves so that we, mere mortals, made of fear and caution and self-preservation, could get out. And there were other gods I could never touch or know, the Western ones who cared—so strange, so incomprehensible—about our doomed destinies. For neither Senator Jackson nor Senator Vanik were Jewish, and yet it was they who wrote the bill, who proposed to trade Jews for grain and set the immigration process in motion; *they* were the architects of my fate, responsible for the state ID card in my wallet, for the Ahi Tuna I now tasted, for the language I called my own spilling effortlessly from my tongue, for this very moment of sitting in a dark New York restaurant, speaking my mind. Better be traded for grain than not to be traded at all.

Still, it stung me that after all this time in the political arena a Jew could still be weighed and measured, exchanged for a loaf of bread— *why, why didn't I know which grain was I —barley, wheat, or rye?*

"Lena, *zachem tyi ehto im razkazyvaesh?*" Alex reprimanded me in Russian. I felt his growing dread—of being found out, of not getting the job, of latent prejudices. But I couldn't contain my mouth, couldn't keep my body from rising out of the chair onto some invisible stage.

"Many people don't know," I went on, "but it's absolutely incredible!"

"Eddie, do you know if Grant wanted the report by Monday?" Sylvia interrupted, turning away from me to Eddie.

But Eddie seemed to see only me. "*I* want to know, Emma, please go on."

"You see, the reason why there was even this amendment, the reason why we were traded for grain, is because in 1970 there was the infamous Hijack Plot Affair or, as it was known in secret circles, Operation Wedding, when sixteen dissidents tried to hijack a Soviet plane to fly to Sweden, and eventually go to Israel. By the time the dissidents arrived at Smolnye Airport near Leningrad, the KGB were already waiting for them. The story goes that the KGB had infiltrated the group and wanted to publicize the fact that Jews were plotting to hijack a plane, but this publicity stunt backfired. Hundreds of people were arrested on that same day, the sixteen dissidents were sentenced to prison, some receiving as long as fifteen years in the gulags, and the two leaders of the group, including the pilot, were sentenced to death. The world was outraged. Everyone from the Pope to Nixon to famous world leaders to celebrities denounced Russia's hard line. To save face, the Soviet government mitigated the death sentences to fifteen-year prison terms, which some said was worse than death. But what the plot did—what it did—was alert the rest of the world to Soviet human rights violations. That's why Senators Jackson and Vanik wrote the 1974 bill, made the deal with Russia to trade Jews for grain and by 1975, there was a process in place. It wasn't easy but there was a process. That's how we got out, how our families got out."

"I never heard this story," Alex said. "How did you find this out?"

"In college. I became obsessed. I read everything I could get my hands on. Autobiographies and memoirs of KGB defectors, dissidents, refuseniks. I found KGB archives at the library and read and read . . . I couldn't believe what I discovered. How we survived. How did we survive?"

"So what happened to your families?" Eddie asked, gazing at Alex and me.

"We got out in August of 1978," Alex said, "I don't remember much. I was very little, never been on a plane before—I was afraid we were all going to die—"

"My family," I cut in, "we were late bloomers. We only gathered the courage to apply for exit visas in 1980 but by then Russia attacked Afghanistan, and the deal was off, no more trades, US-Soviet relations had completely crumbled, the US boycotted the Soviet Olympics in 1980, and the doors closed. My family got out on a fluke in 1982."

"It's amazing how well you both speak in English," Sylvia broke in, looking at me. "I mean I can hear a slight tinge of something but if I didn't know, I'd bet you were Canadian."

"Thanks, I guess," I said.

"Your story, this story is extraordinary," Eddie remarked. His eyes glowed when he looked at me.

"So do you and Alex speak in Russian to each other?" Sylvia went on. "It must be so nice to be able to speak to each other in your native tongues, so romantic . . ."

"Yes, we can speak in Russian quite proficiently," Alex chipped in happily, "and it is in fact romantic, but we both happen to be virtuosos in English, and if there was one quality that I could claim as Russian in me and Elena, it'd have to be our love of perfection. Wouldn't you agree, Lenochka?"

"Russian is such a melodious language," Sylvia went on. "Unfortunately, I only know *'privet.'* I wish I knew some language other than English. I'm so boringly American. I mean, I could have been fluent in French if only I had applied myself, if only my parents had pushed us kids. But we were just so Greenwich."

"Greenwich?" I asked.

"You know, Greenwich, Connecticut—you've never heard of it?"

"Sylvia means rich, very rich," Eddie pointed out, laughing casually. "One of the wealthiest suburbs in America, a haven for investment bankers. Half of Norton resides there. Grant lives there."

"But only after they marry!" Sylvia said with a knowing smile. "Until then, they party it up in Manhattan like good little bad boys."

She took a sip of her wine, as if to stop herself from revealing more.

Eddie abruptly turned away from Sylvia and shifted his entire upper body toward me. "Would you ever want to go back to Russia, I mean now that there's democracy?"

"Go back? To Russia?" I laughed at his simplicity. "It's a horrible place, and this democracy business is just an illusion for the West. Give Russia ten, fifteen years and all these freedoms, this so-called democracy will vanish, and Russia will go back to a dictatorship."

"Why do you say such pessimistic things, Emma?" Alex cut in. "Russia is like America—every country has its pluses and minuses. I hate it when people act like this is paradise."

"I agree with Alex," Sylvia said.

"There's no comparison," I spat, color flooding my cheeks. "I don't care how hard being an immigrant is, we're far better off here—don't you remember the way they treated us?"

"We were treated like everyone else, and we had everything we wanted. So here and there, they mocked our last names, so what, but look at my parents now, you think my mother is happy cutting people's hair when she was a pianist back in Russia, and my father—I mean he was an engineer, and now what—a high-tech salesman, sure he's got money, but where's the intellectual stimulation?"

"What do you mean 'mocked our last names'? Have you no memory, no pride?"

"What are you two talking about?" Sylvia cut in.

I forced myself to turn away from Alex to face her and Eddie. "We're talking about anti-Semitism. That's why we left Russia."

"Yes, I gathered that much," Eddie said with a mysterious glint in his eyes.

"My Russian hairdresser is always telling me stories about how she was mocked for her big nose," Sylvia pitched in happily.

"Yes, of course, us and our big noses," I laughed uproariously as if Sylvia and I had shared a joke and rose from my seat. I muttered something that sounded like "excuse me," and stumbled over people's chairs, keeping an idiotic smile plastered to my face, trying not to knock down wine bottles and dishes overflowing with wriggling seafood. I could feel Alex's anger mounting like a sand storm at my back, and when I found an open clearing my feet broke into a run.

But I was angry too. How could *he* not support me, how, how could *he* not defend me, how could he not say, "Yes, yes, I lived it too"? Even if he with his perennial beauty didn't know exactly what I meant, even if he didn't have the lacerations on his skin to prove it, he had read, devoured everything Russian, taken Russian Civilization in college just like me. He knew, yet still he pretended—why, why—as if I had to ask? As if I didn't smell his fear. Eddie, the stranger who knew nothing, suddenly seemed like a real option, a mind to write my truths upon—instead of this cruel trampling by those just like me.

There were two unisex bathrooms with wide gray doors and large silver handles that beamed like beacons in the dark. I stood listlessly and waited, even though I knew both were open.

"You're an intriguing woman, Emma." I heard a voice inside my hair. "Or is it Lena?"

"It's whatever you want it to be, Eddie, or Ignatius," I whispered, turning to face him.

"You're on a very dangerous path, you know—"

"Excuse me?"

"A dangerous path for people like us," he returned.

"People like us?"

"People who can do anything in this life."

"So what—so what that I can do anything?"

"Then why do what you hate? Why not paint—paint all the time—it's what you really want, isn't it?"

"Because the word 'want' does not exist in my Russian vocabulary."

He laughed.

"Well, you should try to incorporate it into your English one."

"Very funny." I paused and turned to him with sudden anger. "What do you know about me, anyway—we've just met."

"Did we just meet? Because I think La Cote Basque was one of the most memorable French restaurants I've ever been to, and it's not because of the food."

"How quickly did you know?" I felt my cheeks catch fire.

"How could I forget—how could I forget *you*?"

"But you seemed confused—you had such difficulty placing my face."

"I was pretending," he offered victoriously. "I knew within a minute—when you smiled. I was just buying time. How quickly did you know?"

"As soon as you looked at me—I remembered your blue eyes, your strange name—it's only been a few months, or has it been less?"

We stood there at the foot of this other restaurant bathroom, in a warm, saccharine silence, holding each other's gazes, soaking in the pleasure of our secret past. I wondered briefly if restaurant bathrooms were going to become our dens of sin, our dingy out-of-the-way motels, sinks in lieu of showers, toilets in lieu of beds.

"We should get back to our table or they'll get suspicious."

"Hey, you're not upset about what Sylvia said back there—she's ignorant—don't pay any attention to her."

"Oh, I don't know why I start up these conversations! Who cares, you know, who cares that I—that he and I are from Russia—it was a long time ago—it barely merits mentioning."

"Why do you say that? I was riveted."

"By my 'big' nose?" I asked, laughing.

"By you."

We froze inside an asphyxiating silence that whitened my field of vision, replacing all vestiges of reason with desire. He reached for my waist with a hesitant hand, and yet there was surety in his touch, triumph in his face. "Will you give me your number this time?"

"Is she your girlfriend?"

"Is he your boyfriend—does it really matter?"

"We're terrible," I murmured, "terrible together," and my face fell in defeat against his chest.

"That night we met, Alex and I were—Alex is my—" I went on, the word "fiancé" ribbeting like a toad upon my lips, but what came out was this: "Alex and I *are* dating—"

"I don't think I'm too late," he said confidently.

"This won't affect his job—"

"I may be terrible," he whispered, "but I'm not immoral." Then he kissed me—a hard forceful kiss that stayed on my lips for days.

The next day I walked westward to the Hudson River in the icy rain, holding an empty canvas under my armpit, acrylic paints in a bag, my wooden stand across my back. I would paint, paint it all out: the swarming black underground, the tangle of four lost people, the question of what to do next when the stranger would call, for he would call.

People were running back to their crowded apartments, restaurants, shops. Even those hiding under a silver awning grew impatient, scolding and arguing with the rain. In minutes, the pier was empty. I set my wooden stand at its edge and watched water rise to lick my feet. The sky billowed in gray faces and spat upon me, and I watched lightning burn a hole in its center. Pellets of water tapped against red bricks, barricaded warehouses, black tar drying, windows installed but not secured—*tap—tap—tap—* water drops upon my head. Russia surfaced like dead rotting fish in my consciousness. Memories called forth by smells and sights, faces dug out of an unplumbed past. I smelled Usiyevicha Street here, on hot concrete, on sidewalks turning black, exhaling the sweet perfume of heat into the air and twirling in my nostrils like a beguiling witch that took me under . . .

Painting #1

I'm eight and the sidewalk is alive, breathing from the cooling rain. Trees vibrate in green and cobalt hues and smile at the howling sky. It is spring, and my feet and hands are small, and air thickens over the hidden sun. Clouds fuse into a brown sheet and water pours onto my tongue. Rain is on my gums, inside my throat. I rise on toes to touch the leaves that feel like velvet scarves and paint in violet, then red, then purple-black the bludgeoned sky; it roars as though enraptured just with me. Lightning cracks the sky in half and, for an instant, whitens my multicolored world, sending a mingling of fear and pleasure through my blood. Lenochka, Lenochka, I hear my grandmother's voice echo through our artificial forest. She's on the balcony, I know, her forehead wrinkled, her yellow hair matted from the rain. My dress is dripping in my shoes, underwear clings to my stomach, sags between my thighs, makes me want to pee. But eyes refusing to obey are tethered to the purple sky.

I feel a hand against my back—what are you doing here, the boy says. Playing in the rain, I reply, his face and hair wet like mine, eyes sparkle in the fading light. Let's run around the park and dip our feet in mud, he says. Misha is his name, I think, I think I have a crush on him. We run toward the soccer field, now just a brown swamp. Dirt swishes in my shoes, snakes around my toes, and grabs my ankles. He takes my hand and pulls me under, into earth. We sink and splash and scream. Our noses, lips, and eyes are sheathed in bold black stripes, our bodies made of mud. We look like warriors without bows or arrows, like prehistoric children without clothes on our backs. Our stern black gaze disintegrates in laughter. Our laughter rises, harmonizes, swims. He takes my face into his grimy hands and plants a grimy kiss upon my lips. His legs bind mine, slide between my thighs. I slap his cheek, pretend I'm mad, know mad is how I'm supposed to act, but mad I do not feel. Only the butterflies arrive, one two three, a battalion inside my anxious stomach. He jumps away, then runs toward a hill: let's see if you can make it down that hill without falling. We run together, hand in hand, and at the top, we bend our knees, prepare to ride the mud, our shoes are flying through the air. He glides down the hill in perfect form; his back is straight, arms out to the sides, his face a stoic mask, a soldier in a battle. But I collapse along the way, legs shaking, caving from the kiss. My body drowns in the boiling earth, and then I hear his laughter, his grotesque cry: *Zhidko, zhidko, zhidko!* An arrow shoots into my chest—*this* pain I cannot bear—not this again, not him, I whisper to myself. *Zhidko*, he keeps on mocking. Against my will, I feel my tears break free, my throat close, my heart flail in the sky. I run without turning back, a shoe inside each hand, hiccupping, barefoot, steeped in mud, my tears are washing me.

What happened, who hurt you, Grandmother cries out as I step through our front door, dragging mud into the entrance hall. Misha told me I was *zhidko, zhidko*. He called me a Yid, a *Zhid*, I weep. But *zhidko* isn't *Zhid*, Grandmother says, *zhidko* means weak, like a liquid, my sweet silly child. It doesn't mean *Zhid*, the answer lingers on, and Grandmother, to soothe me, smiles. I run out to the balcony and see Misha trailing home, barefoot like me, head hanging low, rain still pouring, peeling mud from his face. I wipe my tears; my crimson skin is burning under dirt. A new unbearable emotion presses in, crushing my ribcage. I'll recognize it soon—the tug of shame.

The Subterfuges of Desire

When Eddie showed up at my door, rain was gelling into snow mid-flight, turning the city's roads and highways into sleet and ice. And I, recalling the imprint of his lips upon my breasts, recalled the shame of my youth, the shame that would spawn all shame.

"Compliments of La Cote Basque," he exclaimed, sporting a wide luminous smile and a bag of potpourri composed of lavender and thyme under his arm.

"Come in, come in," I said and, picking up the bag of dried flowers, stumbled into an embarrassed laugh. "Thank you."

He towered over me in his dark navy suit, his figure elongated in crisp straight lines. Gold-rimmed cufflinks hung at the edges of his sleeves. His gold-flecked hair was layered neatly across his head in glistening crescent waves and his cheeks glowed, as though the skin had been thoroughly cleansed and burnished. The narrow hallway seemed to bow in deference to him, widening at its edges to accommodate the air of importance he carried on his back, and I wondered if there was a touch of the asshole in his demeanor. Rather than repelling me, it made me want him more. I stared at him, unabashedly, without wincing, in search of an objective evaluation of his looks. But my judgment was lost in the quiet beauty of his disproportioned face. Alone, each feature was perfectly designed, but when combined subtle incongruities emerged and lingered like puzzles to be solved. His nose was thin and straight, widening into a flare above a full, sharply drawn pale mouth, its tip seeming to touch the upper lip. The eyes, sunk into the recesses of his skull, outlined by heavy lids and thick hazel brows, danced in vivacious blue-green hues. More than any other feature, they seemed to capture his mysterious appeal, despite their close proximity to the inset of his nose. He was in many ways more beautiful than the classically drawn men; he was a project—a face to explore, analyze, interpret as it changed moods, colors, thoughts. I painted him in my head—part God, part man, part inanimate object.

"You look good," he offered casually, appraising my dress—a black sheath that grazed my knees and was missing one sleeve, so that one white shoulder protruded and drew an imaginary line toward my breasts.

"Would you like some water?" I pointed down the narrow corridor toward the kitchen, but he caught sight of my roommate's private parts staring from walls, the black cracks in the parquet floor and peeling paint, revealing soot and water stains that had turned brown over the years.

"I can afford a better place," I quickly assured him without knowing his thoughts, in case he pitied me or, worse, pegged me as a poor immigrant. "I mean, my parents are always willing to help out. But I want to suffer—to tough it out—I want—"

"You want to feel like a starving artist?" he finished the thought for me.

"Yes, something like that—I want to live like one," I corrected him.

"So let's see your famous paintings," he said, seeking in the labyrinth of the dungeon's hallway my closet of a room.

Inside a murky interior, canvases leaned against walls, and atop my futon bed, next to the sunless window, stood my latest creation: *Prehistoric Children under a Bludgeoned Sky*. A boy doused in mud strung a bow across his chest, and pointed the arrow at a girl's heart.

"This is incredible," he whispered, his eyes glistening. He stayed silent for a while, simply looking. Then he said, "Is the girl you?"

"Me as a child. I paint the past. I paint Russia," I tried to meet his eyes as I spoke, but he only looked at the girl, at the terror in her verdant eyes, at her skinny grimy hands shielding her chest.

"Do your parents know?"

"What—that I spend all of my time painting, that I've got four Incompletes, and that I'm on a date with you? No—and we aren't going to tell them."

I handed him a glass of cold water and he drank it slowly, as if he were drinking me.

"I promise to keep your sins to myself," he said, his wet mouth curling into a grin.

"And what are *your* sins?"

"Isn't it obvious?" He sidled up behind me—arms like two pythons slithered round my waist, across my breasts, down my stomach, and halted between my thighs.

"We can't do this—" I blurted, yanking my body out, pushing him out of my room, back into the hallway toward the door. "I have to work—I have a survey to whip up, a painting to paint, I have a boyfriend—"

"Do you always feel this guilty?"

"Yes, well—"

"The Jews and the Catholics and all their guilt—" He cheered as if we were somehow identical.

"Try being Russian on top of that."

"I'll try anything for you." He grabbed my waist impatiently and held me under his breath.

"What are you trying to do?" I muttered through a haze of desire. "Deflower me?"

"Ahhh"—he laughed—"I promise to be gentle."

"I can get gentle anywhere—what I want is something else— what I want—"

"What *do* you want?" His face underwent an unexpected shift, his eyes turning stark and grim. "We never finished what we started in the bathroom. Someone got cold feet."

"My grandmother appeared on the bathroom wall like an apparition." I tried to explain what really happened, apparently out loud. "'Don't be a slut,' she said, 'or you'll end up like my aunt Irma—alone, old, and childless.'" I paused and looked at his bemused face. "That's when I stopped us."

"And now—is your grandmother on the wall now?" he asked, laughing.

"I want to go now—I'm hungry!"

"Oh, you're always hungry, Emma!"

And then without warning, he plugged my mouth with his tongue and, pressing both hands into my waist, jammed us violently against the wall. And I, as if energized, emboldened even by the sudden rush of pain, gripped his neck and threw my legs around his waist, my body wrapping his. We kissed like hawks colliding in mid-flight, bruising our lips, teeth, tongues, emitting strange and wondrous sounds. I felt my back smash into Natasha's photographs, tasted hair mixed with sweat, heard something tear and then a thud on the creaking floor. He ripped my underwear in half with what felt like a third arm, and entered me, brazenly, urgently, without words or equivocations. I felt my body dissolve and scatter in the air, leaving only one sensation in what used to be my hips and thighs—a loud, protesting, by turns a dying cry. Through a blur I thought I saw the metal door shudder, a shadow creeping in. I imagined Natasha watching us through the keyhole, bursting in to find us thus—bruised and naked in a thaw—and the thought cut my orgasm in half. In unison, we collapsed on the floor of the hallway. Steam rose off our skin, my shoulder blades pulsated with pain, his pants now sported a rip, a slice of broken glass glistened on the entrance rug, and a sly smile sparked in our mirrored faces.

"Now we can go to dinner," he said, his fingers caressing my hair, looking at me so tenderly I had to look away. "Now I can eat in peace; now I can bear looking at you for an hour or so without wanting—without wanting to be in you."

I opened my mouth to say "And I at you!" but instead only a strange silent acquiescence came.

I had discarded the Bronze and Silver Rules.

The next night I put on my giant black winter coat and went to his apartment because I couldn't stop wanting him. My hunger had intensified. The wind howled in my ears as I made my way into the subway and in its glum airless confines I felt at ease with myself, with only artificial lighting illuminating people's empty expressions, their lives ghostly like my own, finite and without purpose. I was mourning something I couldn't put my finger on, battling some undetectable virus in my gut. My diaphragm constricted and all the air I had taken in from the cold had been squeezed out of me, draining my body of breath and will. I stared at the oncoming train—it seemed to taunt me—*jump under me,* it cried, its shrill soothing and familiar. The train screeched and whistled even when it stood still. People poured out and I poured in, squeezing myself between them, their bodies heavy, sinking into my ribs and back, carrying me along with their briefcases and shopping bags and frustrations. How did I turn—or was it jump or leap—from the perfect immigrant child to this, this execrable creature? All those years Grandmother tried to instill morals in me fell away, a waste swirling beneath me—of time, effort, air. I told myself: "Men are incurable assholes, expert boasters and virtuoso complainers, insensitive fools with ultra-sensitive egos—they don't deserve your mercy." I told myself: "Alex isn't doing it with you because he is a chauvinist crusader and sex will be your undoing in his eyes: you're within your rights!" But the more excuses I conjured, the more intense the pain, the further I reeled and bent against the throng, shrinking under my culpability, brandishing my scarlet-letter sin—L for Liar, L for Lena— upon my chest. I felt a thousand eyes dig into me—could they see it blazing there? Through a haze of static the conductor's urgent voice announced: "14th Street up ahead." Then again, "14th Street up ahead." *I should get out here, turn around and run back home.* But I couldn't—something other than sex drew me to the stranger—some arcane force tugged and pulled on me, whispering in my ear of souls meeting through the warped forks of destiny. And who was I to argue with destiny—because wasn't it destiny that brought us to the same gallery, bowing before the same painting, that even, dare I say, brought him and Alex together to the same interview? Who was God but a tactless jokester? Through tears, I saw a man staring at me two inches away. He seemed to be on the brink of flirtatious sympathy and a clichéd coffee request, but violently I flung my head away. He held no interest for me now.

Eddie lived in a loft on the twenty-seventh floor of a sleek black building in Tribeca on West Street, one of the new developments springing up in the area, towering over warehouses and the Hudson River. I had only managed to step through the front door of his apartment when he greeted me, clad only in a towel, and said, "Stay with me, stay as long as you wish—I want us to make love, many, many times, for as long as it's humanly possible before we both pass out." He took off my coat and jeans and boots and we laughed and made love, and watched the sun squeeze between buildings.

After that I didn't leave. At some point I visited the dungeon to get a change of clothes, my toothbrush, shampoo, other toiletries. I returned without feeling like I had ever left or lived anywhere else, without recalling the acute guilt I felt during that first subway ride.

Eddie's days were spent at the office. Only late at night when the traffic would subside into a dull hum would he find me sprawled on his bed, hypnotized by the TV, waiting sometimes into the morning hours for the warmth of his body. He operated without sleep, without respite, moving like a phantom between deadlines. Yet his fatigue would vanish and untapped reserves of energy would be unleashed upon seeing me. In those first heaving days when the newness of each other's bodies palpitated under our fingertips, he seemed intent on having me in public space. We did it on rooftops, in courtyards, in elevators, in the laundry room, and on the indomitable kitchen floor—standing, sitting, lying, flying through the air. Our bodies had become so familiar to one another that when he crawled into bed in the dark, I slid my body into position, my eyes glued with sleep, my mouth already half-opened in anticipation of a wordless cry. At the first pink light, he appeared to be someone else, in his stern dark suits, feet in fine leather, face pampered and perfumed, wrists bedecked in cufflinks, his brisk gait carrying him out the door. And I would roll in his king size bed, imbibing a view of the Empire State Building and the Hudson River, and order food from dingy restaurants down the street and eat in bed, crumbs and salad leaves mashing under my naked skin.

The longer I stayed, the more I felt my academic mind grow stale and dissipate from comfort and sexual decadence. I lost my sense of time and responsibility, forgot to pay bills, skipped classes, and resigned myself to yet another Incomplete. I moved between clashing emotions, wondering one instant if he was a hollow shell with a sophisticated finish and accidental insights into human life, and the next, imagining that he alone understood me, that he possessed truths I had only guessed at. The motion of life as I had known it ended. I no longer went to bars at night. I stopped attending graduate school parties or gazing lasciviously at my professors. I stopped wanting other men, stopped seducing other men in classes, libraries, and coffee shops. If I flirted, it was by force of habit. I even stopped painting, so exhausting, so satisfying, so utterly luxurious it was to simply exist naked, to be aroused and aroused again, to swell from one consuming thought: when will we do it again? Perhaps we were entirely unmatched as people—we did not take the time to find out—but when in bed we swam like eels, our slippery souls intertwining to the deafening motor of unfettered lust.

For three sumptuous weeks, I sleepwalked through my obligations to that other life, the one bustling in Chicago in another tongue. It amazed me how quickly the human mind can adapt itself to moral failure, how natural, comfortable it was to simply forget that out there another person cared for you, longed for you, intended to marry you—how inscrutably easy it was to pretend! How did my parents mollify their guilt, I'd ask myself sporadically, and then with shame, with a bitter salute to my own inadequacy, I'd recall how much they hated each other ideologically. Where was my ideological war? My guilt seemed to recede into some irretrievable cabinet inside my mind, only to resurface through the Pandora's Box, otherwise known as the telephone. Alex, thank God, called with a new penchant for brevity, as he was "temporarily living" with his parents and they were using the phone bill to extract more devotion from him. I told myself to compartmentalize him into my future: a husband I would one day want, dote on, adore, desperately need, and affectionately call "my darling *mudila*," "you unbearable asshole," and "my sweet spineless fool."

On the phone I was the dutiful wife-in-training, discussing Alex's phenomenal array of offers from New York banks. I was *mahaing* and *ahaing* as he mulled over the pros and cons of working at Lehman Brothers vs. Morgan Stanley, but Norton Bank remained a silent vault. No letter had arrived, no one had called, no Eddie. And Alex wondered out loud if the chance meeting at the gallery might have ruined his chances. "I wish you hadn't told them I was Russian—I think that whole story made me look bad." "I'm sorry," I said instantly, because the possibility that Eddie was stalling on Alex's offer began to gnaw at me. But strangely, Alex himself appeared undecided about his future. He confessed that sometimes he dreamed of going to physics graduate school to make a difference in the world, and yet, yet, he wretchedly, selfishly wanted to make money—to be his own man. He peppered me with hypotheticals: he will move to New York, work at Norton or Lehman or Morgan, and we will marry atop Sears Tower next fall. What a wonderful idea, I cried with robotic enthusiasm. There should be liberty and mischief and all the trappings of youth in my situation, I told myself, I have a lover and a fiancé. I should embrace them both, the way I embraced the two sides of my brain that existed in different languages and ran on different tracks of thought. I should free myself from this moral carnage, from this guilt-spewing whale in my brain, but I couldn't.

Sometimes I awoke unable to breathe. The doctor said I might develop asthma soon if I didn't take care of myself. Take care of *myself*? I wasn't taught to take care of myself—*they* had always taken care of me. Mom and Grandma told me how to think, what to think, when to think. But now, on my own, what a chance I had to separate myself from their incessant, caring, worrying intrusiveness—to become myself! Yet without their wills to guide me, where were my ideas, mores, ethical certainties—where was my feminist roar—under what boulder hid my will? I felt morally naked, stripped of opinions, lost in a plethora of choices, unable to pinpoint or even ask the question: "Who am *I*?"

When I stopped returning to the dungeon, I started lying to throw Mom and Grandma off my scent. I told them I was drowning in work, that my brain belonged to the library stacks now, that I was interned in a prison we fellow inmates liked to call SPASM HELLHAS'EM! I told them these things to please them—to keep them from hassling me—calling every other night from Eddie's bed while he was stuck at work.

"When are you coming to Chicago to make appointments?" my mother was ripping into me for the thirtieth time that week. "You need to start thinking about a place for the wedding. Everything is usually booked in advance—you remember what it was like for Bella—"

"Because this isn't one of your hoodlums," Grandmother gleefully pointed out, "this is Alla Bagdanovich's son—we know these people, we go to Moscow Nights with them, we see them at every noteworthy event: Alla is friends with everyone and related to everyone. We might as well go into exile if you screw this one up."

"Everything happened too quickly with Alex—maybe I'm making a colossal mistake."

"You never last beyond a year with any man," my mother noted. "It's a tragedy," Grandmother added.

"I've been with Alex for over a year, over a year and I still don't know if he was nine or ten when he left Russia or what happened to them there. What is all this 'I-am-so-Americanized' bullshit? Maybe he's a fraud, maybe he's really just Russian underneath his perfectly chiseled veneer."

"Is there someone else?" My mother's voice dropped several octaves.

Grandmother moaned and blackmailed. "I can't take it anymore, Lord, you're squeezing my heart, *Bozhenka*—"

"Alex won't have sex with me—I think that proves he's really *not* American," I said after some thought, giving them a chance to absorb the possibility of someone else.

"Good for him! What a gentleman!" Grandmother recovered quickly. "Tell me, please, that you aren't pressuring him?"

"Where are you now?" my mother asked. "Where are you calling from?"

"Nowhere!"

"Oh, my good *Bozhenka*," Grandmother whimpered.

"Nowhere—nowhere." I kept at it.

"So you're calling from someone else's apartment," my mother stated with confidence. "You've got a lover—am I right, am I right, you have a lover?" She was screaming now, but I allowed myself to imagine that in the shrill echelons of her outrage there was a wisp of nostalgia.

"It doesn't mean anything," I confessed quickly, like an ape ripping a Band-Aid from its chest, "He is no one—just sex." Was there a foot-long needle in my ass pricking me to confess? Who confesses such things to their family members? Who? What happened to manipulative, well-intentioned, nerve-soothing lies?

"What is wrong with the women in this family?" Grandmother jumped in. "I was always a paradigm of virtue, sacrificing my whole life for my children; I tried to teach all of you the difference between right and wrong, and what do I get—a bunch of eternal sluts!"

"You must end it," my mother said.

"What do you mean by 'eternal sluts?' Bella's your golden girl, married to your ideal man, Igor, and the mother of a most gifted child—where is this venom coming from?"

"We believe," my mother announced morosely, "that Bella is having an affair."

"Good for her," I shot back.

"Do you understand what you're saying—she's going to destroy her family—everything she's worked for!" my mother yelled.

Grandmother urgently recounted the evidence: "She's been sneaking out of her house late at night, asking us to take Sirofima in the afternoons and not telling us where she's going, and Igor and his mother are on to her—they're on to her—he's been hiding money from her, trying to keep her from spending it on her lover—"

"You're all crazy KGB agents, suspecting everyone of everything—you're all crazy—have you asked her—have you asked my sister what she's doing?"

"We don't have to," my mother assured me. "We know everything and we're always right."

"Alex is moving to New York, *Bozhenka, oy vey, oy vey, Bozhenka* help us, *help us*! He's moving to New York to be with you—he got the job at that bank—"

"Which bank?"

"At *Norfox* Bank? Or was it *Norfan*?" wondered Grandmother, then with extreme passion declared, "He got all the jobs this time, all the jobs, imagine that: your Alex, your genius! Oh the pay is excellent! Excellent!" Eddie had made Alex an offer after all.

"Oh, I have to go." I heard the door click and Eddie's footsteps break across the parquet floor. I saw him before me, tall and stately, his face breaking into a thousand smiles upon seeing me. My mouth parched, whitening, a loss of breath. The feeling I now struggled to contain climbed up my throat and like boiling water stung my gums, my tongue, the insides of my cheeks, taking me over the pain threshold into numbness. For I could not drink—it held out its hand yet was never mine to hold—someone else's fear of loss.

"You must end it, do you hear me?" my mother's voice belted out of the receiver. "Sex comes and goes but your children, think of your children—"

"What children, what children, mother?" I begged, feeling myself disappear.

"The ones you're going to have if you marry this or any other goy," Grandmother explained with sudden patience, as if I had become in the span of one minute a hapless imbecile.

"Why can't I just have fun? Why can't life be simple and happy? Why can't I fool around a bit, you know, before I have to settle down for the rest of my life?" I asked Grandmother, because as an authority on virtue and most likely God, she had to have a satisfactory answer, one that would settle the moral dilemma of cheating once and for all. Because it didn't seem fair that rising out of the massive spaceship that is New York City, with its millions of faces, banks, corporations, stores, law firms, medical establishments, and other diverse industries, Norton Bank should emerge as a setting for the coincidences in *my* life.

"Because only the honest ones get caught," my mother answered. "Because it's one of God's serpentine ways of teaching moral lessons to the guilt-ridden cheaters. The ones who don't care, who don't suffer, who don't feel any guilt always get away with everything. They never pay the price." Was she implying that despite my admission, I was still good, that good meant sinning and suffering for it?

"Hi, what's going on," I instinctively said, smiling back at Eddie.

"Are you talking to your family—tell them *privet* from me," Eddie said and closed his eyes.

"Do you hear him, do you hear him, Sonichka," my grandmother wailed, "an American —he's an American and a goy and most likely a hoodlum! Semeyon is going to have to support everyone again. That Alex is golden! If he only knew what a flippant hussy you are!"

A Catholic would never do, I told myself as I watched Eddie get undressed, as I listened to Grandmother rail, starting from the Stalin era to the current ABC coverage of the Israeli-Palestinian conflict, against ancient hatreds and conspiracies, dooming the world with her every breath, unveiling before me (as if for the first time) the anti-Semitic strain that like an incurable virus corrupted the blood of every individual on earth. But all I could think was why couldn't Eddie have been a Protestant, like the other goyim I dated? A Presbyterian, a Methodist, a Quaker might have been more palatable, more feasible, for the Protestants as a lot seemed less attached to their religions and eminently more convertible. The Catholics, on the other hand, rose before us like fierce Christian warriors from the Middle Ages, like Crusaders, like the Spaniards who exiled us; their grandiose churches and ostentatious rituals, their guilty conscience and penchant for constantly asking for forgiveness gave them an insularity against other faiths and an eerie similarity to Judaism, making them ironically as blood-bound.

Yet as I watched Eddie drifting into sleep, with half-closed lids, as I caressed his cheeks, kissed his forehead, ran my fingers through his thick crop of hair, as I observed his flaring nostrils and his breath ballooning in and out, in and out, from this peculiar angle, I thought, *no*, no one, no one would do. Not even a secular Protestant or an exiled Mormon, not even a philandering Southern Baptist like Bill Clinton or a fun-loving Buddhist like Richard Gere!

For what we were in America we had never been in Russia. My father would pose rhetorical questions at dinner parties. "What are we? A religion? Us, Jews, a religion, what nonsense! God-worshippers when there is no God! Are you trying to tell me that other people now want to become us—us—whom everyone wanted to kill for centuries? What a glorious country America is!" They thought it was surreal, unthinkable, an insult almost that a person could pick up the Jewish bible, take a few classes in Hebrew, read a few texts on the Holocaust, court the local rabbi, light the Sabbath candles as if the very wax could alter the genetic makeup of their blood, and miraculously—in one swoop—be proclaimed a Jew. So much so that their children would now be indisputably Jewish, and even their sketchy pasts, pasts no doubt filled with offenses against these very Jews, would be wiped clean. "We, we," my father would yell, "we are a people, a race!"

I hung up the phone and Eddie's eyes popped open.

"They don't know about you," I told him with sudden urgency, "because if they did, if they did—well then—"

"What then," he asked with a laugh, "would they disown you—cut off your allowance?"

"I enjoy you like an addiction," I offered, "nothing more."

Silence came between us and he rolled to the other side of the bed to face me.

"Is that how you feel? Nothing but this?" He pointed at my breasts, and I grabbed my shirt for cover.

"We're having fun, right? Isn't that what all men want?"

"Is this your brand of feminism? You want to turn yourself into a man?"

"Tell me, tell me what's the difference between us—between man and woman? I can want sex just as much as you, and not care, not want you for anything else. Maybe I don't even like you. Hasn't that ever occurred to you, or has every woman you bedded want to be welded to you at the hip? Maybe you think we all want marriage—well, not me! Not me!" I yelled, yelled the way my mother yelled at my father. But he didn't react the way my father did; he smiled exultantly, and said, "Ah, I see, I've hit a nerve. If I were to make an educated guess, I'd say you like me too much already."

"Oh, please, your arrogance doesn't surprise me—"

"What if I told you I don't like *you*, what if I switched places with you and said, I want *you* just for sex—how would you feel?"

"I'm coming at you from a position of powerlessness, a history of powerlessness—women do not have the power! The reason they protest—the reason they want to numb their emotions is that we're always trying to regain the power that has always been denied us."

"Why are you so intent on equating yourself with men? Why is that power? Look at men: blind and lumbering fools who don't see anything until it's too late. In my life, women have always had all the power—far too much power—"

"I want to paint, to cut everyone off, to cut—"

"Me off?" he offered.

"Yes."

"I can't stop you," he said. "I'm a great believer in freedom. But how about something in between, a compromise, a male gift, you might say—"

"What?"

"We can see other people—and still see each other."

"I'm an all or nothing woman," I shot back. "We either commit, or this means squat."

"Ah, so you want to do whatever you want but imprison me in you. How so female of you!"

"Explain the term 'other people.' Apprise me of the rules of your game."

"We see each other, but when we don't and are presented with the opportunity for sex, for meaningless sex, as you say, we take it. We take it because we don't really like each other—right? How does that strike your appetite?"

"Brilliantly, a brilliant solution—a wonderful solution!" I rallied with zeal. "I'm perfectly happy with that arrangement—I'm always getting propositioned."

"Oh, I'm sure you are."

The next morning I returned to my dungeon physically drained and in pain; the memory of our awkward sex, of our naked bodies stiffening from some unspoken mutual animosity, gave me a feeling of closure. Inside my room, drowning in the stench of garbage trucks and bleating groans of cars and trains, I returned to my adolescent brood. My temples felt as though they were being squeezed in a metal vise and the world was convulsing in an existential spasm. The bliss of the last three weeks, after being torturously reexamined, emerged as a state of delusion, so that I could no longer say with certainty whether I had actually experienced pleasure or only imagined it.

I lifted my head out of this torpor long enough to see two messages blinking on the answering machine. "Great news, I got the job—I've been wanting to talk to you all morning. Call me." Beep, beep, then another one: "Oh I'll be working with that guy Eddie we met at the gallery. Can you believe it? I'm moving to New York just like we planned. Call me."

That weekend Ignatius did not call me. Red bumps flared on my neck and chest and ankles, causing itching attacks. The rash would scorch my body and then miraculously disappear, alternating my skin from a white hue to a bulbous pink-red within ten-minute intervals. Visiting the doctor seemed like a mortifying ordeal, as I envisioned our exchange. "You say you have a rash—where is it now?" "It comes and goes," I reply as the doctor searches inside his forehead for that one anomaly he came across in medical school. Of course, I didn't go to any doctors, for even I suspected that I was a prototypical hysterical woman, right out of Freud's case studies, suffering on account of my indecisiveness. Who caused my itching, I asked myself like a diligent psychoanalyst: Alex or Eddie? Was I stricken with fear that Alex would demand that wedding invitations go out tomorrow, that we reserve the top of Sears Tower and Sears Tower would say YES? Or was it Eddie whose absence sent my body into convulsions? Eddie who wouldn't call—who shouldn't call! Time would wipe him out and relegate our brief affair into that happy category of "hot fling."

I woke up the next morning to Alex announcing that he was at O'Hare Airport, en route to JFK, en route to me. The sky was dull and white, submerged in winter. The city was under siege from a blizzard that raged for days, blocking roads, blinding traffic. The plane, however, had not been delayed, as if Destiny Herself had cut a clear path in salt. "It's only been three weeks, only January, a cold inhuman month, let him go," I muttered to myself, the phone nestled at my ear, my fingers dialing, hanging up, dialing again.

"Hello?" I said, "Hello? Is Eddie there?"

A woman's voice answered, "Can I help you?" and I promptly hung up.

I picked up a long thin paintbrush and it began to dance.

Painting #2

I awaken in a ray of light, in our government-appointed Moscow apartment, in an aquarium brimming with human flesh, or is it fish—don't you see the resemblance?—we're mermaids without tails. Whispers of a celebration reverberate through permeable walls, and tables fill with breads, potatoes, salads, caviar, *kolbasas*. Green pickled tomatoes and mayonnaise-filled eggs sit atop delicate crème plates painted in sapphire tulips, the china Grandma saved from Stalin's goons that belonged to her great-ancestors, the German "aristocrats" whose superior manner and confidence she brilliantly embodies. Mother chops radishes and peppers as she hums a gypsy song, her fingers tap in quick methodical steps to Grandmother's precise directions. The sun turns scarlet-orange and slides behind the horizon, and in its stead, the ocean rises above our heads in webs of blue-green algae.

Our neighbors upstairs leave Russia in a week but the husband tangos with the KGB, a dance of amiable conversations and the stench of threats. He resells furniture for higher prices, engages as they say in *spekulyatziya*, a Western pastime but in Russia it's a bona fide crime, punishable by incarceration. Mother's throwing them a bash, a romp of vodka, debauchery, and envy. The lamps outside our windows flicker and the light creeps in, peering through the cracks inside our curtains like yellow eyes.

Now we fly in, the children, a multitude racing from room to room, wiggling between the adults and the food and coils of smoke. Already thudding, tapping, stomping to foreign music—such tiny tots already mouthing infectious Western songs—in defiance of proscribed sleep. We're lifted high on arms and necks, and there's Andrei, the handsome son of KGB-watched neighbors, one of my suitors, looming like a Tsar upon his father's head. He screams: Englit, I speak Englit, and everybody nods in awe. His youth and careless tongue glow in their eyes like promises of freedom. We too, my mother whispers, can be them.

A cocktail of vodka and anti-Soviet jokes and rowdy laughter flows through our aquarium of captured fish, and suddenly, the lucky youth, whose parents will be arrested in forty-eight hours, has closed his eyes. My father carries him into our middle room where all the other children lie perpendicular in slumber.

But not I! Not Bella! Although they've brought us to my room and flung our nightgowns on, our lids are obstinate, awake, and so we crawl like thieves through passages between the drunken bodies that smile and grab our cheeks and ruffle our hair. Not us! We know that ardor flares after midnight and Cinderellas lose their slippers at the ball. Not us—why wasn't I invited, a neighbor thinks, because you're not a Jew, because you cannot know the whispers that pass from tongue to tongue of relatives we'll never see again, of friends we'll soon forget or perhaps run into in a supermarket in Iowa, LA, Chicago, or Brighton Beach. Because our neighbor Dina will catch us in the act of disappearing—where's your furniture, she'll cry, poking her long snout into our hall. We're leaving Russia, emigrating to Israel, Grandmother will reply. Well, well, so traitors live next door to me, she'll bridle— why, it's a shame Hitler didn't finish all of you!

For can't you see—we do not know who or what we're truly saying goodbye to. Except for our belongings! Our books, our hard-earned sofas, laminated oak tables, embroidered silk, sapphire rings, gold necklaces, tulip china, emerald wallpapers, burgundy velvet curtains, ancient chests and carved steel beds will still remain as though here lies and eats and dreams a Jew. But once sold to other lives, our belongings will be stripped of us: our stains, blemishes, fingerprints, and spit washed, polished, excised from the glass and wood and metal. We'll disappear without a trace, without a mark left of our lives.

My mother shuts the curtain and commands: simmer down, simmer down, but no one hears her except my grandfather who frowns from his throne, the green reclining chair. I told you not to have these celebrations any more, he warns in an ominous low voice, but my mother longs to dance and sing, for she's young and glorious and thirty-eight. And Bella's streaming in—she too is young and glorious and fifteen. Away from Mother's gaze, my sister jumps upon two chairs that lean against the southern window and begins to sway. The moon's ethereal white light touches her hair and dissipates the gown's cotton shield, snaking around the child's waist and burgeoning breasts.

The men, enticed into a silent thrill, glance at her wearily from guilt and hunger, and in their eyes, a question flickers: is she a child or a nymph?

She's supposed to be asleep, my mother screams, both girls are supposed to be asleep! Put something on, she screams at Bella, where's your shame? Dear God, they can see your breasts— you're not a child anymore! The nipples poke the gown like two stern arrows about to shoot into the heart of every man. They are beside themselves, the men, they cannot look but yet their eyes, as though unfastened from their sockets, navigate the room and land upon her swaying shape. She does not know herself why she wears this yellow gown, why no shame crisscrosses her cheeks. She does not blush but smiles—grins—caresses with her eyes their faces and seeks her prince.

He has a look: a handsome talker with profound eyes—she's painted him for me. Oh, feverish, implacable adolescence—she's dancing on her bare feet. Barefooted, my mother moans, get her shoes—take my shoes, a woman says, and Bella's feet slide into high blue heels. She now seems older, taller, like an almost-woman. There's not a drop of makeup on her face.

A man appears out of the smoke—an apparition, maybe. Like a hawk, he swoops down to our Bella, circling her body with his hawk-like bulging eyes. He has a predator's wide mouth, claws for fingers, and fur for skin, but she—she cannot see.

The morning after blood stains the yellow nightgown. What have you done, my mother yells in terror—how could I have missed it! Ah, when the castle had fallen into a deep, deep sleep, the sleepless beauty was lured into the sorcerer's lair, and there, in innocence, in faithful homage to the gods of love, to princes of her beloved fairy tales, she gave him—how do they say in adult-speak—her soul! The child-mermaid swears she is in love and there, arrested by her pain, melts into the wall like silent foam.

Wanting and Not Resisting

Alex was delighted to be in New York, working at the prestigious Norton Bank, living on the swanky Upper East Side in corporate housing, and dating "a catch," who was apparently me. I was now taking a cab from my dungeon to 87th Street and Lexington Avenue, to a high-rise cookie-cutter apartment building, spending evenings and nights with my fiancé.

We would kiss languorously for hours, speckled with gentle caresses, but at some invisible juncture, he would repeat his usual refrain: "Leave something to be desired, my dearest Elena, leave the best for last." By which I assumed he meant marriage. Our lives now consisted of the daily monotonous routine of moving toward marriage, career goals, visible achievements we could bring home to our families and declare as trophies, won fairly in the American marketplace of success. Our peculiar celibacy would remain till marriage, Alex said, till it was all settled. But what needed to be settled, I didn't know, I didn't ask. I simply acquiesced in this arrangement, the way I acquiesced to everything else in my life. Even art, under Alex's prodding, had to be abandoned for the far more urgent task of completing my statistics degree. "You need to think about making money," Alex said. "We'll have a two income-household, and then after you have children, you'll go back to work with a ready-made *remeslo*, an expertise." I locked my unfinished paintings in my locker at NYU and registered for Probability and Stochastic Modeling for spring semester, the class I had already failed once before. I felt a perverse pleasure in following his orders, in negating my feelings, my creativity, my sexuality—my essential self.

Memories of Eddie stayed in me and intensified: his taste, his scent, his touch, all of him consumed me. In the midst of some discussion with Alex, I'd imagine Eddie moving inside me, the sharp hook of an orgasm spreading into an unbearable longing in my gut. I'd steal away and hide in the bathroom—to breathe in the images undisturbed. Time, I told myself, would cure me.

Except for one strange inescapable fact: Alex now worked for Eddie. After almost a month at Norton Bank, Alex's daily sustenance—his grandiose obsession—became Eddie. He described an alarming image of a ruthless tyrant hell-bent on driving Alex into the ground and burying him before the age of thirty. "I'm telling you he loathes me with inexplicable rancor!" Alex would exclaim between hurried sips of late evening tea. "You're exaggerating," I'd offer, painfully recalling my last conversation with Eddie. "They're all so stupid, he's stupid, everyone is just so stupid!" Alex would declare. Yet he wanted me to figure out, with my "brilliant social mind" (his words, not mine), what every facial tic, declaration, casual remark uttered by Eddie symbolized, and when, when, Alex begged, would he get on his good side?

Eddie kept Alex in the office till late, assigning him more and more work, overburdening him and, according to Alex, treating him worse than the common intern.

And the astonishingly long hours, the menial work, the endless spreadsheets, the complete disregard for his superior brain were taking a toll on Alex's enthusiasm for making money. Even when his check arrived at the two-week mark, he felt it failed to attenuate his humiliation at the whim of Eddie's whip. Though the sudden and complete extrication from the arms of his parents—this feeling so beautifully bound up in the American concept of independence—did allow him some measure of happiness, he felt "virally disaffected with the corporate world." He had become a shadow of his previous self; his voracity for life, for adapting to sundry social environments, for playing Victorian courtship, for tepid foreplay with the express purpose of, as he put it, "inflaming the undergrowths of our mutual desires in anticipation of sexual bliss," for inverting his Russian pessimism into a madcap hyperbole of American optimism seemed to be waning. He had grown thinner, paler, more subdued; the working world most certainly interfered with his excellent digestion, and I wondered out loud if he might not consider quitting.

I can't remember how many days passed, but soon after I deposited this idea in his head, Alex came to my dungeon and before even crossing the threshold announced: "I've left that putrid swamp." He couldn't take it anymore, he confessed, and called Eddie a "nefarious asshole," among other things. Although he had all sorts of explanations for what happened—he was too brilliant for them all, Eddie was "rancid" with jealousy, the clients were imbecilic, there was too much "ass-licking" and not enough thinking, he always returned to his favorite sound bite: he and he alone was waging a war against ingrained American stupidity (forgetting, naturally, that he considered himself one).

"Anyhow, I'm moving back to Chicago—I'm still waiting for replies from physics grad schools," he said after a long pause. His olive-colored skin still glowed in angry hues, adding a touch of pink rouge to his complexion, and I marveled absently at his beauty.

"What about us?" I asked.

"You know my situation, Elena, I can't afford to live in New York without a job; my parents don't have *that* kind of money. We'll live together when we get married," he went on. "I figure it'll take me three—four, max—years to finish grad school and then I'll get a professorship, and hopefully we can settle in Chicago near our parents, so that when we have children, it'll be easier for us to take care of them."

Feebly, I protested, "But what about me, my art?" I hadn't picked up a paintbrush in weeks, but still his speech about our future struck me as severely unjust.

"You'll get a job in statistics—you'll be so much happier in the work world, Lenochka. You're so good with people. And as for painting, I've already told you—and please don't take this the wrong way again—you're no Dali. Keep it as a hobby, on the side— we'll decorate our living room!"

I'm no Dali, I whispered to myself, *I'm a hobby on the side, on the side, I'm hanging in our living room*, I whispered to myself, and thought of my painting, *The Child-Mermaid* I'd call it, my painting of Bella growing a corn-colored tail and long mesmeric curls and fantastical breasts. The fused thighs and knees were shrouded in scales, and the face took on the hue of a cobalt ocean, out of which two eyes beamed like violet suns. I thought of her, my sister, and pitied myself.

"I want you—us to live in New York!" I pleaded with him, terrified by our impending separation.

"Are you listening to me, Elena? I don't want to be an investment banker anymore—I am destined for greatness. I'll be making real discoveries that will impact science, not some algorithms that'll make more money for people who already have too much—"

"Is that the Marx in you talking? What about capitalism—the very beauty—the very artery of this country?" I objected but so weakly that the sides of my mouth seemed to be drooping from exhaustion.

"Is that our parents in you talking?" he snapped.

I turned away from him, but he reached for my hair and ran his fingers through it tenderly, making me purr like an old cat.

"Oh, c'mon, forget all this silly ideology. Stop picking fights with me," he said. We sat down on his queen-sized bed and held each other for a minute. Then I laid myself out and closed my glum, dissatisfied eyes, and let his aristocratic hesitant fingers traverse my body: up, down, sideways, in, out, and in again. After finishing (i.e., finishing off) the business of lethargic, sleep-inducing, what-is-still-edible-in-my-fridge foreplay, he zipped me back up and triumphantly declared a new variation on an old refrain. "At the end, always leave something to be desired. Always keep a man guessing, running back for more!" And I wondered to myself, where's my orgasm—where's my incentive for *not* thinking about Hungarian salami on pumpernickel bread or herring Grandma-style, straight up? We lay together afterward in a tranquil, tender embrace, and I felt the heat of my future approach me, the heat of regret and children and old age and clogged arteries.

Then he got up to pack his clothes and philosophize about his future while I watched. He had a flight at ten o'clock that very same night. I returned to my apartment, feeling drained of myself. February was giving way to March and droplets of warmth crept into the air like magicians, enticing us to throw away our coats in our mad rush for spring. I walked out of the dungeon as I was, in my jeans and sweatshirt, and at midnight found myself in an underground S and M French boutique shop three blocks from Eddie's apartment. In the cramped, moldy dressing room of La Femme Libre, I tried on bizarre revealing dresses I decreed to never buy. As I watched my body in the mirror squeeze into glittering red leather pants, petite jean skirts bedecked in spikes and zippers, and necklaces that looked like collars for a German shepherd, it occurred to me that life situates us in categories that over time turn into self-enclosed squares: once shaped by others, now maintained by us. There we stay locked and content, becoming incapacitated and unable to cross the very boundaries we've built around ourselves. At that very moment, I knew I could do anything, go anywhere—*I* had enough willpower to break out of *my* square. I walked out of the store wearing a burgundy velvet sheath that matched my hair, drew curvaceous lines around my hips, and cut a heart-shaped hole across my back. It was dark and windy outside and I hadn't eaten anything all day. Hunger gripped my stomach in its iron fist, making me feel hollow. I stepped inside the dingy pizza parlor across the street from his building and nursed hot Lipton tea in a Styrofoam cup, sipping with ardor this miserable piss-twanged liquid and inhaling five slices of burned pizza adorned in canned mushrooms and lifeless olives. Surreptitiously I watched men in navy suits pass in and out of the parlor after midnight, eating their slices on the go, standing or leaning against the dirty pink counter, hoping that one of them was *him*. But upon closer inspection, only strangers gazed back at me, their eyes glinting with desire as if to mock me.

At one in the morning I stood at the edge of his formidable lobby, with its heavy revolving door and a black awning that guarded its residents from the street. Through the thick glass I saw Clarence, the gray-haired doorman, frozen in contemplation behind the podium. My body lunged back and forth like a seesaw, caught between pride and desire, reeking of its perennial uncertainty. The wind lashed against my naked back and legs, and with its cold wide palms pushed me inside the marble-floored vestibule.

"Hello there!" Clarence straightened up and smiled without seeming to recognize me, which is why his next statement made me stagger. "You must be looking for Eddie—well, I've been here all night and I haven't seen him." How many of us faceless women were looking for Eddie?

"He must be at work," I offered nervously.

"Works hard, that Eddie. Do you want to wait for him?"

I leaned against the front desk, hesitating, my eyes fixed on the swiveling door. No one was coming in, and small drops of rain started pelting against the thick glass.

"I'll wait," I said and headed for the black leather couch that occupied an isolated corner at the back of the lobby.

I must have fallen asleep because when I opened my eyes the sky was breaking in pink and yellow lights and Eddie's voice was bouncing off the ceiling.

"Hellooooooo, Clarrrrrrence!" he exclaimed, laughing, "and how was your night, my friend!" His speech was by turns clear and muffled, ringing in loud hiccupping tones. He was clearly drunk and a tall woman trailed behind him, a long-haired brunette on high black heels, swathed in a short black dress, her features round and small, her lips pouting in a child's frown.

"Mr. Beltrafio," the doorman muttered in an official tone, visibly discomfited, "Emma—Ms. Kaulfield's waiting for you." He pointed toward the back of the lobby at my still lying form. I closed my eyes and pretended to sleep.

"Ah, the tortured artist is here!" Eddie's laughter reverberated through the lobby, and then the wind swallowed their voices. He and the woman stood in a huddle and whispered, and I caught Eddie leaning gently into her ear. A jealous claw burrowed into my abdomen. From one half-opened eye, I saw the woman clank her heels against the floor and twirl out the door, her long thin figure flailing in the wind, her short dress flapping against skinny thighs—a model out of a catalogue, I thought wryly to myself.

"C'mon, you faker," he said into my ear, grabbing me by the arm, "get you on up—Up—Hop stairs to my bed."

"What's wrong with you?" I burst out and my sweaty palm landed on his cheek, leaving a red imprint. He stared at me in disbelief, then broke out in a thunderous, convulsive laugh.

"Oh, my dear lady, thou hath no right to blow me such expressions of your love!"

"Shut up, who the hell was that?"

"Who the hell was that?" he exclaimed in a mock imitation. But his face turned from laughter to rage in an imperceptible second. "That was my mistress, my business, my time away from you—and what have you been doing with your time away from me?"

"Thank you for the male gift—I hope *you* enjoyed yourself."

Still shouting, we dove into the palatial gold elevator.

"How are the wedding plans coming along, my little sphinx? So you're the marrying feminist, suffering not from male oppression, it seems to me, but from bizarre contradictions."

"Oh, I forgot to tell you—Alex is my third fiancé—it's much safer to be my lover." The doors opened on the twenty-seventh floor and we walked in silence down the hall.

He fumbled with his keys, struggling to unlock his apartment, and I breathed into his back, exhaling my fury. Yet everything about him excited me. Even the smell of alcohol seeping from his mouth, his clothes, hair, face, punctured me with desire. Outside the wind turned into a torrent of rain and smashed against the floor-to-ceiling window that covered the southern wall. I had the sensation of being doused in water.

He plopped on his gray leather couch and, in a hoarse voice, muttered, "I need coffee."

"Let me make it for you," I offered.

"Just sit here—sit here! So you had two other poor chaps who planned their weddings with you and you left them at the altar?"

"Yes, they're always poor chaps when we women dump them, but they're *men* when they dump us! Isn't it right, Ignatius?"

"You know what boils my blood—it's this goddamn self-righteous air you put on, as if you're some kind of victim. Like you're on a warpath to avenge all men for the wrongs they incurred to other women, but clearly not to you!"

"Alex is leaving New York, he quit his job, and he's taking me with him," I said.

"I don't want to be your punching bag, do you hear me?"

"Alex couldn't take you, apparently. Said you were a horrible boss. Said you were only interested in me."

"Did he—is that why you came to me tonight, to find out if I was interested in you?"

"I came to you tonight—I came to you tonight to ask you why you mistreated him—you promised me you wouldn't be horrible to him—"

"Look, I think this game has gone a little too far: you want to keep fucking me, you want to marry him, and then force me—I assume as a just reward for getting to fuck you—to give him his job back so that he can make money and support your artistic aspirations."

I couldn't see clearly; I could only feel spite and rage flooding my nostrils, spewing from the rims of my eyes. I swung my palm through the air and slapped his other cheek, the one that wasn't pink yet.

"With such a temper," he retorted without moving away or giving up a millimeter of space, "Alex can't possibly be what you want or need."

"No, you're right: what I want is a raw motherfucker—straight up tuna sashimi! No soy sauce to confound me."

"Oh, I do like your imagery, lady," he came back at me, "but if you're going to compare me to food groups, I prefer to be a slab of meat—a porterhouse rather than such delicate matter as raw fish."

I laughed and so did he. Each second amplified our laughter, unified our voices, our open mouths, our smiling eyes. After a while we didn't know why we laughed, and how, without being conscious of it, we got caught in this moment of perfect mutual understanding. Then, as if on cue, we stopped with one look of hate.

I pried open the living room balcony door and stepped into the rain. Water pummeled my head and deluged my dress and seeped inside my bra. I watched the color strip in its first washing, gathering round my toes in blood-red pools, and stuck my tongue out from a childish habit of wanting to taste the rain. How could I explain? Twenty-seven floors below, dots of human beings hid under umbrellas and merged with one another to create an interlocking web of ominous black heads. I thought of him again, the boy-crush from childhood and what my mother told me years later in America—that *zhidko* could mean both a dirty Yid and weakness, that the two could be synonymous, that his parents loathed Jews, that Grandmother concealed the truth from me. Lightning from my childhood struck the side of the building and, for an instant, seemed to torch me with its sharp white tip.

"Emma, get in here for Christ's sake—" I heard a voice blaring, a figure at my back. I couldn't recognize the language for an instant, for in my head everything swam in Russian. "*Ya ne ponimayu*," I wanted to say, "I speak no English—English no speak!" I stepped back into the apartment and whispered, "It smells like

Russia out there, in the rain. The sidewalks and the gray buildings—everything is somber and gray like Russia."

"Have you lost your mind—do you want to die?" he screamed, a coffee mug in his hand, his red-rimmed eyes zigzagging and awake.

"I—I—"

"Take the dress off and put something dry on—here—" He came back with a heavy white robe and, without speaking, pulled down my soaking dress. "Take everything off," he commanded and I obeyed, my mind revolving around the same stubborn sentence that wouldn't come out. Only when I stood naked before him, with not a cloth to hide behind, I said, "You—I want you—I don't care how or where or what—I want you and I don't want you to see other people."

He didn't answer so I went on, by this point, completely pride-deprived. "How many women have you slept with this month, this month that you haven't called?"

"How could I have called once I found out you were engaged to Alex—you were sleeping with Alex?"

"What do you mean 'sleeping with Alex?'"

"He boasted—"

"Nonsense! He has a colorful vocabulary, that's all—empty words! Alex couldn't get beyond my bra," I exclaimed with a sudden laugh.

"So you think this cleans your moral palate, this makes everything all right?"

"How many women—how many?"

"What's it to you?"

"Before I give us a try, I want to know what I'm trying—how many other people I'm sleeping with."

"Lady—you're fucking the whole country!"

"I can never marry you," I threw back.

"Oh, and have I proposed?"

"You know what I mean. This will be temporary—this—us—*must* be temporary until we run the natural course of falling in love."

"So you think love has limits?"

"Love is a concept," I replied firmly, "an illusion for the masses like religion; love is a question of willpower. You can plug it or you can fan its flames—all is controlled by reason."

He turned on me with a grim face. "So this is all because I'm not Jewish?"

I wrapped his robe around my body and sinking into its warm protective layers, I muttered, "I'm tied to them in ways I can't explain. They suffered too much on account of being Jewish for me to betray them. They're my baggage."

"Everyone suffers," he said, "everyone has baggage."

"I'm not talking about something that can be resolved in a few therapy sessions!" I let out a quiet mocking laugh. "I'm talking about a world where you can't get out, where there's no recourse but full submission—"

"How wonderful it must be to be Russian! If you ever fuck up, you just say, 'Hey, it's not my fault, it's my damn culture.' That's precisely the kind of reasoning lawyers use in their insanity pleas for murderers."

"Are you purposefully being an idiot?"

Anger seized his face, constricting his features, squeezing his eyes, so that only faint slivers of blue glared at me from under thick brown brows. "I don't care how you define us—love buddies, sex mates, committed sadists—but I need the truth. If we're going to try this thing, you have to be honest with me."

"Listen to me: I'm not Russian anymore, not anymore! I don't want to be Russian, not after everything I've done to become American. My family is my Russia now and all that's left of it— the language and our passionate tempers and our singing. They're wonderful, you know . . ."

"Are you going to let them decide who you fall in love with?"

"I owe them my life," I cried.

"In all my years of dating, I've never been driven this crazy by a woman. You give me a headache, you know that?"

"That's only because you feel like you can't have me. If you could, the headache would be mine."

He let out a laugh. "Dating is a cutthroat sport, and you and I—we both like to win." I felt the floor swivel beneath me, switching our positions in this game of high-stakes chess. He caught me by the elbow, caught my fear with his eyes. "Let's not anoint the winner just yet. Let's go to bed and do what we do best—basic training!"

We circled each other like two enraged bulls in a ring. It was splendid, awkward, painful to be ravaged by the gnawing sensation of being led nowhere, just its own circular motion of wanting and not being able to want. I couldn't feel his flesh or mine, only our bones mashing underneath. And at the moment of complete compression, when I could barely breathe, he disengaged from me with a start, and traced with a single finger the curvature of my exposed form.

"There's been no one," he spoke at last. "No one since you."

"I too, I've thought and wanted—I've dreamed only of you," I whispered, and felt it in my eyes and heart and back, a loud, grating knock, my body tossed on waves against a gale and dropped mercilessly on shore. I felt regret spread inside my chest, regret for speaking, for feeling, for lying here bare like an animal about to be pried open for a feast. But his countenance was startlingly kind, and his lips like two ambassadors of peace joined together in a smile.

There was something healthy and optimistic in that smile, in the blue spheres of his eyes, and in the very color of his skin—a golden brown that made one think of sand under the sweltering noon sun. He had a strong thick body that gained texture from the brown curls sprinkling his chest, and his delicately woven back tapered off like an inverted pyramid into long slender legs. As I pressed my lips against the smooth brown terrain of his stomach, I tasted salt and sweat, his inner world on my tongue. Here, here, I thought, dwelt the American spirit—inside the ridges of his muscles, sloping up his chest into his shoulders and across his elongated arms, inside the sharp squares of his jaws and generosity of his smile and shapeliness of his calves and thighs, grounding his perfect posture in the ample width of his feet, marking the shift of his body from side to side, even conveying humility to his swagger. It seemed to reside in all his indiscernible qualities that couldn't be pinned to any specific characteristic, but simply acted as a collective, defining us according to the soil upon which we're born. And in kissing him, I felt myself as other—the other walking, smelling, smiling, taking in the American landscape, reinventing it as my own life.

PART II

An Ode to Soap Operas

I t was the May scorch in Chicago. My father suffered his seventh major stock loss and began transferring money into a
secret bank account in case of a crash, which came to him in a
dream; my mother, to celebrate designing her first corporate office
space, spent thirty thousand dollars without remorse on a Russian
sable jacket, claiming it was a summer sale and not entirely disregarding the sensitive condition of my father's brain (a floor-
length coat would undoubtedly have inspired more stock-related
dreams); Bella was now openly sneaking out of the house to meet
that same non-existent lover (or lovers) after sunset and returning home starving and exhausted, which convinced Igor's mother
(who in turn convinced Igor) that the lover was forcing Bella to
perform unseemly sexual acts and join him in debauched orgies;
Grandmother had sent the plumber away under the pretext of
not wanting to be alone with a strange man, but in reality she
suspected him of being a KGB agent disguised as a plumber (the
stock loss could not have been a random accident); and Alexei
Bagdanovich, Grandmother's ideal husband incarnate, had moved
back to Chicago to live with his parents, freeing me to date Eddie
in New York without fear of discovery, and ironically freeing me
to plan my wedding with Alex without forcing the poor man to
have sex with me.

An unanticipated perfection seemed to abet the unfolding
of these events, as if the Lord Almighty had personally devised

a challenging obstacle course for me and I was excelling at every jump with Her seal of approval (for surely, God was a woman in my book). Alex quit his job on Thursday, packed his clothes, bid me goodbye, and flew to Chicago all on the same day, leaving me to spend the entirety of March and April with Eddie. And out of concern for Alex's well-being, out of guilt for sampling every five-star restaurant in New York including the exquisite Jean Georges (where after finishing a bottle of champagne, Eddie and I fondled each other under the uncomfortable round table and the waiter in his snooty primness cleared his throat like an old headmistress spanking us with her ruler), out of pity for his scantily concealed feelings of defeat, I suggested to Alex that we must light a forest fire under our parents' asses and reserve a place for the wedding, thereby not only creating an illusion of wild enthusiasm but also sealing myself into a deadline. Alex begged me to come to Chicago and search with him, but unlike every other truly committed bride on planet America, I left the decision entirely in our mothers' hands. "Nothing will go wrong," I assured him. "Our mothers have exquisite taste." For two months I postponed the inevitable trek to Chicago to approve the wedding plans, for two months I basked in the unparalleled bliss of Eddie's devotion to my body, for two months Alex and I held conference calls with our parents to dissect wedding logistics: whom to invite, where to seat them, and whom to snub. I delved into every detail with the ferociousness of a greedy accountant, disregarding the fact that these discussions triggered an overproduction of mucus in my nasal passages.

The reality of May 12 set in, the day the spring semester was over and I would be arriving in Chicago to see my family, my fiancé, and the magnificent ballroom at the Drake, overlooking Lake Michigan where our wedding was to take place. "This will only be a two-week sojourn into my family's womb," I explained to Eddie on the way to the airport, "a regular pilgrimage I *have* to make to relieve their anxiety about the perils of my sudden individualism." "Is 'sudden individualism' a euphemism for fucking me?" "Precisely," I said, chuckling with glee, "you're my secret individualism!" He kissed me with such audaciousness in the American Airlines terminal that my fellow travelers appeared thereafter to be suspended in sensual reveries of their own.

But the switch in atmospheres, already palpable on the plane, seemed to alter my sensitive organism. I breathed differently in O'Hare Airport than in Manhattan, walked differently, felt the relaxing retardation of my synapses, the inexplicable joy in open uncongested spaces, and the soothing kindness in the measured smiles of my old Midwestern compatriots. The sudden flood of thank-yous and excuse-mes unwound me, and I said to myself, close your eyes and taste without fear that white-processed flour and saturated fat in your chocolate glazed Dunkin Donut because life is easy, easier than you think, easier than you want to make it. Without the smell or pulse of New York, without his lips on my mouth and breasts, I could feel myself regressing to a state of pre-infancy, my embryonic brain firmly embedded in the family's thick placenta. I felt it coming on like some abysmal incurable disease—the state of frailty and helplessness coupled with an absurd happiness that was stripped of sexuality and desires outside the family hearth. I was surprised at how simple it was to switch gears. When I violently raised my arm in the air to hail a yellow cab, preparing to push people aside as they ran to form the infinite taxi line, I halted from sudden shock: in Chicago the cabs were not uniformly yellow, no one ran or pushed each other aside, and a short, stocky man was standing at the curb, buried under a sign that said, "Elena Kabelmuffer, Velcome!" This was my father's private limo driver, and one of the numerous family perks now bestowed upon me for staying (yes, staying!) engaged to Alex. (It was Grandmother who felt that I needed incentives not only to marry Alex, but more crucially *not* to sleep with the mysterious hooligan she and mother regularly questioned me about.)

As the limo raced down I-94, I kept my eyes peeled, watching for stop signs and yield signs and sky signs as to what I should do. It seemed so obvious on the surface, obvious to anyone who did *not* know me, that I should run to the lover and we should flee society together and find ourselves a thatched villa on the island of

San Domini. We might stay for a month, or a year, or a century on some abandoned stretch of white sand, imbibing ocean air, wine, soft-shell crabs, and freshly-caught Branzinos from the Adriatic Sea. But as I read each exit sign, I saw only this: Alex, with all his idiosyncrasies and flamboyant language and irritating views of the world, was dear to me; he was the comfort zone where I was not at war with myself. He would accept me as I was—broken, deceitful, sexually progressive, full of billowing pride; he would forgive my every inner ugliness as God's just reward for my outer beauty and my perfect English pronunciation and my ambition to attain a statistics PhD. Alex was the immigrant in me.

We had arrived in Chicago in July of 1982 at the height of the Cold War, when Reagan called Russia the "Evil Empire" and James Bond was battling the KGB in movie theaters. Our first apartment was in a drug zone, although we—the newly arrived immigrants—had not a clue. There was a cluster of us Russians living in an American mix of whites, blacks, and Hispanics on the North Side. Our neighbors downstairs welcomed us with tea and tales of our new motherland. The man said, "Don't worry, this is an excellent neighborhood. At night, though, there may be some shootings, and the lady in the building right over there"—he pointed out the window—"was killed only yesterday by her husband—a spat of the most sensitive nature." And we believed him: not that there was crime, but that there was adultery, just like there had been adultery in Russia. We took long walks, two or three families at a time, sometimes at midnight, all the way to the lake in our relentless search for fresh air. Suspicious characters were wary of us, of our boisterous voices, our irreverent mannerisms, and our foreign tongue. The lake was a sanctuary away from our congested apartment, where two broken air conditioners buzzed and puffed out warm air.

I imagined I was born there, at the tender age of nine, in a one-bedroom apartment that our uncle Yakov had chosen for us because we did not speak any English. Mother and Father slept in the living room, while Bella, Grandmother, and I shared the bedroom, staring out of two small windows truncated by steel bars. Our kitchen was a narrow windowless hallway, darkened by grimy lamps and overhanging oily brown cabinets. It was partitioned from the living room by a row of white colored bars, closely spaced together, smacking of a prison cell. The walls were spotty with fingerprints and grease. When the moon shone meekly on our linoleum tiles, cockroaches emerged from caves under our carpet and held banquets on the kitchen counters. The view from the eating area was of the garbage dump and a parking lot with a predilection for criminals. When I pressed my face hard against our steel-barred window, I could see drug dealers cashing in on the lucrative cocaine buzz of the early eighties and sometimes, to my great joy, getting arrested by fancy-looking police officers who looked astoundingly like the ones inside our television screen.

Telling people you were Russian resulted in a variety of patriotic responses such as "Are you people really KGB spies? When my mother told a waitress in a pizza restaurant that we were from Moscow, the waitress never returned with our pizza and eventually, after waiting for two hours, we left.

My mother's English was a complicated amalgam of Russian and English adjectives and nouns, with very few verbs which resulted in communication disasters with the well-meaning Midwesterners. My father's English was superior to my mother's, in that he spoke in a British dialect and was arrogant enough to believe he was on the brink of fluency. But in reality, he spoke a language that was at best a distant cousin of English. He blamed his inability to understand Americans on their pedestrian usages of grammatical structures and their constant reliance on slang, and glibly argued that their uncomprehending faces were typical American reactions to a sophisticated British accent. But it was Grandmother, while staunchly remaining "non-fluent," who alerted us to the serious anti-Russian rumblings in our building. There was the family upstairs, a divorced mother with two teenage children, who advised us to go back to Russia and periodically dumped reeking garbage at our doorstep. There was the lonely widow next door who hid her cat inside her shirt upon seeing us, fearing that we might contaminate it with our foreign eyes or perhaps eat it. And there was the crazy old man downstairs who literally thought we were aliens descended from Soviet UFOs and waved cardboard sabers at us if we happened to cross his path.

I understood early on that the only way to camouflage myself was to eradicate all traces of Russia from my tongue. I was only nine, but like a dedicated investment banker, armed with three successive editions of Oxford dictionaries, five grammar textbooks, and countless English-Russian tapes, I embraced the American work ethic: keeping insane hours, drinking caffeinated pop sodas, and abnegating all childish pleasures such as doll-playing and cartoon-watching. I fell asleep with headphones wrapped around my head repeating such words as "theological," "thespian," "realignment," and "insurmountable," words whose meaning escaped me, but whose sounds reverberated in my ears and mangled my tongue and jaws, forcing Russian out of my dreams and replacing it with the male monotone from the tape recorder that over time resembled a lullaby of "th's," "l's," and "r's." I pored over impervious vocabulary lists and constructed sentences with my new triumphs: "Will you please alleviate me of my elocution?" or "Didn't I discern you a fortnight tomorrow?" Nor was I shy about sharing my knowledge with my elementary school classmates, who received me as any sane children might in the early 1980s, as a Soviet humanoid sent to entertain them. But their mockery only fueled my resolve. "I will become fluent, I will become fluent, I will become fluent," I chanted in my head as they laughed at me. Within two years, my Russian accent vanished and I began to pass for an American, even before I changed my name to Emma Kaulfield, before I stopped wearing all my Russian clothes, before I knew any slang. And even though fellow Russians stopped recognizing me as one of their own—the highest form of achievement for an immigrant child—I felt as if my world had been splintered, my mind lost to the incessant dance between two languages and two cultures. When accompanied by my family, my tiny victories felt like betrayals; waiters in local diners and fancy restaurants alike engaged only me in their long summaries of specials and jotting down of orders, their eyes conspicuously avoiding my mother, grandmother, father, and even my sister. Behind their painfully cheerful veneers, I could see mockery and dread of meeting the eyes of the unspeaking—the aliens pattering in some unfathomable tongue.

During the holidays, we suffered from nostalgia. We had lost all of our Russian holidays and knew nothing about American ones, so we existed primarily as observers, outsiders passing by windows with giant dazzling Christmas trees and stately menorahs. We discovered that Americans believed in a being called God and spoke to Him at every turn, thanking, blessing, demanding things of Him. "This is called freedom," my father explained to the family, "the freedom to be real Jews." "And who were we before?" Grandmother snapped. My parents enrolled me in an Orthodox Jewish school, not because they wanted me to learn about our religion, but in order to avoid sending me to a drug-infested public school in our area. God appealed to me instantly, replacing the omnipotent red-haired, half-balding Lenin with a more ambiguous though still theoretically human visage, featuring prominent Roman features and a magical silver hairdo. And I brought Him home with me, lecturing Mom and Dad and Grandma on the do's and don'ts of our new identity, pointing out that being Jewish isn't just about anti-Semitism; it is also about *not* eating pork hot dogs, *not* combining turkey and cheese in the same sandwich, and praying to this new God daily out of simple gratitude, a concept so foreign to our hyper-critical existence that I was instantly subjected to my father's personal take on his beloved Karl Marx: "Religion is for people with underdeveloped left brains."

But by the time I reached adolescence, the strict religious tug of Judaism lost its grip on me, and pop culture beckoned— with its incessant whir of eighties music, movies, fashion, and neon-infused coolness. The greatest sign of my Americanization became my quick sexualization. By the time I reached eighth grade, I had already made five separate announcements that I had no intention of "waiting" till I was married, that this was a "dumb" idea, and that sex was out there to have, to partake in, to enjoy as though it was a hot red borscht. Much of this rhetoric, I admit, I stole from soap operas, which Grandmother and I watched religiously, and which contributed to much of my phraseology in English. Although Grandmother was wary of soap operas, wary of their high sexual content symbolized by red lingerie for women and muscular chests for men, she nevertheless demanded that I translate for her, and thus inadvertently sped up the maturation of my raging hormones. While none of us spoke English, we understood that the color television, yet another hand-me-down from my uncle Yakov, was a box filled with sexual secrets that like a magnet drew us—the unsuspecting immigrants—into its force-field.

From our TV I learned that sex was a long, tongue-involved kiss between two tan blond human beings, preferably well-oiled, or just plain wet. And as I was meticulously honest—a Communist value I had dragged with me to the States—I informed my mother and grandmother that I needed to get kissing over with, considering my pitiful age: fourteen. Grandmother warned that kisses led to terrible things, foremost of which was sex, and sex inevitably led to eternal slutdom. And as I did not want to be doomed to eternal slutdom—all I wanted was to interlock tongues with John Stamos or Jack Wagner or that pure fount of sensuality, Prince—I settled for a substandard kiss in a roller rink with a guy whose face I can no longer remember and whose name I never knew, but whose slobbering tongue has remained embedded in my memory, reminding me that my transformation into a true American had to start there—at the moment when Grandmother's advice on kissing lost its effect on me.

By that time Bella was in college, leaning toward economics, a major so practical and noble that Grandmother conveniently forgot all of my sister's sexual escapades and saw her as a newly minted saint, while I had metamorphosed into a lascivious devil in the garb of a teenager. Grandmother tried to keep me away from R-rated movies once she figured out what R-rated stood for, and if we happened to be in one, she'd reach over with her large palm and block my eyes. But nothing could stand between me and gratuitous 80s love scenes; when confronted with Demi Moore and Rob Lowe buck naked in red candlelight and a plethora of sexual positions in *About Last Night*, I almost ate Grandmother's hand in an attempt to catch every last scintillating detail. When Grandmother grew particularly worried about me (this occurred on average three to four times a week), she'd sacrifice her own enjoyment of soap operas for my moral benefit. Whenever *Dynasty* was on and Alexis was luring a man three times her junior into her sagging arms, or oily sex was being simulated on *General Hospital*, or Rachel Ward was struggling to free herself from Richard Chamberlain's arms as part of their inevitable beach-inspired sex on the peerless *Thorn Birds*, Grandmother would splay her body across the television screen and yelp in horror: "Pornography! Obscenity! Smut! *Uzhas!* This is what they're teaching children these days—that's why there are so many teenage pregnancies in this country!" "Please, please, I can't see, *move away*," I'd plead. But she only moved when a commercial went on. Grandmother knew better than anyone else in the family that these shows were the root of my libidinal yearnings—the founding mothers of all my sexual fantasies—and to bring an end to them, she had to be forceful, persistent, and most importantly (as is true of all educational endeavors) repetitive.

Yet despite all of my vocal mutinies, I was a very obedient teenager and remained a virgin far longer than anyone in the family expected. I attribute my heroic effort to the guilt I felt on account of the aforementioned God and, naturally, my family members, whose suffering during those early years preyed on my conscience like a debilitating odor, obfuscating my desires and guarding my vagina with the will of the entire Russian emigration. For to be an un-virgin was to throw yourself in the cage of the "many," as in "how many men have you been with?" and whether there were only two or twenty, I knew that in our world the collective opinion would not be merciful or kind. In my virgin state, I believed that sex could surface on your face like leprosy and thus out you to the entire Russian community, forcing my parents to endure yet another bout of public humiliation.

It was enough that they embraced their "new careers" with all the indignity of people who had become inexplicably blind. My professor father was now moonlighting as a gas station cashier, driving cabs, and lecturing us about how much he loved "working with his hands." "Sure, they complain I go too slow," he would say of his customers, "but they know when they're with me they're not going to get hurt." My father was terrified of oncoming traffic, so he always drove too close to the curb, or to other cars, which resulted in one side of his cab having long, ugly scratch marks. The drivers honked and gave him the finger as they passed him, and my father responded with his new affinity for Russian swearing. "Go to the dick," or "Go to the ass" he would say with a belligerent smile, and I would know at once how much he missed his old sedentary, intellectual life.

My literary mother threw herself into manual labor without the slightest pretension of having any useful skills other than those that required scrubbing and nodding: she was now cleaning toilets at the local high school and making beds at a nearby Holiday Inn. She was also taking classes in manicures, pedicures, and hairstyling, the preferred profession of intellectual Russian women who had once been doctors, dentists, engineers, pianists, and linguists. If you did not speak English and were not willing to return to medical school, cutting people's nails and hair seemed like an excellent alternative to cleaning, washing, making beds, and wiping the asses of rich crippled ladies. My mother did a great deal of cleaning in our apartment as well, as if her job did not sufficiently satiate her soul. A stench of piss and mildew emanated from our mysterious beige carpet and my mother scrubbed it with Comet. The skin on her soft, aristocratic hands crinkled and cracked, and her eyes watered and reddened from the blue particles in the air. She preferred the stench of liquid soaps and chlorine to the grime and insects that crawled under our feet.

We always had the feeling of being watched. It was one of those things you import from Russia, like decayed Beluga caviar, or a moth-eaten cashmere sweater. My grandmother always locked the doors twice: the first time to pay homage to an old habit, the second to confirm it into fact. It was a case of divine intervention that Chicago apartments had front and back doors: Grandmother was now locking us in four times. My father periodically checked our phone to see if it was tapped, although with him it was more an act of nostalgia rather than fear of KGB infiltration. When my mother raked her fingers through the carpet hairs, I used to wonder if she was checking for wires.

Modern medicine had no cure for what we had, and we hadn't been in the country long enough to mollify ourselves with shopping like the other Russians had. Although they had been in the States only a few years longer, the other Russians seemed as alien to us as the native Americans. Their memories seemed to have been wiped clean by the purchase of houses and cars, by discussions of lawn mowers, VCRs, surround-sound stereos, and annual bonuses. No one seemed to remember how they fled or why. The only things they did remember were Visotsky's ballads and parties that lasted into the morning hours, orgiastic drinking and seducing each other's spouses. Their primary complaint about Americans was that they were boring and inhibited, stuffed shirts who held beers in their hands and thought that dancing was a matter of swaying from side to side. Ahh, the way *they* had once danced, drunk, loved, recited Pushkin to their mistresses and lovers, imbibed fresh tomatoes and strawberries they had picked with their bare hands, and drunk vodka nectars from the breasts of gods. Although my mother had her own memories crowding beneath her consciousness—of the gods who roamed birch forests and the brook she swam in as a child, fried potatoes and her beloved wild mushrooms, luscious boysenberries, and red-nosed Fedya—you would never catch her mentioning the past with anything but a frown of disdain. To her, Russia was dead, along with its beauty, romance, debauchery, and wild nature.

For the first five years, we watched other immigrants buy houses in the suburbs and endured their relentless boasting. But in 1987, my father bumped into an old student in an all-you-can-eat Chinese restaurant, and the man said, "Why, Semeyon Romanovich, you should really be working with your mind again."

Although this remark deeply injured my father's ego, he marvelously recovered when this very same student, who happened to be a manager at a major bank, offered my father a whopping salary of fifty thousand dollars, an unfathomable sum in our young struggling Russian community. We thought we had been transformed into millionaires overnight. Bella was instantly enrolled in music and dance schools, and I was allowed to take art lessons at the Art Institute of Chicago, to make up for lost years. Grandmother sent money and presents to relatives in Russia who had never been very fond of her. My mother quit her cleaning job and immediately aborted all plans to rise to a full-time pedicurist at the downtown salon; she decided to decorate the house instead, which was how her passion for decorating was born. While other respectable immigrant women were moving on to more realistic careers in computer programming, engineering, hair styling, medicine, real estate, and accounting, my mother, to the shock of all who knew us, took an unpaid internship at a fancy suburban furniture store. An unpaid internship was, after all, a purely American concept.

With each year, my father got promoted, his English improved, and the money poured into our bank account like a slowly accumulating lava that formed a divide between us and the other immigrants still paying their dues. When we bought our first house in the suburbs, accomplishing the most critical stage of the American dream, the backyard alone seemed to signal a new era of fresher air and uncharted possibilities. My father would gently murmur (out of my mother's hearing range), "Look at our forest, it's like we're back in Russia." Our rise in status was instant and meteoric, prompting rumors that we had smuggled diamonds from Odessa (even though we were from Moscow). But the simple truth was that my father had made money the healthy, old-fashioned American way: by gambling on the stock market. Ever since he had been promoted to senior mathematical analyst at his bank, helping to construct formulas for predicting the market, he itched to dip his own hand in the gold pot. He was cautious at first, investing minuscule amounts in reliable monoliths, but over time he became a barracuda, chewing chunks off his salary all in the name of the big win, losing thousands of dollars he and my mother made on their jobs, seizing on the riskiest companies, resembling the poor souls on talk shows who denied their gambling addictions, until that rather ordinary, sunless day when his investment of twenty thousand dollars in a dubious Internet company quintupled. My father strode into our house like a man who had exchanged his sanity for a gilded crown. I can't remember how many times or in how many octaves he had sung, "I told you so," but from that moment on, we did not question my father, and he, with great bravado, buried himself in stock reports that were now treated like sacred artifacts by my grandmother. Steadily, my father lifted us into the firmament of thickly woven millions. When our green-eyed relatives and friends watched my parents build a mansion from a mere blueprint on the prestigious Winnetka shore, with a wooden Jacuzzi, they plummeted into a depression unique to all immigrants: why them, why not us?

Grandmother spoke with despair about jealousy. She was a great believer in the evil eye, and therefore there was an explanation behind every ailment in the family. "We didn't knock on wood enough," Grandmother would say, or "we should have washed our faces with urine after they complimented us." When my mother bought a new triangular purple couch and people visited and complimented the couch, Grandmother became worried. "You don't want to believe, but look at your mother—she looks terrible and has a high fever when only yesterday she was gorgeous and healthy. How can it be?" Jealousy and the evil eye reigned over our world, constricting our tongues, our actions, our purchases. We lived in constant fear, suspicious of Misfortune, which could strike at any moment and whose precarious laws did not subscribe to any gods, but belonged to some force wielded by human beings themselves, hating one another and sending curses on each other's heads.

Each year the memory of our one-bedroom apartment on Morris Lane was further blurred into unreality, a dream not unlike the dream of having once lived in Russia. We were living fully now, breathing so to speak the American life; only I could never tell exactly what we were. None of us could, except perhaps my grandmother. She, who stuffed Russian traditions down our throats, who lived as though Stalin could walk through our front door and arrest her, who spoke of Grandfather's death as though it were yesterday, who knocked on wood religiously throughout all conversations, who never looked in the mirror while she ate, who lacked even a basic grasp of the English language and because of that never passed her American citizenship test, believed that she had always been an American in her soul. The rest of us were still stumbling to define our peculiar intersection of cultures—Americanized Russian Jews, or American Jews originally from Russia, or Russian-Americans who are also by the way Jews. As I passed construction sites about to soar into rows of houses, into future suburban enclaves, I imagined that we, the immigrants, started out as mere blueprints, then over time became the raw materials—mortar, wooden planks, steel—and eventually, brick by brick, parquet floor by parquet floor, rose into family-sized houses with charcoal rooftops and winged windows and rich mahogany doors.

The Art of Not Offending Anyone

The dining room in my parents' house had never sparkled in so many festive colors as it did on the night my parents officially celebrated my engagement to Alexei Bagdanovich. Our fancy dining table was a delicate piece of Brazilian cherry wood on skinny carved legs, an antique my mother snagged for a whopping twenty thousand dollars. Grandmother said its solemnity reminded her of the war and brought out our red embroidered silk tablecloth, which my mother felt bore a stark resemblance to the Communist flag. The other colors of the evening were due entirely to Mrs. Bagdanovich's hair. Alla had taken auburn to a new level of mauve, which she said gave her the oomph she needed to seduce her husband, Fima, a plump bald man who had long ago transferred his sexual energies to cars.

The Bagdanoviches arrived in style, in their best jewelry—their beloved new silver Lexus that Mr. Bagdanovich purchased despite the threat of divorce. Unlike our family, the spender in their family was the father, who, they say, loved pleasure the way only a woman can. The mother was the saver, the accountant, the overseer of all things purchasable and unpurchasable, and the whip that kept the father from plunging the family into bankruptcy. It was no secret that Mrs. Bagdanovich was dissatisfied with the fact that her perfect fingers, a pianist's treasure, were now being wasted on cutting Russian women's hair. Mr. Bagdanovich was happily employed as a high-tech salesman at Able-Soft, a dwindling corporate conglomerate still making Apple computers, a job at which he did not excel and that no one knew how he got (as he was neither exceptionally presentable nor fluent in English), but which had a pernicious influence on his frail, vain psyche by refocusing his energies to Armani suits, Porsches, Jaguars, BMWs, underwater watches, and full-service condominiums in Naples, Florida.

The family was "shit-deep in debt," in Alla's famous words to her manicurist, and unless she squeezed Fima's throat in her manly fist, their poor son Alexei would have to fend for himself in the world.

One had to admit that Alla Bagdanovich was a selfless mother. When Harvard called to say that Alex had been accepted to their PhD program in physics (as did Cal Tech and MIT), Mrs. Bagdanovich thought she had gone to heaven and returned to earth in a diamond choker. "If you don't go, then you're a fool," she told him, sacrificing, like all good Jewish mothers, her own well-being and sanity. "What do you want to be for the rest of your life—a buzyman?" She said the word "buzyman" as though she were describing a garbage collector. When Alex protested on account of his parents' financial crisis, she protested back: "Fima and I are done for, our lives are finished; we now live for you." She also spoke of true Greatness with a capital G and universe-altering scientific discoveries. "What if you're going to uncover the mystery of quantum physics? Do you want to lose that chance? Or teach the world about time travel?" Such things did not fall flat on Alex's egotistical ears. When he quit Norton, he felt fully empowered by his mother and even sang to her in a middle C: "*Mamochka*, I just sent forty-five dollars to HARRR-HARRR- HARRR-VAAAAAARD."

The joy unleashed in the Bagdanovich household seeped through their walls into their neighbors' ears and down the wide highways that led to the houses of their Russian compatriots, their fellow sufferers in the struggle to reach the apotheosis of American success. Having appealed to the universe, claiming that the survival of the human race hinged on Alex's Harvard PhD (MIT and Cal Tech were unilaterally dismissed on account of other Russians' greater familiarity with Harvard), Mrs. Bagdanovich felt that she had personally succeeded. Her suffering as a hairstylist and part-time piano teacher—as a "nobody"—her nostalgia for the art of performing (straightening her broad back, arching her imperious brows, assuming an expression of godliness as she crinkled her skirt on the stage before settling at the piano), and her year after year exhaustive rush to churn out meat blintzes for Alex's finals were at last justified. Happiness palpitated like a warm fuel in her heart.

My father rose warily from his chair, and fixating on Mrs. Bagdanovich, proclaimed: "To our two children, may they bring us *nachas* and lots of grandchildren!" Then he clinked his glass against Mrs. Bagdanovich's, and the two immediately exchanged a knowing smile, one that promised an ongoing flirtation into old age.

"Yes, to our children," my mother added, "may you love each other wildly, passionately, honestly, and remember: the most important thing in marriage is the implicit understanding between two people."

"Very well stated," Igor announced in a somber tone. Bella was seated next to him in a gold shimmery dress, holding five-year-old Sirofima in her lap and feeding her *blinchiki*. (Bella and her husband and child lived on the third floor of my parents' mansion, separated from Grandmother by a large sitting area, a quasi-balcony that featured stacks of romance novels and a miniature refrigerator, because as Igor pointed out, "Why spend unnecessary money on our own house when your parents' house is so big!")

Alex and I nodded with exaggerated enthusiasm, and Fima Bagdanovich cried out, "Touché, touché," like a demonstrator rallying for the eternally misunderstood.

Everyone clinked glasses with one another and reached over the appetizers to make sure that no glass was left un-clinked.

A moment for heroism presented itself. Alex couldn't reach my grandmother, so he rose gallantly from his chair and, circling the table, sidled up to my grandmother's outstretched arm. As they clinked glasses and beamed at one another, I saw Grandmother's mind, that complex organ of pristine virtue and flawed logic, zeroing in on a joyous, palliative thought: all her devotion to my moral upbringing had not been in vain.

"Well, well, well, Sonichka," Mrs. Bagdanovich exclaimed, taking a considerable helping of Olivier salad and stewed eggplant, "you really didn't have to go all out on our account. We just wanted simple tea and dessert, but this looks wonderful." Alla Bagdanovich was a plump woman with excessive layers of bright pink lipstick on her thick emotional lips and globs of mascara, a gold choker of a necklace, and that fashionable black dress meant to pinch fat into submission. She had once been a beauty, it was said, but overeating and nerves over her failed career and her husband's insolent spending habits had caused wrinkles and puffiness around the eyes, so that now only makeup could retrieve her features. Still, she accepted her corpulent figure, with its rolls of fat across the entirety of her back and her constantly deepening, fluid cleavage, the way only a Russian woman could: with pride and majestic deportment. (At times, one hoped for a little less pride when she wore skin-tight black dresses and pressed her bosom ardently into the dinner table.)

"Lenochka, which of these delicious dishes did you cook?" Mrs. Bagdanovich inquired.

"I—oh, I don't know how to cook—" But before I could finish my sentence with "Russian food," my mother valiantly interceded:

"Our Lenochka is concentrating on her mind now—cooking will come later."

"A woman must be able to do everything well," Mrs. Bagdanovich observed.

"So must a man," Bella snapped.

"Our Sashenka is full of hidden talents. Just the other day I discovered what a wizard he is with the lawnmower. Fima couldn't make heads or asses—excuse my language—out of our broken lawnmower, but Sashenka with his excellent knowledge of physics and mechanical prowess immediately saw that the problem was with the motor and threw it out, announcing that it was unsalvageable." His mother gazed wide-eyed at her son with the sort of admiration that could make a rock blush. Alex remained unperturbed.

"I told you hundreds of times that we needed to get rid of that piece of shit," Fima barked at his wife, "but no, you have to save everything. Do you realize that my wife"—he turned to my grandmother as if she was the only authority on lawnmowers—"has kept not one, not two, but three old couches in our basement in case all our *mishpucha* drop in from the motherland and where will they sleep?"

"Where *will* they sleep?" Mrs. Bagdanovich broke in with passion.

"Not to mention all the *drek* we've kept from Russia—torn seventies *shmatas*! The basement is our oyster—let the damn rats eat the cashmere already!"

"Must you embarrass me everywhere we go?" Mrs. Bagdanovich sniped.

A traumatic pause invaded the dinner table, and Alla Bagdanovich blushed a deep pink that matched her mauve hair.

"Sasha tells us that your daughter has extreme ideas about *feminiiiism*," Fima said, addressing my mother in a formal tone. "There's nothing wrong with a woman having a strong opinion per se, as long as she doesn't try to push it down a man's throat."

"I couldn't agree with you more," said my father.

"Are you implying that our daughter is pushing feminism down your son's throat?" my mother exclaimed, then, twisting her neck in hatred at my father, added, "and you're agreeing with this impudence!"

My father's eyebrows rose to his hairline and he only managed to produce, "Ah, what?"

"You're misinterpreting me, Sonichka." Fima came to my father's rescue. "I was speaking about American women who have clearly had a pernicious influence on this country."

"I, for instance, do not in the least agree with *feminism*," Mrs. Bagdanovich exclaimed, even though she worked after Alex's birth, was a wizard at plumbing, packed, carried, and lifted all their Soviet suitcases supposedly on account of Fima's bad back, and oversaw all the money transactions. Although it was socially promiscuous for a Russian woman to support feminism in public, in private, feminism was alive and kicking, in the form of criticizing, emasculating, and manipulating any random male.

"And thank God for that." Fima nodded at his wife, then turned a stern eye in my direction.

"Americans have stupid views: they think if you give a woman equal pay she'll turn into a man. But that's just idiotic! Consider the Bible, which says a woman came out of a man's rib, that's why she has weaker muscles and could never be a plumber or a car mechanic or bricklayer. Give me one example of a woman we know who's a bricklayer!"

"Wonderful point, wonderful logic, you're my hero, Fimochka!" Alla cried out with emphasis on "hero."

"You can't argue with biology!" Fima said.

"Sure I can." I almost leapt out of my chair. "According to your biology we were once savages who tore animals apart with our bare hands, ate with our fingers, slept on the ground, lived in caves, died at the age of thirty, beat our children and wives with sticks, and ate each other if survival demanded it! We outgrew barbarism, although that's still debatable, and now it's time to outgrow chauvinism."

"My dearest Lenochka," Mrs. Bagdanovich said with a suspicious smile, "there's no need to get so excited. Men will always be animals, who will never voluntarily wash their dirty paws before dinner unless you nag. And, of course, impotent men will always be asserting their superiority over women. Be smart, Lenochka, speak in a softer tone—apply soft pressures to the man's insecure brain." Bella winked at me. She, too, had caught the word "impotent," and with an irreverent laugh downed her vodka.

"You must learn to be more feminine," Alla said in my ear, her tongue practically tickling my earlobe. "You say too much of what's on your mind—men don't like that. My Alex is a very sensitive individual and you must learn to handle him because I assure you"—she stared meaningfully at my profile—"talk of feminism will get you nowhere."

"Take more *kabachki*," Grandmother urged Alex, while eyeing Alla with grave mistrust.

"Speaking of feminism," Igor joined in, "what does everyone think of that prostitute, Monica Lewinsky?"

"She's certainly not a feminist," Bella noted.

"Grotesque," Grandmother offered, referring not to Monica herself but to oral sex.

"Poor Beel Clinton," Alla murmured as though he were her lover. "I feel sorry for him."

"Me too," my father said, "a man has a little fun and the whole country wants to burn him alive. Don't Americans realize that all politicians lie—they have to lie to subsist! I would have lied in his shoes!"

"She's to blame!" Grandmother cried.

"Who—Monica?" Bella asked.

"No, Hillroy Climpton—"

"Hilllllllarrrrry Clinnnnnton," my mother corrected her.

"It's all Hillroy's fault," Grandmother went on. "When your man is a chronic philanderer, you need to be on guard. Keep your eyes peeled open and a frying pan nearby—for his unfaithful head."

"Which brings me to an important issue!" Mrs. Bagdanovich galloped in to insert her seven cents, "Let me begin by saying that I'm delighted our children are getting married and next May is as good a month as any, but there's something I must get off my chest. My experience in life tells me that if I don't speak, no one ever will." She quieted down to give the guests a chance to prepare for the inevitable scourge of the evening. "The Drake is very expensive, and although I accompanied Sonya on this decision, I feel that I must protest—Fima and I simply don't have the same resources—"

"Allochka, I told you, not in front of people," Fima murmured.

"These aren't mere people"—Mrs. Bagdanovich pointed with her manicured forefinger at my mother—"these are our future in-laws—why, they're practically our family!"

"No worries—I'll take care of it—I mean we, my wife and I," my father stammered, glancing fearfully at my mother, "will take care of the bulk."

"That's very generous of you, Semeyon, but I can't have that," Fima said. "I must insist."

"With what money do you want to insist?" Mrs. Bagdanovich cut in. "Everyone knows we're nose-deep in debt! Like pigs in manure!"

My father swiftly raised his glass before Alla could elucidate and said, "I'd like to make a toast to a very special young man—to our very own Alexei—who I'm proud to call my future son-in-law. May your genius flourish at Harvard!" My father abhorred confrontations of any kind, despite his propensity for them, but the ones about money in particular riled his stomach acid, resurrecting his Soviet-era heartburn.

"May it flourish, indeed," my mother said. Then she rose from her chair and aimed a suspicious gaze at Alex. "Lena tells us you really loved working at the bank. So I was wondering why you only stayed there for a month or was it less?"

Alex stood up as well. With his shot glass embedded in his palm and in a sonorous baritone, he announced, "First, Sonya,

Semeyon, and of course, Zinayida Genadevna, I want to make a toast to you for raising such a remarkable and beautiful young woman."

"*Nu, nu, molodetz,*" my grandmother exclaimed, "now that's a toast for you!" And with that, everyone downed their glasses, eyes shutting from the desire to momentarily escape each other.

"As to your question, Sonya," Alex went on, "I think Lena is mistaken. I loathed the bank. Mindless cruelty is what it amounted to—slavery for a thinking individual—"

"Well stated, son!" his mother effused.

"Our children have become such idealists! I wish I had the luxury to be an idealist," Fima put in.

"I wanted greater things for myself than what the corporate world had to offer. I have a fantasy—of a personal greatness." Alex addressed only my mother.

"You don't have to explain yourself, Sashenka," Mrs. Bagdanovich said.

"I could have stayed on indefinitely, Sonya, if that's what you're implying—I was supremely successful at the bank! And Mother," he said, turning to her with all the gentleness he could muster, "you have nothing to worry about—I have plenty to contribute to the wedding."

"What a wonderful boy!" my grandmother remarked, smiling at Alex. "What a heart."

In reality, she was bemoaning this state of affairs: a mama's boy, a wet rag, possibly not even a real man . . . but there were so many other blessings, like his pristine Russian and his verifiable Jewishness!

"Look, we're getting ahead of ourselves," my mother said. "Let's hope everything works out—"

"Well, why shouldn't it work out?" Mrs. Bagdanovich directed a scouring gaze at my mother.

"Oh, I mean no offense, but a wedding requires superior planning. When our Bellochka was getting married, it was pandemonium in this house. What with the dress fiasco, and the flower people, who tried to rip us off—"

"They were homosexuals," my father put in.

"We have nothing against homosexuals," my mother quickly added, "but—"

"They're a blight on the human race," Grandmother summed up, her cheeks filling with warm mauve tones, "espousing their ideology on every corner and corrupting the young with their unnatural ways."

"What do you suggest, Grandma," I shouted, "that we do to homosexuals what they did in Russia—put them in jail? Or kill them, like the NKVD killed Tchaikovsky?"

"Don't *you* tell me about the NKVD—I knew the NKVD before any of you were born—dear Lord, what they did to our family—" Grandmother's voice cracked and her eyes moistened. The dinner table entered a moment of silence, to mourn Stalin's victims, of course, but more importantly to assure Grandma that all her views were admissible on account of her unsurpassable suffering.

"I have nothing against specific homosexuals," Grandmother said. "And *Swan Lake*—everyone knows is my cure against insomnia—no doctor can explain it, but when I get to the second act I drop off like a corpse, *every time.*"

"As I was saying," my mother cut in, "we have nothing against anybody, but when the orchids arrived, they were wilted, practically brown from age—"

"Oh, our mother exaggerates," Bella declared, "my wedding was a royal affair—no expense was spared."

"I've already told you—I will never make as much money as your father, so stop dreaming!" Igor barked at his wife.

"My darling Igoryek"—Bella adopted the amicable playfulness of a kitten (for we had a saying: if there's a prick in the family, no one else has to know about it)—"have I ever complained about your career—you've done brilliantly!" As she scratched the back of Igor's head, her fingernails, like the needles of an acupuncturist, seemed to cure his nerves.

"Honestly, we can do something simple, modest, and elegant." My mother looked apologetically at Alla, baring for the table her guilt and kindness. "We don't have to have orchids; we can just have roses. White ones or crème, or a wild theme in red like that actress, I forget her name. It all depends on the children. What do you want—Lenochka, Sashenka, what do you two want?"

"Oh, I leave such matters to the ladies," Alex announced, warming my grandmother's heart. Real man, real man, real man . . . she chanted through closed lips.

"I'll be right back," I said and rose from the table.

Alex lunged toward me. "Do you want me to come with you?"

"No, Sasha, please, I'm going to the washroom."

The table quieted down for my departure. In a panic, instead of using the downstairs bathroom, I ran up our winding wooden staircase and ducked behind the gargoyles perched on the banisters (my mother's homage to old Victorian homes).

I plopped on my bed and felt my heart zigzagging inside my body, heat gathering in my armpits and under my closed lids. I pleaded with God: *Aveenu Malcheynu Haneynu Vi Aneynu Vi At Anu Maasim.* The Yom Kippur prayer had stayed with me since Hebrew school, since I first learned it as a nine-year-old child, since I practiced it in secret, without letting my family know that I still fervently clung to this elusive God we had denounced in Russia. The melody unlocked a refuge in my head, and from the Hebrew I offered it to myself in English: *Forgive me, Lord, for I have sinned.*

For here it was, barreling through my heart, an unexpected exhilaration in the act of lying. Lying as the postponement of commitment, of choosing, of being owned. Lying not conventionally defined but as the ultimate act of self-bifurcation, the precise condition of double identity, a near perfect simulacrum of two parallel languages and cultures swimming side by side within one mind. I switched between them as I did between the men, with a heightened devotion to each—a full transformation from my inner thoughts to the outer placement of my tongue. I luxuriated in the fluency I now possessed in both languages, in this ability, now fifteen years later, to move seamlessly from one state of being to the next, to pretend to be "one of you," so clearly differentiated from "one of them," and yet continued to feel the brunt of alienation within the very language and culture I found myself in. I was a stranger unto myself, at once at home in each world and an alien in both, never belonging.

My fingers tapped against the phone, and with each click I felt the muscle from my cheek to my brow tensing, my tongue hardening, my jaws readjusting and locking into that familiar position of the Other—my American self.

"Hello," I said into the receiver, "it's me."

His low, crisp voice was tinged with exhaustion, yet it gave me immediate release.

"I've been thinking about you," he said.

"I'm dying."

"Of horniness?" he asked.

"That," I submitted, "and madness: my family is driving me insane."

"What are they doing to you?"

"Nagging. Plotting out my life. Secretly getting disappointed," I replied.

"Am I still your secret goy?"

"You are," I confessed warmly, staying approximately ten kilometers away from the actual truth, and then I added a tender lie on top of it: "I haven't had the courage to tell them."

"Don't—I like being your sin," he said. "When are you flying home?"

"In three days, if I don't lose my mind."

"You won't. And if you do, I'll fuck you back to sanity."

"Can you do that? Can you cure my depression with your dick?"

"I can—I am that confident!" He laughed. "Now think of me on top of you and scream as loud as you can, 'Fuck me, Eddie, fuck me!'"

"I'd say keep everything except the name. Eddie is too common, too prosaic. I should scream, 'Fuck me, Ignatius, fuck me, your royal highness, fuck me properly!' That way when they accuse me of whoredom, at least I'll be seen as an aristocratic whore, a throwback to the days of the educated courtesans, those rare birds who knew how to hold a fork, recite poetry, and lift their skirts with just the right modicum of modesty."

"Is that what you aspire to be—a courtesan?"

"In my fantasies of you, yes. I aspire to be *cortigiana onesta*."

Eddie laughed. "I'm glad I'm having that effect, my honest courtesan."

"You know what it means?"

"You sound surprised whenever I know anything other than my subfields of econ and finance," he said cheerfully, "but I happen to be an avid admirer of courtesans. You're my Duchess Du Barry. Grand, extravagant, stunning looking—like you. You look like her."

"I look like Duchess Du Barry? How strange of you to think that. We are talking about the last mistress of Louis XV of France, the one who was beheaded during the Reign of Terror?"

"Same one," he said.

"I only know everything about her because Vigee-Lebrun painted her and I studied female artists who are missing from history books."

"There's a painting of her in London—in the National Portrait Gallery. I'd like to take you to London with me one day to see it."

"I'd like to do that: paint a portrait that will one day hang in a gallery. I want to paint as if it will matter in the future—I want to paint you, Ignatius—naked."

"When I see you at the airport, I want you to scream 'Fuck me Ignatius, your royal highness, fuck me—I'm your *cortigiana onesta*!'"

I laughed. "Should I be in costume?"

"Yes, in costume!"

"In a black corset and no underwear under the poofy skirt?"

"God, try to have mercy on me: I'm painfully erect already."

I smiled to myself, then said, "I want you miserably."

He breathed into the phone. "I didn't realize until after you left, just how much, how much I would miss you."

"It's like there's a hole in my stomach and I can't quite plug it."

"I keep thinking I forgot something and then I realize it's you," he said.

My entire body seemed to convulse with longing, and tears broke from my eyes. No, I thought, I take no relish in the lying, in the pain of bifurcating love, of splintering myself: I feel only one thing, for only one man.

"Two more days," I said.

"Yes, I—I—" He seemed on the verge of saying something more, but instead he only said this: "Two more days. Forty-eight hours. Two thousand, eight-hundred and eighty minutes."

"Oh, please don't stop counting—give it to me in seconds. It's such a turn on!" He laughed and I laughed, and we hung up.

I went to the bathroom and splashed cold water on my face. Mascara globs ran down my cheeks and chin, and my green eye shadow spread into my forehead. In the dark, my features undulated in the mirror and changing monstrous physiognomies swam across my face. I sipped the water running from the faucet—let pollution kill me!

"Have you lost your head?" Alex was standing in the doorway. "Why are you here in the dark, drinking tap water? Who drinks tap water anymore?"

"I'm so *glad* to see you, Sashenka," I cried, hurtling at him like an offensive tackle. How it was possible to long for one man one minute, then to pretend so convincingly with another; that's right, I was now smooching Alex's celestial features as if we had been temporarily parted by the Iron Curtain. How could a woman compartmentalize herself so unceremoniously? I thought of *them*: the courtesans. Could I have been one of them in another life?

He caught me in his arms and, balancing us on my lacquered maroon dresser, murmured: "To what do I owe such a vigorous sensual advance, my love?"

I detected a shade of fear in his loving gaze and dug in at once. "I can't believe you told your father about my feminist views!"

"As if you would have sat quietly as he made his absurd, tired speech! Do you realize that there isn't a single Russian woman in Chicago who hasn't had to endure his evolutionary theories? You're the only one who's dared to oppose him."

"Well, that's just pathetic!" I said.

"They're simply more devious than you, that's all. You need to learn to maneuver language to appease all parties. Mother is an extremely sensitive individual, and she takes offense easily."

"Oh, Sashenka, why is everything so difficult? Mothers-in-law never like their daughters-in-law. It's a golden rule."

"Don't be ridiculous. They're like anyone else—they can be plied and buttered up, and told what they want to hear. You're just so damn stubborn. You think everything is a cause."

"You're probably right," I replied, collapsing my head on his shoulder. "I always want to prove things to them—to make them see—"

"Let them be," he chided wisely. "We can never change them. They are what they are after years of swallowing Soviet propaganda. It's astounding they've adjusted to this country at all."

"Yes, they are what they are," I agreed. This conversation—this implicit understanding of our mutual families, our common history and struggle, our balancing act between two worlds—could never take place between Eddie and me, I noted.

"Don't be nervous about me going away to Harvard. I'll make every effort to see you."

He kissed my forehead, and his lips gently traveled down my cheek to my mouth where they lingered, his tongue soothing and warm. "Is something going on? Are you having second thoughts?"

"Yes, Alex, you're right, I'm having second thoughts—with the deposit already put down on the Drake and the invitations already in the mail, you can practically map my escape route!" I laughed hysterically.

"It's not an unreasonable thing to ask—I don't want you to feel forced into this—I know your grandmother is pushing, but my dearest Lenochka, I want you to want me for *me*."

A sharp pain stirred within me. Tears fell from my eyes, and the fierce tenderness I felt for him swelled for a moment into a magnificent flame.

"Oh, my dearest Sashenka, I've just been under enormous stress—"

"I know just how to cure you! I'm ready for you, Lenochka. Let's activate the volcanoes, *moya krasavitza*, rouse the gods from their sleep! We've waited *long* enough and now that the wedding is iron clad—"

"You feel morally liberated—"

"Yes, from my evil nature," he murmured. "It was *you* I had been trying to protect."

Protect yourself, I thought in silence, protect yourself, and settled quietly into his arms. You can be sure, patient reader, that we did not have sex that evening.

The Artist on a Corporate Playground

When I got off the plane in LaGuardia, I instantly reverted to a New Yorker. The congested, overcrowded terminal pumped my body with adrenaline, extinguishing the last remnants of guilt I had been dragging through the neon tunnels of O'Hare Airport. I wasn't merely moving forward, I was gliding, sashaying, daring men to look at me. It was difficult at first—these men were busy with their newspapers and meetings and their Nokia phones, but with a kick of an effort, with a look of Fuck-Off amiability, with a stern mouth, a swiveling round butt in white jeans, with breasts pointing upward in the blue gauze of summer, with strident legs on sharp heels, with hair grazing the gloss of my crimson lips, the men as if one by one got caught in my circumference—my nifty butterfly net. From the side, from behind, from up ahead, determined pairs of eyes landed on me. I amplified my walk, added more seductive juice to my frame, as if I couldn't get enough—because I couldn't. I felt a pang for one man, then another, then a third, then a fourth; I could have any one of you, I thought imperiously.

I could be the first female sultan with a hundred husbands—a *sultaness*, you might say. Men would line streets to be chosen by me: buff sportsmen begging to lie at the footstool of my lavish elephant-bone bed, untested virgins offering me their ignorance in exchange for slavishness, brilliant savants supremely educated in the sciences, literature, history, philosophy itching to stun me with their insights, and sensual Tantric yogis renewing my spirit with their stress-decreasing techniques. I would grow old too, amass wrinkles and sag, my breasts flat like lasagna sheets, knees crackling from arthritis, back stiff from osteoporosis, and my vagina sapped of its youth, rage, vigor. But the men like loyal round-table knights would still bow at my feet—mesmerized, wanting to possess my decrepit decaying body; yes, yes, I could be the female Hugh Hefner bedding hard, blond bodies at eighty, or the female Howard Stern devising raunchy contests to determine which man got to have his naked ass spanked by me. Ah, the world in reverse!

I imagined Eddie's naked body splayed on the tarmac, hands tied above his head, ready to be ravaged by his sultaness, and then I saw a tall figure quickening toward me, his blue eyes flickering from afar. I almost ran toward him, almost climaxed from the anticipation of being touched by him, when I stopped short; close up, he looked foreign, unrecognizable. His face was unshaven, hair plastered to his forehead and streaked in oil, his body demarcated by torn jeans and a T-shirt featuring a lewd red tongue and the word HOOTERS on its front. His empty gaze washed over the surroundings. He looked despondent and lost, and in need of someone to hold him, and it scared me suddenly to approach him—to be forced to deal with his needs.

"What's wrong?" I asked, touching my stomach from fear, imagining that he'd uncovered the truth—any truth—about me.

"Nothing, just tired. Haven't slept for two days finishing something for a client. And I have to go back tonight." He took my backpack off my shoulder and produced a closed-lip smile. "How was home, how was Grandma?"

"In excellent form—nagging and interfering as usual," I exclaimed as my stomach lurched again. "So you won't be able to be with me?"

"No," he replied without emotion. "I'm sorry. That's the way this damned job is."

"This seems worse than usual."

"I have a limo waiting for us. I'll be free—if all goes according to plan—on Monday night, latest Tuesday. You can stay at my place, if you like. I have a ton of sushi."

He got my luggage off the conveyor without looking at me, and outside a limo driver waited.

The black leather interior with its tinted windows, gray TV screen, and low roof reminded me of a coffin in an eighties prom movie. "To my place, Felix," he said into the intercom. He turned to the window with the same blank stare that had greeted me. I touched his shoulder but he didn't seem to feel me. I didn't seem to feel myself—what terror now possessed me—did he suspect me of reneging on my promise? Cars, trucks, taxis leaving the airport were melting under the corrosive glare of the sun. The heat streaming from the outside intercepted the cold breeze of the air conditioner, and the contrast between the warmth and the cold, the pain of it, seemed to echo the strange incongruities in Eddie's face—the luminous smile disappearing under a look bereft of feeling, sunken under gloom.

"What's going on, Eddie?" I pried against my better instincts.

"Nothing unusual. Nothing."

I imagined that he had spies follow me to Chicago, that these nefarious creatures hid under our Brazilian dining table listening to our toasts, that there were secret tracking devices attached to my clothing. Did Eddie somehow catch my tender moment with Alex?

"I should have been a philosopher," he broke out in an unfamiliar tone, "with a concentration in Machiavellian ethics—it would have been more useful. Did you know I once fancied myself a photographer? I even have a portfolio—what a joke! Now I contribute money to *IMAGE Magazine* and visit art galleries—to assure myself I'm not completely devoid of culture. When I have time, that is, when Norton lets me off. When the client takes the bait and we shake hands and celebrate by drinking and staring at depressed strippers—our mandatory doses of healthy debauchery—that's when I'm free. Some people sleep, others masturbate over Internet porn, the humans go to St. John's, and I catch up on culture—culture in small doses—how long, no, that's the real question, how long have I been working at Norton Bank? Six years if you don't count the MBA. Six years, plus an MBA—eight years of my life dedicated to what? Spreadsheets! All I know is this fucking hellhole with its 'golden' perks; no one tells you in Sunday school that hell is made of Italian leather and black marble and brainless dogs—no one tells you that you're one of those dogs!" He turned to me suddenly and touched my face.

I sat in silence, my face strained from concentration. His eyes were vacant, darkened by bluish-mauve circles stretching from the bridge of his nose to his brows. At long last, I asked what I had wanted to ask so long ago: "Second time we met you told me you wished you could take pictures again. When I heard you speak about that painting in Nebu, I thought to myself, who is this man—he's so interesting and different, amazing-different. I never met a guy who talks so intelligently about art—who thinks deeply about this world I so love. Don't you dream of doing something else one day—of leaving all this? What about art, poetry, philosophy?"

"Yes, of course, I thought about everything. I still do—about leaving. I have a box of books labeled READ WHEN YOU QUIT!" He laughed with the look of someone who's just said something wildly outrageous. "I used to spend hours in my red room—my parents let me have it in the basement—during my junior year. I'd fantasize that my photographs were gracing the cover of *National Geographic* and people were talking about this or that image for years to come."

The limo's air conditioner spilled freezing air against my bare feet and calves, and I wished I could cover myself in a quilt.

"Do you still take pictures—I mean, do you have a secret red room?"

"Good God, Emma, that's all lost to me now." He stared at the traffic ahead. "There's no time for daydreams. I'm on a timer—can you understand that—I could lose this job. This guy at work—an underling—a vengeful idiot—humiliated me today in front of the client. Do you see what I'm saying: it's the sense that you've wasted yourself on something that can be taken away from you in a snap of a moment!"

"It's not too late to change your life—that's what you always tell me—"

"Oh, but it is, Emma, it's too late for me. My blood runs through that fucking bank. I've given too much, sacrificed too much to leave now. Not now when there's still a chance. Besides, I could never forgive myself if I failed, if I turned out like my brother—failed poet, musician, philosopher, sadist."

"I didn't know you had a brother—you've never mentioned him."

"We don't speak. He's my fraternal twin." He clasped his hands together and the fingers turned red from the pressure. "He's the lucky dilettante in the family, with two kids, a wife, and no real job. He 'works' at my father's company. No, I think one dilettante in the family is enough.

"No philosophical text, no perfectly captured image could have done for me what this—this—" he pointed at his torn Hooter's T-shirt, forgetting momentarily, I imagined, that it wasn't his suit, "has done for me."

He looked away for an instant, and when he turned to me, his cheeks burned.

"Work cured me—by frying my brain. That's how I got relief—by *not* having the time to think. And the money too, the money cures too. Like gluttony—you can never have enough—the crazy spending sprees, the sense of importance it bestows on you—I won't lie. But when the hours worsened and my purchases just sat inside unopened boxes, money began to pass through me like air. I couldn't feel anything—days passed without distinction, each compounded into the next, days blurred into piles of stock reports and dreary cocktails parties and lack of sleep. I'd wake up in the morning and think: what hell am I in—what name do I give this antiseptic purgatory?" He put his hand on my open palm.

"Do you still feel that way?"

He gave me his entire face now, met me with gentle eyes. "Not when I'm with you," he said. "I touch you and feel everything."

I threw myself at him. "You can't imagine, you can't imagine how much I've missed you!" The car jolted forward and with each violent stop, we attempted a kiss. His hands sat limply round my waist and ventured periodically inside my shirt, fingers clammy and stiff. I felt cheated. When the car stopped in front of his building, he seemed to sigh with relief.

"I have to go back. You'll be all right?"

"I'll be all right." I stepped out of the limo in front of his building, a glittering black tower rising into the sky. His keys jangled in my pocket and heat singed my air-conditioned skin. Hot swaths of air streamed into my lungs, and I smiled at the traffic around me, stunned and gladdened by my sudden loneliness. Only hours had passed without my speaking to Mother, Grandmother, and Alex, and already they had faded from my consciousness. I felt a new truth burgeoning in my chest. I wondered if I could ferret out the feeling known as love in the intricate labyrinth of my organs, if it hid somewhere between my ribcage and my heart, not knowing whether it would be expunged into the open air and thus freed, or sucked in by that four-ventricled organ—that arena of human hell. Even so, even as I crushed it on its way out, I felt liberation and breath flooding in, and I was able to push apart the metal bars of my cage and let an arm or a leg hang out.

I spent two days alone in his apartment like a Neanderthal deposited amid civilization. I did not shower, brush my hair, or smell my armpits, though I did stare at myself in his spotless mirror (he employed an ambitious cleaning lady from Brazil) for untold eons of time, whereupon I took the liberty of popping a few significant blackheads on my nose and investigated the state of my skin, on the prowl for wrinkles, freckles, and invisible pimples (which have a curious habit of becoming visible after such long investigations). I noted without regret the way beauty can succumb to a guilty conscience, depression, and obsessive-compulsive tendencies, and thereby vanish, to be unfortunately (or perhaps, in my case, fortunately) replaced by hideousness. I watched TV by incessantly skipping channels and battling guilt during commercial interruptions, devoured cold sushi in bed as though it were hot fries, spilling soy sauce on his fancy linen without feeling apologetic, and supplemented my Omega-3 diet with pepperoni pizza, which induced heartburn-associated nausea. I felt quiet ecstasy roil through my veins as I imagined Grandmother's horror in catching me in this state. By the time he returned on Tuesday afternoon, I felt cleansed of Chicago, gratefully amnesiac and spiritually renewed, which goes to show you just how deceptive appearances can be, for I also sprouted unruly oily hair (smelling unsurprisingly of pepperoni), exuded garlic breath coupled with soy sauce, and brandished a few critical red patches on my nose (from my self-executed facial). Clad in the same tank top I had worn on Sunday night, I felt that sex appeal was still within my reach.

He, on the other hand, looked spectacular; his suit glistened, his skin looked polished, and an enormous smile hung on his lips.

"You are the hottest woman on earth!" That's how he greeted me upon opening the door.

"You're just sleep-deprived," I said, wondering how it was possible to look spectacular without sleeping for forty-eight hours.

"Everything went off without a hitch! It was an unbelievable success! The client loved my presentation, and tonight Grant, our boss, wants to take the three of us out—Eric, Sylvia and me. I want you to be there. I just need a few hours to sleep—two or three will do. But before I sleep—" He grabbed my legs and wrapped my body round his as if I were a rope, and I thought—how strange men are! Success is what turns them on, rendering them dumb and blind; they'll see an angel, a beauty, a model in any woman who happens to lie in their bed, and yet that very success, if taken away, can set their brains in reverse.

For my initiation into the corporate world, I wore purple because the shirt, with its triangular cut in the front and sleeves that opened at my wrists like bellbottoms and tightened round my waist over low-cut jeans, gave me that paradoxical look of innocence and lust. "Are you preparing to seduce my co-workers?" Eddie asked, eyeing the exposed inch of my navel. "Are you already jealous?" I asked, pretending to be irritated. "No, but I'll be watching your trips to the bathroom tonight," he said.

Two buff bouncers in black T-shirts blocked the entrance. The women, decked out in trendy cut-off miniskirts and stiletto heels, were sporting indifferent expressions and non-descript men. The line stretched for the entire block of 23rd street, but we got in without waiting because Eddie nodded at one of the bouncers as though he knew him personally, and then slipped him a heavy green bill. The bar was called Aqua, as it resembled an underwater aquarium, if not literally, then metaphorically; water ran inside stained blue glass walls and shark heads protruded from the ceiling. But the sharp smell of cigars wafting from private rooms, the black leather couches, and mahogany coffee tables set against blue walls created an aura of sophistication and wealth.

A man hailed us from a nearby couch and Eddie rushed toward him, pushing through the crowds as though he were about to miss a train. Two men and a woman I immediately recognized as Sylvia were seated around a square coffee table, talking. An older man in his early fifties was puffing on a cigar, sipping a drink. The other man looked extremely young, as though he had been recently plucked from a frat pledging ceremony. He sipped frenetically from his Corona. Sylvia was coquettishly eyeing her cosmopolitan and puffing on a skinny cigarette. All I knew about her was that she and Eddie had casually slept together before he got involved with me. She appeared pale and less lively than when I'd first met her that night at the gallery, and I began to suspect that during the last couple of months the corporation had chewed years off her life.

Eddie immediately ordered us drinks, and although I would have preferred a hot Earl Grey tea with lemon, I ordered my usual: cranberry juice with vodka.

"Why don't you be brave and order what I'm having?" the older man said and winked at me.

"Is it very sweet?" I asked.

"It's just right," he said and without waiting for an answer, called out, "Old Fitzgerald Very Old," which, I saw in disbelief on the shiny black menu, cost over three thousand dollars per bottle. Then he turned to Eddie. "You didn't tell us you had such a beautiful girlfriend!"

"That's why I didn't tell you—I know how you are, Grant." Eddie laughed, offering Grant an approving smile. The two men exchanged a secret glance that sent a sliver of pleasure through my stomach, reminding me once again that my feminist ideals did not sufficiently guard me against the serpentine poison of politically incorrect flattery.

"I'm Grant," the older gentleman said and extended his hand. Eddie had already informed me that Grant was known around the office as a mild philanderer, who "dabbled" in other women, but not with any serious intention of leaving his wife. His wife was not only fifteen years his junior, a former *Sports Illustrated* model, and a formidable hostess who knew exactly how much cleavage *not* to show, but she was also the mother of not one, not two, not three, but four (an entire posse by Manhattan standards) children. Grant engaged in what could only be described as the blithe, insensitive flirting of a self-satisfied executive: occasionally winking, ogling, and grabbing a butt cheek or a heavily armored breast of his loyal secretaries, who in turn were devoted to his generous bonuses. Only when there was an impossible deadline or an unreasonable client did Grant feel the need to request a discreet blow job. He was good looking in the way rich men tend to be good looking—lacking perfect features, symmetry, and a built physique, but endowed with an air of having been cleansed, brushed, massaged, polished, buffed, tanned, dyed, and sexually fed.

"Emma," I said. "A pleasure."

"The pleasure is all mine," he murmured like a fox devouring its rabbit prey; although he kept his eyes on my face, I felt as though he were fondling my breasts.

The other man rose and extended his hand. "I'm Eric." The woman sat in silence and nodded her blonde head. "Yes, we've already met," she said after a long pause. She was wearing a sleek black dress that revealed nothing except two hard pointy nipples.

"Yes, we have, at the art gallery with Eddie," I said.

"I didn't know Beltrafio liked art," Eric exclaimed and without waiting for an answer added, "There's so much crap out there today for millions of dollars—who buys that shit?"

"Emma paints," Eddie offered idiotically.

"Do you?" Grant raised his brows at me. "Do you paint in oils?"

"Yes, and acrylic, and sometimes watercolor," I replied with effort, my tongue parched from nerves.

"I just bought myself an expensive watercolor by this guy—perhaps you've heard of him—Grayhart?"

"Really, that's amazing—what a small world! He's actually my teacher."

"You study?" Grant asked, raising his brows.

"Yes, I'm at NYU—I mean I take art on the side," I muttered with embarrassment.

"Very good, very good! Everyone should study. When I stare at his painting I feel at peace. Partially, of course," Grant noted, "because it reminds me of just how much nonsense I can afford. Sure it's pretty and it makes me think of fall, and my happy childhood in rural Vermont, but I ask myself, couldn't my thirteen-year-old daughter have drawn it just as well?"

"I couldn't agree with you more!" Eric chirped. "People are always trying to shock us nowadays but what you get is some asinine idea that any dolt could have come up with—a black blob for a canvas or salad leaves on top of a brown sac—I swear that was an exhibit at the Guggenheim! Does that sound like art to anyone?

"Speaking of being bamboozled, could you believe Robertson today?" Eric went on excitedly. "Just on Friday he was fuming, but today he bought everything—results, numbers, even recommendation—hook, line, and sinker. I mean, after Friday's fiasco, I didn't think we'd get off the ground with him."

"Well, disasters do happen," Grant said in a reproving tone, "but Eddie did a superb job this morning. It just proves what a little social finagling can do.

"You turned the whole situation around. Robertson was actually beaming! I couldn't be more pleased. The way you handled that, Eddie—that was pure genius!"

I caught Eric's eyes narrowing, envy rising, spreading from his forehead to his chin.

"Well, Eric and Sylvia were indispensable," Eddie said.

"It wasn't my fault," Sylvia blurted out, appealing to Grant. "Eric handed me the wrong report. That's why Eddie had the problem with Robertson in the first place."

"Is that true?" Grant demanded. "You almost lost our biggest client?"

"I had nothing to do with it. My stupid secretary gave me the wrong report, that fucking idiot!" Eric snapped.

"No, it was you," Sylvia insisted. "You tried to make me look bad in front of Eddie."

Eddie scanned Sylvia's face, then in a neutral tone, said, "Don't worry, we'll figure this out." Tears gathered at the edges of her eyes, and I leaned in, wanting to touch her forearm, but she reeled from me.

"No one's accused you of anything," Grant said to Sylvia. "We'll get to the bottom of this."

Eric laughed violently. "Women! They're always so dramatic! Relax, Sylvia, I'll fire my secretary."

He resembled a toad that had been imprudently placed on top of a tall, muscular body, and although that gave him a disconcerting presence, his toad-like face, with its bulging eyes and a rather extensive mouth, brought one relief. Had he been outright handsome, he would have been difficult to bear, but in his case there were no discrepancies between appearance and personality.

"Forgive us, Emma, we always revert to shop talk." Grant turned to me with a smile and extended a bowl of peanuts. "Did you know that this bar is *the* hot spot for all the white-collar professionals of this city?"

"Oh, is that why no one's dancing?" I exclaimed.

"Of course, because as a general rule white-collar professionals are expected—actually required to be exceedingly boring. Do you see that group over there gulping their drinks—those are the MDs popping antidepressants and drinking themselves to death!" He laughed and pointed toward a distant section of the bar where three men and two women huddled together in conspiratorial postures. "And those mousy heads over there with slouching backs and ghostly faces are the lawyers—pathetic nerds with little money and enough bitterness to sue us all into bankruptcy. They work harder than we do, and make ten times less."

"And what are we by that estimation?" Eric asked, looking up at Grant.

"We—We are the Gods," Grant replied in earnest. "We rule this city."

"Ooooh, I like that," I cooed, smiling at him.

"So how did Eddie convince you to go out with him?" Grant flirted back.

"Eddie—convince me? He leered at me from a table of white-haired Gods."

"Our clients," Grant laughed. "By the way, I'm an excellent leerer!"

Sylvia skewered me with her light blue eyes. "So, how's your old boyfriend, Alex?"

"How would I know?" I shot back.

"Are we talking about the same Alex, Alex Bagen?" Eric burst out. "He was a great guy—such a riot, with his wild yellow and pink ties, man, those ties killed me! It's a shame what happened to him."

Eric stared at me with sudden interest. "Wait a second—you're not that Russian chick, Lena—are you? The one Alex was going to marry?"

"Same one," I replied, my heart somersaulting in my chest.

"You sneak," Eric taunted, "dating our Eddie and marrying good old Alex on the side. Now that's what I call the new wave of feminism in the nineties!"

"We broke up months ago."

"Of course you did. I'm just pulling Beltrafio's leg!"

"I've always said there's no tougher mind than Eddie's," Grant observed. "If there's a loose end, he'll tie it up; if there's a loose cannon, he'll get rid of it."

"Oh, c'mon, Grant," Eddie protested. "I did what had to be done."

"It's a good thing you got rid of him, Eddie," Sylvia murmured, gently brushing Eddie's forearm with her fingers.

"Still, getting fired after what—a month, a month on the job— is brutal. Shit, I'd be pissed as hell," Eric said.

"Who got fired?" I recalled my mother's suspicious eyes circling Alex as he insisted, in front of everyone, that he left of his own accord—for a fantasy of personal greatness.

"I guess Alex didn't tell you," Eddie remarked casually. "That doesn't surprise me."

"No, no he didn't, but why didn't you—why didn't you tell me?" My voice quivered from sudden indignation on account of Alex; stung to my very bones, I felt as if I too had been fired, as if the whole lot of us, the immigrants, had been fired. I bit my lower lip to steady it and said, "I hear from my family that Alex is going to Harvard in the fall."

"Is that so?" Grant exclaimed, "Doing what?"

"PhD in physics," Eric said with a smile, winking at me. "We've kept in touch."

"I didn't know you two were so close." Eddie scanned Eric's face with mistrust.

"Oh, you know how it is, Beltrafio, when you're both starting out in the copy room."

"No one put you in the copy room," Grant rejoined (Eric was Grant's nephew by marriage, as Eddie earlier explained, and this job was a happy meeting between guilt and nepotism). "I gave you a good position right away. There are tons of people who'd kill to have your job!"

"Sure, and I'm grateful," Eric conceded with open sarcasm. "Let's get another round of good Old Fitzgerald—for the special lady of the hour." He motioned at our waiter.

"Well I, for one, am glad for Alex," Grant remarked. "He was a solid guy. He meant well, anyhow."

"He belongs with the academicians," Sylvia observed. "None of them have any social skills."

"Neither do business people, for that matter," Eddie admonished.

"Yeah," Eric cut in, cackling. "Look at you."

"I never knew you had such an eye for detail, Conners—you should have been an interior decorator!" Eddie shot back.

Everyone broke into a booming laugh, and Eric, burning in pink, giggled like a school girl whose ass had been unexpectedly slapped.

"Hottest girl I ever dated in college was Russian, but then again she dated everyone!" He chuckled and the malicious grin rippled across his toad mouth. "Did you and Eddie start dating while you were still dating Alex—I mean I was just curious if Beltrafio here didn't fire Alex out of that alpha male need to get rid of the competition? I mean what the f—excuse my language, ladies—did Alex do to get fired?"

"Technically it was me who fired him," Grant said.

"These things *are* confidential, Eric," rebuked Sylvia, landing a protective gaze on Eddie.

"Sure they are!" Eric laughed.

"What competition, Conners? Sparks flew when Emma and I met!" Eddie declared like a man brandishing a flag.

"There were sparks between you two even when you were still dating me," Sylvia noted. Her injured face was meekly angled at Eddie as if she were still ferreting out remnants of his love.

"I'm sorry," I stammered, and our eyes met over the men.

"Hey, you did me a favor," she said. "Everyone around here knows that Eddie is quite the playboy—what did you tell me, Grant, he's dated every model in the Village, and every struggling B-actress as icing on the cake."

"No need to be cruel, Sylvia, sweetheart," Grant purred. "Everyone knows my weakness for office gossip. A guy as good looking as Eddie—why the secretaries practically stalk him like the paparazzi!"

"I have no secrets from Emma," Eddie announced. "She knows the truth from gossip, and she doesn't care."

"Does she know about your ménage à trois with a trapeze dancer and an ophthalmologist?" asked Eric. "Now that was the best frigging story I ever heard, man!"

"The best gossip you ever heard," Eddie retorted with typical confidence, giving me an apologetic look. "Besides, Emma isn't the jealous type: my stories amuse her."

"All women are jealous when their men stray," Sylvia pounced.

"The only cure to straying men," I said, swooping in, "is to cheat ourselves—and why not—our desires are no less magnificent than theirs."

"Oooh, I like her," Grant murmured. "Where did you find her?"

"In an art gallery, of all places!" Eddie exclaimed.

"And did she speak English then?" Eric pushed on, his mouth curving unattractively into his cheekbones. "What I mean is— were these sparks the international language of love or were they based on some bullshit Eddie fed you about a painting?"

"How did you guess? Not a word of English—I just grunted— *da, nyet*," I snapped, "and as to your second question, I thought you knew that Eddie has a master's degree in bullshit?" Eddie and Grant and even Eric laughed, but Sylvia kept a tight grin. "That's the problem with women today," she said sternly, "they're willing to overlook everything—"

"What I want to know," Eric cut her off (her half-parted mouth seemed to be on the verge of illuminating the full extent of her pain, making me want to erase all the men in the room and shroud her in a pink flannel quilt that would symbolize our universal feminine solidarity), "is if *I* had met you at the gallery first and drooled over some asinine artist who didn't know a paintbrush from his dick, would there have been international sparks between us?"

"Now that's a thin dick!" Grant cried, chuckling.

"Galleries are excellent pickup joints," I enthused, "honey wells for the horny elite of this city. Only beware: you have to fawn over artists as if they were your own children."

"For you, I'd trot around naked and proclaim myself an exhibit," Eric offered.

"I wouldn't want to see that turn into reality." Grant laughed.

"Are you flirting with my girlfriend, Conners?"

"I didn't know you were so territorial, Beltrafio—I heard from Sylvia that you date to sample, not to hog."

"I'm starting to think your interest in my love life is a little unhealthy," Eddie remarked, and he and Grant exchanged glances.

My face ignited from sudden shame. I rose from my chair, overcome by a yearning for the abandoned dance floor.

"Are you leaving us?" Grant touched my arm.

"Oh no, I just love that song," I said, discerning with horror a disjointed confluence of beats and melodies, which quite possibly included "Le Freak," "Bust a Move," and "I Will Always Love You." As I pushed past him, the room began to spin, and Eddie ceased to belong to me: he had turned into an indistinguishable particle in the complex self-propelling organism known as "men."

Only the stage, a desolate stretch of brown wood under flashing strobe lights and an outdated silver ball, beckoned to me. A dejected DJ clad in a pirate's hat was holed up behind a protruding black podium that once must have been intended for dignitaries and informed lecturers. The music jumped from hip-hop to Madonna to seventies disco, remixes roaring from two giant speakers. Women in cliques around the bar waited for the men to approach them, as they sipped tall drinks and chatted with feigned indifference. The men stared concertedly at the women, measuring their faces and bodies, weighing their own desperation against a gauge of who they could and couldn't get. Some were already mingling, conversing, passing their numbers on wet paper napkins, but no one danced. No matter how many tequilas, Kahluas, vodkas, bourbons, beers, cosmopolitans, martinis, Bloody Marys, Sex on Kitchen Counters, and Naughty Orgasms they had had, nothing seemed potent enough to break through their inhibitions.

The dance floor belonged solely to me: a breathing, pulsating organ, sprouting thorns that pricked my feet in evenly timed beats. Brown velvet vines rose from the ground and entwined my ankles, my entire body held captive by the sounds vibrating on my tongue. The floor *is* music, *is* flesh, its inanimate surface infuses the willing with life. The DJ-pirate, catching my fever, plugged in "Bust a Move." As I flailed and tapped and twirled and shook my head and chest from side to side, screaming "Something Fellow, I am Yellow," eyes began to turn my way, out of curiosity, or perhaps to see if the wild beast on display could tap into their own primordial instincts. Men and women interrupted their conversations to look at me, and I was no longer alone with the music, but I was with *them. Feeling triumphant, triumfucknant, thinking I'd transcended everything—the dance floor, the bar, the men, even my very predicament. I was the sultaness again . . .* Like gnats their eyes landed on my skin, their superficial perceptions stinging, invigorating my blood, swelling my vanity; I moved faster, faster, until the disparate parts of my body seemed to fly off my torso, and my legs, moving by themselves as if disconnected from my brain, cut across the dance floor and burned it with my heat.

Then I felt a sweaty hand squeeze my elbow:

"You're a wild one," a voice cried into my ear. Eric's reptilian countenance materialized inches from my face.

The abrupt cessation of movement brought me to a sudden awareness of other people. The dance floor had miraculously sprung to life; the same stationary bodies that had lavished me with their disdain were now laughing and thrashing against one another in an ecstatic communal dance.

"Don't you dance?" I spoke at last, relieved.

"I'd need a gallon of beer before I could do what you did up here! You got this whole place in a frenzy—impressive!" He surveyed my face with his invasive toad eyes. "So, you're getting married to Alex and screwing Beltrafio on the side. I like that, but it's not *that* original."

"I don't know what you mean—"

"Alex has already sent me an official invitation to your wedding. But I promise I won't tattle tale; it's quite the opposite. I want you to go out with me. Hell, if you're dating two guys, why not add a third? Now that would be original, wouldn't it?"

"Don't be insane," I cried.

"I find that Russian women are excellent in bed, and very submissive in the kitchen."

You're an astounding idiot, an idiotpanarama, a mudila, I was on the verge of saying, but instead, I merely observed, "While others are frigid virgins and don't know what a spatula is, right?"

"That's what I like about you, Emma—you like to joke around just like me. You need a fun guy, somebody who can party hard with you and take you dancing, not that self-important asshole over there you call your boyfriend. He doesn't know what the word 'fun' means—he drives us all crazy with work, and he fired Alex for nothing, I tell you, for nothing. I wouldn't be surprised if he was plotting to oust me as well. Do you see what I'm saying?"

"I can't see anything," I muttered, and suddenly, without thinking, without knowing if it was true, without harnessing my mouth, added, "I'm in love."

"Then why marry someone else?" he asked. He was genuinely befuddled.

"It's complicated—"

"Well why don't we ask Eddie—hey Beltrafio, get over here before I ask your girlfriend out on a date!" Eric screamed across the dance floor and within seconds I saw Eddie moving through the crowd toward us. His gaze gripped me from across the room.

"What are you doing?" I muttered in fear at Eric. "What do you want from me?"

"I told you what I want," he exclaimed with sudden cheer. "I want to fuck you—you fuck me and I won't tell!"

I laughed at him uproariously—because Eddie stood within inches of me.

"Is Eric entertaining you?" Eddie asked both of us, but his eyes were glued to mine.

"I was just complimenting Emma on her dancing," Eric said. "Did you know she's a professional?"

"No, but it wouldn't surprise me—" Eddie's features constricted from an inability to hide his contempt for Eric.

"I've taken jazz classes in college—"

"Hey, Beltrafio, I may look dumb but when it comes to women, I'm fucking Sherlock Holmes."

"Hey Eric, I think Grant over there needs you," Eddie said, pointing at Grant and Sylvia leaning into one another, with bourbons in their hands.

"Listen, Beltrafio, Sylvia seriously fucked up, I'm telling you. It wasn't me."

"Let's discuss this later," Eddie said with irritation.

As he started to walk away, Eric called out to me, "Remember what I said to you Emma. Anytime!"

My palms froze from congealed sweat when Eddie touched them, and I held the tears back.

"What did he say to you?" he asked.

"Nothing—he—"

"You shouldn't dance like that—"

"Why not?"

"Because I can't bear it, I stop functioning—I can only think of you."

"That's the idea."

He put his palm on my sweaty neck and then reached inside my shirt, his fingers running down my ribs. Eric was watching us, pretending to move, but his face was turned sideways, his bulging eyes peering from the sides of his face.

"Don't—Eddie, not here, not now. Not in front of them—"

"I can't control myself—I don't care about them!" he decreed triumphantly. "They're all just jealous. Jealous vultures, all of them, ready for a feed."

"They'll get the wrong idea—they'll talk about me at work."

"So what, let them, let them talk about you. Stop caring so much about what people think." He pulled my face in and kissed my mouth and licked the sweat off my neck and gyrated his hips to the staccato beats, moving with me—to me—his hands caressing my back, my behind, whispering in my ear: *let them stare.*

When we finally strode out into the brightly lit night, a yellow cab awaited us like a magnificent carriage to whisk us away. I closed my eyes and landed in Eddie's safe arms, and ached to tell him the truth—a truth—any truth, the final-sale truth that would have no return policy: *You and I are a grim obsession, a sexual confluence of unmatched souls meant to move past each other, but not to converge.* Too kind, too sugarcoated, I thought, so I went further: *You mean nothing to me, just sex, a sexual fanaticism, a gripping infatuation, a crush, a crash.* Then I'd sidle up to a finale: *I'm still engaged to Alex, engaged despite your cry for honesty, engaged so irreversibly there's a wedding in the offing and betrayal-grime on my heels...* The horror of the moment, its stench, loss, desolation, even these very words seemed to carve themselves into my consciousness as though I'd already committed the act of confessing. But somehow I smiled, a hideous smile of someone so internally contorted the lines of her face begin to unspool at their seams.

The cab raced down West Side Highway, offering us glimpses of the black river snaking beneath construction sites. When the cab came to a jolting stop and we unfolded ourselves onto the sidewalk, Eddie said, "I'm sorry."

"What are you sorry about?"

"The chauvinist assholes, myself, Sylvia—I'm sorry you had to find out about Alex this way."

"It wasn't pleasant," I replied. "What did he do?"

"I'm not like them," he said. "Oh, maybe I am, but in my mind, in my mind, I imagine I am made from a different cloth. There's an act that's required of us, and when need be, I put it on."

"You didn't answer my question," I pressed as we entered the building.

"If it's over between you two, why do you care?"

His cerulean gaze met mine with longing and I felt a rush of power to my veins, power foaming between my thighs, power in the very spot his fingers were now probing. We were in his elevator, just the two of us and the camera above our heads. I grabbed his tie and brought his face closer to mine. We fell through his front door onto the marble kitchen tiles, his breath gaining upon me like a wild boar on my trail. How he struggled to peel all the skin-layers I wore to cover myself up; that's how I was able to see *him*—by not letting him see *me*. Beneath his barefaced desire, jealousy and mistrust spilled from his eyes onto his suit. It was this suit—the navy jacket and slacks lit by a maroon tie, the rustling surfaces and multiple inner folds, the perfectly ascending lines that defined his features and delineated his jaws, the starched coarse texture intermingling with the soft surface of his fingers and knuckles—that aroused me. I imagined that not he, but *it*—this rigid symbol of power and wealth—had pinned my hands against the floor and swallowed me in its corporate jaws. A mask in navy stripes grew out of the jacket lapels and fell over his face, so that his features no longer surfaced as distinct elements but as continuations of each other, blending into the dark ceiling where only his eyes—greedy, transparent, crisply blue—peered at me. As the coarse wool rubbed my breasts and the slacks fell into the crevice between my legs, the suit seemed to lose its conventionality, its stiffness, its very association with a structured life, and as *I* straddled *him* now, I creased and mangled it to the point of decimation.

I returned to the dungeon the next morning and lay on my futon with a wet pruned face. On my wall above my desk hung the To-Do List.

1. Choose wedding theme color: pink, red, or violet. Choose wedding theme flower: roses or orchids.
2. Choose menu: Russian (shrimp, lobster, *kotleta*, blintzes, and herring—grandma wants) or American (steak au poivre, braised Cornish hen and arugula salad—mom wants).
3. Decide on band: Russian (ABBA, Alla Pugacheva, Gloria Gaynor, and any Celine Dion) or American (The Doors, Jimmy Hendrix, Blondie, The Bee Gees and Hava Nagila).
4. Invitations already out!!!!
5. Call Mom with final decisions by Friday.
6. On Tuesday hang yourself.
7. If still alive by Wednesday, confess everything to Mom and Grandma, down to the detail of when you and Eddie did it in the alley behind his building. You'll feel better.
8. Start a slow regimen of vodka. (All artists were/are alcoholics.)

Concentrating on the last bullet point, I made my way to the kitchen, where I found Natasha's bottle of Stolichnaya in the fridge and poured myself half a mug. She kept it there to keep up with her transformation, or as she liked to call it, Russofication, forcing herself to drink at least a shot a day, and working hard to overcome her true preferences, Corona beer and white wine. I went to the living room, where Natasha's iguana hissed from the cage and sat on the floor beside it. The animal stared at me from one side of its face and opened its mouth as if to speak. She was a creature of stunning beauty, with cobalt blues dancing on her back and two turquoise spheres gathered round her strange evocative eyes. A purple wave zigzagged along her jagged spine and came to rest upon the top of her head, creating the illusion of a purple crown, as if to hint of royalty and glamor in a past life. I raised my shot glass to her highness. "Nazdarovye!" I said, *to your health, you strange beguiling being,* and took one tortured sip. Instantly, I felt bold, energetic, even artistic. Yet I was again confirmed in the knowledge I already cemented from previous such sips: I could never be a plate-throw-ing, toilet-hugging, acidly witty drunk. The embarrassing truth was that I loathed alcohol of all colors and odors, pretended at parties to have a low tolerance, and announced such profundities as "I need a drink, preferably vodka without frills" to fellow grad-uate students to show my hyper-funness, my laissez-faire attitude, my ubiquitous, authentic Russianness!

I unlatched the cage as I had often done when Natasha was not home, and the creature followed me to my room, settling her heavy awkward body in the middle of the floor. Natasha warned me against freeing the iguana, even for a few hours at a time. "If you let her taste freedom, she'll become aware of her cage." But I grew attached to the animal, a strange bond had formed between us, and on the days when Natasha spent away from the dungeon, I let the creature watch me paint.

I took out my palette, my expensive brushes, tubes of acrylic and oil paints, and the ancient silver bottle of turpentine. I mounted a new canvas on a wooden stand and ran my fingers along its crisp white skin, feeling my own bristle with desire. I inhaled the odorless emptiness, and the images came in spurts: my mother in crimson, my father in orange, the sky in gray. How the colors mingled with words—how loud they had been! How often had I thought of them as they were then: young, rebellious, exuberant souls waging war against each other.

No, I don't care anymore, I screamed at the walls, at the iguana, I welcome *your* world of irate souls who never meet, never inter-sect, never run into their other halves. There is no one out there for me, only desolate bars, cafes, streets, libraries. The supposed men I meet and love turn into paintings that cannot speak but stand in silent mockery of me. Everywhere I look, people settle for someone they do not love, for irritants whose inner thoughts are diametrically opposed to their own. Love does not exist, only its illusory doppelganger grows in our collective consciousness, feed-ing on hype and wielding ceremonious reign over our hearts—a capricious tyrant that leaves us crushed and barren.

Painting #3

The colors leap onto my stage—a blackish blue sucked out of the modules of memory—and I, a calligrapher writing on white snow, a paintbrush skipping in and out of consciousness, am no longer here but there. I hear the gurgling of the lily stream, smell the aroma of burning leaves, see her—a tiny thing, a tiny *me*—running through the white birch forest in the Camp for Intellectuals before it all went down . . .

Lenochka, I have the perfect stick for you, my mother mutters and appears, a magic fairy out of an old oak tree. She's in white cotton that blends with her pale skin, and puffed white sleeves flap like wings upon her arms. The giant gray galoshes make her legs look skinny. The ground is bathed in autumn dew and I sink in, my nostrils drunk on grass, elms, lilacs, pansies, pines, Russia's voluptuous nature. Take the stick, my mother says, and hands me a broken branch that's half my size. She leans against her own, a crooked ancient staff. My guiding light, she calls it, lead me to the mushrooms! I mimic her; *I adore her.* Like wizards with our magic wands, we steal into the verdant darkness and peel away moist earth, discovering a prickly quilt of brown pine needles below. One moment she's my *mamochka* and the next she's a princess, a queen, a goddess, a gold-flecked mermaid shedding her disguises into the bellowing green sea. She can fly and sing and swim underwater and somersault through clouds and read my thoughts.

We carry empty mushroom bags tied around our waists and mock each other—I will gather more, I shout, no I will gather more, she shouts. Hunched and lurching forward, I stay close to the ground, straining my eyes for the commoners—creminis and *maslyata.* Look carefully at pine trees, my mother teaches, *maslyata* hide in swathes of fallen needles under arching roots—their heads are moist and sticky, their bodies small and fat. But have your eye out for chanterelles, the lovers of my heart, their yellow-orange heads will bunch together under stumps or hide beneath the birches. And don't forget the King Bolete—*Beliy Grib*—the thick white stem and golden russet head that lives under the sprawling oaks; it is the rarest, thickest, most delicious mushroom of them all. We'll fry them on a bed of onions and potatoes, my mother cries, oh, most of all I want chanterelles. But all I find are standard brown heads: short, plain-clothed and glinting wet, with pine needles stuck to their skin.

Then suddenly I shout: I found a chanterelle and bring it to my mother. I don't know how I saw it, I mutter in delight, but her face cringes, breaks in half—I recognize that face—a sheet of pale terror. She grips my wrist and squeezes it with sudden force—the mushroom cascades to the ground. She takes my bag and empties the creminis and *maslyata*, and stamps them out with her foot. Poison, my mother screams, you found a *poganka*. I told you to watch closely! God forbid you'll poison us all! You must remember the first law of mushroom picking—people die of them! I bring my face close to the killer on the brown earth; its torn leg and broken head is mixed among the body parts of innocents. They mimic the chanterelles, she says in a conciliatory voice, it's difficult to know the difference but you must watch for a thin stem and round skirt upon its neck, and a dull umbrella head that crumbles as you pull it from the ground.

The sun snakes through the trees and warms our heads. I make a circle round each mushroom now; my bag is empty. I smell them, breathe on them, brush aside the leaves and stare in fear. There are *poganki* under every tree; they are omnipotent like gods and omnipresent like the ants that crawl between our fingers; they seem to multiply and vanquish our shiny, stubby, brown-headed heroes. Dejection slips into my heart. Nothing is alive or edible or real—only poison, death, a grumpy angry forest—I throw my useless wand against the ground and suddenly my eyes catch Him: the King Bolete—Porcini—*Beliy Grib*. He sits proud and still, leaning like a retired general against a thorny shrub. The needles prick my skin and latch onto my hair, but still, with bare hands, I forge ahead and pull the *Beliy Grib* out whole, my fingers clenching its regal, portly stem. I found Him, I scream in joyous trepidation, tears tapping at my eyes, but my mother doesn't hear. She's singing to herself or is there someone else?

A crowd's gathered round my mother. Sonichka, Sonichka, they exclaim, the forest air does you good, you're glowing! The sun draws specks of gold upon her skin, her rosy cheeks pinch into a smile. A man stands at her back, tickling her ribs, her neck; his fingers play unabashedly with my mother's hair. Dimochka, she murmurs, blushes, this is my daughter, Lenochka; Lenochka, he cries in shrill delight, but only looks at her. And I feel small and frail in a yellow blouse, my skinny legs drowning in tattered jean overalls. I'm the mushroom in the ground hidden in my mother's skirt, shielded by her stalwart body. But Dmitry sees me now and lifts me in the air and seats me on his shoulders. My *Beliy Grib*, I thunder, but he laughs, they laugh so hard I want to cry.

At the bonfire, there are so many chanterelles and *King Boletes* that my paltry contribution seems only fit to feed the camp's old dog. Pans are frying on the fire and mushrooms crackle, glistening in browns and orange-reds. Potatoes sizzle and sparks fly through the air and black bread blackens on jagged sticks. The taste of charcoal permeates my tongue, and I feel the pangs of a supine, mirthful hunger. The mood infects me and I laugh from nothing, from the air, the breeze, the fire, from guitars strumming, songs spilling from crimson vodka-laced lips, from voices harmonizing and diverging like seals quaking out of tune.

My mother radiates at its very center, flocked by men, by women, even by the old camp dog. She laughs and downs shots and sways and cracks clever jokes, stringing the words and innu-endos so seamlessly together that her eloquence seems almost invisible except to me. She sits on one man's lap and curls the hairs of another with her soft, long fingers. Someone else's hand is rubbing her arching back, her swan-like neck. Ooooh, Sonichka, you have such lovely skin, a bald-headed man says. Sonichka and her luminescent aristocratic skin, her stunning face, those sky-blue eyes, why, she's every poet's dream, a woman from another time, from the Renaissance, a woman painted by Renoir. And Lubochka, what a glorious body you have, what breasts, what waist, what thighs, Dmitry coos, grabbing another woman's hips, you remind me of Catherine the Great; this is my mother's closest friend, a voluptuous blonde beauty, these two *devushki* are the ladies of the ball.

Their husbands, my mother's and Lubochka's, are in Moscow: working, huffing, puffing, cheating. The wives have been exiled to the outskirts of the city—to camps and dachas—to soak in the summer nights, cleanse children's lungs of fumes, imbue their bodies with the sinews of Russian nature—the healing evergreens, judicious oaks, blushing birches, and alluring eves. Yet each wife is here for a purpose: Sonichka's part of the *Collective Farmers* sojourn. All the editors at her journal have been sent to pick potatoes, sunflower seeds, corn stalks so that they may understand—viscerally connect to—the hardness of a farmer's life. Physical labor, as the saying went, never did anyone harm. There are other intellectuals here—publishers, scientists, columnists, professors, teachers—amassing hours as farmers: The Workers' *Collecteev* Unites! They'll return to Moscow refreshed, invigorated, their stubbed fingernails and calloused hands and new earth-sown wrinkles will herald their physical prowess, their Communist values, their hatred of snobbism, intellectualism, capitalism and the evil West. Only the doctors, dentists, and nurses come here to work as doctors, dentists, and nurses, a special privilege handed through connections, to give their children fresh air and keep out of their spouses' reach.

My mother is Carmen tonight, a puffy black blouse frames her chest and shoulders, and from her narrow waist a crimson skirt unfurls into a fan around her legs. Her fiery auburn curls bounce on her pale cheeks. She's done duets with balalaikas, guitars, flutes, even violins, but at this moment the only instrument's her voice. She sings Carmen's seductive "Habanera" a cappella, and rising from the men, unclasps her hands and frees her body from their grasp. She snaps her fingers and throws the skirt up in the air, showing a smidgen of white thigh. She shakes her shoulders, chest, and hair; the blouse rides the crescents of her breasts. Her feet *tap-tap-tap* against the moist black ground, her belly undulates before our eyes. Her voice crescendos—a spear—a warrior's jubilant cry.

The others join in. The men accost her, their arms like legs of octopuses squeeze her narrow waist. Why didn't I see you first, a man says. Sonichka belongs to me, another claims. My mother laughs, her laughter quavering in high soprano. The air stings and crackles on the open flames, and in our eyes, life gathers into a single moment, embalmed in startling blue joy. Across this fire I watch her and wonder if I'll ever be free like her. Come to me, Lenochka, come dance with me, she picks *me* from the crowd. I wiggle arms and legs and arch my back into a perfect bridge. The crowd roars in boisterous approval, shaking its medusa head. And I shake mine together with my mother and feel the music teach my body how to dance. Give my child a microphone, my mother screams, and someone throws a stick. I grip it like a pro, and out of my mouth Alla Pugacheva streams, the chords of "Where Does the Summer Go?" Longing and melancholy issue from my lips, and thou behold, my figure assumes the adult pose of seduction. My audience grows quiet, their faces coalesce into a blur.

The next day when my father visits, my mother looks exhausted, her hair disheveled, eyes swollen, closing as she struggles to keep them wide awake. He's brought her a box of chocolates and she thanks him meekly, but their eyes only briefly meet. You want to sleep longer, he whispers, climbing into bed with her. I watch them, pretending to be asleep, one eye a slit for catching secrets. The covers slide, I see his fingers on her thigh, sneaking inside her nightgown. She turns to face him and there's a kiss I cannot see, but hear saliva swishing, lips smacking, the whispering in between. My father squeezes her behind, have you missed me, he wonders out loud, and she says, shhhhh, of course I've missed you, it's terrible you can't stay longer. You look tired, he tells her, you look tired, she tells him, and they laugh, as if they both know what they're tired from. They kiss again, only it's lighter, gentler now, like cautious tigers circling their domain, afraid to stir their underlying wrath. But suddenly, there's an invasion: my father's hand abruptly pulls down mother's shirt and one breast falls out, a white pear with gray creases round a soft pink nipple. Don't, Semeyon, Lena might awake, my mother whispers and shrouds her body in the sheet. She's asleep, he says. She's always awake, my mother counters, even when I think she's asleep, her eyes are watching me. I wonder what he wants from my mother, why does he nag her, push her so, why should he want to see her breasts. You're imagining things, he says, I've missed you, he says, I need it, he says. Later, later when it's dark, when it's night, she promises.

I'll prove it to you, my mother whispers. And in a voice of mischief, she says, now what do you think we should get Lenochka for her birthday—a huge stuffed poodle or Anderson's fairy tales or a set of watercolors I saw last month at Gūm. Well, I was thinking, my father picks it up, of not getting her anything at all—after all, she's been misbehaving a lot lately. How have I been misbehaving, I jump in, and my parents break out in a laugh. Sneaky sneak, my mother says and runs to me, and lifts me in the air and throws me at my father, and I laugh and laugh, and jump up on their bed.

But by lunchtime, my mother and father can barely exist in the same room, and I can't remember who said what to ruin our burst of bliss. I backtrack through the questions, tones, remarks, acrid glances—investigating like a detective what catapulted them from love to loathing, between sunrise and mid-noon.

First, mother asks: how are my parents?

Fine, Father replies, but already signs of irritation snake across his lips.

I don't know what your father is trying to do, he says, but he's putting us all in danger.

He's gotten emotional in his older years, my mother offers, no one knows, it's his own thing, it doesn't involve us, so don't worry.

Are you crazy, of course it involves us! Just saying hello to a dissident on the street is enough to get arrested but this! There are informants everywhere, the KGB are crawling out of every mouse hole, and when you're like me, like me—*a professor*—they watch your every move! I watch what I say in every class I teach, every staff meeting and dinner I attend, I'm extra, extra careful but what good will it do me if your father decides to be a hero, operating of his own accord. I told him, Gregory Abramovich, you better stop your nonsense or I'll throw you out on the street!

How could you say such a thing to him, to an old man, my mother cries.

What do you think he did, my father mocks, he laughed in my face: what—you think you're the boss of me now! Sonya, you better tell me what your old man is doing—

I can't tell you if I don't know myself, she says.

You know, you've been in cahoots with him for years, you and he in your cry of suffocation against the Soviet Empire—are you involved in it too?

Have you lost your mind, lower your voice or we'll be arrested on the spot!

You better not be doing anything to jeopardize our lives, my livelihood, what do you think life will be like for your daughters, I wonder?

I'm not doing anything, my mother pleads, maybe, maybe he's at it again. Maybe Father's having an affair.

That's old hat, my father retorts, he's always having an affair.

But this time, this time, my mother says nervously, it's with a dissident woman, I don't know her name and it's better that way—that's why he goes to those meetings.

For fuck's sake, my father shouts, what meetings?

Shut your mouth in front of the child.

I don't fucking care anymore, has he lost his fucking mind? A dissident? A dissident? Well, you can forget about your precious America, you'll never get out with a father like that, my father says, his voice entering an ominous calm.

Mudila, that's what you want, you want to imprison us here forever, my mother yells, but then her voice drops as footsteps thump across the hallway, near our door. Her face blanches, her hands shake.

I'm not going anywhere, I'm not leaving my country, my father says quietly, I've already told you.

My mother collapses her head in her hands, and through a web of fingers, looks up at him: please, Semeyon, perhaps you thought about it, perhaps you've understood me. Aren't you tired of being afraid? Let's apply for Lenochka, for our girls, for their future. She grabs both of his hands and pleads, her eyes burning like gold-rimmed sapphires, tears deluging her cheeks, muffling her speech. She drops to her knees and throws her arms around his legs, and a high-pitched cry soars from her lungs.

Sonichka, please, stop with this sentimentality, with all this melodrama, I can cry too, you know. You know how I feel. He's pulling her up from the ground but she won't budge. I've already told you, No! No, I will not submit! I will *not* submit to you on this. Not on this. It is too much, too difficult. You're asking me to change our whole lives, our whole lives, my whole life, our children's lives, you're asking me to relinquish my mother, my culture, my tongue, my books, my friends, my ties, all things that make it a life, that make me a man, that make me human. We'll never be Russian again, my father laments, don't you feel Russian, don't you feel that your soul is Russian?

Jewish, Jewish, my mother spits, rising from the ground, rage displacing sadness—my soul, *my soul*, she screams, is Jewish.

Jewish, Russian, my father says, what's the difference? Who are we but Russians first and foremost—what do we have in us that is Jew, what do *we* know of Jews.

Blood, my mother roars, here, it lies here, she points to the breast I'd seen, in here, everything lives, breathes in here, I can't explain—

Well if you can't explain it, my father snaps, if it's in your heart, how can I listen to a woman's wild emotional fancy?

Don't disgust me! Don't twist my words around, don't take what I've given you freely, openly and turn it ugly—

My father pleads, you're loved by everyone here, admired by everyone; you're the belle of the ball—an editor, a person of literary merit with such deep knowledge of the Russian language. You adore it! What will you be there but a recluse, an outsider, an alien, deaf and dumb, a mute; you'll never speak as mellifluously in English, as brilliantly, never write with such wit, never joke as you do in Russian.

In that, you're right, my mother whispers, the language I will lose, but I'll gain freedom, passion, myself. I'll no longer suffocate from the blackness of all this censorship, this propaganda—don't you know what I deal with every day when hapless writers get axed and hacked and chopped, and the truth—there's never any—just lies. And who knows, perhaps I will conquer English. I'll work like a dog to gain eloquence!

Speak it, yes, my father says somberly, but you'll never own it, you to whom language is like blood, like the liver and lungs and heart inside your body.

Oh, don't you see, I don't care, I don't care about my insides anymore! Can't you see the outside creeping in, corrupting our organs, our very blood—can't you see that I'm rotting—that we'll all rot? My mother collapses on the bed and dinner congeals into a cold mass, untouched by either parent.

I'm tired, my father says, I can't talk about this anymore, I'm all talked out; we spend half our lives thinking and talking about leaving, about life elsewhere, instead of living our lives now. *Here. Now.*

I don't want to look at you, you repulse me, my mother bristles now, her voice quiet and deadly. You're a traitor, a snake slithering in my domain for you understand nothing! I want you out. I want a divorce and I'm taking the children with me.

I'm leaving, my father announces, leaving you! But the children stay in Russia, with me! Tears cloud his eyes.

Don't you start getting pathetic on me, my mother bites back, always weeping like a child. Take yourself in your hands and be a man! Then she looks at me. Lenochka, why don't you walk with your father, he needs fresh air.

So I take him to the pine forest. Do you want to pick mushrooms, I prod his solemn gaze, desperately wanting him to smile. We walk through a sandy path that leads out of the staff's complex into an open meadow. Chocolate and lemon butterflies, wings splashed in plum and lilac flakes, zigzag over tall grass and land on wild dandelions and pansies. I dive toward them but their wings are fast and brisk, my fingers only graze their dusty limbs. My father catches one—a purple wonder with bold black loops and golden specks—and gives her to me. Grab her by the wings, he whispers hoarsely, or she'll die. See her throat, her eyes, her stomach: don't squeeze her there! Only the wings are ours to touch but eventually we must let go. The colors rub against my fingers, mottling my skin, transforming me into the insect, and the insect into me. The wings flap, loosening my grip, but I don't let go. I breathe on it with my mouth open, with my childish hunger to possess it, to keep it forever in my palms, to watch it lose its strength, power, beauty—to watch it die. To metamorphose my own body into the butterfly, to grow wings instead of arms, silk instead of skin, to fly . . . always craving to fly. Let go, my father commands. No, I say, no, then I let go.

My father smiles as though he's forgotten my mother, and he's laughing, running after me, tickling me under my armpits, throwing me up in the air, lecturing me about the birth and death of butterflies, their quest for beauty, their counterpart ugliness like our own human nature. We all have ugliness and beauty in us, he says, he repeats himself, my father. But it is only when we reach the center of the meadow where the grass rises to my forehead, tall and thick and sharp, cutting into our skin, hiding our faces from each other, that my father's voice breaks and he starts to cry.

How to Eat Trout Without Chewing

By the end of June I had moved into Eddie's loft. That was the summer of media's lustful affair with the president and his intern, when instead of health care, Medicare, poverty, world peace, world hunger, the devastated and now defunct Yugoslavia, the Middle East, and the looming threat of bin Laden, we engaged vicariously in yearning glances and sexual escapades under the Oval Office desk. We longed to hold the First Lady in our arms and murmur "c'est la vie," without the French accent; realized that cigars, besides being cancer-causing agents, are, according to a recent study, a major source of infidelity in men; and that semen is *not*, as some men would have you believe, a sweet ambrosia from the gods, but a viscous substance that can ruin a perfectly conservative dress.

Eddie and I spent that summer making love and watching the Monica Lewinsky scandal unfold through our post-coital, glazed eyes. That summer, with its immodest heat and bone-baring air conditioning (for everything seemed to gaze back at us through sensual goggles), wiped Chicago from my mind. My fiancé and family grew into an undergrowth in my memory's warehouse. Intermittently I'd see their disapproving faces catching me in the act, frazzled and in lust, and my eyes would blink, shutting them out.

Because of my abysmal record at SPASM, I enrolled in summer courses and promptly began to fail Probability and Stochastic Modeling for the second time, in spite of the endless hours I spent listening to my advisor, Professor Gerald Lee, explain such concepts as mutually exclusive events and unconditional probability. He was a serious man who noted my body-hugging turtlenecks with enough dismay to deflate any woman's breasts. Why are you doing this, Kaulfield, he asked me one day, why are you torturing both yourself and me? How are you ever going to come up with a viable master's thesis if you still struggle with permutations? He knew better than any of my professors that I understood squat in mathematics, that probability concepts could not be screwed into my imagistic brain, even if you were in possession of an industrial drill. He saw at once that I did not belong among the rejected geniuses of SPASM (insecure exiles from pure math and physics). But these were the glorious, affirmative action days of the nineties and, as the only woman in the department, even if I failed Probability and Stochastic Modeling for the third time, no one would throw me out.

The thrill of being the only woman left in an all-male program, ignited by my mother, was steadily dissipating. Homework induced epic REM sleep and lectures gave me a chance to sketch profiles of comatose students. During my free waking hours I roamed the city streets, wondering how I would swallow this career for the rest of my life. The notion that each step, each job, each human interaction was to revolve around graphs, survey questions, formulas, hypotheses, geo-sexual-social-medical predictions brought on waves of nausea. Was I in fact only doing this for *them,* the endemic plural of my singular family? Was this just another circuitous route to unceasing praise and syrupy ego-stroking, case in point, my love of Grandmother's cry: "Our Lenochka is studying matimatiku!"

But I couldn't please them anymore, not because I didn't want to, but because it was impossible. I had finally acknowledged that my brain was an average Joe, a lowly agent in a hierarchical, genetically preordained structure, a lonesome warrior fitfully groping in eternal darkness. Welcome, the brain seemed to blare, to the abyss of your stupidity!

Failure grew into an all-consuming, obdurate reality. I had striven and lost. I was a pathetic truant, a rare gem from the Idiots-Incorporated Collection, and all at once my straight A's, honors, scholarships, accolades were drowning like shit in the proverbial toilet. I had no idea what to do with my life if I pulled statistics out of the equation. For a person who was always sure of her step, confident in her brain—this new ambiguous era signaled a full-scale immersion in Russian hell, *Ad* as it was once conceived by Dostoyevsky.

One night Eddie came home at midnight (a regular hour for us) to find me sprawled on the kitchen floor, statistics texts tucked under my buttocks, graphs staring out of wrinkled open notebooks at my dejected face. I was wearing his oversized Columbia sweatshirt and his boxer shorts (my own clothes were overdue for an emergency visit to his very own washing machine). I looked at him with my wet, self-pitying eyes and, without speaking, leafed through the notebook pages, where superimposed upon graphs and plausible survey questions were driblets of black acrylic paint strung in random patterns that resembled hideous faces.

"This—this—this—is—shit—this shit is what I've been doing instead—instead of—" I gasped out, adding hiccup after hysterical hiccup.

"Calm down, calm down, Emma." He put his briefcase down and, crinkling his black pinstriped suit, lowered himself to the floor next to me. "We've been through this before. How many times have you told me that you're unhappy in your program?"

"Many," I replied like a child being tested on her basic developmental skills.

"And what have I told you?"

"To quit."

"And what have you done?"

"Not quit."

"You act like such a baby sometimes," he said. "Listen: you have to treat yourself seriously. You have to take your desires seriously. You talk of feminism, but I don't see it—'a woman in her own right, a woman exercising her own free will'—where is she?"

"Don't you see, that's exactly what I'm doing—statistics is my ticket to financial freedom! But with art, where will I be? I'll never make it—and then I'll be dependent upon my family for the rest of my life—or worse, dependent on some man." I remembered my half-baked plan to start painting full time after I married Alex and gave birth to our first child.

"You can make money as an artist—it's possible. You can get an MFA in art, meet people in the field, make connections, get a job in a gallery, work as a graphic designer—"

"I don't want to be a graphic designer or a cartoonist or a beggar. I want to be a real artist—I want to see my work on display—I want to create—oh fuck, what does it matter what I want!"

"Or—or—or I could support you," he offered tentatively.

"And where would that get me—from one man's pocket to another's! Oh, who cares, why are we even having this conversation? I'm not good enough to make it as a 'real' artist!"

"Are you actually asking me this? Because you know what I think—"

"Tell me again, please."

"I've told you before—your work astounds. You're the real thing, Emma, the genuine article. You can't keep second-guessing yourself if you ever hope to make it. You have to know the way I know—in your gut—that you have the gift. You know you have it. You suffer because you can't escape the pull—"

"To paint, constantly, relentlessly—"

"But you have to believe in yourself."

"Where do you get such incredible confidence, why can't I have it, feel it?" I wanted him to teach me the way one might a child.

"The only reason you doubt yourself—as an artist—is because you don't know if you have what it takes to sell yourself. You have to promote your own work nowadays—"

"No, I never think of selling. I doubt myself because there's an inner critic inside my mind that constantly barrages me with notes and points out my flaws—flawed technique, flawed color, not enough depth, tells me I can do better or, when it's more deadly, tells me I'm not good enough."

"You have to battle this inner critic, silence him. Understand—believe—what talent you have! Your work can extract a drop of blood from your viewers. Your work will make them cry—I've cried."

"You've never cried—don't flatter me!" I laughed through tears.

"I did too—the first time I came to your apartment and you showed me those muddy children—"

"You mean my *Prehistoric Children under a Bludgeoned Sky*?"

"That piece belongs on a gallery wall, not under your bed."

"Oh c'mon, you're just buttering me up—"

But his expression altered, his eyes swam to me. "When I saw that painting, I became so nervous, I thought—I thought you were so, so talented. I thought: who am *I*—what can I offer *her*?"

Strength, I wanted to say, you offer me strength, which is everything.

"Eddie, I need to—I need to tell you something—"

Eric still buzzed in my ear and his threat hung in my mind like a knife periodically puncturing my abdomen.

"I want to be honest with you about everything."

He leaned down and closed the statistics books sprawled on my lap.

"I want you to paint," he said. "Personal truths can wait. You were meant to do *this*—to create universal truths. I believe in you Emma."

Tears pricked the corners of my eyes and he took all the statistics and math books from my hands and stacked them neatly against the wall.

"This," he offered, straightening the pile, "we can send to your parents with a note: ATTENTION MOM AND DAD—THIS IS NOT MY LIFE."

His words reverberated in my head like battle cries, awakening me from my immigrant slumber. He took me from the humdrum of my parents' practical ambitions to such grand terms as destiny, ability, debt to oneself, duty to one's "God-given talent." He took me from struggling and puffing angrily over my statistics homework to wanting to paint without respite, to paint through the night, to once again feel the pain in my joints, the knots in my back, the numbness in my fingers, the happiness.

One night I returned to the dungeon to retrieve all my acrylic and oil paints, my pastels and blank canvases, my huge collection of brushes—I suddenly needed everything at once and it couldn't wait.

Natasha greeted me in the doorway.

"Someone's been calling you non-stop. Some guy named Eric." She handed me a piece of paper with a number on it and I dialed.

"Hello, Eric?"

"Hello, Emma—so glad you called!"

"What's up?"

"I was just wondering if you're doing anything this Saturday night?"

"I'm busy," I replied.

"Yes, you are, very busy. I just told Alex I'll be coming to your wedding—how do you like them apples?"

"I'll ask him to disinvite you—"

"He complained to me that you're very busy. So I said to that dumbass, 'Oh, I'm sure she's longing for you—she never goes to bars or has fun, never!'"

"Please leave me alone!"

"That's not possible," he said. "You've had—oh, how should I put it—you've rocked my world!"

"What do you want?"

"You," he said. "I want to try you—I want to sample you the way you sample a tasting menu—has Eddie taken you to these fucking pretentious restaurants—has he impressed you?"

I remained silent, then in an abrupt threatening voice, he spoke again. "Drop Eddie."

"Why?"

"Ever since you, he's not the same. He suddenly cares. No more fun, no more strip clubs. What the fuck did you do to him?"

"What—I—I didn't do anything—"

"Don't play the victim card with me, you little Russian immigrant gold-digger, probably trying to see which of these two losers will make more dough and then you'll decide! But I'd be careful if I were you. If I were you, I'd suck more dick to keep up the status quo—like my dick for instance and—" I don't know what he said next because I couldn't listen anymore. Perhaps I should have paid attention to his threats, to the shrill desperation in his voice, but I couldn't stop smiling, couldn't stop replaying the words in my head: *he's not the same, he suddenly cares* . . . I felt my heart swell and my mind burst and the colors on my palette start to dance, and the dungeon's drab walls glow in a beautiful pink light. The world momentarily turned inside out and all the suffering I harbored in my past was swept away by this indescribable feeling of happiness, this exuberance for this other individual who seemed to possess within himself the key to my life.

Eddie set up a semi-studio for me in his loft, demarcating the living area with an opaque burgundy curtain behind which I could store my supplies and work. I set up my world inside the curtain's circumference, with all my acrylics and oil paints and brushes and various palettes arrayed on the windowsill and floor, and watched the sun set and rise from a sliver of window embraced by the curtain. He would awaken at four in the morning, and catch me bent, gaunt, crazed, with my paintbrush in one hand, yellow-purple-red stripes on my forehead and cheeks, muttering inscrutable incantations under my breath. He would watch me from the curtain's edge, sometimes ten, twenty minutes at a time, waiting for me to feel him. But I never could. I was so lost inside. Only when he'd speak, when he'd say, "It's amazing watching you work," I'd turn, for an instant unable to recognize him, and then I'd smile in gratitude for throwing away the chains I couldn't cut on my own.

One night he appeared in the shadows, holding an enormous Nikon camera with a long thick lens protruding into space, and started snapping pictures of me. I was painting them, my mother and father fighting in that wooden cabin, their war reemerging on canvas as a child hiding under a mushroom tree. I called her *My Secret Chanterelle.*

"You inspired me," Eddie said, "I haven't touched this camera in years. But every night, I watch you, I watch you and want to capture you." I was wearing a long sleeve blue button-down shirt, one of his old relics, torn and worn out, unfit for the office, and nothing else. Specks of black and gold and red paint sat on my face and thighs and calves, even between my toes, and the shirt itself resembled a cheerful Jackson Pollock masterpiece.

"I want to take you somewhere special," he said, his voice quiet as though he was confiding in me.

"A new swanky restaurant in East Village?" I cried with delight.

"No, something even better—"

"A wild discotheque in Queens?"

"I want to take you to a special place—to my secret cottage in the wild woods of Maine—it's like your Russia, like this painting."

Everything fell away, my heart grew quiet, my mouth watered, my tongue hung free. I imagined he only took his most prized lovers there, to swim in the freezing lakes of Maine, where water nymphs glow on waves and he, a satyr, stripped of his banker's garb, clad only in verdant robes of nature, carries his Nikon over one human eye shooting arrows into goddesses—leaving their hearts—*my heart*—in tatters . . .

"I don't think that's a good idea," I said.

"Are you still scared of me—Emma—is that it? Are you scared of getting too close to your secret goy?" He laughed as if *we* were a joke, treating our intimacy as we often did—like an ongoing project in ill-fated humor.

"I'm just not ready, Eddie, for such a concentrated dosage of you," I replied with an easy laugh.

How long did I have to sow my oats, how long did I need to get *it* out of the system (as men so triumphantly claim) before I could enjoy jubilant domesticity with Alex? I couldn't take this protracted fling, this ephemeral love-tryst, into the echelon of driving to secret cottages because if I did, if I did, I'd be leading Eddie to a dead end. I checked myself quickly, retracing my steps—didn't I tell him that I enjoyed him like an addiction? Didn't I plainly state my case: I can never marry you, you a hot gentile, me a sexy Jew, you a wanton fiend, me a temptress-feminist? Didn't I try to tell him—only a moment ago the truth was sliding off my tongue: "I have not broken up with Alex—I am not free to love you!" I patted myself reassuringly, and yet I was aware enough to know that I was lying unremittingly, blatantly, willfully, lying through omission, lying to him, to Alex, to myself—that I was lying to keep *him*. How did I allow it to happen: how did my desire to make something of myself, something unique, staggering, satiating, become so bound up in him that I awaited him now with my whole self, not just that hackneyed animalistic pang between my thighs?

As the taxi approached the restaurant, located directly opposite the Metropolitan Museum of Art, my skin turned wet and prickly, and my stomach contracted from nerves. I took comfort in my outfit: black rayon pants, a silk white blouse, and a black blazer that I felt was conservative enough to survive lunch. Still, nothing on me ever closed properly, and the blouse cast a shadow around my breasts, its white waves lingering obstinately over my nipples.

I wore tiny leaf gold earrings that belonged to my great-great-grandmother, who had hidden them in her mattress during Stalin's collectivization raids, and periodically fingered the jagged spikes that cut into my earlobes; *I'm Russian*, I whispered in my head, *I can take anything*.

I was buttoning my top button and straightening my pants when Eddie suddenly unbuttoned me. "Don't—don't play someone else with her. I want my mother to see you as you are—sexy as hell."

"I can't believe I agreed to this!" I cried, wondering how I managed to say "no" to the secret cottage and "yes" to meeting "The Wicked Witch of the West," his words, not mine.

"Does your mother even know we're practically living together?"

"This is my world, Emma, not yours. And in my world, my mother is not my keeper. You can say and do whatever you want." He said this with such belligerence that I suspected the truth was hiding somewhere underneath, mingling with this lie.

"I want to get out of the car—stop the taxi," I exclaimed with sudden horror. "I can't do this—"

"I thought Russians weren't afraid of anything," he goaded, but with a smile so wide and generous that it washed over my upper intestines like a gallon of Maalox.

Across identical white tables and elegantly dressed women, I spotted a great head of light brown hair. The woman was looking out the window, her face turned away from her husband's.

We approached them briskly, urgently, like two cops who've spotted their suspects. "Mom, Dad, I want you to meet Emma!" Eddie announced, shattering her reverie.

She twisted her long neck and languidly rolled her eyes over my body and face. "We've heard so much about you, Emma," she murmured warmly.

"It's a pleasure to meet you too, Mrs. Beltrafio," I said.

"Please call me Cynthia," she corrected me, the first of the many corrections to come.

At close range, I could see that she was a woman of great height and perfectly sustained skin. She had an elongated face and her dark brown eyes were shaped almost precisely like Eddie's. But her face, like a vacuum package carefully wound in wrapping paper, was the antithesis of Eddie's expansive and gratifying expression. Each feature had too little room to maneuver, so that her speech and emotions were confined to scant millimeters of space, dooming her to one invariable state—grandiose politeness.

I wondered if her cramped physiognomy was the result of Botox, which Eddie confided was one of her secret spa addictions, or something else, something more insidious.

"I'm so happy you could make it, Emma," she said. "Eddie was telling us you were very busy." Then she relieved her face with a smile, a smile that like her other attributes was constrained at the outer edges of her jaws, leaving the impression that she hadn't laughed in years.

"Harold, but everyone calls me Hal, even my children." Mr. Beltrafio stretched out his hand and shook mine. "It's so nice to meet you." He was an inch shorter than his wife, with an amicable easy smile, kind hazel eyes, and soft, round cheeks that smacked of a jolly childhood. Yet he resembled Mrs. Beltrafio, the way a dog might resemble its owner, not in the details, but in his peculiar stunted demeanor, as though he had been trained for years to keep his emotions within the boundaries of hers.

The four of us looked at our menus for a long time before anyone spoke, an utter impossibility in my family. They flashed before me, my querulous, loud sextet, spouting their contradictory opinions and impossible demands on waiters, and I was struck with a sudden yearning for them. *He's not looking me in the eye,* Grandmother sang in my ear, *just because I don't speak English doesn't mean a waiter can't look into my eye! Look at that contemptuous physiognomy! What kind of chefs are these—no one says anything, no one complains, that's why the food is so horrendous—is this chicken or rubber?* Her lively voice was drowned out by the silence of the Beltrafios. Their lifeless concentrated faces perused their menus with a sense of purpose—could I ever be a part of *this*?

Mrs. Beltrafio was shrouded in several layers of yellow satin, bordered by a navy jacket. Its left lapel featured a gilded scorpion brooch that perfectly matched her blouse and added a glint to her invasive black eyes. She peered at me over her menu to assess my face, or was it my soul she was assessing? "I highly recommend the fish, it's always fresh here," she said, "and the scallops for appetizers."

"Mother is a fish aficionado," Eddie remarked. "She is always eating fish in every restaurant."

"I love fish," I trilled, attempting to please her. "I'll take the tuna and the scallops." Only moments passed before I realized that I had chosen the two most expensive items on the menu.

"I'll have the trout," Mrs. Beltrafio announced, the trout being only twenty-three dollars, while my tuna was thirty-two fifty. "And I think I'll skip the appetizer," she added after pausing distinctly on the prices.

"Oh," I said, feeling as though my tongue was hanging from a scaffold, "perhaps I'm ordering too much—" Even when we were poor, living with cockroaches, my family never skimped on food. My mother made sure that the expensive items on the menu were tried by at least one member of the family, and if we were taking people out to dinner, it was a matter of honor that they would never feel our lack of resources, our private money woes.

"Don't be silly," Mr. Beltrafio said, stepping in, "order as much as you want. Eddie is going to order an appetizer, aren't you, Eddie?"

"Yes," he said, stroking my back as though for support, "I'm getting lamb, and the tuna tartar, and the scallops. I'm famished."

He met his father's eyes and added, "Hal, this is my treat."

"Don't be ridiculous, Edward, your mother's always dieting."

The silence resumed, only to be broken by her: "Isn't it a lovely place? These paintings are really quite remarkable. I believe these are reproductions of Odilon Redon—how lovely!"

"How's work, my boy?" Hal turned to his son.

"Good, we just closed a merger between Gladdon Oil and Exxon—I was in charge for the first time. The stress was incredible, Hal, like nothing I'd ever experienced before."

"But you did it—you succeeded," his father announced as though this were an irrefutable fact about his son, a branch he could grab onto in a world where everything else wobbled and fell apart.

"Ignatius, have you had any more thoughts about starting your own hedge fund?" Cynthia inquired. "Doris's son, Nathan, said he'd be very interested—he's like you, an ex-investment banker, and Andy could certainly use a more stable job than running your father's business."

"That's just it, son, your brother isn't running the business—he's getting a free ride," said Hal.

"Mother—we've had this discussion before and the answer is still the same: I have no intention of starting my own company and if I ever did, I would never hire Andy."

"Oh, but then you'd be on top of the world," his mother went on, "instead of what you are now—just a cog in the wheel."

"He's doing just fine, Cynthia, he's doing great! You should concentrate your efforts on Andy. He's the one who needs to grow up—"

"Try to calm down darling, it's not good for you," Cynthia said this kindly, but her perplexed gaze seemed to chop off his tongue.

"Nothing ever changes," Eddie grumbled. "Why don't you sell the business, Dad, and just retire? Or get someone else to run it for you—fire Andy, for Christ's sake."

"Ignatius, please don't take God's name in vain," murmured his mother, the rebuke carrying the same calm tone as her appreciation of Odilon Redon.

"We're making a profit this year, son, we'll be all right. Don't you go worrying about us—"

"Your father's a dreamer," his mother remarked with a laugh. Her mouth remained suspended in a crooked smile that I knew she produced specifically for me, but her eyes stung Eddie's face. "And where do you suppose your brother could go if your father fired him? What would his children eat? He has a family to support, you know—you're the one without responsibilities."

"How long are you going to defend him, Mother? Andy has to learn to make his own way in the world."

"I'm not defending him, Ignatius, I see *all* his limitations. Oh, poor, poor, portly Emily—that woman has a heart of gold and of course, no dignity, practically hanging herself around your brother's neck to keep him from running off to the city to be with some doe-eyed Barnard student. And imagine this—telling your father and me he's making 'connections' for the company, building up 'clientele' in the city! Does he really believe your father is *that* naïve? We're not the sort to interfere but Emily, poor girl, just doesn't understand him. It's not my place to educate—all Augustine wants to do is restore his manhood—"

"Do forgive us, Emma"—Hal suddenly turned to me with warm smiling eyes—"for talking so rudely about our private family affairs. This lunch was really just to get to know you."

Cynthia nodded her great brown head at me and said, "Yes, we understand that you come from Russia—from where exactly in Russia?"

"Moscow," I replied as if I was at my own deposition.

"Ah, my second favorite Russian city—I have always preferred Leningrad—to me, of course it will always be Leningrad." She shifted in her seat, and the quiet, almost intimate disrobing of her jacket seemed to take me into her confidence. "You really don't look Russian at all, your features are quite astonishing—almost American Indian I'd say—such excellent cheekbones and so skinny. Typically, Russians are rotund in their faces and a lot more voluptuous in the hips."

"Mother, please—must you air your racist views in the first ten minutes?" Eddie hissed.

"How many times have I told you, Ignatius, that I'm an observer of human nature, like say a botanist—I've never claimed to be its judge!"

"I'm Jewish," I said suddenly.

Appraising me with her narrow brown eyes, she replied warmly, "Of course you are—you didn't think I was so ignorant as to believe that you defected here like that ballet dancer—what was his name—Godunov?"

"Our exit was just as dangerous—"

"Well, certainly, but from what I understand, Jewish people were being legitimately released by the Soviet government on account of the many people in this country who fought for your freedom—I think our accountant Gary Schneider wore a bracelet that said FREE SOVIET JEWS, and even marched in Washington. Isn't that right, darling? Wasn't Gary just such a maudlin, sappy liberal—everything he said—" Her face suddenly underwent a perceptible shift in color. "I'm sorry—do you know what 'maudlin' means, Emma? It's like dripping with sentiment, exaggerating one's feelings."

I felt her thoughts running under her skin: my impoverished vocabulary, my backward immigrant mentality, my potential grammatical errors, my lack of familiarity with her favorite Mother Goose rhymes, like "Sing a Song of Sixpence" and "Mary, Mary Quite Contrary."

"You're quite right, Mrs. Beltrafio, about me not looking Russian." I spoke too soon, my old immigrant indignation rising to my throat. "I think my features changed when I became more fluent in English. My jaws sharpened from working the mouth too much. I believe the Russian language is *interveludian*."

"Do you mean *antediluvian?* I'm not sure you sure you're pronouncing that correctly," Mrs. Beltrafio noted, her countenance pinched from some deep internal discomfort.

"No, no, I didn't mean antiquated. I meant *interveludian*," I went on with a crooked smile. "It's an old British usage; it means that the words operate on the inside of your mouth rather than the outside, the way English does. When you speak Russian, your tongue and teeth stay hidden from view, sentences are formed within almost closed lips; but in English the lips are open, the facial muscles work constantly, the tongue dances in plain view." *Interveludian*, my ass! I had my own unique dictionary, in use for several years now to confound fools: *largodick (*pronounced as it's spelled; translation: *large ego, small dick*), *fantasmobullet* (meaning fantastic bullshit) and *idiopanarama* (self-explanatory).

"That's very interesting," Mrs. Beltrafio remarked, appraising me anew with what I guessed was a modicum of respect. "Very, very insightful! I've always loved the French language—but until now it hadn't occurred to me that their lips get all bunched up, like they have a little mouse dancing on their upper lip. I wonder if there's a special word for *that*?" Then she smiled, but the sharp corners of her lips cut into me, and my heart accelerated with fear. "Hal and I used to go to Paris all the time, when we were still traveling to improve ourselves. Now we just sprawl on some Caribbean beach and drink strawberry daiquiris."

"We haven't been to the Caribbean in over ten years," Hal said.

"I know, darling, you're too tired now to go to Australia or Africa, I know—I'm not complaining." She appealed to me again. "You see, Emma, the flights wipe my husband out, and so he prefers Jamaica. For me there's nothing there but a kind of heavenly deadness. Moscow is a wonderful place to visit—do you remember it much?"

She propped her pale manicured fingers under her chin and flashed me a sliver of motherly anticipation.

I didn't know what to say. The three of them looked at me with throttling curiosity, and the question, posed in this emptiness of context, hung before me like a strategically looped rope.

"I remember the street I was born on," I spoke with sudden candor, "our neighbors' white poodle barking in the mornings, the dark elevator in my building that always broke, the walk to school in the snow—strange things. Here and there something will come to me: the five-year-old girl whose parents were drunk all the time, a golden-headed little creature always naked, pressed against the window pane, crying. Behind her we could see her parents throwing books, vases, chairs at one another. And we'd watch, crouching on our knees, the whole building, because the parents were so loud and violent but no one dared to call the police. The fear, I remember the fear."

"Yes, that's the way memory is," Mrs. Beltrafio murmured in a mellifluous voice, "that's the way it is for me, you know. I can remember as if it was yesterday my sons squirting each other with those toy green guns—they were all the rage then. I don't think there were any siblings on our block who got along quite so splendidly. Ignatius excelled at math and Augustine in the verbal department, although neither really lagged behind the other in any subject."

"That's terrible," Hal said to me, "what you remember, what you must have endured in that awful country."

"Russia was miserable," I said to Hal, "but I have good memories too: memories of fresh strawberries and raspberries I picked with my own hands at our dacha."

"How I loved our raspberry shrubs—do you remember them, Hal? We had them in our old house. It was a mansion, really, a magnificent piece of luck that Mrs. Luftcourt sold it to us."

"I'm afraid, Emma, my wife tends to idealize the past."

"Do I? Perhaps Emma should know the truth about us," Mrs. Beltrafio announced, her expression undergoing a stark, terrifying change.

"Oh, don't start, Mother," Eddie said.

"We're a broken vessel, that's what we are. We're the remains of what once was; fossilized artifacts of a happy family. Do you really think, Ignatius, that the money you're sending us can make up for the pain I endure every day—every minute of every day?"

"Stop—stop this, Cynthia—you do this to all his girlfriends," his father blurted out.

Eddie glared at his father but the latter merely hung his head like a man depositing his already severed head at the guillotine. I wanted to cup it and force him to look at me, to show him that I too felt his powerlessness—a weakening of limbs, the separation of mind from flesh, the easy floating of one's consciousness above the conversation below. But I was caught in their family's trap: a series of tests administered to every girlfriend like tiny vials of poison where the end result, without exception, known to all the participants, is that no one survives.

"I didn't mean that," Hal murmured, his pale lips shivering. "I was only trying to get us back to you: we tend to forget, you know, other people . . ."

Cynthia swirled her head to face me, and her eyes thickened with tears. "Perhaps you'll have better luck with Ignatius, Emma, than I've had. Easter just came and went, and I had to figure out a way to split the festivities in half. Ignatius refused to come to church with us—he doesn't go to confession anymore—he's given up on God." The accusation turned into a plea. "Andy is willing, he's forgiven you; all you have to do is say the word!"

But Eddie merely frowned in her direction. His gaze was clear and unflappable, and it occurred to me that her tears and pleas were familiar to him, like a play he'd had to endure for years. "Dear Mother, you know very well that reconciling with Andy is not an option for me."

"So, Emma, we hear you're in some confusing program," his mother interrupted, her entire being reclaiming its serene stateliness, "but that you really want to be a painter—what a wonderful aspiration it is—to be an artist!"

"SPASM," I announced proudly, "that's my program: it stands for statistics, probability, and survey modeling."

"Why, that's like swallowing a suitcase." Mrs. Beltrafio giggled with pleasure.

I couldn't understand why despite the fear of *my* family's disapproval of Eddie, I wanted *her* to fall in love with me, why I then made this desperate stab to defend myself: "There are so, so few women in math and science—that's why I want to be part of it."

"So you thought you'd sacrifice yourself for the greater good?"

"I thought—if I have the talent for numbers, why not? I felt like I owed it to women to tip the balance of power. In my Intro to Statistics class, there were forty-eight men and four women, and I was one of the four. And in my program, all the other women dropped out—except for me."

"Impressive," she returned with a strained laugh. "No, no, not that you're in statistics, but that you're so passionate about something you don't really want to do—it demonstrates serious willpower."

The table fell into its habitual silence again. Only this time it was as if something terrible or profane had been uttered, as though Mrs. Beltrafio had reported on someone's untimely death. In the absence of language, I took it all in: her keen evaluation of my soul, my soul splayed open like the trout she was meticulously chewing, and the sensation of myself being chewed.

"Emma is an extraordinary painter. Each piece takes your breath away," Eddie broke in.

"Parents must never force their children to give up their dreams," Mrs. Beltrafio noted absently. "It just so happened that Ignatius chose a very practical career, but I'd have certainly supported his every endeavor, even if he decided to become a trombone player like he dreamed of when he was twelve—"

"My parents didn't force me into anything either." I offered my parents like pork chops on a skewer. "They don't even know that painting is my dream."

"It must have been freezing in Moscow!" Hal quipped cheerfully, but I knew that he simply wanted to save me.

"You must forgive my husband for his ignorant remarks," she said. "He seems to be under the erroneous impression that Moscow is Siberia."

"Yes." I was grateful for some juncture of commonality with her, and so, betraying Hal, I said, "Most people don't realize that Moscow winters are dry and not that windy. It's much colder in Chicago."

"Russian winters always make me think of *Dr. Zhivago*, that excellent movie with Omar

Sharif and Julie Christie. Love only works when people can't be together. But when they're together they want to rip each other's throats out—are you a fan of *Taming of the Shrew*, Emma?"

"I am." I nodded.

"Why, I'm surprised, given your feminist bent—do you remember when Petruchio plans to deprive his wife of sleep and meat? Do you remember what he says?" She paused, giving my mind a chance to assemble itself and awaken from its shock. Then, clearing her voice and acquiring an actor's precise aplomb, she leapt into it: "'And if she chance to nod I'll rail and brawl/ And with the clamour keep her still awake./ This is a way to kill a wife with kindness/ And thus I'll curb her mad and headstrong humour./ He that knows better how to tame a shrew/ Now let him speak . . .' Wonderful, isn't it? What a flawless meditation on marriage!"

My brain felt hollow, emptied of all the books I had read, and the play itself, which I vaguely recalled from my senior year of high school, surfaced, its words like multi-shaped forks now scoured my subconscious and dug up memories I had long since drowned. How many hours did I stare into that dictionary, the Webster's, the Oxford, the English, sleep with it, coddle it, loathe it, throw it against walls, wrestle with its parade of meanings—ancient and modern, colloquial and formal—until it grew on me like fungus, like a lover I could never discard. I conquered Shakespeare eventually, in college, swept through him like a wildfire, scorching the rabbit holes of their double-meanings.

"My favorite play is *Anthony and Cleopatra*," I chirped suddenly. "Now there's a woman I could bank my theories on . . . 'Age cannot wither her, nor custom stale/ Her infinite variety.'"

Mrs. Beltrafio grinned and turned to her son. "You've always had taste, my dear Ignatius."

"Emma is my girlfriend, mother, not an escargot."

She reached for my hand and squeezed it, but her eyes stayed squarely on her son's face. "My darling son, I would never dare compare your Emma to any food group—she's like a magnificent bird."

The waiter finally deposited the check upon our table, and I breathed a sigh of relief.

"We've got to go, Mother," Eddie said, grabbing the check even as Hal loudly fumbled with his own wallet.

"You are truly a delight, Emma," Mrs. Beltrafio murmured, picking up the mercurial voice reserved especially for me, her eyes lucid and angelic. "I've had such fun bantering with you about Shakespeare—so few people nowadays care for the classics—"

"I hope we see you again, Emma," Hal said, cutting her off.

"It was a pleasure to meet you both." I nodded meekly at them.

"No, indeed, the pleasure was *all* ours," Cynthia returned. I wanted to say something more, my mouth hung open for her, but Eddie had pulled me—dragged me, really—out of the restaurant and manually fit me into a cab. There, for the first several minutes, I sat in a daze, staring at other cars clogging our passage forward. I thought of our first days in America, days that dragged in murky silence, when we couldn't speak or hear, when we woke up as mutes, when the world around us was a choir of unfathomable, grating sounds, when the faces we encountered on the streets were objectively human, but not human like us. We were no longer visiting other countries, no longer passing through Vienna or Italy; this alien planet was our new home.

It was only when I heard my name, "Emma, Emma, what are you thinking," that I remembered that I too lived on this planet, that *I* spoke its tongue.

Eddie was grabbing my thigh and maniacally caressing it.

"We must have sex as soon as possible," he said, "otherwise the bad taste she's left in your mouth will remain for weeks."

"She wasn't so bad," I remarked without facing him.

"You don't have to be polite about her." He stuck his hand between my thighs and began to rub feverishly like a man about to be carted off to prison.

"Is it true that you send them money?" I asked, pulling his hand out of my irritated thighs.

"It's not a big deal—I give it to them for emergencies. My father refuses to take it, but my mother makes him feel that they don't have a choice."

"Do they?"

"My parents used to be rich—that's their Achilles' heel. Mother talks about it now like she'd been a movie star, about her furs and cars and reserved seats in fancy restaurants, and her beloved country clubs. She never recovered after they lost their wealth. My father's best friend, partner, our godfather—Russell Walters—decided that he had had enough of civilized life. He started funneling funds to Switzerland and God knows where else, stealing from the company, planning his escape. He had been in charge of the books. We still don't know where he is, though he's been on the FBI most wanted list for fraud and counterfeiting for years."

"That's terrible," I whispered. "I'm so sorry, Eddie."

"Oh, it was years ago. I don't care now. I have shitloads of money. That's the stink of it for my mother—to feel that she—*she*—the Grand Duchess of Larchmont is at my mercy."

He turned to me; his face was open, decisive. "When my parents lost all their money, my father had a nervous breakdown. That's what you witnessed between them. She can't help exercising her muscles once in a while—her reign, you could call it, over him. My father had an honest-to-God meltdown; he spouted inanities, laughed at inappropriate times, cried randomly and walked around the house with shorts on his head, singing the national anthem. It sounds funny, I know, but believe me, it wasn't. My brother and I were starting high school, and my brother wanted to bring girls home but couldn't. And my mother became cruel. She couldn't take it. She strove to control her environment; her days to the tiniest minutia were always carefully planned. It wasn't just the loss of money, it was the loss of everything she held dear—no more parties, no more socializing, no more late-night cocktails on the porch with her country-club friends. She told people Father was ill with cancer—she would have done anything to keep it a secret. But our world was small and my father—well, he didn't know left from right anymore—there wasn't a mall or a grocery store where he didn't end up pulling some stunt or bellowing an incomprehensible rant, and they'd call my mother to take him home. She almost had him committed to a mental institution. The psychiatrist placed dad on antipsychotic drugs and he got better. But my brother and I were certain it wasn't the drugs that did it—it was Mother and Mother alone who forced him to snap out of it. With her kind intentions!" He let out a bitter laugh. "My father has been like this ever since: quiet, submissive, a pathetic sight, but indisputably normal."

"Have you brought other women to meet her?" I asked.

"I was once engaged—"

"Always a fiancé," I said, laughing, "never the groom!"

"That's the way my mother likes it," he muttered as if to himself.

"Then why—why did you bring us together—"

"Are you so blind? You had to meet her—because, because I thought if there was ever going to be anything between us, if there's any hope for us"—he paused, lowering his eyes—"you'd have to meet her. You'd have to know that if you ever wanted to be with me, you'd have to deal with her."

My face collapsed into his shoulder and melted into the beige cotton of his shirt; tears effaced my lids, brows, nose, cheeks until there was nothing left but raw exposed flesh. "*Ya lublyu tebya,*" I whispered. I saw *it* writhing before me—this feeling of being tethered, trapped, of love reduced to its colorless, flavorless essence. I wanted to say it in English, for "I love you" seemed kinder, gentler, more humane, less fatal in its demands on my soul, but it stayed on my lips in Russian—*Ya lublyu tebya*—searing into my skin its heavy, metallic texture, desiccating my tongue.

"What did you say?" he asked.

"Nothing, it was nothing," I replied and shut my lips.

The Caged Iguana

When I entered the dungeon, it appeared darker, smaller, more claustrophobic, in the grip of loneliness. The walls seemed to have grown muddier, yellower, and a rotten-broccoli stench emanated from the living room. Natasha was lying on the fake Oriental rug next to the iguana. Her red-rimmed eyes went through me as if I had become transparent glass. As I came closer, I heard her chortle bitterly, "The iguana is dying from insanity—schizophrenia reptilian style." "What does that mean?" I asked, approaching the animal. "Poor thing doesn't know she's caged—thinks the metal bars are tree stumps and all she needs to do is just burrow through them with her teeth and nose until—well, take a good look at the carnage—for the metal never bends, the freedom never comes . . ." Natasha appeared drunk or high, her eyes partly closed, breathing heavily through her mouth. I could smell her and the iguana swimming in some strange communal odor. But upon closer inspection, I realized that it was the iguana's breath whirring, spreading, sucking every last bubble of air into her heaving, malfunctioning lungs. Her blue scales were peeling, unveiling the dull gray hue beneath, her ribs were protruding, her red tongue was parched and now hung loose from her jaws. Her habitual frenetic hissing and violent purple tail appeared anesthetized. The most telling sign of her emotional state was a mangled lacerated bloody nose, fatally injured by her inexorable attempts to break free of the cage.

"She'll die soon, poor girl," Natasha said. "You never let her out, did you?"

"How could I—I'm never here," I said, feeling unsteady, thwacked by guilt.

I went to my room and sank my limp body into my bed.

Two feet away, an unfinished canvas stood in judgment of me, one half stark white, the other gratuitously black. If only I could tell him this, this indicting, haunting memory, he'd understand. He'd understand why I could not go on a second longer, not splintered thus in half, my mind frayed, depleted by its own dichotomy, by this merciless invasion of two selves. This double life, which once thrilled and terrified and opened up my veins to emerald wilderness and raw possibility, had sown a prison over my head. I couldn't wriggle any parts of me; from both sides, I was now spoken for—so that I had lost the freedom to devote myself to one or the other man. I couldn't ride it like a wave, like an intrepid surfer, like a free-wheeling hedonist, because I wasn't one. I had been carefully circumscribed into a moral box, abetted on every side by limitations and fear of an omniscient God. I needed to cleanse my moral palate of this debris and rot, and to do that—to do *that*—I was certain I had to lose both men. *That* ought to be the price for my sin, and yet, yet . . . how there was always a "yet!" If I told Alex the truth, I'd destroy the one chance I had for a happy, unobjectionable family life. And if I told Eddie the truth, I'd destroy the rare chance life handed us for truly selfish pleasure, for the kind of temporary ecstasy women remember long after they're married and saddled by children, sipping their midday glasses of white wine, reminiscing with their female friends of that thing they did—that thing they did when they were carefree and young and brimming with reckless lust!

I reached for the phone and dialed.

"Alex, Sashenka, there's something I must say—we need to speak in person. I need to come to Chicago," I said.

"Wonderful, let's activate the volcanoes, I'll prepare the grounds," Alex cried, and my father purchased an emergency ticket for me to Chicago.

I pushed the phone away and drifted into a dream. I must have fallen asleep because I was awakened by a loud thump at the door. With half-opened eyes, stumbling through the dungeon's corridor, stringing together slivers of my dream, I made it to the front door and thoughtlessly unlatched it. I was wearing a white T-shirt that barely covered my buttocks and revealed the lace of my pink underwear.

"It was as if you knew I was coming!" the man said. It took me several minutes to place his face but the toad resemblance was unmistakable. Eric stood before me, clad in a shiny black suit.

"What are you doing here?" I pulled the T-shirt as far down as I could but it snapped back into place.

Within seconds he was in my hall, loosening his mauve tie.

"It's not fair, it's just not fair that he should get everything, fucking everything—"

"What are you talking about?" I looked around, hoping to see Natasha, but she had left. I was alone.

"Your Eddie—that fucking star—Grant is going to make him managing director soon—"

"What does that have to do with me?"

"Oh everything, everything has to do with you!" His mouth curved downwards. He advanced toward me with sudden speed.

"There's a picture of you in your element—painting—on his desk. Very pretty! I told you to dump him, didn't I?"

"Have you lost your mind?" I staggered backward.

I stumbled into my room but before I could slam the door in his face, he was inside.

I felt my knees buckle and opened my mouth to speak, but only saliva fell out. I was five foot six and 110 pounds, and he was at least six feet, twice my weight, with muscles protruding from his chest and arms. His physique, if it were to be painted, would turn opaque on a canvas, robbed of human shadows, a one-dimensional object held together by crude black lines.

He threw me on the futon edging into our feet, his legs already in a straddle. With thick thighs, he squeezed my body and flattened me into the mattress.

"You owe me! You owe me!" he screamed. "I warned you if you don't behave yourself, I'll treat you like a common Russian whore! I offered you a deal!"

"What deal? I don't remember any deal." I replied, as if this were a sane exchange between two civilized people.

His eyes raced wildly, but he wasn't actually looking at me. "I gave you many chances but no, you didn't listen! No more Mr. Nice Guy! Now you owe me big time!"

I blinked and in a flash I saw it: an anthropomorphic steamroller, its weight, its height, the mass of its robotic muscle, its power grid and dirty stench, its metal inhuman fingers creeping up my legs, its front roller heading to my vagina, ripping out my hair, squashing, pulling, raiding the private parts of me. I couldn't see through the blur of pain, pain accumulating in my ribs and abdomen, pain in my chest. I was breathing sporadically, in gusts, hiccupping, inhaling, exhaling grim loud sounds—of dread. Vomit rose up my throat and I yearned to burn him with my stomach acid, to disfigure him, bring out the ugliness I saw. But I was helpless, powerless, numbed. Each act was a quickening, a fermenting of the thing to come, a breach of more personal space, I heard a zipper open: his pants dropped. My diaphragm contracted into my back. I can't breathe, I whispered. One arm was still loose and I pushed him up and off of me, but he sank in deeper into my lungs, until I saw it—his white boxer shorts within inches of my face and I was suffocating in it: the stench of penis and balls—a mixture of cologne, piss, and sweat—clogging my nostrils, closing my throat. At last a pool of vomit spilled out.

He noticed and laughed uproariously.

"Get off, you motherfucker! I owe you nothing!" I let out in a hoarse voice.

His expression froze, his eyes menacing.

"You know, fucking can be traumatic if you're not wet enough. Dry and bloody! But hey, you look easy—what—a hot-blooded

Russian bitch like you? A little naughty immigrant? I like all of it, all of you little multicultural bitches. And you're so fucking pretty—how did you get to have such a fuckable face—do you want me to pummel that face in or are you going to talk nicely—with respect?"

He brought a giant fist to my mouth and chuckling, hovered it there, pretending to strike. When I reeled back in fear, he pulled his erect pink penis out and said: "Now suck it, you ungrateful bitch! Suck it!"

I lost my tongue; it hung limp inside my mouth like a cold dead animal. He grabbed my hair and pulled it, together with my head and neck, to his penis, my mouth landing painfully on its tip.

"Suck it! Now!" He screamed, pushing his dick against my closed lips and teeth.

My skin burned, my heart a wild zigzag in my chest.

NO, I screamed, *rape*, I screamed, *how did I end up here*, I screamed, *No, No, No,* I screamed, but none of it was out loud. I was afraid that if I opened my mouth, he'd get in.

In an instant, I was transported to my childhood, to Russia, to fleeing the KGB. Survive . . . escape . . . think . . . run, someone's following you, they're behind you, run . . . think, think, *dumay, dumay bystreye, pridumay chto-to*, I broke languages inside myself. *Lenochka gde ty*?

My transformation was sudden and radical. My synapses relaxed, my neck loosened, my eyes opened. I winked at him, at it. The words "Relax, Eric, relax, all in good fun" came out of my mouth. My voice changed an octave, acquired a lewd tonality. A seductive hue washed over my face. My eyes retrieved their habitual sensual blurriness, then landed on his erect penis. With the loose hand, I stroked it, moving it away from my lips.

"Nice," I said. "I never would have guessed you're so well endowed."

His entire body pulled back, away from me, and the pain across my chest and breasts dissipated. I breathed again.

"Really? You like him? I call him Spiderman."

"That's adorable, Spiderman," I murmured, looking only at his organ. "I think if we're going to make this *fun*, we shouldn't do it here. It's too missionary, too prosaic! I can talk Russian to you if you like."

"Ooooooooh, that would be such a turn-on."

"I think we should head into the living room. More space. Better lighting. I like to look when I suck."

"I knew it, I knew you'd be fun!" He appeared to change into a little boy, eager and excited.

"Can you put something sexy on?" he asked.

"Sure," I said, "but you go into the living room and wait for me."

"No, I want to watch."

I pulled a short leather dress out of the closet and stood there.

"Well, put it on, take off your T-shirt, take off your underwear."

"Oh, c'mon, Eric. Don't you know about the art of seduction? You Americans! Let me teach you somezhing." I spoke suddenly with a Russian accent. "Close your eyes and turn around. I want zhis to be slow, special."

He obeyed. My hands were shaking.

The dress was tight and difficult to pull over my head but once it stretched over my figure, accentuating every curve, it infused me with an instant jolt of power. I put on leather high heels with spikes, a miraculous find in a shop in East Village, and clicked loudly against the wooden floor.

"Keep your eyes closed," I commanded and led him to the couch.

"When can I open my eyes?" he pleaded.

"Wait, I said, wait!"

I tiptoed across the living room to the cage and unlatched the lock. Upon rolls of dried grass and leaves, the iguana was sprawled in all her fat glory, wheezing, shrouded in sleep.

I stroked her broken nose and her right eye popped open and stared at me, watering, as if in comprehension.

"Now you can open your eyes," I said to Eric.

I stood upright before him clad in leather and artificial confidence, my legs spread in a military stance. My time was limited: his penis had grown fully erect, and he and it stared imploringly at me, like two siblings separated at birth. I imagined the tip of his penis to be the tip of his nose—I painted the image in my head, face superimposed on a penis, penis protruding from a face.

"Wow," he said, "you're so hot, so fucking hot."

I swung my hips from side to side and snapped my fingers, like my mother, like Carmen at the bonfire, raising my skirt, dancing, you're dancing, I told myself, tapping your feet to the rhythm of *this* stage.

Suddenly, I heard it: an echo, a shuffling sound trailing the beat of my heels against the floor. The iguana had climbed out of the cage and was now hissing, heaving, moving sluggishly toward me. I wondered if he could see her. She was almost five feet long if you took into account her purple tail.

But he couldn't. He only saw me.

"Enough, enough fucking foreplay!" His voice turned acrid, the muscles in his jaws and neck visibly twitched like denuded wires. "Now drop on your knees and suck my dick, you Russian bitch!"

"Of course, as you wish."

I felt the animal at my back. I made the motion to lean down but instead I jumped away from him, sideways, in a violent jerk, tapping the iguana's bruised nose with my sharp heel. The animal screeched and turned wild, thrashing her terrifying jagged tail, reaching wide stretches of space. The movements were so quick and bellicose that I barely had time to comprehend: the iguana's triangular turquoise head drove directly into Eric's penis. He let out a high-pitched shriek, but I wasn't sure if it was from pain or shock. The animal had climbed up his leg and froze in position, its claws digging into his pants, as if she and I had planned the entire attack in advance.

"What the fuck! What is this freak show? Is this your pet or the product of a radioactive experiment?"

He tried to push the iguana's face away but she hissed, its bottom jaw unhinging to reveal a set of perfectly aligned, ghoulishly sharp teeth.

"Get this hideous monster off of me." His eyes narrowed, fear shone in his gaze. But the iguana slammed her tail against the floor with defiance, and amid flight, the tail's sharp jagged edge caught on his pant leg and cut the cloth, revealing a sliver of his calf.

"Oh God, did it cut me, am I bleeding?" he whimpered, attempting to look at himself.

The animal turned her deformed face toward me, as if awaiting *my* command. I made two steps toward the iguana and then I bent my head to hers. The tail stopped moving; her breathing grew calm.

I stroked her head. Tears rose up my throat but I pushed them down, down into the underground of my subconscious, locking them in my secret vault of memories. I stared menacingly at Eric and waited.

"Please," he begged, the irises of his eyes watering, "please, Emma, get this thing off of me."

"Don't ever return here," I said. "Do you understand me?"

"Yes."

"Shut your mouth. I don't want to hear you speak. Just nod once that you understand."

He nodded.

"Next time I'll tell the iguana to bite your dick off."

I clicked my heels, turned toward the hallway, and began to walk. Heaving and hissing, the animal followed me into my bedroom. I could hear Eric get up after a minute and then run down the corridor and out the door. A loud slam reverberated through the apartment and pierced the walls of my room. The iguana shuddered. Then she collapsed, sinking her weary, corpulent body into the floor, nestling between my paintings, as if painting herself in. I took my heels off and stroked her bruised face and wept.

The next day I flew to Chicago, postponing seeing Alex, shortening my calls with Eddie. I'm not feeling well, I told them, I think I have the flu. My voice was hoarse, shaky: they believed me. The repetitive circle of violence, I thought, the way it chains us to its vicious circumference, from childhood to adulthood, the way it sticks like glue to our souls. I walked along neatly manicured lawns unfurling before identical luxurious red and white and yellow brick mansions, and then veered down a hill to a muddy-colored lake, our Lake Michigan in the heart of Winnetka. The wind was soft, soothing, but I felt nothing on my skin, only the nagging dull pain poking periodically at my ribs and climbing up my throat. I didn't know whether to feel triumph or devastation. I escaped the ultimate violation, the entries from inside, his stampede into my mouth, my vagina, and yet I could not escape the feeling of having been imprisoned nevertheless: the physicality of the assault, the repulsiveness of his face, his corrosive sweaty touch, the putrid stench of him infected all my senses, as if he had been etched into my flesh, the memory of his words hurtling themselves at my head like bullets—quick, hard, repetitive.

Five days later Alex picked me up at my parents' house because he couldn't wait any longer. "I don't care if you cough on me," he said, "I have an excellent *immunitet*!" He was meticulously dressed in causal starched khakis and a light blue shirt that accentuated his vivid brown eyes. His skin glowed in peach hues as though it had been lightly stroked by the sun. I caught myself gaping at him, the instinct of possession overtaking me.

He gave me a rudimentary peck on half of my mouth and said, "You look exhausted."

"Do I? I feel exhausted," I murmured.

"It's about time you came back to Chicago—how long has it been? More than two months? You missed my mom's Fourth of July party!"

"I'm sorry. Are you angry about something?" I asked robotically.

"No, I'm not angry—who said I was angry—but you haven't done anything for the wedding. Mother tells me plans have virtually come to a halt since you—since you gave some sort of 'career' excuse—"

"I've three Incompletes, Alex—I need to finish them if I ever hope to even get a master's in this field. I can't move forward until I finish—"

"Well, you've got to pull yourself together—you've got to get organized."

"You sound just like my dad," I retorted, turning away from him.

"I don't want to squabble," he said softly, patting my arm. "I've missed you and I'm so, so glad—well, that you've finally come around." He pulled two tickets out of his pocket to Shubert Theater where they were staging a revival of *Fiddler on the Roof*.

"I love *Fiddler on the Roof*," I said absently, and imagined us cuddling under a polyester blanket to watch it, not in some impersonal red-velvet theater, but on his VCR, with a steaming glass of Earl Grey at our lips, a remote control at our fingertips, and me wailing "Sunrise, Sunset" at my whim. (As an afterthought, it occurred to me that this was the type of fantasy I'd never have about Eddie.)

We drove to his house in the heart of Buffalo Grove. Small white and yellow houses were pressed against each other like identical portly companions peering from identical miniature squares of grass and dilapidated driveways. He clicked on the remote clipped to the overhead mirror several times before the door jangled upwards. We drove into a dark, cluttered space, where the stench of garbage and diesel fuel assailed my sensitive stomach, and his hand reached for my thigh. "Please, let's get out of here," I begged. "You're not wearing any makeup," he whispered in my ear as he pulled me into their kitchen and examined my face under a harsh fluorescent light. "Is that a problem?" I asked.

"Just noting that you're still desirable," he chirped, "—good sign for the future," and I wondered suddenly, was he always this annoying?

The spotless white eighties kitchen opened onto a carpeted living room, where two black spheres (otherwise known as footstools) abetted a phallic-shaped glittering red leather spaceship (otherwise known as a couch). The sexual imagery was not lost upon me. A narrow staircase, leading to his room, was crowded with his degrees, awards, and gold statues for fencing competitions; an enlarged 15 x 20 photograph of his face hung brazenly on the central wall next to the bathroom, invoking comparisons to presidents.

He approached me slowly, tepidly, each move tentative, with a corollary revision to each step, indecisiveness warping his face. His hands shook as he unbuttoned my jeans and raised my black T-shirt above my head, and I let him, because his hesitation soothed me, allayed the memory of Eric's uninvited assault on my body. His eyes were magnificent and dark, his expression stoic like that of a warrior in confining metal armor. He bit his voluptuous lower lip, as if the process of undressing me produced acute pain. His deference and beauty devastated me; I felt a pang of desire for him, desire that seemed to flow directly from the well of his fear of me. I wanted to scream: *existential crisis here—woman on the verge of imploding!* But, as in all good stories of confusion coupled with the act of betrayal, this intense feeling was followed by the still more intense feeling of a rope tightening round my throat and suffocating me, which could also have been a reflex to body odor, which in Alex's case was DKNY cologne for men.

Alex robotically removed his clothes, retaining the purple Calvin Klein underwear and alas, he was practically naked. "I'm all yours," he declared, "but before we proceed—let me serenade you!" And with that *let me,* Alex spread his feet shoulder distance apart, took a deep breath of air, and let out a sound. It took me a few seconds to realize that the instrumentals for *The Phantom of the Opera* were issuing from his stereo, and that Alex was singing, in a gorgeous countertenor, "The Phantom of the Opera is here inside your mind!" and marching thunderously in a quartet of steps to the titillations of his own voice. Only a Russian man could perform a Broadway tune and lightly tap (barefoot) without wincing, without, for an instance, worrying that he might appear gay if anything, his features strained as though he were performing massive masculine feats, such as lifting boulders or impersonating the Terminator. Still, I had to admit: like his face, so was his body proof of God's virtuosity and commitment to perfection—and not surprisingly, Alex also had a superb voice.

Who would have guessed that he had once dreamed of the stage like Bella? That in Russia he had taken ballet and tap lessons and envisioned himself the next Baryshnikov or Godunov with a jazzy edge, that there were piano, voice, and guitar lessons woven into his daily schedule of advanced math, physics, penmanship, and German by his ingenious mother? Were we all, these children of immigrants, doomed to nostalgia for our youths when we were tiny gods, doomed to perform only in the close quarters of our lovers while longing for packed houses of adoring audiences—for their enthralled eyes and exuberant applause to placate our perennial inferiority complexes? Wouldn't I want to be married to a man who could regale me with tunes from the *Sound of Music, Les Misérables, Cats*, and, most vitally, *Fiddler on the Roof*? How many times while lying in the arms of a boyfriend did I wish (albeit in my subconscious) that he would burst into "If I were a rich man, Yabadabadabada!"

Soon the instrumentals turned to "Think of Me" and Alex exclaimed, "Think of me—join me, join me, Lena, before I say goodbye." Although it felt preposterous and remarkably unsexual, I jumped off the bed (who was I to resist a chance to perform?) and, hitting my mezzo-soprano, thundered: "Think of me, think of me, Alex, when I say goodbye, remember me once in a while, la, la, la if you try la la . . ." My clothes miraculously dissolved in an act of jolly solidarity. I was in my brassiere and, farcically enough, as if I had planned the entire thing myself, purple polka-dotted underwear. Alex's hands were now busily attempting to rip through the complex architectural design of Victoria's Secret's Brassiere #5: God's gift to virgins.

A trickle of laughter spilled from the corners of my mouth, but I held the bulk of it in and summoned an austere, properly aroused expression for to my shock—Alex's penis had become erect!

But it wasn't until he produced a gold-tinted condom and waved it jubilantly in the air that the horror and absurdity of this moment came to me.

His fingers crawled over my breasts and then snuck ever so gingerly between my thighs—naturally, to prepare me for his grand entrance. And what did I do, ladies and gentlemen of the jury, what did I do, mothers and grandmothers of the high moral court: what did *I* do? I burst into cacophonous, plug-my-own-ears laughter. I was laughing so hard my stomach turned into a trampoline that might have given him a considerable flip if he stepped on it. Thank the Lord Almighty that my underwear was still covering my vagina, and though one nipple had shamelessly popped out of Brassiere #5, the other breast was fully cloaked. I pushed the nipple back in, and oddly enough, burst into an even more crippling laughter. *Oh, thou a silent mute with parted jaws and globular tears.* Secretly, I hoped this would disgust Alex or scare him, or at least stop him in the midst of what appeared to be a steel-willed determination to consummate the act. He was desperate for consummation, for a wrapping up, if you will, for confirmation that he could do this and that I wanted him. But it was too late. I wanted only friendship now, only a sympathetic ear, or just an actual ear canal into which I could holler: *I am in love!* I don't know why it took me so long to admit it outright, to Alex, to myself, or why I had to wait till Alex danced in the nude to *Phantom of the Opera*, till he was rubbing his gold member between my thighs, till the comedy of my predic-ament seemed to pry open my subconscious and spill its contents out like vomit triggered by overeating. So there I lay and there *they* lay: my feelings unfiltered through any notion of what should or should not be but simply bare, simply here, as they existed inside my mind, as they gurgled and fermented and *became* true despite myself. I was in love with Eddie—with Edward—with Ignatius Cyril Beltrafio. And it was not merely love caught in a moment, of the sort I felt in the aftermath of meeting Mrs. Beltrafio, which may have been gratitude for not taking her side, but the daily sort, the nagging sort, the stomach-churning sort, the smiling-blithe-ly-and-idiotically-into-empty-space sort.

"Did I do something wrong—is something the matter, Lenochka? Maybe this was a tad over the top, I admit it, but I—I wanted it to be spectacular. Are you not aroused?" He slumped down on the bed next to me and stopped the music with a slipper that seemed handily nearby. I was thankful for this little miracle.

"Oh, no, no, no, Sasha, this is wonderful and very stimulat-ing—you *are* spectacular—it's not that—I'm just a horrible, mis-erable, abominable person."

"You seem to find this very amusing—this depiction of your own character—or is it me—have I made an utter fool of myself? Tell me honestly."

"No, it's not you, Sashenka—it's me—it's all my fault. I've been—despicable—"

"Believe me, Elena, I've already forgiven you, whatever it is—"

"You're not making this easy for me, Alex. I don't know exactly how I arrived here—I was trying to please everyone, trying to do the right thing by everyone—by you especially! And I didn't want to hurt anyone—well, the long and the short of it is that I've been—"

"You've been naughty!" he returned with a sudden belligerent laugh.

"What—wait—what?"

"I've known for quite some time," he said, turning away from me, his laughter subsiding into startling gloom. "The worst of it, of course, is that it's Beltrafio—that's the worst of it."

"How long? How long have you known?"

"Oh, I started to suspect you a while back—I'm not Russian for nothing!" he cackled, his gaze menacing. "When you stopped actively pursuing sex with me, the notion that you were with someone else began to haunt me. But that it was Beltrafio—that I couldn't have borne on my own—"

"Oh God, oh God, that toad Eric told you—"

"You should never underestimate your enemies, Elena Kabelmacher—how un-Russian of you!"

"I thought my feelings would change, I wanted them to change."

"A few days ago Eric called me to say he won't be coming to our wedding—that it was morally repugnant to him. He said you're still with Eddie—is that true?"

"Eric is a vile, vile person—"

"Answer me—"

"I thought you and I were perfect for each other. I was planning to dump him, I was planning all the time, but then I—you see—I—"

"So dump him now!"

"How can you stand to be with me? How could you take it—all that time talking to me, sharing yourself with me, knowing, knowing that I was with him—how you must have hated me!"

"Oh, I've never hated you. I'm a realist, *moya dorogaya* Lenochka, or haven't you realized by now? I pride myself on being a postmodern man, on having serious insight into human nature, into the putrefaction of desire. I want you to dump him now. I don't care about the past. We'll get married as planned and never mention him again."

What a glorious option he was giving me—saving me from myself, forgiving me, giving me what I'd always wanted in life: a clean slate. Oh, if only I could clean Eddie out—if only there were a detox program for people like me: a special spa treatment, like a man-exfoliation mask or a turning-a-new-leaf bath or just simply a laser to dull my obsessive, cantankerous, lovelorn brain. But no such spa existed nor ever will. As the case remained, the idea of never seeing Ignatius again made me sick, quite literally. I endured actual symptoms: rapid breath-depriving inhalations otherwise known as "the no-more-fabulous-sex asthma attack," a bout of extreme stomach nervousness otherwise known as "abandoned lover's diarrhea," and even the old enigmatic rash otherwise known as "the incurable liar's hives."

"I wish that was possible, Sashenka, but unfortunately I've—I've fallen in love."

"You just think you're in love with Eddie because you've been copulating with him. Once we make love—don't you see—we must make love!"

"But you're too late—if only—if only then in November when I begged you . . ."

"Haven't you understood why I've been so reticent—what a fool you've been! I wanted to wait, not for all the stupid reasons I gave you, not because I was afraid for you—I was afraid *of* you."

"Of me—why—what do you mean?"

"I didn't want to disappoint you and I wanted it to be special, phenomenal! I wanted you to always remember our first time, to look back on it with fondness. I had such romantic ideas but more than that, I was worried that you were experienced and I—well, I not so much."

"You're a virgin?" I asked with horror.

"If you must put labels on things, yes, technically I am."

"Good God, Alex," I murmured, "I had no idea, I thought—oh, Sashenka, I'm so very sorry! But you should have told me right away."

"Mother always said: be cautious with women, women are very sensitive about sex—she just never prepared me for how sensitive I'd be."

"And to think how much you argued with me! If I had only known, I might have—I might have acted differently." I paused, choking on this possibility: I might have never looked or touched Eddie or entered La Cote Basque's bathroom had Alex had enough *sechel* to be upfront with me; it would have been morally implausible to abandon him then. I thought of destiny, of its imperceptible forks in the road, a slight tilt to the right instead of the left, and with our own free will, we alter our fate irreversibly. Eddie was my irreversible fork.

"Can't you just do it with me? Can't you do me that favor—you owe me at least that."

"I can't!"

"I'm better than him in every way. I'll be better in bed. I'll be a feminist for you—do you want me to pledge my devotion to feminism—is that what's holding you back?" Melancholy spread from his eyes into the rest of his face and swam there, under his skin, like a thousand muted gray fish. "I need you," he whispered. "I need you in my life."

"Are you listening to me? I'm in love with him; I'm so in love with him I don't know if I'll survive . . ."

"Do you seriously expect me to pity you? God! I just kept thinking, 'this is her last hoorah before marriage, her last man before me, before our forever vows.' I wanted to give you space, time. I thought you'd come to me with worldly understanding, with appreciation, you'd feel so lucky to have me—never, ever, in all my calculations did I ever assume you'd choose him over me."

"You assumed too much, Alex. Didn't you know anything about the draw sex has on a person?"

"What's sex when the rest of your life hangs in the balance? If you *try* to marry him—why, your grandmother will eat him for breakfast!" He struggled to maintain civility but his voice snapped. "Weren't you the one always thundering about what you went through in Russia—all your purported anti-Semitism? How could you *ever* conceive of yourself with this, this, this ignoramus?"

I grabbed my clothes and began to dress manically, laboring to get inside my jeans and shirt. Love didn't seem to matter; love was a pragmatic notion, maneuverable, forgettable, and reversible. He reminded me of the way I had once spoken of love to Eddie: *Love is a concept, dependent on our wills . . .* spoken before I knew love, before I had fallen.

"I know what he is," I murmured. Ah, but alas, the true blow was not in the telling but in the way a single memory, a single image of Eddie kissing my face goodbye at the airport, surfaced and thawed my face. When I opened my eyes I saw that Alex had become alarmingly white. He glared without seeming to see me, and his mouth, at first failing to emit sound, began hurtling words at an accelerating speed: "Whore! *Blyat!* Who does such a thing to a person? To a man? What kind of monster are you? *Chyort*, what are we going to tell our parents—what about the invitations? All the fucking invitations have been sent out already! I'll look like a degenerate. Do you realize what you've done to me—this will ruin my mother!"

"I'm so very sorry, Sashenka," I mumbled in fear, "you can tell her you left me—"

"Don't you dare call me 'Sashenka,' you've lost that right; second of all, I'm not a liar like you. Oh, how you snowballed my mother, oh, how she cooed about you—Lenochka this and Lenochka that, and she may be outspoken, but she's gorgeous and what an excellent person!" He waited for my response, but my mouth wouldn't open. "Do you know what that asshole did— he fired me, fired me for nothing, so that he could have you all to himself! When he finds out what a prevaricating *blyat* you are—an egomaniac like him—he'll dump you faster than I am going to walk out that door!" He pointed at his own door and briskly walked toward it, his beautiful bare chest still on display, and there he stood, wavering, as if there were one more score to settle, one extra tidbit of evidence to present: because he was a good person, after all, my Sashenka! "Fool—you're a fool! Don't you know how many women he's been with? Traded a good guy for a bad one, you foolish bitch!" And for lack of the other slipper, he hurled a blanket at his stereo, which accidentally clicked from *Phantom of the Opera* to *Eurythmics Greatest Hits:* "Sweet dreams are made of this . . . everyone wants to use you!" Alex twisted the doorknob with the heavy air of a man who's been stabbed and shot, and from across the threshold, cried, "I should have guessed that all your feminism was bullshit—you're just an ordinary whore!" Then, as if infused with new energy, as if he could already see flames engulfing me in hell, he raced down the staircase, cackling, his contorted visage igniting in me an irrepressible urge to strangle my own neck.

I crawled across the room to his desk on all fours like a CIA field operative and, surreptitiously removing the mammoth receiver from the dinosaur-era telephone, dialed my house. To my great relief, Bella picked up.

"Bella," I said, "I need you now! I'm at Alex's house."

"I smell a rat," she exclaimed happily, for she always wanted to smell rats as a long sufferer of housewifely ennui. "What's wrong?"

"We're done for—broken up!"

"You're just in time. Alla Bagdanovich and Mother just agreed—at long last—on pink orchids."

"Oh Lord," I mumbled.

"Relax, melodrama queen," she said. "I'll get you in ten minutes." By which, of course, she meant she'd drive the twenty miles at twice the speed limit, because Bella, with her spectacular face and blonde hair, never got tickets, not even from female police officers.

Bella arrived in seven minutes, exchanged a few civilized pleasantries with Alex, who was concentrating intently on the TV, and safely ushered me into the driveway without his supposed notice.

"Confess," Bella demanded once she locked the car doors and turned the air conditioning on full blast. "Confess all your sins to your older and wiser sister."

"Sins, what can be my sins?"

"That you have a lover in New York you're mad about and that's why you won't marry Alex." She flashed me a wide, insinuating smile.

"How—how did you—"

"Oh, I didn't; I was just fantasizing!" She laughed freely and unreservedly, holding her stomach, stuttering, "Oh, Grandma, Grandma will be in—ha, ha, haaaaaaaaaa—in—purgatory, and our poor, poor, poor mother, hah, hah, hee, hee, will be blamed for everything."

"I'm a terrible person, Bellochka," I whimpered, collapsing my head on the dashboard.

She started the engine and drove out of Alex's driveway with a violent screech. On the highway we passed every car in our path with style, swerving masterfully around them, and rolled down our windows to feel the hot July wind in our faces.

Then looking at me from the corner of her eye, she said, "We're all terrible people, but at least you're taking your life into your hands and saying the fuck with everyone else."

"Am I—then why did I get engaged in the first place?"

"Cuz we're all alike, all trying to do the right thing for the wrong reasons, or the wrong thing for the right reasons, who knows? Because Grandma buzzes in our brains like a well-meaning bee—"

"Don't blame her—it's my fault—ours. She can't change her ways, we've always known that."

"Yeah," Bella sighed, "sometimes I think I'm a lot like her. I hate men as much as she does."

"What do you mean?"

"I laugh at them in my head. I look at them, fawning over me, making fools of themselves, but do any of them know what goes through my head—do they have any concept of how smart I am. And this lack of realization on their part—their blindness, their stupid senseless dick-driven desire—makes me want to trample them under my feet."

"No wonder Igor has been looking like a flat pancake lately," I said, laughing.

"Oh, him, he's not great enough to be spoken of in such a tragic manner. You see how marriage ruins beauty; remember how he gawked at me when we dated, slobbering over me, 'oh you're so beautiful, Bellochka, can't believe you're so beautiful, I'm so lucky!' And now five years later—does he even see my beauty anymore?

"I don't care, Lena, you hear me—I don't care if he *never* looks at me. The point is that marriage dulls the senses and your beauty means squat—your beauty that had once meant so much to you when you were young is suddenly obsolete, like an old fancy towel you've used so many times it's turned into a rag."

"So why not have an affair?" I asked.

"Because affairs are overrated—banal, commonplace, and most of all boring. Am I so foolish as to think I won't run into the same problems with a lover as I do with my husband? Sure, they court you when you're a mistress and sure, it's exciting, the way jumping out of a moving airplane is exciting, but it wears off—everything wears off—everything but the stage."

"Do you think I've betrayed them? Do you think they'll think I've betrayed them?"

"Two different questions! Am I supposed to answer that for you, *I*, who picked so abysmally for myself?" she exclaimed, impaling me with her eyes. "Only one thing I've learned—you can't let what people say and think affect you. If he understands half of you, then you've already found something rare."

"But I've been lying to him—sleeping with him while still engaged to Alex—"

"Details! Look on the bright side—at least you haven't been sleeping with the two of them at the same time! That should count for something!" She burst into a generous, soothing laugh and infected me with it. All at once our eyes were watering and our stomachs contracting, our cheeks stretching as we laughed silently and then again with gusto, as if everything in the world had become hilarious: the windshield, the dashboard, the street, Alex, Mom, Grandma, my predicament, and Bella's sad, sad life. And as I laughed harder and harder, keeling over, wanting miserably to cry, I thought about Bella, about a young life that seemed to have spanned centuries and taught one so little.

Pushkin, Arrogance, and Beauty

Pushkin, arrogance, and beauty conspired to alter Bella's fate at the irascible age of fifteen. She had long fantasized about aristocratic men so struck by her looks that they would leap into Tsveytaeva's illicit verses. She felt she should have been born in culturally superior Leningrad and believed, like all good-looking children, that the world was a land of well-meaning fairy godmothers and princes who would adore her, pamper her, and relieve her of the suffering others must endure. In the year we were to receive our permission slip, Bella had been courted by just such a prince: an older man whose age was somewhat of a question mark, who may or may not have had a wife, who may or may not have been a KGB operative, and whose name may or may not have been Nicholai. He lacked the features of a prince (in fact, put together, his features invoked the likeness of a goat), but being tall and surprisingly well-built for a Russian man, as they neither worked out nor refrained from vodka and fried *salo* (fried bacon fat eaten with the same regularity and enthusiasm as fried potatoes), and conversant not only in nineteenth-century Russian literature, but in sexually subversive foreign texts as well, such as *The Interpretation of Dreams, Lady Chatterley's Lover*, and *Lolita*, one could safely say that he possessed princely endowments.

Bella met him at my parents' "going-away" party for the Avenbuchs. Although no one could remember inviting him, he insisted that he had met my father during Gregori Margulis's lecture on lattices in Lie groups, and thus obtained an invitation. This explanation was so laughable that it was instantly seen as a veiled threat.

Bella and I twirled to ABBA and Boney M., shook our knees to Elvis, closed our eyes provocatively like the adults to the Doors, but when her beloved Louis Armstrong burst into "I Say Tomato, You Say Tomato" Bella fully unraveled, becoming in her wild frenzy the dance floor's sole proprietor. Other women stepped aside to grant her dominance, and the unsuspecting men mistook her childish antics for the demands of a grown woman. They came at her, these roosters with their feathers all riled, wanting to lead, to teach, to subdue her movements under their will.

Only Nicholai made no attempt to impinge on her dancing. He was of the verbal seduction variety. Spreading his arm leisurely across the sofa, he recited an entire stanza from Marshak's translation of *Taming of the Shrew*, as if at once to laud her looks and criticize her behavior (a popular Russian male strategy for winning women's hearts). And our Bella, who imagined herself the heroine of every novel, poem, and play, dissolved. Or fell in love. Or fell into that stage of adolescence I like to call premature deflowerment. For they had done it the very night they met on the staircase of our building, her back pressed against cold brick, and although it felt "horrible," Bella believed she was bound to him, that "something beautiful" happened—beautiful, that is, between their souls.

Normally, after such an act the man would never call or pursue the woman—her *submission* to him would be deemed a grave act, proof that she was a *blyat*. But Nicholai embarked upon a serious courtship; he brought dazzling roses and tickets to the Bolshoi for my mother, hard liquor and Italian sausages for my father, oversized jars of Beluga and pillars of *vobla* (a salty dried fish that could only be considered a delicacy in Russia) for my grandmother. He invited himself over to dinner. He was too moneyed, too well-groomed, too finely dressed to be your typical Russian man. Only the KGB, my mother told Bella, have imported leather coats and fragrant perfumes on their chins. But Bella refused to listen. Nicholai had proposed that she remain with him in the Soviet Union, for by then he had learned of our plans. As my grandmother would say years later in America, the job of getting the whole family out intact was not for the weak, and so she, the Hercules of the Jewish people, had to apply all her muscles to transport my sister's lovelorn head.

Bella wept, denounced the family, and threatened to commit suicide. With tragic aplomb, she ended it a month before our secret day. By the time June 2, the day of our departure, rolled around Bella had turned into a shadow of her old dancing self: a depressed little girl deprived of her prettiest doll. Despite her supposed sexual awakening, Bella seemed sedated, drained of her vibrant sensuality and budding confidence.

My grandmother blamed my parents for Bella's incurable state; after all, for three years before we left Russia, my parents were divorcing one another. The word—*razvod*—flew like a sword in the air, none of us knowing where it would land. Even after they severed ties with their lovers, even after we boarded the plane heading west, my parents were still divorcing one another in Austria and Italy.

In Vienna we were greeted by handsome Israeli officers and brought to a gated mansion, which had been a sanitarium in its finer days. There had been terrorist attacks on Russian Jews in the city, and a new security policy stipulated that we needed to be "contained" for the duration of our stay, which in real terms meant being locked in a mental health facility. We were stuffed, ten families per room with bunk beds, and guarded by large Austrian women in white robes who used to guard the mentally ill. Sometimes a husband or wife slept beneath or above someone else's husband or wife and the rules of privacy were ignored. In the dark, when the lights were shut off, you could see the silhouette of a woman's slip and her jiggling breasts, a man's white underwear and his black socks reaching for his calves. Bella and I lay awake at night, huddling next to each other on a narrow bed, listening to husbands and wives fight, to infants weep, to the groans of the old, holding pain inside their mouths, to my parents quarrel about the rest of our lives.

Vienna turned out to be a strategic stopover; we were allotted five days to decide whether to go to Italy, en route to America, or to take a flight directly to Israel instead. Moved by the beauty of the Israeli men, whose glistening brown skin, lean long bodies, and dazzling blue eyes burned holes in the anti-Semitic images Russia imprinted upon our minds, whose mastery of the Russian language seemed in perfect harmony with their divine faces and the paradise they painted of life in Jerusalem, we women became ardent Zionists, with my mother leading the pack. "We should go to Israel," she urged my father, "it is the only sure way to escape anti-Semitism—to truly embrace who we are." "Yes, yes," Bella echoed (the men's flirtatious gazes became her therapy), "it's the only way I'll ever be able to love again." But my father was livid: "First you tortured me with America—now Israel!" he told my mother. "I didn't leave my mother, my job, my friends, my life so that I could live in a Jewish desert—it may be Jewish but it's still a desert with Arabs and constant war!" When my mother continued her protests, my father abandoned the language of reason and resorted to his favorite phrase: "Over my DEAD BODY!" My mother did eventually surrender. "No one wants your dead body, after all," she told him on the fifth day.

It was during our two-month sojourn in Italy, waiting for our visas to enter the United States, waiting for my parents to end their war, that Bella's sexuality surfaced again—or, as my mother liked to put it, "erupted."

Italy was a hot sumptuous interlude, a simulacrum of a vacation from the Soviet regime, with no home to return to, only the consciousness of flight. The rest of our lives hung in the air like magnificent optical illusions. We could have applied for visas to enter any Western country—England, Canada, Australia, France, or we could have remained in Italy if the Italians would take us. But after much hypothesizing and poking in the dark, we followed the original plan that first stole our hearts upon reading Yakov's letter—America! Only America took in Russian Jews without any pre-conditions, without demands for higher education, without questions about our age or skills. Our visas to the United States were practically guaranteed, for our status—as political refugees—elevated us into Cold War's highly charged political realm. We were human proof of Soviet oppression, the unsuspecting players in America's strategic battles with the Communist regime. Still, there was a wait. And for a people who came from a world where a contract, a document, a newspaper, and the words "truth," "promise," and "fact" had long ago lost their meanings, "waiting" became a euphemism for uncertainty, a joke God played on His most audacious dreamers.

Italy whispered of forgetting, of starting anew, of abundance, of untapped possibilities, but we couldn't embrace even these quiet hopes; we had no money, no language, and no knowledge of where we would one day end up. Our nerves, strung like poorly tuned violins and snapping from the slightest irritation, prevented us from delighting in the grand vistas of nature and the ancient ruins of the Roman Empire. We sleepwalked through the crumbling Coliseum, the majestic Pantheon, marveled absently at the antiquity and beauty of the Roman Forum. We roamed its luscious, emerald terrain like phantom beings, invisible to the loud, colorful Italians streaming past us, invisible even to each other.

Our first destination was a dingy hotel in Rome, a red-carpeted remnant of antiquity that stank of mildew, piss, and rose water, and creaked under our feet. We were given one room for a family of five, but the exquisitely carved wooden chests and wardrobes dating back two centuries tantalized us with fantasies of Western grandeur. The bathroom was the centerpiece, an open space with a resplendent boudoir and only a velvet red curtain to offer a semblance of privacy. The hotel was paid for by Jewish organizations in America, who provided us with a minuscule allowance for which we were deeply grateful but which did not prevent us from starving. Having sold our belongings in Russia to pay off the KGB, we were then allowed to take a thousand American dollars per person and survive on it for an unpredictable period of time.

My mother wanted to spend the money on travel like the other Russians were doing; she had dreamed of Venice since her romantic adolescence, imagining herself in cafes by the water, or enfolded in the arms of some handsome Italian in the Gondolas. But my father painted a grim picture of our future in America: "You shall rot in poverty! You won't have anything to eat or a place to live in your American paradise! Capitalism," he held sternly, "requires money." We knew plenty of unfortunates stuck in Italy for months, their money trickling away into the abyss of Western seduction, of bureaucrats in America and Italy mixing up documents, of relatives in Los Angeles and New York forgetting to sign some obscure page and thus prolonging the wait. My father cleverly played on my mother's fears until he scared her into complete submission. Not only did she excise all romantic getaways from her mind but she denied herself, as did my father and grandmother, the delicacies of Italy: aromatic strawberry ice cream, a divine dish called "pizza," and, of course, our long-awaited Western prize: "Coca-Cola."

Every morning in Rome we drank coffee and ate delectable free rolls with butter. My parents ordered nothing else, and with shame blazoning on their faces, they surreptitiously stuffed purses and bags with extra rolls, knowing they would last us all day. We did not even have water on our trip to the Vatican. As we stared in hundred-degree weather at dead popes resting in tombs behind glass walls, we politely refrained from fainting; after all, if we could survive Russia, then we could certainly withstand a little Italian dehydration.

Through the immigrant grapevine, we heard that the secret to happiness in Italy was selling. Bring your dresses and shawls, fancy linen and towels, and your lingerie if you have nothing else because that's where the real money hid—selling Russian goods to the Italians. So on a wide expanse of grass near a major avenue, parents and children and grandparents were selling their clothes, linen, *matryoshkas*, handkerchiefs, shawls, and cashmere. *"Quanto Costa? Quanto Costa?"* the Italians would scream at us. But my parents were poor salesmen. They spoke in judgmental tones of the indelicacies of selling, of pushing and deluding customers, of the impolite nature of asking for more money than what it originally cost them, and blushed at their broken Italian.

"But I've worn that shawl," my mother would whisper, "it's Great-grandmother's—I wore it to the Bolshoi, how can I sell it? It's dishonest." "I can't sell this fountain pen," my father would say, "it's my only memento from college—it's priceless." Every morning they laid out my great-grandmother's silk black shawls painted in scarlet and pink roses, white embroidered linen, sterling silver spoons and forks, and simple gold earrings the KGB security apparently felt were worthless, and every evening they returned with all the items still jiggling in their suitcase. Nor were my parents alone in their embarrassment, for our fellow countrymen were engineers, linguists, physicists, dentists, pianists, computers scientists, chemists, violinists, writers, teachers, and doctors, who scoffed at haggling and begging, terrified that this might be a first glimpse of their future in America.

The only person who wasn't humiliated by the process was Bella. She spoke in voluble tones of the necessity of survival and urged my parents to abandon their "girlish shyness," "their communist views of the world," "their persnickety habits," and embrace capitalism with spiritedness and dignity, and feel, *feel* that acute sensation of being free! Grandmother championed Bella's cause in private, but in public she only yelled at the poor Italians to stop groping her mother's priceless linen; "*Von, von poshli ot syuda* ," she'd yell from behind the table as though she were dispersing a pack of wild cats. Only Bella, clad in white shorts and tight purple tank tops, lounging lazily behind the table with her long sturdy legs and full bosom on display, understood the art of selling. "*Ciao, come stai*," she would say to Italian men, and the men would reply, "*Bella, bella donna!*" She would spread her flaxen mane on her bare shoulders and grin and nod without knowing what she was nodding to, and the men would write out phone numbers, attempt to embrace her, or propose marriage on the spot in Italian, while Bella would push an embroidered pillow in their faces and murmur "*Grazie, grazie*" as if the men had already purchased it. While my mother trembled at her daughter's feats, the men flocked to our table like seagulls to fresh fish. By the end of those two months in Italy we had sold enough of our belongings to eat pizza and ice cream and drink Coca-Cola twice a week. I believed in those years that Bella could alter the state of the universe.

She had a miniature waist, womanly hips, a voluptuous bosom, and gorgeous healthy legs, Russian style: thick thighs, round knees, and tiny ankles. Not too tall, not too plump, and not too skinny, she was woman *perfecto*. Her features, although small and distinct, came together in almost superhuman symmetry so that she appeared at first glance, as she did on a prolonged one, to have a flawless face. Unlike my mother, whose strong voice and penetrating gaze made one feel that her features were merely the tools she used to express herself, Bella's power was inextricably tied to her appearance. Her serene blue eyes floated beneath crescent lids, harking to the beauties of the Renaissance, and a perky nose reminded one of farm girls in the Russian countryside. Her beauty was strangely at odds with her rough-edged, rambunctious personality that thrashed like a prisoner inside a demure innocent face.

During our fifth day in Rome, a certain Veronica Rabinsky (aka Rabinovich) set her sights on our Bella. After spying on her for several days, she barged in on my parents in the midst of a tumultuous debate: Russian Jews were being transferred to two coastal towns to wait for their entry visas to the US.

"Ostya is cheaper, I heard from the Bershovskys," my father was saying.

"But the Ladispoli apartments have better access to the beach," my mother held.

"No, no, you mustn't even consider Ostya—everyone from the provinces is going there!" Veronica announced from behind my father's back. "All the Moscovites are going to Ladispoli, end of story." My mother broke into a glowing smile and instantly offered Veronica a seat next to her.

Veronica moved like a samovar on legs, wide-armed and confident, zealously determined to control life's chaotic trajectories. Naturally, the first victims of such zeal are one's family members; her husband and her only child, Igor, were jammed deeply under her thumb.

"I hear all the Moscovites are off to Florence," she said, vigorously exploiting our common bond, and failing to mention that she herself was originally from Mogilev Podolsk, a small town in Ukraine.

"I terribly want to go," my mother murmured and threw a menacing glance at my father.

"Well, we decided to play it safe." Veronica softened her voice, picking up on my parents' strife. "My husband"—she pointed at a skinny gray looking man sitting next to an even skinnier boy three tables away from us—"says Florence can wait."

"Now that's a smart man!" my father thundered.

With that, the Rabinskys transferred themselves to our yard sale table permanently. Two weeks after our sojourn in Rome, all the Russian Jews were transferred to seaside towns to await their entry visas into the United States.

We ended up in Ladispoli together with the Rabinskys, our apartment two floors above theirs. Veronica's pimply son, Igor, was a miniature version of his mother, only without the vitality or the charm. At eighteen, he was a surly, negative character who never spoke unless there was cause to criticize: the Italians were loud and mannerless; the people from Kiev and especially Odessa chafed at his perfect Russian; and the conditions in the apartment were below his expectations of the coveted "West." Only Bella had the ability to brighten his complexion and raise his eyebrows into a semi-circle above his glum eyes. Besides the defect of his skin (which made his father and mother lovingly refer to him as "our leper son"), Igor had excellent features—a straight thin nose, rich brown eyes, coarse copper hair, and gaunt cheekbones. He smacked of the emaciated Jesus and the depressed Raskolnikov. During our communal excursions to the black-sanded beaches of Ladispoli, Igor trailed after Bella like a tail she couldn't quite cut off her ass. He neither addressed her nor looked at her, but zeroed in on her breasts, which offered him solace. He would stand in perfect stillness, his feet sinking into the burning sand, his hands clamped against skinny hips, a white dry film caking on his lower lip. And she would laugh and run into the water, her breasts bopping up and down, falling out of the tiny red scraps designed to hide them. "What do you think of him," I asked once when we were alone. "Who?" "You know who, pimply Igor, I mean, would you like him if he wasn't pimply?" "He's a bore, a depressing, long-winded bore," she cried out. "You miss Nicholai?" "Don't speak of my Nicholai in the same breath as Igor!" "Nicholai was an even bigger bore," I told her, recalling his silly recitations from *Romeo and Juliet*. "You little twerp, what do you know of love, of its sublime pain!" "Nicholai raped you—is that the pain you mean? He raped you that first time, Bella, why do you pretend he was so wonderful?" I yelled but it was wasted breath—Bella would never speak of it, never admit to having been abused; such weakness of spirit was not to be tolerated in our home. She looked at me defiantly and said, "Besides, I have my eye set on a fancy American." "You don't know any fancy Americans," I pointed out. "Oh, yes, I do—I just saw him on TV. His name is Tom Brokaw!"

It just so happened that we received our visas to America earlier than the Rabinskys, and despite "tearful" goodbyes and promises to reconnect in the States, I never thought we'd see Igor and his parents again. But two years later, the Rabinskys showed up at our one-bedroom apartment on Morris Lane to have tea and never left. Had my mother known that Veronica Rabinsky had planned in 1982 to marry off her pimply son to our Goddess Bella, she would have banished Veronica from our yard table back in Rome. But no one fathomed, not even my grandmother, that a woman could have that much foresight. No one imagined that Veronica's incessant praise of my grandmother's cooking and my mother's excellent looks and my father's brain were stepping stones to a successful merger—a plot devised, after all, by a provincial brain.

Besides, given Bella's quick Americanization, we assumed she would end up with an American. High school brought Bella euphoric popularity and an infinite array of suitors. Bella dated the crème de la crème of high school: the muscle-sprouting, beer-guzzling, God-fearing, sexually advanced football players. She paraded them in our home like daggers to stick in Grandmother's gut. With her smug smile and manicured fingers pressed under her chin, she welcomed our grandmother's roar: "Sex—I hope you are not having any sex!" But it fell on deaf ears. Not only was Bella technically doing "it" (she did not fear Grandmother's wrath, venereal diseases, or getting pregnant—she only feared needy men), she was enjoying it, and threatening Grandmother with a life dedicated to casual screwing, drinking, and the stage.

For Bella dreamed of becoming an actress. She would jump on my bed in her underwear and bra, cradling an invisible microphone and mouth everything Madonna, and I would brim with pride, imagining her face splattered all over *US Weekly, People Magazine,* and the *Enquirer.* She rebelled, not like other children of Russian immigrants rebelled, by smoking pot on the sly and still becoming computer scientists, or by crashing their parents' cars into the neighbor's fence after a drunken party and still ending up in dental school, but by doing the unthinkable: leaving.

What ensued during the year that Bella turned twenty-two would forever be dubbed in the family as Bella's *mishugas.* Bella received her BA from Northwestern University with a respectable major in economics and a minor in drama. Igor was still buzzing like an irritating fly in her hair whom she swatted repeatedly but couldn't quite kill. He endured her serial dating and indifference to his longing glances with the stoicism of a monk. He accepted, after his fourth proposal of marriage, the state of "friendship" she offered as a final peace offering, and endured as a loyal "friend" her tales of exploits. After a bevy of interviews, Bella had several offers from major Chicago consulting firms. All of her friends from college coveted these jobs, and Bella beamed at her unexpected success. She didn't even seem to mind that Veronica Rabinsky, her husband, Kiril, and Igor came to our house to celebrate her success, or that following dinner, in the close quarters of our library, Igor prostrated himself once more with a fifth marriage proposal. Marriage, as he put it this time, would be a binding of mutual admiration between them, if not love, a statement suggested to him by his clever mother who believed that the gates of womanhood could only be broken down by dogged persistence.

That night after everyone retired to their private quarters to knock on wood in the jittery anticipation of a wedding, my sister sneaked into my room dressed in travel gear and rolling suitcase. "Don't panic," she preempted. "I'm going to New York. There's a one a.m. flight. A girl I know from Northwestern said I could stay with her." "New York," I cried, "it's midnight—have you lost your mind?" "Keep your mouth shut!" "But why—you can have all these prestigious jobs—what are you doing?" I was seventeen, dreaming of college, dreaming of emulating my sister's GPA. "I've turned them down, every one of them—including Igor. Fuck it— fuck it all," she said, "I'm going to be an actress—on Broadway! I've already signed up for classes at the New School." "New School? I've never heard of it." "You haven't heard of a lot of things," she chided. "Oh, Bellochka, you can turn Igor down but you don't have to run away to New York—there are classes here. This just seems so radical, so final, as if I'll never see you again," I muttered in fear, "Grandma will have a fit—" "Look, if I don't do this now, I'll never get out. I'll be stuck here like every other child of Russian immigrants, making money, bearing children, buying big houses, and hating my life—" "How do you know they all hate their lives?" "They may not, but I will," she said. "Say goodbye to them for me." She kissed both my cheeks and her figure receded into the black void of our palatial hallway.

I presented the note to the family at breakfast the next morning: "Dear Loved Ones, I've decided to try my luck at acting in New York. Will call from there! Kisses, Bella." It unleashed such a foul-mouthed tirade from Grandmother, a person who had denounced profanities as the terrain of the basest simpletons and goys, that I thought a provincial demon had entered her body. My father proposed to call his contacts at Friendly Airlines (whose stock was part of his portfolio) and manually retrieve her. Grandmother, never being one to half-ass an operation, demanded that we contact the FBI. Only my mother remained calm and, if I wasn't entirely hallucinatory, quietly elated for her daughter. "What do you want us to tell the FBI," she said, trying to reason with Grandmother, "that your granddaughter needed to flee to another state to be free of you?" But Grandmother didn't see the logic in this. "Freedom! Freedom!" she yelled. "What an imbecilic, idiotic, godforsaken, *meshugganah* word!"

A year later Bella returned from New York, silent and dour, with a new cropped hairdo, maroon lipstick, and a black ripped T-shirt in the style of eighties punk. She did not speak about what happened, and whenever Grandmother would question her, Bella would say, "Nothing happened, I just didn't get lucky." All Bella told us was that she shared an apartment with a girl from Northwestern, a graduate student of English Literature who loved theater as much as Bella. But she never described her auditions or talked about her job as a hostess in some fancy restaurant. We knew she barely made any money because my father incessantly complained about having to funnel money into her bank account. Although he threatened to cut her off if she didn't come home, we knew that Bella could have stayed on—she always read our father correctly—but when her lease ran out she packed her bags and left New York on the first available flight. She showed up at midnight on our doorstep, her face drawn and fatigued.

Igor showed up a week later with a dozen red carnations, cheap and already rotting, but they had a strange effect on our Bella; she wept, welcomed him with open arms, and upon his sixth proposal of marriage, she agreed.

After they were firmly engaged, Igor began to openly reminisce about his walks in birch forests, his parents' dacha on the outskirts of Moscow, "real" kefir, nitrate-free hard salami, and non-alcoholic beer, known as *kvac*. Igor turned out to be a repressed Russophile, who spoke of Russian literature as though each text was a woman he once loved, and vowed to make their future children read Tolstoy by age six. I blamed my mother and grandmother for Igor. For them, his irksome qualities were outweighed by a heavily touted resume. He ended up at MIT almost as soon as he arrived in America, placing not only out of all high school math and science requirements, but the first two years of college math and science as well. Although he struggled with English, he managed to graduate with a 3.8 GPA and entered a

PhD program at Northwestern University to study artificial intelligence. During the summers he tackled the English language with something bordering on fanaticism, and after four years in America, he spoke in perfect grammatical structures with a grating accent that was neither Russian nor British, but his own brand of universal snobbism. Every time Veronica waltzed through our front door, she recited his achievements to my grandmother as though she were depositing a magic potion into Grandmother's hypothalamus, which kept her in a state of inane ecstasy for hours.

After Bella's interlude in New York, Grandmother became convinced that Igor was the rock that could tether Bella to the ground and keep her from falling down the bottomless pit of "the American Dream." "I know he's an insufferable *mudila*," Grandmother would say when I brought evidence against him, "but he'll make your sister happy! He'll be a good husband. He'll keep her head straight and keep her away from all those artsy ruffians without a future." These invisible artsy ruffians were the men that Bella must have slept with, the New York men she must have met at bars and acting classes and auditions, the men who never stepped through our door, but we knew they existed, as certainly as we knew that the year Bella spent away from us existed. "Why don't you give Igor another chance?" Grandmother would nudge me. "He's brilliant, and he's not bad looking."

Igor was in fact not good looking. His face, after years of pimple therapy, was still pimply and gray, concealed from the world by oily reddish hair. His features had lost their youthful delicacy and proportion, perhaps from battling Bella for so long, and he had grown, we all had to admit, uglier over the years. He was always seized by some interesting idea about society or computers that was too sophisticated to be understood by the ignoramuses around him.

But when in Bella's presence, Igor's large brown eyes seemed to glisten from a secret fount of happiness. He diligently asked her about her feelings, goals, dreams. And Bella told him that she longed for the stage—an actress, a singer, a dancer—anything that would make her feel that her beauty and talents were not being wasted in life, that there was a reason behind her flawless nose and sapphire eyes and a gold mane so naturally shiny that Russian beauticians wanted to use her in their salon ads. She lamented her degree in economics, her "stupid" year in New York, and she shared Igor's love for Russian literature, although she read most of it in English. Igor listened to Bella with such concerted admiration that she mistook it for love. "No one could love me the way he loves me," she confided in me. "But where's the lust, the desire?" I asked. "All you care about are looks—I've looked into his soul, and there's beauty within," she insisted. "Empty words," I shot back, "you're not in love with him." "I don't think I fall in love as easily as you," she told me.

To this day, I keep returning to that very moment, replaying it over and over in my head. And in each reenactment, I remind her what Igor said when she confessed her longing for the Broadway stage: "You'll grow out of it." In each reenactment, I say decisively: Igor is a viper, uglier within than he is on the surface, he'll eat your flesh and once he gains entry, he'll devour your soul. He'll lock you in his immaculate prison of intellectual puff and moral righteousness, in his intellectualisms and realisms and chauvinisms, stinking, all of them, of hypocrisy and vapidity, and then he'll swallow the key. He will carefully plot out the passages through which you'll inevitably walk but the doors will close, one by one, extinguishing your last flicker of hope, your plan B escape route. I scream at her: Imagine your life five, ten, fifteen years into the future. Run while you still have legs, run while you still have a will. But in each reenactment I fail to speak, or if I speak, I fail to move her. And I see that Bella's future was strangely sealed.

Now, as we drove up to my parents' mansion, I said, "I'm going back to New York."

"To your forbidden lover?" She spoke with joy, her small mouth breaking into a warm glowing smile, her beauty spilling all around me.

"Yes, to Eddie," I said, speaking his name out loud for the first time.

"Wait until tomorrow, tell them you're leaving. You need to tell them you broke up with Alex."

"No. You tell them. It's my turn to run. I don't want to talk to them anymore. I just want to pack and leave."

No one was at home. I called Eddie and said, "I'm coming back, I'm coming back to you. Now. Today. I want to go with you to your secret cottage in the wild woods of Maine."

Within minutes, he purchased a ticket for me to New York on that same day, and Bella drove me to the airport. As the car approached the terminal, screeching against the onslaught of traffic, we turned to one another, Bella and I, looking in silence until tears rolled out of our eyes.

"Never be afraid, never give up, *derzhis*!" She said what we said to each other as children, children going into battle, children hiding, children learning to survive.

Escape from New York

The city receded slowly behind us as we crawled along the George Washington Bridge. Cars grunted and grazed each other's backsides. I rolled down a window and breathed in the diesel fuel with mysterious pleasure. I was smiling. My face burned from the glare of the hot August sun. He sped, passing every car, his eyes taking on a lion's ferocity, his hands barely on the wheel. "I want you right now!" I said, as an empty highway unfurled before us.

I grabbed his thigh, his erection already swelling between his legs, and the sudden thrill of wanting and being able to have silenced me. *You are here for me, for me, for the taking. And I, at last, am here for you.*

Eight hours later we entered Acadia and the road narrowed, taking us into dark, uninhibited nature. Black mountains soared at our sides, pockmarked with yellow, orange, and red stones as if to signal the dawn of fall, and wild flowers peeked out of uneven grasslands in sweeping fuchsias, lavenders, and whites, bowing intermittently to make room for giant pines and evergreens. Brown earth unfurled at the feet of majestic orange-leafed oaks and naked birches swayed like emaciated ballerinas attempting flight. How did I get here, I wondered with a mingling of rapture and trepidation, how did I manage to grab this piece of happiness for myself—to do that which seemed impossible one year ago, one month, one week ago?

The car finally came to a halt, but there was nothing in front of us except more trees and road.

"We need to stop here because the road is too muddy up ahead," he said.

"I love it here."

"I knew you would—*you* belong in wild nature."

"I'm practically Thoreau," I chuckled.

"When I read him in college, I thought—that's it, that's what I need—nature." He broke into a bitter laugh. "That's why I majored in econ and moved to the city."

He led me through the groves into a gold-speckled meadow. Overlooking a bay, nestled among evergreens, stood his cabin. Daisies and goldenrod swayed among the weeds, and a narrow dirt road led to the mouth of the ocean. Waves crashed against mud-colored sand and ringlets of foam scattered across it like blackened snowflakes. I imbibed the air and my childhood appeared, my lips parted to drink it, taste it, this brisk, clear, unpolluted air, air squeezed from the boughs of pines. I saw a tiny scrap of a girl, a blurred face and body; only my eyes retained the same lime-hued clarity and joy. The outside world emerged as those eyes had caught it: running up the rickety steps of our dacha, bringing stalks of corn for Grandmother to boil, huge sunflowers rising over our heads and our tongues maneuvering seeds out of cracked black shells, and laughter—mine and other children's intermingling in the vines of memory with something vile, unthinkable. I grabbed a handful of brown earth with my fingers as though I were reaching for my past, and smelled my childhood through my nose. I turned to him to say, "My childhood," when he turned to me and said, "My childhood—it reminds me of my childhood." His eyes glinted and his mouth was parched from the long drive. Yet there was something inconsolable in his face, framing it in the softness of a twelve-year-old boy's.

"I bought this place a few years back because it reminded me of my childhood on Martha's Vineyard. My parents used to own a beach house before they lost their money and my brother and I would run wild in the dunes." He pulled me toward the door, but I resisted. The memory from my childhood returned me to *them* at once, and I could hear Bella's voice ring like an echo inside the trunks of ancient trees: "You must tell Mom and Grandma; you must tell them you're serious about this lover." My breaths grew quicker, shallower, evicting the sweet aroma of pines and salt water and warm wind, leaving me only one mordant thought: none of my other betrayals—betraying Alex, betraying Eddie, betraying myself—could compare in scope to my betrayal of *them*.

"C'mon, let's go in! It's getting cold out here," he said, jumping up the porch stairs and opening the front door. The inside of the cabin was made entirely from wood, wide auburn planks stretching from the floor into the walls and crisscrossing the ceiling. The hue filled me with serenity and warmth, transporting me mentally into an oversized sauna. A compact, dark living room gave way to a smaller dining enclosure where three wall-to-ceiling windows brought in the evening light. I felt myself sinking into him—into a world I barely knew.

A steep staircase led down into a marvelous high-ceilinged basement he had transformed into a library; books lived everywhere—on coffee tables, peering out of corners, stacked in piles on the floor, crowding shelves built into walls. The pristine books, untouched by human hand save to purchase them, were those dealing with history, biography, presidential memoirs, trendy business texts, and sundry modern novels I had never heard of. But on the opposite wall, a walnut bookshelf with finely wrought engravings protruded into the center of the room. There Euripides, Herodotus, Plato, Marx, Kant, Mill, Weber, Smith, Descartes, Nietzsche, Jane Austen, Balzac, Stendhal, Henry James, Tolstoy, Dostoyevsky greeted me like old friends, and like old friends, they had been thumbed, underlined, ruffled and bent out of shape. The lower three shelves were devoted to photography and art, fancy hardcover books that too looked stricken and aged from overuse.

Every remaining inch of wall space was covered in paintings. I recognized some abstract artists from trendy galleries and along one wall hung the *Abyss* by Michael Cobb, the one that in my mind brought us together. It seemed peculiar that the walls and bookshelves in his city apartment were glaringly bare, except for a few business texts he never opened. I imagined that there were two of him, and the half that lived in the cottage perfectly coalesced with my soul.

One corner of the library was devoted exclusively to his photographs. They were arranged in a chronological order to showcase his development from childhood until the college years, which was the last time he luxuriated in "the idle exercise of snapping pictures." The earlier work displayed a view of Manhattan from a yacht, and the one adjacent to it was a study of a cluster of rocks in Cape Cod. But huddled together, protected from the rest of the room by a mammoth walnut credenza, was an array of black-and-white photographs, his last work. There were naked backs, two thighs stuck together, hands shrouding breasts, a profile flaring against a black void, and detailed palpitating lips that exhaled desire. But you couldn't see their faces, their eyes; you only felt the chill of abstractness—the women's anonymity.

"You're very talented," I said quietly. He had stood behind me as I looked at the women through the fog of my own desire. I too wanted to be watched, analyzed, photographed, my body deconstructed, limbs and neck disjointed from the torso.

"Will you photograph me? I want you to photograph me. For real this time."

He turned away from me and walked over to the fireplace, picking up a box of matches to light a fire.

"I don't do it for real anymore," he said. "I used to think of myself as an artist but that was a long time ago, when I imagined I was some kind of Don Juan."

I peeled off my shirt and jeans as if they were old skin I was shedding, and he stood askance, watching me, his hands clasped behind his back.

There among pictures of his women—I did not ask who they were—we fell together in one swoop, in one gesture of defeat onto the black fur rug at the mouth of a fireplace. At first he seemed to be barely breathing, lying spent beneath me until a fierceness overtook him, and he threw me on my back. I looked up and saw them—his women, their hidden faces, concealing stories, stories I quickly wrote for them. In this room he and I were not alone, but we—he and I and his women—were clustered together, black and white repainted in color, bodies dancing in orange, red, and yellow flames, their souls fusing with mine.

"Look at me, I want you to look at me," he whispered, "nothing matters but you and me. No one compares to you. That's the past, and it's buried there behind the glass."

I closed my eyes and laid my head upon his chest. The musty odor of the wood spiraled through my lungs and I imagined he was made of the same matter as his cottage. Stripped of his polished surfaces, his essence was built from plain, thick, wooden planks: stationary, good, unbreakable. I can invest my whole self in you, I thought, I can trust you. And then a hobbling afterthought came: because at last I can trust myself.

"What happened between you and your brother?" I asked.

"It's ugly—I'm embarrassed—"

"That's ridiculous," I muttered, smiling, bringing his hand to my lips and burrowing my mouth, wet and full of feeling, into his palm. *I love you, there's no space between us now—I've taken all the impediments out. There's nothing you can do to embarrass yourself. I'll take all your secrets, your baggage, and your terrible family members, and carry them on my back.*

Out loud I merely said, "It doesn't matter, Eddie, you don't have to tell me if you don't want to," as if my curiosity weren't squeezing the very gut of me.

But that's precisely when he let it out. "Every stupid high school cliché begins like this, but yes, there was a girl. My first love was a strange beautiful creature. For her, small talk was akin to torture. People said she was pathologically shy, said her parents were very strict—someone even told me she wasn't allowed to date, that she was waiting for marriage. So she danced in order not to speak. Every school production gave her a solo—you couldn't tear your eyes away from her. Perhaps if things had turned out differently she would have gone on to Julliard. She had the bearing of a ballerina too, long neck, straight back, the way she stared down at us, us—dumb horny bastards. She wasn't popular—girls didn't take to her, never invited her to parties, but the guys—secretly we all wanted her.

"She sat next to me in algebra. I offered to help her with math once and when she thanked me she got all red and flustered. She brought me oatmeal cookies the next day. That's when I knew, when I saw the anguish in her face—it didn't matter who I was—she would say yes to anyone. Anyone who made the effort. And God did I make an effort! I offered to help her with algebra every day. Every day we met for lunch. Every day I thought about kissing her. I asked her to the homecoming dance and she accepted with a silent nod. Maybe it was gratitude, maybe desperation for some sense of normalcy. But I was so in love by then, I couldn't see straight. After that initial kiss in the October twilight, leaning against her parents' car in the driveway, I'd feel this awful pain in my chest when she'd miss a day at school or was away at dance rehearsal or I'd see some guy talking to her in the hallway. We became an item quickly. Sometimes I'd kiss her in public—she hated that. I was always fighting for her.

"We had been together for close to a year but we hadn't had sex: she was a virgin. I told her I'd wait forever." He laughed. "I masturbated a lot then."

"Who didn't?" I said. "So did you eventually lose your virginity to her?"

"No, no, that's the thing." His gaze drifted, discomfort climbed across his face. "She lost her virginity to my brother."

"What?"

"Yes, my brother, my twin, the philosopher-playboy." He spoke with such acrimony in his voice I thought the voice itself would disappear. "He was suave, juggling two, three girls at a time. You had to be a fool not to know Andy wanted her. He always wanted virgins, always wanted what he couldn't have. I didn't trust him but I couldn't imagine he'd ever make a move. Inside I did get jealous when I saw her laugh at his insipid jokes and look at him the way girls did, like they just couldn't believe *he* was talking to *them*. And in our home too, he was my mother's blond God. She used to call him Aries, or Augustine, his Christian name. She named us after saints but I always suspected that she named my brother after an emperor.

"He was a champion swimmer—the best diver our school had ever seen. This one ability gave him instant fame. Mother had hopes he'd win Olympic gold one day—our whole household made sure Andy ate right and slept right. But he was a dunce in school: lazy, inattentive, a clown. He needed my help in everything, except English. He saw himself as a bohemian philosopher. One day I came home and found him fucking my girl in our room, the room Andy and I shared. I vomited on the floor right in front of them. She just lay there, staring at me with her petrified eyes. Her clothes were still on her. The only thing I saw was his bare ass shining in the dark. I couldn't understand it—my first instinct was to kill him; she looked like she was in such pain, like this was torture. But was the torture in seeing me or being with him? I didn't know. She told me later through tears that she detested him, but felt she needed to do it with someone she didn't care about so it'd be 'special with us.' 'Special with us!'—I knew those were Andy's words. Andy had said, 'you'll lose him if you don't do it soon. Being a virgin gets tiresome for guys, don't you know that? Don't you know you sound like a self-righteous bitch? I can teach you. I can teach you to suck cock and act like you want it.'

"I even thought I could forgive her when I heard that. But the pain was so intense, you know, I couldn't look at her. I probably would have forgiven her eventually if I hadn't—hadn't done what I did."

"What did you do?"

"Andy and I weren't speaking to each other for maybe two weeks when my mother decided to have an intervention, a mediation, whatever the fuck she called it. So we stared at each other with my mother between us, and I said, 'This fuck won't even apologize!' My mother, who never allowed swearing in the house, said, 'Good, Ignatius, you're letting your feelings be known.' And Andy looked at me and just laughed—there were no human feelings there, nothing other than self-adulation—and he cried, 'You're such a self-righteous prick! Serves you right to know you were hot for a whore!' And I snapped—I reached across the dinner table for his collar and just began to pummel him. I had so much rage I couldn't stop—I probably would have killed him if my mother hadn't called the police."

He stopped speaking for a moment, his voice cracked; tears surfaced, then retreated behind his pupils.

"The thing is, the thing is—Andy was in bad shape—I broke his left arm and two ribs. All I had was a bruised eye, a bloody nose, and a police warning. Mother wouldn't let them take me to jail, though one officer recommended it to teach me a lesson. After that, we didn't speak at all—it was as if we had ceased to exist for each other. I moved into the basement, and Andy had pot feasts in our old room, right under my mother's watchful eye. It took him a while to recover, but when he returned to swimming, he couldn't regain his old speed. Diving became an exercise in public humiliation, and eventually the coach asked him to quit the team—'for everyone's sake.'"

"God," I murmured, "how horrible for you, Eddie!"

"Oh Emma, my story doesn't end there," he said, pausing for an instant, his eyes closing momentarily as if to shield me from some unspeakable horror. "At the time, there were rumors in our school that someone had cheated on the SAT exam, and we were all under scrutiny. Some guy paid another guy two thousand dollars to take the test. The problem was that I had one of the highest scores and I, not knowing this, was immediately placed under high suspicion. A month after I beat up my brother, he marched into the principal's office and declared before the entire administration that a guy paid Eddie Beltrafio to take the SAT for him. 'I know this,' he said, 'because I'm his brother.'"

"But why would anyone just believe him?"

"Andy made a convincing case—he said our family was still suffering financially from my father's mental breakdown, said I wanted to be the head of the household, said I desperately wanted to make money to help my mother out. I was completely rail-roaded. I had no idea why I was being questioned or what they were accusing me of. They had found the kid who didn't show up to the exam—Luke Wallerton—and they pulled my test score to compare it to his. The results were stunningly similar but only because we both had close to perfect scores. Luke refused to give up his coconspirator, and I—*I* who had studied so diligently, who had done, it seemed, everything right—had nothing convincing to say in my own defense.

"Andy made no pretenses about wanting to avenge me. His life was ruined without the swimming, without its luminous future; he was still popular but in a kind of pathetic way—a has-been—people still wanted to hang with him, girls wanted to sleep with him, but they'd never, ever consider *being* with him. These girls were headed to Stanford and Harvard and Yale—and Andy—where was he headed?"

"And you—where were you headed, Eddie?"

"I was suspended for three weeks from school, my acceptances from Harvard, Yale, Princeton, and Columbia were all placed on hold, and I was asked to leave the football team. I became a social pariah—no one spoke to me. I was ostracized and suddenly suspected of stupid things like stealing library books or not paying for my lunch. It was horrible. I, who had been such a success, turned into a failure overnight. But the thing is I'm not sure I would do anything differently," he stumbled, his mind seeking a way to withhold something he suddenly felt was unbearable to reveal.

"I couldn't forgive the girl—not for sleeping with him—but for the unseen consequences of this one act—the way it ruined all of our lives. I hated myself most of all, hated my life, hated my brother, hated the memories of being in love, hated my mother for feeling sorry for *him*, hated myself for hating the girl, for blaming her for everything."

I reached for his hand and held it in both of mine—I didn't know what could be done to soothe him. But he smiled awkwardly at me. "Oh, don't feel bad for me, Emma. I'm the only one who made it out of the mess alive. By June, miraculously enough, the true culprit came forward and I was exonerated. Of course. I lost my place in all of the schools except for one: my mother's alma mater, Columbia. They took me in, because the Dean still fondly remembered the money my father had once donated to the school in his heyday, and I studied harder than I had ever studied in my life. I lost all ability to live—or care for anyone. I just wanted to succeed."

"And your mother—where does she stand now—I mean whose side—"

"Andy's, of course, but she never tires of trying to get us to reconcile." He closed his eyes when he said this. "My brother was destroyed by the incident—his future obliterated. He got into drugs, dropped out of high school, and just failed at one career after another, until my father gracefully gave him a job at Beltrafio Movers and Shakers, where he does absolutely nothing. He married a girl he once rejected long ago, and now cheats on her regularly. But no one expects anything from him—they all just feel sorry for him."

"But not for you," I said, "not for you."

"No, not for me and no thought was ever given to my girl, no care, no feeling to what she was going through.

"My relationship with my family is still classically dysfunctional. I don't go home anymore. I've boycotted all holidays involving Andy. It works both ways. He hates me just as much. He's still waiting for my apology, or so Mother says, and I—I guess I'm still waiting for his."

I breathed through my mouth for fear of hyperventilating so incomprehensible, so terrifying this story seemed. For whatever prison I had with my own family, at least I could count on them to protect me from the outside world, at least I knew we were safe in each other's arms.

"Do you ever want to be on speaking terms with him?"

"No," he said, "lives have been ruined, and I can't turn *that* off in my head." He looked at me and tears streamed from my eyes, and as if receiving my permission, tears streamed from his.

"The girl never danced again," he said, burying his face in his hands. He let me hold him in silence.

A Girl Named Sarah

He led me by the hand the way a dog guides its unseeing master into a dark palatial room. When I opened my eyes, I was confronted with a giant Jacuzzi rising out the floor like the parted jaws of a whale. The walls, floor, and even the tub were encased in a gleaming black reflective marble, giving one the unnatural sensation of being seen from every angle. Only the silver framed black-and-white images of cliffs and oceans, with their opaque white calm, allowed one's gaze to escape self-scrutiny.

I laughed at once. "What a chick magnet—did you design this yourself or did it conveniently come with the property?"

"I like to think of it as the intellectual man's den of sin," he said with a self-mocking grin. "Anyways it's not my fault—it's from the eighties."

He lit white candles on the windowsill and looked at me with renewed desire, his melancholy dissipating into steam. We were naked, wrapped in blankets, and we dropped them simultaneously and climbed into the black gurgling water and intertwined our legs, our bodies sliding against each other.

But I couldn't relax. "I was just thinking something strange, something I've never thought about any American: my life seems strangely easy in comparison to yours."

"I told you everyone has baggage," he said, but in an instant, his gaze was cloaked in rage. "My family life is nonexistent. You have a rare thing—real love in your family. But for most of us, parents and children are thrown accidentally together—people who are so different from each other forced to live in unwanted intimacy. That's what I've got—a terrible mismatch. I want to create my own family—"

"Oh, Eddie, don't—don't look at me like that—I'm an impossible case."

"Sure you are—that's why you're for me, the only one for me."

Tears gathered at the corners of my eyes. "Oh, Eddie, you don't know me. I'm lost and confused and I've been broken so many times I don't know how to put myself back together—I've never known how to do the right thing."

He appealed to me in silence, waiting.

"There are things from my childhood that no one knows. There are things . . . I believe they are better left unsaid. And yet, yet I want to tell you—I don't want anything to be left unsaid between us—I don't want to keep such secrets from you."

"I want to know everything about you, Emma, everything," he murmured, caressing my body in the water, his fingers gliding over my wet calf.

"When I was a child, oh God!"

I looked up at the black ceiling and through a skylight saw clusters of stars sitting like conspiring deities across the glass. I covered my face with my hands, covered the tears scorching my cheeks. What else could I tell him! What else breathed with such horror, what else constricted and unraveled and explained me all at once—as I was now—as that moment when I was so happy and innocent and seven?

I began to speak but after a while I couldn't feel myself talking, couldn't remember his responses; the memory overtook me. I returned there, to the wild meadows, to the birch forest, to the time when I was a child at a special camp with my mother, a special camp for intellectual children or rather children of intellectuals: a camp for the progeny of writers, journalists, newspaper columnists, TV personalities, editors. A camp for the elite, where we were taught the arts and sports and survival skills, a distinctly Russian take on the ancient Greek gymnasium. Interspersed among us were the children of the KGB. Though we were Jews, my mother's position as an editor at the preeminent Communist establishment, the Soviet Union of Writers, gave her unprecedented access—to all the coveted privileges of the KGB. In addition to the usual infusions of special passes, Beluga caviar, and an array of German salamis, my mother was offered this camp—a wonder, really, a beautiful place with a deep clear river and meadows of irises and daisies where we would gather bouquets and weave wreaths for our heads and fry potatoes and freshly picked mushrooms over campfires.

Painting #7

I cannot paint yet: I'm still piecing it together, still sifting through memory, still avoiding the explosions of color. I can't remember which day, which hour, perhaps it was toward the end of August, on a Sunday, a day of unification between parents and children, a day I mark in memory with sunlight, heat, buzzing bees and butterflies, a day magnified in my mind's eye by startling beauty. My mother and I are playing in a lilac meadow surrounded by a birch forest—rows upon rows of delicate white pockmarked trees ascending in straight lines, their branches holding hands with pines and ancient oaks, the generals of all forests reaching for the sundrenched sky.

I'm making a wreath from daisies for my head, when out of nowhere three teenage boys appear—I've seen them before at roll call. They're smiling at me. Then a dark-haired boy says, "What a nice wreath you made—do you know what the word *pizda* means?" "No," I reply, smiling back. A blond boy smiles and the others egg him on: "Do you want to know what it is?" I nod. "Because we really want to tell you but you have to come with us into the woods, just for a second," the dark one says. I rise and follow them without any hesitation. I wonder if *"pizda"* is a mushroom I haven't heard of, or a special tree. The blond boy is handsome and he puts his arm around me.

They bring me into the heart of the forest where the thin white birches are so beautiful and close, you feel your eyes water and your mind grow still. I inhale deeply as though I'm underwater.

I see her immediately in the distance tied to an old massive oak: a girl, naked, ropes round her ankles and wrists, ropes wrapping the thick brown trunk. Her face is wild, eyes unfocused as if blind. I only know one thing about her, she's older, eleven years old, and a Jew like me. We're not friends, our activities don't intersect, except at night when we sit with our mothers at the bonfire, and comb the ground with our mushroom sticks.

At roll call every morning the counselors call out everyone's name: the normal names like Petrokovsky, Yagodova, Pomidorov run though our ears like water, then ours appear like plugs. She is the butt of all jokes: Sarah Fichtshtein.

In those years, no parent names their child Sarah. Why did hers? The name itself is used to mock the Jews—pronounced Sa-r-r-ah—giving the "r" a Yiddish tint. Stalin wiped Yiddish out. All that remains is the "r" and "h" in Sarah and Chaim. You're "Sa-r-r-ah" if you are acting too "Jewish," or "Chhhhhhaim" if your nose is crooked or too long. The Fichtshteins came to Moscow from Tashkent; they didn't understand the cruelties of modern city life.

The counselors cough, mix consonants, crack up as they call her name. My last name gets the same treatment. When your name is called, you say "present." Sarah and I always whisper, and the counselors yell, "Louder, I didn't hear you, Fichtshtein! Didn't hear you, Kabelmacher!" I scream "present," she screams "present," and all the children laugh. Sometimes I'm spared on account of my mother, sometimes on account of the smile and the small-doll like features they say reminds them of *Snegurochka*.

But Sarah never smiles, she's never spared; she has thick black hair and a long thin nose with a sharp tip. Her brown eyes are elongated almonds, Roman eyes with pronounced lids, full of anguish. She's beautiful but not in the Russian sense. Hers is the face I paint, the face of my subconscious. But she envies me. "You're lucky," she says, "they look at you and they forget."

God, she speaks like everyone: you don't look It! You're too pretty for a Jew. Too light skinned for a Jew. Nose too small for a Jew. Eyes too light, too green for a Jew. Personality too lively for a Jew. You never complain like other Jews, you're not greedy, manipulative, dirty like a Jew. Maybe you're not a Jew—maybe you're a Slav or at least half of one, a hybrid, a half-breed, a trickster!

Her parents applied in 1976, people *v podache*—waiting for exit visas, three years later they're refused, they're the official *refuseniks*, in the flesh, in our camp. Why are they in this camp? Rumors swirl, no one knows. They're the devoted Jews, the Jews' Jews, going straight to Israel, not America. In Israel she'll say "Sarah" with pride.

But Sar-r-rah is treated like a beloved scarecrow, everyone's relief and mockery. Even the staff and camp leaders and theater directors mock Sarah. She loathes Russia and Communism and isn't afraid to say it, but I tell her to be quiet, to keep her trap shut. Now she's hanging from a tree, tears streaking her cheeks like rivulets of blood.

"We want to show you what a *pizda* is," the dark-haired boy says. "So why don't you take off your underpants like Sarah and then we can all play." I'm wearing a short white summer dress decorated in tiny pink tulips. And instinctively, I pull the hem down, my mind in high alert. I want to run and get help but they surround me—the blond one and a lanky boy named Grisha.

"Where are you going, Kabelmacher," they taunt, "isn't that your name? What's with you people and your unpronounceable names? Why must we mangle our tongues? You always make life so difficult for everyone, you stinky kikes!"

"But she doesn't look like a Jew. Can someone explain that puzzle to me?" the blond-haired boy exclaims, staring down at me as though I'm an algebra equation he wants to solve. "Why do some of them look it and others don't?"

"Probably because their moms fucked one of ours, that's why, but they're all the same underneath," the dark one theorizes.

"Hey," the lanky one says, "some of us are different."

"We're not talking about you, Grisha," the dark one assures him. "Besides, your father's the kike, not your mother."

Grisha grins and says, "What are we gonna do with these two?"

"Well first we gotta get this cute one to drop her panties."

"I ain't dropping no panties for you! Get Sarah down," I yell. I imagine myself to be a great menace. "When my mother finds out," I shriek, shaking my forefinger at them, "you're all going down with a good beating!"

"Ha, ha, ha, a good beating, ha?" The blond one breaks into laughter. "I highly doubt it, little fool, do you know who my father is?"

"If your mother finds out"—the dark-haired boy grabs me by the collar of my dress and lifts me in the air, his grip choking me—"we'll kill your mother, you understand me, you little Yid?" I want to cry but I tell myself to be strong for my mother—crying is for the weak, the stereotypical Jews.

"I tell you what," I say, "I'll show you my—my—my *pizda*—if you get Sarah down and give her her clothes back."

"So you learned some anatomy today, right there between your thighs," Grisha says, pointing his finger toward my crotch.

"You first," the dark one says, "show it first."

Only the blond boy shifts on his feet, grows uncomfortable. "I think we've had enough fun," he mutters, "let them go now. They're too young. We need some real tits."

"Oh, she's got tits, that Jew up there." Sarah's wrists are blue and her sides have red scratches running along her ribs and buttocks. She has two pointy red nipples sticking out of small mounds of flesh. The black-haired boy and Grisha pick up sticks and start poking Sarah between her legs. But it's the black-haired boy who sticks the end of one stick in, right between her thighs, into her vagina, and as she cries out from pain, I see blood drip along the side of her leg.

"That's where the *pizda* is located, little one, you see that— that's the blood of a dirty Yid," the black-haired boy says.

Grisha drops his stick and grabs the boy by the arm: "What are you doing—you're going too far—you're gonna seriously hurt her!"

"What—what did I do wrong—I did her favor, took her virginity from her! Why? Are you chickening out, or are you sympathizing with your fellow Yid? Do you want to be a real man?"

"I'm not chicken," Grisha says, "but—"

"Now I'm gonna make this little cute one lose her virginity," the dark one announces. "Do you know what sex is, little macher kike?" he cries out, laughing, looking down at me. Then he pushes me on the ground and jumps on top of me and straddles me and laughs and laughs. "Oh, I could really start to like this little kike! Are you scared, little one, are you?"

"No!" I punch back, stare at him defiantly. I'm not afraid; I only feel fumes in my gut, fumes of loathing. "I'm going to put a spell over your head, a Yid spell, an evil eye to make you suffer! May you eat shit all your life and pee in your pants—I hope you die, you stupid weasel-brained *durak*!"

"And I'm gonna hang you up there like Sar-r-rah, ha, ha, ha," he screams through laughter and I spit in his face. He wipes my spit with the sleeve of his shirt, and his face changes from laughter to hatred in an instant. He lifts my dress and tears out my underwear with a small pocket knife that seems to materialize out of nowhere. He presses the knife against my thigh and pricks the skin.

"Do you think I'm afraid of your little knife?" I say but my voice falters.

"Let her go, Vladik," the blond boy commands, "let her go."

"But Sarah stays," the dark one retorts, submitting halfway, because the blond boy's father holds a high position in the Politburo.

"Agreed," the blond boy says, nodding. "This one's too little. You don't know, Vladik, she may not even be a real one."

"Yeah, that's true, have you seen her mom—now that's a hot *blyat*! I want me some of that cunt!" It seems miraculous, but they aren't looking at me any longer—they're speaking with one another about other cunts they want, other girls they'd like to hang up on that tree, interspersing their desires with pragmatic subjects such as sticks better suited for picking mushrooms, their fantastically idiotic counselor, and how to elude the important

Politburo father who is too strict. I can only exhale—I can't inhale air into my lungs. I consider sprinting at the tree and somehow pulling Sarah down, but her wrists and ankles are securely tied and the boys will string me up, too, if I try. I grab my underwear and run in my torn dress through the white birch forest, tripping over stumps and leaves, falling, picking myself up again, twisting my underwear in my fingers, tears pouring down my face in a torrent. I must bury the evidence—the underwear—I whisper to myself, I must find a place to bury it, to keep it a secret from my mother. The white-black trunks blur into a mass of gray, and the leaves, so sparse, seem to expose me to the burning sky. I'm afraid of the sky, afraid to be seen by it.

In the clearing I see my mother talking to the art teacher and other girls weaving daisy wreaths. I stand still, feeling the warm breeze on my arms and goose bumps pricking my skin. I feel safe again, but only for an instant—for the fear settles all at once like a giant black cloud in which I'm forced to breathe. The sides of my legs are wet from pee, and I keep thinking what a horrible thing I've done. Grisha and Vladik and the blond boy will kill my mother if I talk so I need to shut my mouth, glue my lips together. When my mother finds me crying I say I fell and wet my panties and bruised my thigh and a tree stump scratched my arm. She carries me back to her cottage and caresses my hair and covers my cheeks with kisses, and says, "I told you to stay near me, but you're a firefly, you're always flying." And I smile at the thought of my red wings—I'm *Zhar-ptitsa*.

I inhaled air as if for the first time, as if I had just been saved from drowning, and met Eddie's eyes.

"Sarah was found late that evening by an old fireman who lived in the woods," I explained. "She never returned to that camp."

"You were a child—what could you have done?" he said, but I was still stuck there.

"I was a coward, been a coward ever since."

"It's terrible what happened to you," he murmured, "but you need to heal."

"How I wish—" I took in a quick breath, and went on. "I can't be a coward again. You have to know the whole truth."

He looked at me in confusion.

"I told you almost everything but the final, invidious little detail I meant to keep to myself—because the shame of it, the shame of it—" I felt my heart multiply in my head until there were five, six, seven hearts all thumping in different parts of my body.

"I hated it. I hated being Jewish. I couldn't digest it, couldn't understand it. Even the horrible boys who harassed Sarah said I didn't look it. How terrible it was, I had thought then, not to look it and yet be punished for it. But that was no excuse for what I did—" I met his gaze in a blur. "You see what I neglected to mention was that after the incident Sarah had reported the boys to the camp authorities, and named me as a witness."

I closed my eyes and fell down the rabbit hole, down, down into a bottomless subconscious, the putrid undergrowth of memory—surfacing, festering, ugly.

There was a tribunal at the camp. The head honchos, the men, were going to excavate the truth, dig it up from the well of lies we all lived in. They alone were going to catch it, this elusive thing with butterfly wings and a fox's tail and a horse's ass . . . In an enormous starkly painted room, ten men were seated behind a long black table, notebooks with identical pens arrayed in front of them. I was placed in the witness chair, a small wooden stool facing the men and the audience, made up of camp counselors and staff. From my perch, I could see Sarah and her mother in the empty auditorium, clinging to each other. I could see my mother watching me, biting her nails, her consternation so extreme that her features appeared to fuse together. Everything was a blur, faces merged, features swam, switched places, danced with one another, coalesced into one terrifying glob. I couldn't figure out where I was, who I was, couldn't remember my name. Fear with its big fat capital F invaded my senses, knocking Memory out with one hard blunt punch.

In the days preceding the tribunal, the entire camp as if in a singular magnified voice had whispered, "Did the Jew lie?"

A bald man centrally placed began the proceeding. "We begin with our witness, Elena Kabelmacher. Octobrist Kabelmacher, tell us what you saw in the woods. Speak freely and honestly."

Everyone's eyes were upon me. That's when I felt it, the dirt, the grime, her sticky blood dripping through my fingers, infected with the Jew disease, blood on my hands, *will these hands never be clean*, and if I'm not careful, if I don't wash hard enough, I might catch it.

I washed my hands with my replies. "I saw nothing, I did nothing, I saw nothing," I repeated, again and again. And Sarah screamed, "No, she's lying! They did it to her, they harassed her, they tore her clothes, they tortured her, she wanted to save me!" But the men commanded her to quiet down: "Wait until your turn, pioneer Fichtshtein." She wept for the injustice and betrayal she endured, not in the hands of the judges, but in the hands of her fellow sufferer—in me. She turned on me. "Why are you lying? After everything we've been through, why are you lying?"

Don't cry, Kabelmacher, ne plach, I told myself, *don't let them see you* (dear God I was only seven), *don't let them know what a coward you are.*

"The boys were only joking around," I insisted. "Sarah just didn't understand them."

"Was she naked and tied up to a tree?" an older man, closest to me, asked.

"She was wearing her dress when I saw her," I said, "and as for being tied to a tree, I do remember that there *was* a tree in the forest." Everyone laughed, and I blushed. I blushed and lied some more.

"Why are you making up such terrible things?" the men demanded from Sarah. Oh, how she wept, hysterically, painfully, her entire body convulsing, tears bursting from her nose and mouth. I thought she would choke on them. "I'm not lying, *ya govoryu pravdu*—I speak the truth." I heard the words muffled but clear. "Coward," she had yelled at me as she left the room. "Coward—we, Jews, are all cowards—that's why they hate us so much!"

I was afraid of everything: the men at the tribunal, the boys' retribution, even my mother, but she—Sarah feared nothing, no one, not even this brutal humiliation. For afterwards, the tribunal exonerated the boys and recommended to Sarah's parents that Sarah be placed under psychiatric evaluation.

After my mom and I returned to Moscow from the camp, I lay in my bed and drew in the new sketchpad my father bought for me. I'd heat up the thermometer and claim to my grandma that I was ill with fever. Grandmother said, "A fever is no excuse for keeping secrets," as if she knew. She seated me on a chair in the middle of our biggest room, and said, "What *really* happened in that swamp for intellectuals?" She probed me for hours. "There are things you're not telling us. Never conceal! Tell the truth, it's the only way to recover." We practiced therapy intuitively, Russian-family style, by pelting people with commands. The truth at last poured out of me, and for the first time since the incident, I cried. The guilt lifted for an instant, like a freight train riding off my chest. "Everything Sarah said was true," I told my mother and father and grandmother. "The boys poked Sarah's body with sticks, pushed sticks into her breasts, stuck sticks in there, inside her *pipka*, until she bled. They tore off my underwear, and said they'd tie me to the tree, like Sarah, if I talk, if I open up my big Jew mouth."

I looked at my mother. "I lied to protect you. They said they'd kill you if I told the truth." Grandmother groaned: "*Bozhe moy, Bozhe moy, Bozhenka pomogi nam . . .*" My mother's face contorted and turned bright red—it was one of the few times in my life that I had witnessed *her* crying.

But it was only for a moment. She wiped her cheeks, and the tears disappeared. "But where was your courage? What you did you must undo!"

"But how?"

"You must find Sarah and apologize to her," my mother told me. Sadness and disappointment swam in her eyes, and then I saw the flicker of guilt, as if it was her fault, not mine—the fact of Sarah's betrayal.

But by the time we found their address and phone number in Moscow, we reached only Sarah's aunt, who told us that the Fichtshteins had already emigrated to Israel. That was the turning point in our lives—that irreversible moment when the truth is revealed and can never be taken away. That was when my mother said to my father, "Is this the life you want for our children—a life where they're forced into betrayal, where heroism is snuffed out before it's had a chance to bloom?"

"My God, how terrible, you were so young, how could you understand these things? Such cruelty to children!" Eddie broke through my memory.

"The irony, of course, is that this incident is why we're here," I explained.

"What do you mean?"

"We applied for an exit visa right after the incident. My father finally agreed with my mother: that to remain in Russia would be an act of great inhumanity to us, the children."

"Yes, well, I'm glad he did," Eddie said, but I could see his mind drifting through my story, not fully comprehending it.

"Jews were being refused left and right in 1980," I said, "and there we were, just beginning our wait. I don't know how we got out—on a fluke, I suspect. By 1982 no one was being let out. But there we were. Here I am."

I looked at him beseechingly, seeking in his eyes something soothing, ameliorating.

"It wasn't your fault," he said, "you have to recognize that."

"Oh, but it was. I could have told the truth. I was a coward."

"You were a child, Emma, a child! And you were terrified. Your mother was wrong to reprimand you."

"I betrayed Sarah. If I was tortured the way my grandfather or great-grandmother or great-great uncle were tortured by Stalin's goons, I would have spilled the beans before the stick would ever hit my face, before a single nail on my pinky would be pulled out. I was weak—yes, a child but already weak of heart."

He lifted my chin with a single finger. "Look at me," he said, "look at me. You are not weak. You are incredible and strong, and I didn't understand—"

"No, no, you still don't understand—the rot is in me! It wasn't just that society that was horrible and rotten, but us—each individual couldn't help but become infected by that disease. I got infected. The rot crawled into me and I'm not sure I've gotten it out yet. I too was possessed, but not just with fear—with hatred. I hated Sarah for her weakness, for crying, for revealing her feelings at the tribunal, for being so sensitive, even for telling on the boys. But I hated the boys even more—flies, I thought in my head, insects, hideous vermin, you are beneath us. In my mind, I took Sarah's hand and we flew above them and mid-flight turned into dragons and then descended on them all—the boys, the men, the audience I imagined, our wrath spewing out of our mouths and consuming the whole room in a great purple fire. We will triumph one day, one day . . . That's why I told myself I must hide, must keep silent for now, must remember and then transcend. Transcend and then what? Transcend what, whom exactly?

"Can't you see I can't get past this? I'm stuck in a cage, and every time I try to claw my way out, I fall right back in. And somewhere deep inside I'm not *me*—not the person I appear to other people, not the woman you see before you, but the child still hiding, peering out of this adult body."

"But you don't hide," he gently contradicted. "You reveal yourself. You announce who you are—you are far stronger than the sum of your past events."

"What I reveal is only a tiny fraction of what I am—"

"It's strange, but I know exactly what you mean—the feeling of never fully sharing, never being able to fully express—"

"You and I are not the same, Eddie."

"Look Emma, we create the cage *ourselves* with our bare hands to punish ourselves for the things we did and did not do, for the sake of punishment itself. You've got stop blaming yourself, not just for your past, but for your present—you've got to paint! Paint it all out, that's your only chance to heal. Paint that scene—the child in the forest—paint it as you see it inside your head."

"I can't—I can't face the possibility of failure. I can't devote my whole self to this only to find out that I'm mediocre, that the coordination between my mind and hands is adequate at best, that the emotions bubbling within are true and deep but can never appear on the canvas as they do in my head. I am so afraid—you can't imagine such fear—afraid that I will bleed out trying, that my failure will be the end of me. My humiliation will result in a full retreat . . ."

"Are you prepared to wonder your whole life what it would've been like to paint full time? Nothing is easy, Emma, certainly not the life of an artist, and this coordination you speak of is a matter of practice and sweat and grit. To do something with your whole self means working on these images for the long haul, for months, even years—imagine how far you could go! What's the alternative? Not painting at all? Painting as a hobby? You're not equipped for that—the compromise will kill you."

"Yes—but how is it that you know this—you, who's known me for such a short time, know the very root of me? I never thought such a man could exist!" I could feel the tears and the gratitude and the gushing joy intermingling with wonder and disbelief, all rising to the surface.

"Life is not supposed to be this easy," I cried out. "Who said human beings are supposed to be happy? Who said *I* had any right to bite into this pie?"

"Americans," he replied, laughing.

"Yes, yes, Americans, America!" I rose out of the bathtub and pressed my breasts onto his lathered chest.

"You're gorgeous, simply gorgeous," he said, smiling, as if relieved to return to our first, our most vital bond. Tentacles seemed to grow out of his black pupils and wrap each breast, and trace the curve of my stomach to the contours of my waist. His eyes devoured, absorbed me, infused me with confidence and power. Through his eyes I saw myself billowing, growing taller, more beautiful, and I balked at it—the male gaze—and turned the female gaze on him. His skin was brown and silky, and the water slid down his chest as if gliding on a stone surface. I traced his muscles with my fingers as though I were mapping out my cre-ation, my sculpture, my ideal man, reaching deep into the water. Only intermittently, through his muffled moans, did I catch my own skin against his, my own whiteness against his brown expanse. The contrast was so extreme that I flinched at the sheer physical distance between us.

I was whiter than anyone I knew, white like my sister, mother, and grandmother, whiter than the underside of arms on my pale American friends, whiter than a fresh new canvas. We burned in heat on gray days, blistered in the sun, peeled and heaved with pain, our skin populated by wild rashes. It was the only physical aspect of myself I couldn't erase—my own sense of my distinct Russianness, and when my hair darkened in the water, losing its reddish and golden hues, the contrast against my face was so extreme that my features intensified and increased in size, taking me from my Russianness to my Jewishness. And I wondered as I watched us in the marble reflection if he knew what I was thinking, if he knew how madly I desired the merging of *our* contrasts, if that alone—this difference in skin and features—was what drew me to him.

"I want you so much I feel like I could burst," I said, my lips moving along his chest. His eyes glistened and he pressed me so hard against himself I felt my skin gluing to his skin.

"Marry me," he said, kissing my face, "marry me, Emma."

"I—I—"

Suddenly a noise erupted from my purse, a grating ring tone that I instantly recognized as my new cell phone, drawing my swelling heart out of my body like a powerful magnet and then deflating it mid-flight. In an area where cell phone service was practically non-existent and few towers had been built, that sound could only have meant one thing: Mom and Grandma had erected a virtual cell tower with their formidable Russian telepathy in order to cross state lines and yank me from the arms of the "wrong" man. Because Life, with a capital L, was not simply about the diligent upkeep of misery and suffering, but about the swift eradication of all seedlings of happiness.

"I have to get that," I said, rising from the tub. "It's my mom and grandma—they don't know where I am and if I don't pick up, they'll think I'm dead or have been abducted by the KGB."

"Tell them you've been abducted by a goy," he cried out, laughing. "How can you leave—you can't leave me like this." He lay there naked and erect under the black water. As I wiped myself with a white towel, I felt a sudden desire to weep. I held the phone in my wet hand and a familiar voice said, "Lenochka, *gde ty*? You must come here right away—we have an absolute pandemonium here." It took me a few seconds to place the tonality, to remember that the only person whose lilting voice could move as easily from Russian to English as my own was Bella. "They know," she said at once, and then the line went dead.

PART III

A Gentile on Our Lawn

By the time Mom and Grandma and Dad were presented with the disturbing news that I was now co-habiting with a certain Catholic hooligan/investment banker named Eddie; that I had already, without informing them, canoodled with his parents during a fancy lunch; and that—here's where heart-related emergency room visits were being heavily touted—I was in love, a concept so laughable Grandmother spat on her kolbasa, they were too exhausted to fight. Anger over Alexei Bagdanovich and disappointment over not being able to attend our wedding had taken a vicious hold in the Russian suburbs of Chicago (which included but was not limited to Buffalo Grove, Long Grove, Downers Grove, the entirety of Grove Meadows and Des Plaines, and critical patches of Highland Park). Our fifth-removed cousin, Svetochka, called to complain that it was impossible to sit through a dental cleaning without overhearing some assistant call Lenochka a flaky *blyat*. For my grandmother there couldn't have been a worse fate.

Valiantly, she defended me against the naysayers, and to restore my honor, spoke of my future as a professor of mathematics and my new brilliant boyfriend, neglecting to mention that he was an American, a goy, and had no plans to get a PhD in any scientific subfield. It was, of course, an irony if they'd ever heard one: Zinayida Genadevna trying to buoy her granddaughter's reputation by pretending that any other boyfriend could be *as* brilliant as

Alex! The other irony was that no one cared that he wasn't Jewish half as much as my grandmother did. Lots of immigrant children were intermarrying. There were Jewish-Catholic weddings with bickering priests and rabbis; secular weddings between agnostic Jews and non-churchgoing WASPs officiated by rabbis disguised as non-denominational chaplains or, in Jewish speak, Reform rabbis; Indian weddings between a Jewish man and a Jewish woman, but her first love was an Indian man whom she was forbidden to marry, which accounted for a wedding menu of tandoori chicken, samosas, naan bread, and rogan josh. A smattering of other unmarriageable men could be represented by, say, spring rolls, tuna sashimi, and a generous helping of kimchi. For a woman who had fallen in love with a black man, there was always relief in music: a rendition of "Hava Nagila" that sounded suspiciously like Bobby Brown's "My Prerogative." Most popular of all were the Russian weddings gripped in an identity crisis: there was the mandatory *chuppah*; an officiant who wore a yarmulke and claimed to be a rabbi, and spoke Hebrew as if he were yelling at his wife in Russian; an abundance of lobster, shrimp, and ham-accented dishes; Russian 70s music; numerous bad renditions of "Shalom Aleichem"; and possible performances by (1) belly dancers, (2) ballet dancers doing *Swan Lake*, (3) ballroom dancers doing the tango, or (4) any of the invited guests performing any of the above.

Grandmother loathed them all. Grandmother's loathing was particularly pleasing to the Russians now that the Kabelmachers appeared to be in an identity crisis of their own. After all, who could forget the way my grandmother, that righteous and indignant prophet, called every intermarriage a blight on the Jewish community, flushing with the wrath of a wronged woman?

What a hypocritical fool you turned out to be, they seemed to be whispering in her ears! It seemed right to them—in fact, an excellent opportunity—to poke at our sensitive underbelly and avenge us for making so much money. At parties, there was veiled mockery of Zinayida Genadevna, phony sympathy for her predicament, and jabs at the Kabelmacher women; just as no one knew where their money came from, so no one knew "what spells their daughters cast over men," which in translation read, "yes, we know, and it is sex." No one envied my mother and grandmother now, and still the evil eye roamed freely, causing my mother migraines and my grandmother heartburn-related insomnia that even Tchaikovsky couldn't cure.

Grandmother and Mother retreated into a deep depression and turned inward, specifically on me.

"You've fallen in love with everyone—couldn't you have fallen in love with a Jew?" my mother asked during a three-way conference call, while my father and grandmother hummed loudly.

"*Bliny ob'eylas!*" quipped my father, which roughly translated into "you're crazy!"

"Bring him here," Grandmother simply commanded. "I want to see this goy who's ruining our lives!"

"If you have to marry a goy," my mother warned, "he better be truly great to make up for the fact that he's not Jewish."

For five minutes, Eddie and I stood at the door, ringing the bell, listening to voices booming, trickling through the brick exterior. I felt only relief and gratitude that Americans were unilingual and that my Eddie did not know an ounce of Russian, except for a few choice words I chose to teach him.

"You are Eddie! Giant pleasure to meet you!" My mother opened the door in a glittering black sweater and silk black pants.

"Same here, same here, I've heard so much about you, Mrs. Kabelmacher."

"Call me Sonya. No need for being official."

"Sonya," Eddie repeated, smiling. He had prepared for this moment in advance, practicing each name in the taxi from O'Hare Airport, and in his arms he held a 1990 Château Lafite Rothschild, a bouquet of fresh lilacs, and an egg-shaped box of Truffles from La Maison Du Chocolat.

"Vaw, I speechless! Sank you for your romantic thoughts," my mother exclaimed, even though she had no idea how expensive these romantic thoughts were, for we were neither wine drinkers nor chocolate eaters.

In the background I could hear my father shouting, "Is he here? Is he here? I can't find my brown pants—Sonya, where are my brown pants?" and Grandmother groaning from the living room in Russian, "Oy, gevalt, may the Lord save us all—the goy is here!"

"I assume that's me—the goy," Eddie said, laughing, plucking out the one recognizable word.

"*Maman*, everyone can hear you," my mother exclaimed, arching her voice above a tolerable decibel.

"So what!" Grandmother bellowed back, "I want him to know that *we* know who he is!"

But my grandmother's rough antics melted as soon as she was confronted with Eddie.

"So tall," she murmured as she came closer with a slight skip and proceeded to scrutinize his face, "and handsome—very handsome. Almost blond, yes, a hazelnut hue in the hair, and the eyes—are they blue—in fact, they *are* blue." Then, blushing like a schoolgirl, she extended her hand and announced, "Zinayida Genadevna Guildenshtein, *ochen priyatno*."

"Ignatius Cyril Beltrafio, but everyone calls me Eddie," he said, shaking her hand.

"Nice To Meet Voo," Grandmother belted out the four English words she knew.

"The pleasure is all mine," Eddie said, flashing his splendid smile.

"Are ze women bozering you already?" My father materialized from behind my grandmother, as though he had been secretly sniffing out the situation before stepping into it, and announced, "Semeyon Kabelmacher—ve chave been awaiting impatiently for you!"

"Zere's not much in fridge," my mother said, "we're going to big event tonight. My brozer-in-law just bought Moscow Nights from previous owner and now he vants to make it more fun, better dance music, and has surprise for us."

"Is that a club?" Eddie asked. "You're all going to a dance club?"

"No," my mother replied with a laugh, "it's a restaurant vhere we eat, sing, and dance."

"Oh," Eddie looked confused.

"But if you hungry now," my mother offered, "we have meat soup and steak stew, or salami and bologna—very tasty if you like?"

"You don't have to worry on account of me—I'll have whatever Emma's having."

"Who?" my father exclaimed in a derisive voice.

Grandmother joined in. "Tell him we don't like the way you butchered your name."

"Grandmother wants you to call me Lena," I interpreted for Eddie.

"Lena is an excellent name," he quickly corrected himself.

"Oh, don't listen to my mozer—I love her new name," my mother said.

"Yes, yes, both are great names!" Eddie let out a smile that froze midway, like a physical manifestation of the stalemate within my family's political climate.

Moscow Nights was an enclave of the happily un-Americanized Russians. They arrived in cheerfully gaudy outfits, drawn by nostalgia to the surplus of vodka, the exclusivity of the Russian language, and the mutilated American songs that now resembled depressing Russian ballads. The dance floor was illuminated in flashing pink squares, and sprawling gold-plated chandeliers practically grazed bopping heads. Red tablecloths, ornate gilded vases of red roses, and a gold minidress on the lead singer perfectly rounded off the restaurant's ambience. Women pranced around the dance floor like proud roosters, their multicolored feathers perfectly arrayed after a full day of primping. Their excellent features, accentuated by heavy strokes of makeup, gave them at once an air of inaccessibility and of sexual friskiness. Their hair was dyed either in a glistening yellow, a sleek bluish black, or a bright red hue that varied from eye-popping orange to a sultry auburn. And their bodies, voluptuous if they were married, reed thin if they were single, were stuffed into a size smaller than what your humble Midwestern saleslady might suggest. Their cramped black dresses revealed wide expanses of undulating breasts and backs rolling with fat. They were Rubenesque figures shaking with mirth and flirting indiscriminately with the old, the young, and the middle-aged. The men, untouched by the homophobic fears of American men, strutted across the dance floor looking busy and ambitious in bright orange, yellow, and purple shirts, either with ties or a few buttons undone to show off their masculine chest hair. The waiters generally spoke only in Russian—they were recent arrivals who as a general rule had been either speech therapists, economists, or depressed intellectuals in the Soviet Union, and were not too happy with such demanding customers as my grandmother who wanted to know if the Cornish hen was fresh, or if they were just saying that as part of the restaurant policy? One clever-tongue replied "We didn't kill it with our bare hands a few seconds ago if that's what you're implying." "Hoodlum!" Grandmother fired back, "hasn't your mother taught you manners?" At moments like these Bella and I were quietly ecstatic that Grandmother did not speak a word of English.

An enormous white table, offering an unobstructed view of the stage, awaited our family. Yakov, his wife Katya, and son Larry (aka Valery) were already seated there in silence, decked out in their shiniest royal attire. At the other end of the table, Igor hovered, paranoid, over his daughter. Sirofima wore a puffy satin white dress and her blonde hair was braided and wrapped around her head like a wreath.

Eddie caused considerable commotion as he passed through a throng of people gathering around the dance floor. I could hear them murmuring in Russian, "There goes an American," with a note of derision and respect, and in some of the female faces, I caught faint envy.

"I'm Sirofima, but Americans call me Sam!"—Sirofima was the first one to greet Eddie with a note of caution—"but grandma thinks it sounds mannish so don't call me that in front of her."

"All right," Eddie said, smiling and gripping her tiny hand, "but just between us, it's nice to meet you, Sam." The child curtseyed, blushing, and ran back to her seat.

"Nice to meet you," Katya said.

"We xhrespect Americans," Yakov announced, shaking Eddie's hand with unusual zeal.

Katya leaned into her husband and unashamedly pinched his thigh under the table, so that he winced as he spoke. As she was a quiet woman with a round face and dark serene eyes that were difficult to read, she resorted to pinching her husband under tables to demonstrate her dissatisfaction with some utterance he made, an occurrence so frequent and powerful one felt that it held their marriage together.

Larry was Katya's stepson, a young man at odds with his surroundings. It was true that he loathed his father, but he loathed his stepmother more. The two parents were so concerned over Larry's lack of a girlfriend that he called them, to their faces and behind their backs, "well-meaning sadists." They bombarded him at dinner with such torturous questions as "Why aren't you married yet?" when hapless Larry hadn't been on a date for seven months (he was now twenty-nine); "Why aren't you normal?" when Larry had difficulty with concepts such as "sociable" and "likeable"; "What is wrong with Galya, Nadya, Helen, etc. . . ." and many others they had set him up with, when the aforementioned culprits had not even returned his calls. Larry got his bachelor's at the California Institute of Technology (a school not known for its abundance of females), majored in material engineering (a major in desperate need of females), and was now working in a mostly male division of a highly specialized subfield at Maletura Corporation (whose single female was ten years older than Larry. She wore black-rimmed glasses that gave her that *je ne sais quoi* ugliness and Cleopatraesque allure. Larry feared her more than the flying dinosaur, *Pteranodon*).

If Larry ever gets married, my mother liked to say, it'll be because some woman tied up his hands and feet and held the wedding ceremony on her bed. "A *shmata*," my grandmother called him, "a soaking rag!" But I didn't agree. I always believed that if Larry ever did get tied down, he would untie himself eventually, and his true self—the essence that hid behind his hard black eyes—would emerge and gain power over time, squashing the girl's independence the way his father squashed women.

For when Yakov first fell in love with Katya, one could argue he had gone limp in the brain. Although he had blithely cheated on his first wife (Larry's mother died when Larry was nine, giving birth to a stillborn son, and it was her absence, everyone believed, that directly impacted Larry's social barometer), Yakov lost his philandering instincts upon meeting Katya a year later. A man who cared deeply about money, prestige, and women, Yakov became blind to the fact that Katya was poor, that her parents were uneducated farmers (they worked as cashiers at the vegetable market on Lenninsky Prospect), and that she was not Jewish. Nor was she a beauty. But her features were large and evocative of suppressed sexual desire, and she did not like to speak, a quality that has appealed to men since the evolution of the *Homo sapien* barbarian. For not only does the woman's silence give men free rein to pontificate on any topic, it confirms their belief, flowing directly from their mothers' breast milk, that they are geniuses. Yakov yearned for such admiration, so much so that when his beloved's parents called Jews "blood-sucking thieves, money-grubbing kikes, and dirty mannerless *zhlobs*," he had to pretend his hearing was impaired. "I couldn't quite make out what they said," he'd tell my father, "maybe I misheard!" After all, they assured him he was different, embraced him with vodka, open arms, and flapping, flattering tongues like Pavlovian dogs at the flicker of gold coins. Yakov had enough money to save them and their daughter ten times over from abject poverty. They encouraged her to marry him even as she protested that she did not love him. Love in Russia was never a requirement, and Katya quickly understood that her petulant demands for love needed to be submerged under larger considerations, such as the fact that Yakov wanted to go to America, and this—for a Russian, a non-Jew who could never leave the Soviet Union "legally" the way Jews were leaving—was a dream.

Two years after they married, Yakov, Katya, and Larry boarded the plane to Vienna on their way to America. Larry had always secretly suspected Katya of grave insincerity, but when he mentioned it to his father, the latter simply replied, "Women are capricious creatures, my son; one moment they loathe you, the next they want to scrub your feet and lick between your toes." His father's prediction, in all its ribald irony, came true. After twenty-two years in America, Katya was now jumping around like a poodle, excited by the slightest gesture her husband made, pampering him with lavender oil foot massages and dead-sea-salt baths, perhaps out of his exponential ability to make money or perhaps out of that human tendency to grow, over time, welded to the choices we make in life because we stop seeing other ones. But when Yakov repeated, "We xhrespect Americans," and Katya pinched him again with excessive force under the table, she reminded us that for a Russian woman, the power shift was never *fait accompli*.

Yakov neither cringed nor blushed, for he was accustomed to unexpected pain. He merely cackled loudly for support.

"What my husband mean is we very please to meet you!" Katya exclaimed, spreading her round face into a smile.

"Good to meet all of you," Eddie said, without guessing how many meanings "xhrespect" had in a Russian mind. On the one hand, Russians courted Americans, behaving like pathetic lackeys; on the other hand, in private, Russians skewered and mocked and poked holes in their generic definition of the "American character." I could see silent laughter in Yakov's eyes, throbbing at the quagmire his brother was in.

"I chave surprise for you!" Yakov spoke as he poured vodka into our glasses.

"Where's Bella?" I asked.

"Zhat's surprise!" Yakov let out ecstatically.

The music began clamoring in the background before anyone could utter another word, and from behind a black door that until this point had masqueraded as a wall, my sister appeared, followed by four men who took their places at their designated instruments. Bella wore a floor-length burgundy velvet gown that created a stark contrast with her golden hair and porcelain skin, and revealed just a hint of a voluptuous cleavage. It was the sort of dress she might have worn for her debut performance of *La Bohème* at the Metropolitan Opera. Instead, her first words were "Money, money, money, always sunny in a rich man's world . . ." My family, as though gripped in a metal vise, could only gasp.

"Uh, that's my sister," I whispered to Eddie as people stormed the dance floor in a nostalgic rush to catch the song that they believed encapsulated the mysterious West.

"What is our Bella doing up there?" Grandmother shouted in Russian. "You miserable lout, how dare you put our child on the stage like a two-ruble whore? Do you know that she has a degree in Macaroni Economics and *Poeziya* from Northwestern—from Northwestern *University*—not some basement college but a university!"

"Don't blame my husband"—Katya jumped in to rescue Yakov—"Bella wanted to earn money and what better way than to sing? It's what she loves to do—you should thank him instead!"

"It's great for business," Yakov said. "This place needed a makeover. We need more people to dance, we need energy on the dance floor! Look at the crowd now—they love Bella!"

"Bella belongs on a real stage—on Broadway—in the theater! Not this, not this—this—this—" My mother's face was repainted in a maroon dye, her cheeks blazing, and with one trembling hand, she shut her mouth to manually prevent it from speaking.

"You repulse me," my father said to his brother under his breath. "All you care about is money."

"You know what? When I had more money than you in Russia, it made sense that you accused me of being a capitalist pig, but now you're a just hypocrite—you're wealthier than everyone. I'm just trying to afford my wife and prepare a dowry for Larry."

"You didn't have to do it with my daughter!" my father grumbled. "You knew how we felt."

"All of you are always feeling, feeling, *feeling* things! When are you not feeling something, and not getting offended?" Yakov yelled back. "Have you asked Bella how she feels?" He downed another glass of vodka and, turning a snickering smile at Eddie, switched to English. "See vhat it like in Russian families, always fighting, always not happy wiz somesing."

Eddie could only nod without comprehending.

"Our daughter"—my mother now addressed Eddie in English—"was trained in Russian Conservatory since she was little girl, it impossible to get into like your Juliyard, but she got in and she was *ochen, ochen* talented. What a voice she had, what a *golos*! And now to do zis, it is so embarrassing!"

The crowd on the dance floor dispersed as soon as the first course of appetizers arrived and "Ochi Chyornye" broke from the instruments. Bella's lips parted and unleashed a piercing cry in her perfect coloratura voice that took the sensuality out of the song, replacing it with a doleful, funereal dirge that made everyone want to weep.

Yakov turned his fury on my mother, as though *she* controlled Bella's vocal cords. "This is the result of your high and mighty attitude, Sonya," he yelled in Russian. "I hire your daughter to sing disco and she delivers operatic arias fit for Bizet's *Carmen*! How can anyone dance to that singing—the whole dance floor has collapsed into a depression!"

"What—you thought you'd hire *our* daughter and tell her what to do?" My father cackled, obviously luxuriating in his child's iron will.

Suddenly hysterical laughter erupted from our table. Everyone looked around in confusion as the laughter rose into the ceiling and mixed with Bella's quavering voice. It was Igor.

"What's so funny, Igoryek?" my mother asked.

"Nothing, nothing, ha, ha, ha—" Igor kept on, his laughter subsiding and then resuming again with greater force.

"Are you laughing at me?" Yakov lashed out, feeling inexplicably insecure.

"No, no, at my wife, I mean not at my wife, but at myself! All those nights she was merely practicing—meeting band mates to prepare for this, for you!" He pointed a finger at Yakov as though the latter was a roach. "She wasn't cheating on me! She doesn't have a caravan of lovers!"

"A caravan of lovers." Yakov burst into a billowing laugh. "Bella, a caravan of lovers! Haven't you understood your wife yet? When a woman is as beautiful as she is, she no longer cares about men. They become mere instruments in her rise to near-godliness. Don't you see—she has one mode of existence: self-adulation. All she cares about is the stage—any stage will do—but a stage it has to be nevertheless. You're a very lucky man, Igor."

"What a stupid analysis of my daughter!" my mother retorted in an injured voice. But my mother's pain was drowned out by the general feeling of goodwill as every person, except Eddie, realized that Bella was not having an affair, and this collective epiphany seemed to suffuse our Bella in a warm, celestial glow (the dry steam that periodically sputtered from the ceiling confirmed one's sense that Bella was literally of the divine).

Eddie had stoically withstood what seemed like an eternity of Russian, without once demanding a translation, and I decided that it was a propitious moment to switch languages.

"Bella has always dreamed of the stage; she even went to New York," I began.

"Are you crazy," Grandmother interrupted in Russian, "are you telling him about her *mishugas*! And don't you dare speak of our suspicions—he's a stranger—why does he need to know anything?"

"Because it's rude," I cried, "because you don't like it when everyone speaks in English, because he's my fiancé." Then I delivered the final blow. "He's going to be my husband!"

"Whose husband?" Grandmother reeled from the table as if preparing to fall backward from her chair. "I don't understand a word you're saying!"

I took Eddie's ring from my purse and placed it on my fourth finger.

"Now zhat's a ring to fist your eyes on!" Yakov observed snidely.

"What's going on?" Eddie asked. "Don't they know we're engaged?"

"Sure, we knew zhat you two engaged. We're very happy for you," my mother said, covering for me.

"Let us make toast," my father joined her, raising his glass, "to our future son-law—may you two be happy, healthsy and wealthsy!" Vodka was instantly poured into every glass and a collective smile invaded the table like an enemy brigade, keeping each mouth taut and wide, except for one.

"Oy, *vey iz mir,* what to do?" Grandmother stammered, parading her frown and yet reluctantly raising her glass. "*Bozhenka,* I don't know if my heart is strong enough to endure more suffering. *Bozhenka,* help me, DON'T LET MY HEART GIVE OUT!"

"What's your grandmother saying?" Eddie asked.

"Oh, she's suffering from indigestion," I told him.

Yakov gripped his stomach and chest with both hands as laughter was bubbling up his wide neck and out his nostrils. In driblets, Russian sputtered out. "Do you—you—you mean to tell me—ha, ha, ha—that your daughter—oh, this is hilarious—is marrying again?"

"Not again, for the first time," my mother upbraided him.

"Right, what's the difference? More invitations, Sonichka, huh, ha, ha, you're going to pay for more invitations! And how much money did you lose on that deposit at the Drake?"

"What's your uncle talking about?" Eddie asked.

Everyone ignored him.

"More vodka—waiter, more vodka," Yakov cackled. "We really need to celebrate—fill the whole room with vodka! And the flowers, Sonichka, make sure you get French—not Spanish, not Chilean, not African, but French orchids!"

"Why is your uncle laughing?" Eddie tried again.

"Oh, he just found out that we're engaged," I said.

"And that's funny because?"

"In my family, anything can be funny with the right amount of vodka," I said petulantly.

"Oh, he doesn't know about the recent one—no, no, I won't say his name," Yakov kept on (fortunately in Russian). "God, women are vicious, they're all *blyadi*! You hear that, Larry, don't get married, all women are *blyadi*!"

"Keep beating your chest, Yakov, but we all know your balls are firmly lodged in your wife's metal grip." My mother stared at him as she spoke, her mouth curving into a strained lethal smile, then she added, "If I hear you insult my daughters again, I'll make sure your discotheque fails! And this time Semyon won't bail you out!"

"Sonichka, *dorogaya*," my father jumped in, "I apologize to you—but my brother has abysmal manners."

"Yes, I forgot you're all very well-mannered aristocrats," Yakov spat. But just when we thought this was a new battle cry, he retreated by focusing on my poor confounded Eddie, and in English said, "Look Andy!"

"Eddie—my name is Eddie."

"Zese people you marrying—zey aristocrats—you Americans don't chave aristocrats, but ve Russians vere raized on zem. Tolstoy and Chekhov really gots to us bones. So zey—Sonichka, your future mozer-in-law, she particularry imagines herself high in sky."

"Yakov, have you lost year head?" my father exclaimed.

"Have you forgotten," my mother joined in, "that Semeyon and I own a percentage of this restaurant. Try to remember that the next time you speak!"

"How could I forget when you never cease to remind me, Sonichka!"

"Shut up, Yakov," my father said, then turned to my mother. "We promised each other that it would belong to him, that we're giving him the money freely, that we're doing a good deed."

"We had an excellent saying about good deeds in Russia"—my mother pointed at our Bella on the stage—"only do a good deed if you want a bucket of shit dumped on your head!"

"I'm sorry, Sonya, for my rude behavior. I sincerely apologize—it was just my bad nerves talking," Yakov announced at last, full of false contrition and fuming with indignant pride, possibly because Katya had pinched him under the table.

Not understanding a word, Eddie stood up, raised a glass of vodka and said, "I just want you all to know that I will try in every way to make Emma very happy, and if you wish it, I will convert to Judaism." He looked with such astounding conviction at each of my family members that they momentarily forgot themselves and refocused their energy on him.

"To our Lenochka, everyone raise your glasses," my father said. "I mean to vhat he just call you—to our Emma!"

"To Lena," Igor stated in his usual drone.

"Eeema? Who's Eeema?" my grandmother echoed mockingly, and downed her shot. "What did he just say?"

"He's offering to convert to Judaism," my mother answered in Russian, taking a cautious sip of vodka.

"Bold fellow," Yakov noted, gulping one shot after another, ending up possibly at four consecutive shots. "I think we make him nervous—we should speak in English more," he added, continuing to speak in Russian.

"Lena says you investment banker." My father began a KGB-style investigation.

"Yes, I work for Norton Bank."

"You worked wiz Alex, isn't zhat correct?" Yakov instantly picked up on it.

"Yes," Eddie said, looking around the table.

"Vhat did you think of him?" my father went on.

"We didn't really spend that much time together," said Eddie.

"We hear he is genius," Yakov inserted for strategic purposes.

"Eddie fired him," I declared, somewhat recklessly.

"Fired! Fired," my mother cried out, "we did not know zhat— he told us somesing else."

"What did you fire him for?" Igor uncharacteristically joined in.

"Let's just say Alex lacked an understanding of corporate mores—better stated, social mores—"

"Not better stated for us," my mother said with a laugh, "what 'mores' mean?"

"What's accepted or expected of you in a certain environment—sometimes it can mean morals, but in this case it's more like rules, social rules."

"You mean he didn't follow your rules?" my father asked, warding off an incredulous laugh.

"He lectured the client on his lack of understanding of basic algebra, and then during this same meeting went off on what a terrible vocabulary Americans have—in front of the client—"

My whole family broke into a roaring laugh.

"That sound just like his mozer," my mother muttered through laughter, "they think they're ze smartest people in ze world."

"Yes, well," Eddie returned with a conscious smile, "I thought it was hilarious. The client didn't think it was so funny, though."

"Well, it true, isn't it?" my father suddenly put in, his face reddening. "Buziness types don't have any basic understanding of math. Alex spoke trus."

"I agree with you, Mr. Kabelmacher. But if you want to be part of the business world, you have to play the game—understand the politics."

"In Russia, vhen I was at university—did Lena tell you I vas professor of mathematics at Moscow State University, Eddie? Anyvays, at my university, we always spoke ze trus," my father exclaimed. "If you were idiot, you were told you were idiot. You needed real knowledge to speak. Here when you speak to idiot, you have to figure out if he has lots of money and if he does, you chave to smile and leek his balls! No trus here, all about money."

"You're right, Semeyon," my mother continued arguing, this time in English for Eddie's benefit. "We did speak trus—I mean truth—only little problem vas zhat truth-tellers were shot on spot or put in gulags. It vas a very honest country!" my mother announced with her customary panache and stood up from the table. "Vould anyone like more Salat Olivye?"

"You exaggerate as always and twist my words!" my father exclaimed, exasperated. "You know zhat I vas not talking about political freedom. I vas talking about American corporate stupidity." He paused, examining his wife's expression. "And yes, please I vould like more Salat Olivye!"

Like Alex, my father believed that he too struggled against corporate imbecility. His exact title, technical senior vice president, said it all: the King of Nerddom! He pored over formulas, oversaw brilliant minions from MIT, Cal Tech, and Berkeley, and together they churned out results only to watch them get pulverized in meetings, where the bottom line dictated every decision. Truth was as elusive in America, my father often argued to the dismay of my mother, as it was in Russia. He felt that the business world lacked intellectual broadness and sensitivity, and now it seemed I had plucked someone from its very core and presented him before Father's throne. That Eddie was not Jewish did not distress my father nearly as much as the fact that Eddie symbolized my father's adversaries—the Ivy-League-MBA-wielding, summarize-it-for-me-in-four-words, barely-out-of-diapers, ladder-climbing corruptors of mathematical truths. Nor had my father reconciled himself to the strange American custom of *not* offering his opinion on everything; while he restrained himself at meetings out of a remote understanding that it might get him fired, he suffered from implacable urges to yell and the nervous tremor would assail his right leg. For, like Alex, he considered himself a superior intellect, the brain that could seize all the other brains and squash them with its proverbial pinky.

"I apologize," my mother said, "for my husband view. I love America, I very grateful to zhis country for opening its arms to us."

"Vhat I can't criticize—if I criticize, point out flaws, zhen I become ingrate?" my father exclaimed.

"Oh please—you fill up viz nostalgia for Russia every day," my mother lamented.

"Zhere's no freedom for man. I can't even watch Russia TV in peace," my father said.

"There's no justice in zhe world. How quickly people forget! How quickly people forget zhe truth! You speak of truth, Semeyon, but you live in fantasy. You remember nozhing about our suffering, nozhing about our children's suffering. I still remember—everyzing!" My mother spoke with quiet menace. Her face had become so red and swollen that I feared flames would break out along her hairline. She opened her mouth to say more but only the words "*mudila, ti mudila*" escaped her lips like a whistling steam.

A thick impenetrable silence settled over the table.

"But that's just it, Mrs. Kabelmacher, I mean Soniya," Eddie stepped in to help reseal the wound now openly festering between my parents. "Alex will be great in a university setting."

"I don't believe a word he's saying," my mother announced in Russian.

"I don't believe him at all," Grandmother backed her up with urgency.

"I haven't been completely straight with you, Sonya, or you, Emma," Eddie said, as if by some miracle of facial tics, he had understood them both.

The table shut down, its synapses, blood vessels, extremities frozen, only the multifarious eyes popped out and landed on him. Eddie scanned my clan without fear, and then he spoke. "I'll tell you this because you should know the truth. We hired Alex because of his fluency in Russian and rather impressive banking credentials. We were in the middle of a deal with a Russian company and we needed someone to navigate between the two cultures. But Alex hated being the 'middleman'—he felt that he had basically become a 'lowly translator' and that Norton wasn't properly utilizing him for his math and econ skills.

"He complained to my boss, Grant, that he was being treated like a 'nothing' during meetings. Alex took notes, translated documents, and sometimes was allowed to be present during critical transactions, but for the most part he was told to keep silent. Then one day Grant relented and gave him more responsibility. Alex was allowed to sit in and participate in the complex merger between this Russian monolith and an American oil company.

During a break in the proceeding, Alex offered his 'financial' opinion to the Russian CEO, in Russian, without giving a single thought to all the work that went into nurturing our clients' relationship. According to Alex, he advised the CEO against a merger that Norton had spent a year putting together."

"No wonder he didn't tell anyone the truth!" I said. "So that's why you fired him?

"I should have fired him then, but I didn't. Because . . ." Eddie paused and looked at me, his blue eyes darkening, making the room vanish. We were the only ones left in some black void. "I was waiting for you to come back to me. She'll come tonight, I told myself, or the next night and say, 'I left Alex; I left Alex for you.' I thought, I'll cover for Alex if I have to—my boss thought the deal fell through on its own. But every day that you didn't come to me, every day that you stayed with him—I realized that I was losing. I realized that I could only be magnanimous if I had you. When Eric told me, 'Did you know, Beltrafio, that Alex is engaged to some Russian girl?' I was done." Eddie halted, his eyes strained, his expression drained of its habitual ease.

"That's when I told Grant, and Alex was fired that same day." He bowed his head for an imperceptible instant, then looked up at me. "I'm sorry, Emma. He couldn't stay if I had lost you."

How I wanted to scream, *because you knew you and I belong to each other*, but instead I simply grabbed hold of his hand. The feeling remained inside, beating under my tongue.

"So you sent Alex back to Chicago," my mother noted cleverly, "vhere you knew he vould lose zhis game."

"So it vas a duel!" my father said, in a mocking tone, with just a hint of nostalgia. "A modern-day duel, like Pushkin—only today zhere are no bullets, just dollars!"

"Yes it's true: I knew he couldn't stay in New York if he didn't have the job at Norton," Eddie said. "But I wasn't as Machiavellian as you're implying, Mr. Kabelmacher."

"Ah, Machiavelli, a genius! I very impressed, an American who knows a little philosophy!" my father interrupted, then added, "Money is veapon nowadays."

"What are you talking about Semeyon, zhis is about love," my mother cried.

"Love and money!" my father noted, grinning at Eddie.

Eddie's gaze was directed only at me: "I knew that Emma would then have to decide—that you would have to decide and when you didn't, when you didn't go to Chicago with him . . ."

"But how did you know that?" I asked.

"I knew his flight, we booked it for him, part of his severance pay was that we paid for his flight. I knew you were still in New York, I was waiting—"

"I came that night—that same night—"

"I waited."

"And the girl?"

"Bait. To torment you."

I smiled strangely to myself, and thought, ah, the torture instruments of love.

"You were that aware?" I said with sudden terror.

"I was *that* in love," he said simply, his eyes watering. "And I had a glimmer of hope—that maybe, just maybe, you were in love with me." No one existed in that moment. I forgot that my parents, my grandmother, my whole family were in the room, listening to us. I brought his face close to mine and kissed his quivering mouth, kissed him with dread and urgency and hunger.

"I see, Eddie, I see: you play to win," my mother broke in.

Yakov suddenly turned to me, saying in Russian, "Wouldn't he love to know that you just broke up with Alex—that you'd been playing *him* all this time? When was the breakup—only a month, two months ago?" He stared at Eddie with the intention of somehow secretly intimating the truth to him.

"Well, I like him—he's a romantic!" my mother announced in Russian, and suddenly the whole table nodded. Eddie's bold confession, his directness, his tormented feelings for me connected to their belief that *they* possessed these qualities, and tapped into their vanity like heroin that hooked and unwound them. Eddie reminded them of themselves in Russia, a man of romance willing to sully his bare hands for that ineffable prize—a woman—like

Pushkin who had idiotically challenged a man to a duel and died for his love. They drifted into memories when they were young, wild, easily bruised, and irrefutably beautiful. And something within them seemed to alter their perception of him, to soften their collective scrutinizing gaze.

My father appeared to forgive Eddie for being purely a "businessman," and my mother's cheeks flushed in a warm glow of admiration. When Igor finished translating to Grandmother, she gave Eddie that prestigious mark of her guarded approval, "A real man, that's what I was afraid of."

"Who's a real man?" Bella's voice pierced through our rumination, and her beautiful figure materialized behind the table like a phantom that's been converted to real mass. Bella plopped down next me, heaving, perspiring, her chest rising and falling, her face exquisitely bent on Eddie.

"Why, it must be you!" she exclaimed, laughing in English, "you must be the real man!"

Eddie squeezed her hand and said warmly, "No, I'm just the hapless American who's dating your sister."

"You've only begun and already you're feeling 'hapless'—just wait till you get married!"

"Ah finally a family member who knows we're engaged," Eddie exclaimed with a jovial laugh.

"I'm beyond happy for you guys but I won't lie to you, Eddie: our family loves to criticize everyone, and Americans in particular, and it goes without saying that we don't ever tell Americans what we think about them."

"Oh, I'm sure I'm failing miserably! My only comfort is that I'm aware of it."

"Well then you're unique in my book—I mean for an American!" She laughed warmly, and Eddie's smile widened further than I had ever seen it, but then again Bella always had that effect on men, a kind of ethereal, otherworldly power to put them in a trance.

"You have a beautiful voice," Eddie said.

"Thank you." Bella bowed her head slightly, glancing at me. "My sister does too, only she's shy."

"Really, I haven't noticed!" He raised his brows, and the three of us burst into laughter.

"Vhat do you sink you're doing up zere?" Yakov yelled at Bella. "Disco, disco, disco—zhat's vhat I hired you for."

"I promise, Uncle," Bella murmured, taking a long drink of water, "that after this number, I'll stick strictly to ABBA and the Village People."

And with that, Bella walked to the stage and ascended with the aplomb of a monarch, lifting her dress as though it were weighed down by a heavy velvet train adorned in rare jewels. She glanced at me from the stage, and the wink in her left eye alerted me to her next move.

While taking a class on film noir, Bella had fallen in love with Rita Hayworth. She must have seen *Gilda* a hundred times, replaying the scene where Hayworth sings "Put the Blame on Mame" and strips only her gloves, her ethereal chalk body spilling from the strapless dress. Bella imagined herself as Gilda, as Rita Hayworth, endowed with *her* beauty and cursed with *her* wretched luck in love. Or perhaps she envisioned herself as Rita's avenger, destroying men on her behalf.

The instruments strummed together and rocked her from side to side. Her voice flowed like white silk, folding in dulcet undulations across the ceiling dome. Inside my head words broke from notes and hung in space like cryptic, solitary black marks that penetrated my thin, sentient skin: *amado mio, love me forever, and let forever begin tonight . . .*

When the song came to its long pause to give way to the instrumentals, Bella pulled away from the microphone and burst into a tremulous dance. The slit on her dress parted to reveal a long shapely leg punctuated by a scarlet heel. The dance floor remained empty. All eyes were rapt on Bella. Her voice, like a mystical incantation, fell over the room, at once soothing and disturbing, healing wounds and then opening them up again. And I felt it too—my sister's voice filling my lungs with air, clarity, with her bounteous courage—how I longed to sing! I jumped from the chair and leapt onto the barren floor, and the words cascaded from my mouth in slow watery cadences, swelling into one consuming, indecipherable feeling: *amado mio, love me forever, and let forever begin tonight.* With eyes closed, I saw us from a distance: two separate figures moving like reflections of each other on two separate stages, with only their childlike wails intersecting and tethering their hearts. When I looked up, she was smiling at me in her strange beguiling way—in gratitude, I thought.

Although the audience didn't seem to be familiar with the song, they clapped wildly for us—Bravo, Bravo, they screamed, Brilliant, Incredible, Magnificent, or was it, Bella, Bella, they screamed, Gilda, *our* Gilda!

When I collapsed on my chair, Eddie ran a single finger along my wet neck. I caught Grandmother's eyes upon him, but whether it was because he meant to defy her or he simply didn't see, Eddie now circled my moist skin in long sensual strokes.

"You were both wonderful, just wonderful!" my mother murmured in Russian, her eyes darting from Eddie's fingers to me to Bella, "I've never seen a restaurant in such ecstasy—"

"I want to sing on stage like mommy and aunt Lena," Sirofima announced in Russian.

"You see where these things lead," Grandmother moaned.

"And why shouldn't she pursue the stage—if you want to become an actress, my darling, you're welcome to," Bella said.

"We'll see how generous you are in twenty years," Grandmother warned.

"Are you going to eat with us?" my mother said, looking cryptically at Bella.

"No, I'm going back to the stage. What did you think, Uncle, can I sing it again?"

"Only if you wear a shorter dress!" Yakov giggled.

Igor slammed his hand against the table and shouted, "Enough, you're not doing this anymore. Your grandmother is right, this is whoring. I have to put my foot down sometime." But his idealized foot was in the air, levitating from joy; still, a man had to maintain his image.

"My darling husband, rest assured that a little whoring never hurt any marriage," Bella purred, and hurried off. This time she obeyed Yakov; she sang the perennial upbeat ballad of vengeance against the male race: "I Will Survive." In seconds, women of all ages and sizes stormed the dance floor like paratroopers descending, marching, shaking, jumping at the ecstatic outpouring of angry memories. They hailed Bella as their new fair heroine. My mother, grandmother, and I, and even Sirofima, instantly succumbed to their feverish spell. The men joined the crowd as well, but they were static wooden soldiers from the *Nutcracker*, impervious to our unifying effervescence. Eddie danced among us, invisible at first. But then with his habitual audacity, he barreled toward my grandmother. He bowed to her and took her hand in his. She blushed but still managed to lead him in a tango waltz to "I Will Survive." So peculiar and odd did they look that the women made room for them in the center of the dance floor. My mother and I laughed, but as the song progressed the eccentric couple remained awkwardly intact, smiling periodically at each other, and then looking away in bursts of self-satisfied introspection, as though they had each done their part in the upkeep of peace. It was impossible to enjoy the song now; their strangeness seemed to radiate from them and afflict our feet, making us linger and stumble. The muscles in my face ached from the strain of watching them. Eddie felt it was necessary, he told me later that night, to make an overture to Grandmother, to intimate to her that he was not afraid. But to no avail. "A real charmer," she said in Russian after he had taken leave of her. "I see how he seduced you. But that doesn't change the facts: he is not a Jew, he knows nothing about you—about us. You are ruining your life!"

Stalin Had Been to My Grandmother's House

Eddie was granted the downstairs couch as a matter of principle, as the moral foundation upon which the family's stringent boyfriend-to-fiancé rulebook resided. But Grandma had her own KGB-esque twist: despite the existence of two guestrooms upstairs, despite the basement where three couches coalesced into a triple leather threat, despite the formal living room where a post-modern triangular purple sofa resembling a spaceship could shield him from passersby, Grandmother threw my Eddie to the wolves of the family room: to be observed, in leisure, from every conceivable angle in the house, because she believed that privacy and that scourge of all unplanned pregnancies—proximity—led to sex. When I protested for the fiftieth time that I was no longer a virgin, Grandmother slathered me in her favorite balm. "You may do whatever craziness you like in New York, but in my house, you'll be turned back into a virgin!" Like partially-boiled lobsters, Eddie and I clung to each other as we crawled into the dark, empty kitchen.

"How long had you kept me a secret?" he asked in a whisper.

"A long time."

"I meant what I said tonight—I'll convert if you want me to—if that's your family's price for leaving you in peace."

"You're very smart, Ignatius, did any girl ever tell you that?"

He grinned slyly. "Nah, I always liked to play dumb—dumb banker, dumb jock—there's only one woman brilliant enough to see through my act—"

"Your mother?"

He laughed.

"But seriously, think of your mother! I can't imagine what she'd do—to what lengths she'd go to—to ruin us . . . would she threaten to hang herself?"

"Never. I assure you there's not a single melodramatic bone in my mother's cold body—florid language, yes, but no real, satisfying drama."

"Does your mother even know we're engaged?"

"Of course she knows. And do you know what she wants? That we get married in a church, that a priest officiates, and that you baptize our children."

"Don't you care that you'd be stripped of your religion, your heritage, that she'd be horrified at the sight of a rabbi?"

"Has it ever occurred to you that maybe I want to jump ship?"

"That won't be enough for *my* parents—you still won't convince them, especially not my grandmother."

"What if I'm not doing it to convince them—what if I'm doing this to—"

"These are not good reasons to convert!"

"No, but loving you is," he said, catching hold of my hands. I sank into his embrace and buried my face in his shoulder.

"You don't have to do this, Eddie, you don't have to convert. I love you as you are. And I want us to be free—of them. To live as *we* want."

"I know, but you're close to your family, your grandmother—you've always told me that. And I don't want you to lose them."

"Oh, Eddie, why does everything have to be so difficult? There's something I need to tell you. I must. I must tell you this thing, this one thing, before we do anything else."

"Whatever it is, banish it from your head. You don't have any score to settle with me: your past is your past. Now that I've met your family, I feel good, secure. I know who I'm dealing with, and I can handle it. I—*we*—can handle whatever comes our way."

"Yes, yes, we are magnificent together!"

We kissed softly at first but I pressed into him, kissing him harder, deeper, our tongues intertwining in the warmth of intimacy. He lifted me and wrapped my legs around his torso and carried me in the darkness. He sat me down on the marble of our kitchen island, beneath suspended pots and pans, and we tore into each other's clothes, ripping them and piecing them back together, fear of Grandmother creeping up our backs. Windows spliced by blinds, lamplight peering from the street, pots and pans clanging overhead, black leaves rustling in disapproval, the ceiling alive with sounds—all ghosts growling from the shadows, watching, reporting on us to some higher entity. We could hear my mother fussing in the bathroom, my father snoring, Bella and Igor arguing upstairs, our pulses spiking, our fingers gaining momentum, autonomy, nerve. He untied my sweatpants with such vigor I heard a tear, and then they dropped to my ankles. He spread my legs across the cold granite counter.

"Are you crazy? If Grandma catches us, it'll be death!" I said without releasing my hold of his buttocks.

"How about we do it in the bathroom, for old times' sake?" He laughed as he unbuttoned his jeans.

"No, no, no—" came out of my mouth as I pulled him closer in. "Uhhhh . . ."

"All right, whatever you want." I submitted, "I'll do it wherever, however you want—"

"Uhhh . . . ahhhh."

"Was that you?" he blurted, jumping an entire foot away from me and zipping up his jeans.

"I thought that was you!" I whispered.

"*Oy, gevalt,* how my legs hurt," someone moaned in Russian and I felt her, then I saw her. Grandmother's voluptuous figure was hunched over the kitchen table.

"Babushka?" I breathed. My sweat pants were on the floor, my ripped shirt was hanging from a frying pan, and carefully, stealthily, I reached for it like a woman in an advanced Tai Chi class, hoping not to disturb the balance of the universe and cause unnecessary banging between Grandmother's frying pan and my mother's wok. As I squeezed my breasts into my T-shirt, I prayed to the Lord for a miracle—that Grandmother's head be dunked in viscous tar and cause her fleeting amnesia.

"Babushka, what are you doing up so late?" I said, trying to rally my own indignation, an almost impossible feat while you're still palpably horny.

Fortunately, Grandmother didn't remember what palpably horny looked like.

"Couldn't sleep—what are *you* doing?" she replied in the singular tense, pretending she couldn't see Eddie.

"Eddie and I were just about to have tea—"

"Oh, Eddie is here," she said with mock surprise. "Well, I'll have some too—turn the light on already! Nothing's better for insomnia than a strong cup of tea."

"Perhaps I should go—I mean to sleep," Eddie offered, awkwardly readjusting himself.

"No," Grandmother said, as though she had understood him, "tell him to stay—I want to speak to him."

"Did you see us?" I asked her in Russian, and pulled all the light switches on simultaneously.

"See what?" she exclaimed, her eyes shrinking from the influx of light. "That my granddaughter has no shame—in her parents' house, of all places? But you say I'm not modern so I'll keep my big mouth shut." She paused for a second. "Are you living some sort of movie fantasy here? Doing it on a kitchen counter like they do in pornography?"

"What's your grandmother saying?" Eddie asked.

"Only telling me what she wants in her tea."

"I thought I heard something about sex?"

"You heard 'sachar,' which means sugar and sounds a lot like 'sex.'"

"Oh," he mumbled with obvious distrust.

"I told him you like sugar in your tea," I informed her.

"You're finally getting smarter"—she offered the compliment as if it were an unsalted omelet—"but when are you going to get real smart and see people beyond your crazy desires?"

"Tell me, tell me then what should I see?" I asked without wanting to know.

"Strength, real strength! Is he strong enough for you? That's the question you should ask yourself. For married life is made of ugliness too. What would happen if he found out what lies you're capable of—does he know about Alex?"

"What are you saying, Grandma, that I should tell him the truth?"

"God forbid," she said, "no, no, I've never been an advocate of airing a woman's secrets to a man. But here's the question—can he handle a lifetime of you—of us—of all this?" She spread her arms and motioned at the black window as if it alone contained all our unplumbed depths.

"Do you think my father has handled my mother?" I asked.

"Do they have a happy marriage?" she countered.

The kettle whistled on the stove and I poured scalding water into our brass teapot over Russian Caravan leaves. Grandmother and I sipped our hot brown liquids from tall glasses (never mugs for the rims were always too thick, too uncouth for the nuanced pleasure of drinking tea). And in the silence she left me, I imbibed doubts with each scalding sip, tasting the acidity—the ugliness—surfacing between us. I didn't dare look at Eddie, knowing that his shirt was crooked, the top three buttons and belt buckle were undone. But he couldn't fix himself because from the corner of her right eye, Grandmother was watching him.

"My grandmother wants to tell you about Stalin," I improvised, turning to him with a forced smile. If there was one thing that Stalin was good for nowadays, it was a glitch in the conversation.

"I'd love to learn more about Stalin," Eddie joined in, happy for a tidbit of English.

"Eddie says he is really interested in hearing about your life under Stalin," I told Grandmother.

"Oh, that, what can I say about Stalin that hasn't already been said," Grandmother muttered, feigning indifference, but I could see her brightening.

"He's really fascinated, Grandmother," I egged her on.

"Well, it's nothing to be fascinated by!" she began.

She settled more comfortably into her chair, took another gulp of tea, and began to speak. And I began my juggling act—of translation—throwing one language up and then another, twirling them up in the air, scavenging my mind for synonyms, idioms, roots, multifarious meanings, until sentences landed on my tongue and I was able to weave a story, hoping to foment a friendship between Grandmother and Eddie, the two most important people in my life.

"We were people just like anyone else and Stalin was loved by us all. No one knew what he was doing to the people. Oh, the things I saw as a young girl, the things I witnessed . . . I was only eight years old when the insanity started—when they started taking people away."

Every time she told this story, no matter what year, what month, what hour, she would stop and let the tears swim in her eyes.

"*Kollektivizatsiya*—have you heard of it, Eddik?" Grandmother asked, but she didn't wait for his answer. No matter what you once were, you were turned into a peasant. And we were starving—that's what equality meant—starvation. No one was better than anyone else, all starving equally—that was Mother Russia.

"It was 1928 when my father was taken away. I never saw him again—men were being arrested left and right, carted off like hens in cages to their slaughter. No one knew who had ratted on him. Rats everywhere in those years.

"We were *kulaki*—we owned land, lots of it, and five buildings, an entire block. But Stalin, that thief, stole everything. The NKVD moved seven families into our house, and forced us, the owners, to live in the upstairs attic, while the peasants, who used to work our lands, now roosted in our palatial bedrooms, slept on our silk sheets, and ate at our oak dining table under our gold chandelier. Have you heard of *The Three Bears*, Eddik, that was us! The attic had been abandoned, cold, moldy, no heat, nowhere to sleep, except a few piss-stained old mattresses and one bathroom for the nine of us. Because there weren't enough mattresses, the men slept on the cold cement floor. Russia taught you lessons the way no parent ever can—Stalin was our father, our mother, the whip at our backs teaching us the meaning of *za-im panyimaniye.*" I translated the phrase in my head: a co-understanding, a so-called mutual regard.

"Now our masters were our peasants. They couldn't stand the fact that not only were we rich but we were Jews. Like acid on an old wound. People thought Jews were slimy merchants but we were—*we*"—she pointed at her heart—"we were aristocrats, Jewish blue bloods with fancy china and diamonds, and emeralds the likes of which you've never seen. As a child I wore dresses made from real lamb's wool—well, everyone in school stared at me with envy."

I tried to translate to Eddie in a hurry but Grandmother waited patiently, letting me know that she wants him to learn, to understand us.

Then she went on, "I don't remember the exact year, maybe it was 1931, I was just a child when the purges started. Stalin was arresting everyone, informants lived inside your walls, under your bed, in your toilet bowl staring up your asshole. Our house was filled with them—cockroaches crawling out of every corner. Each family assumed that only their case was unjust, only their son or husband or father was mistakenly arrested while everyone else was guilty. They didn't spare the women either. Eyes burned into each other's backs, everyone thinking—should I report him?

"In those days, everyone had special government stamps—you couldn't get food otherwise at the market. *Ti golodal.* But my grandmother had sewn gold into the underlining of our mattress for an unforeseen emergency, and against Stalin's decree, kept sugar and flour in our kitchen cabinets. One of the peasants, a fat drunk who could barely function, saw Grandmother open the cabinet, and the next minute, the NKVD were swarming our place; all our trunks and drawers were turned over, clothes and books strewn on the floor and German shepherds barking at us. It was easy to find the flour and sugar—that drunk, that miserable *alkogolik* pointed at the cabinet.

"'How do you have flour and sugar?' the NKVD agent asked us, 'no one has anything—everyone is starving—where are you getting your food, your sneaky Yids—you subversive capitalist swine!' They arrested everyone—my grandfather, Aaron, and grandmother, Aksaniya, my aunt Brina with her three-week old infant and her husband, Issak, my uncle Arkady, my aunt Irma, their fifteen-year-old daughter, Anya, and my mother, my mother Sonya. I was the only one not arrested—I was only eight. The women started screaming, protesting—you can't leave a child alone in the house, but the NKVD weren't human—they were vultures feeding on the flesh of the living. They left me alone in the house, with no food, and they took the flour and the sugar. The peasants living in our bedrooms didn't care either—no one was fully human then. The neighbors would pass me on the stairs, knowing I was alone, only a child, and not utter a word, not one kind word. *Kakaya nespravedlivost!*

"A few days later, they let my mother come home to me. My grandfather and Issak were now sitting in a Moscow jail.

"Together Mother and I sat in our attic and tried not think about food. Oh, how little I was back then . . . how time flies, *Lenochka moya dorogaya, zachem govorit*? I still remember the unbearable pain of hunger, my gut stuck to my back, I was a sheet. And yet I bore it, we all did, like a knife cutting your flesh out but you keep living, you keep thinking, Let me die, *Bozhenka*, I want to die, but God says live and so you do. *Prosti menya*." Grandmother put her palms together and looked up at the ceiling.

"Then one day Grandmother Aksaniya sent a loaf of black bread from Moscow. Oh, how the bread gladdened my mother's heart! 'We will eat again, my dearest *dochenka*,' Mother cried, 'we will survive.' It was as if the hunger had caused her blindness, as if she couldn't see it or smell it: the bread was covered in green festering mold. 'Don't think about it,' she said as she cut it up into little pieces; she even saved extra slices for Brina and Grandmother. We split one piece per day and ate crumbs for breakfast, lunch, and dinner. Worse than not eating at all, eating like that.

"My mother's face turned bluish-gray, her throat swelled, her fever rose. Three days after that she could barely walk or breathe. She only left the bed to go to the bathroom—she was coughing constantly and was in terrible pain. She told me to stay away from her—she was afraid she was contagious. 'Just give me a little more bread,' she'd say and I'd feed her more and more crumbs, eating less myself. Turned out she had diphtheria: it was the bread that killed my mother—the same bread I ate. She died a few days later. But I didn't know what death meant—worse than hunger to lose your mother. I kept talking to her, putting wet towels on her forehead. Thought she was asleep. By the time aunt Brina came home, I had lived on that bread and water for more than a week with my dead mother lying next to me. I was an orphan at eight."

Grandmother had been telling me this story since I was a child, but every rendering revealed new details that soaked into my memory, coloring and conflating my past with her own. As I translated for Eddie, I felt myself deposited into her world, reliving her life—in English.

I wasn't cohesive and suddenly it didn't seem to matter if he understood me. I watched him scrape at the walls of my language, groping in solitude for similar-sounding words, for hints in our gestures and expressions, wanting desperately to know but staying put—at our mercy. And at once I was assailed with an image of my grandmother's muteness. She existed in a vacuum of knowledge, inside the anger that billowed on her face and whipped us like a torrential gale, but was never able to break down the barricade: oh, that wretched English—unpronounceable, inconsistent, unpredictable, obstinate and yet, yet—how this frustrated her—as everyone said and of course she had to agree, easier than Russian! It seemed right that the man who embodied my future should live, however temporarily, in her void.

"What a difficult life you've had!" Eddie said, looking into Grandmother's moist eyes.

"*Shto govorit*—why speak when everything under the sun has been uttered," Grandmother replied. "In America everyone thinks life gets better with time, but in Russia—you get arrested, starve, freeze in Siberia, die, and then Hitler attacks! Thank God we fled Ukraine in 1941; the whole family could've been wiped out—if not in Babi Yar, then in the concentration camps." Grandmother broke off and sighed loudly, tears fogging her eyes. Her entire being glowed like a giant lantern in the dark, blinding me to everything: the kitchen, my own thoughts, Eddie, even love itself.

"When Grisha was attacked—well, by that time, America was all I thought about." It took me a few minutes to realize that Grandmother had jumped half a lifetime forward to my own grandfather, Grisha, and the year was 1981. She mixed decades and people, Brezhnev with Stalin, Gorbachev with Khrushchev; she was perpetually lost in the maze of history, mapping incoherently the traumas of her life.

"My grandfather was attacked by the KGB," I tried quickly to translate for Eddie.

"What does your grandmother think of the new democracy?" Eddie asked timidly.

"Democracy—Shmukracy," Grandmother said, picking out the most important word. "What you think is democracy is not what Russians think is democracy. You couldn't go to the bathroom without having to bribe someone to make sure the sewage system traveled down instead of up your asshole!"

"American businessmen should be careful when investing in Russia," I translated for Eddie.

"That's true, I know people who've lost millions there—" Eddie wanted to say more but Grandmother quickly cut us off.

"In the hospital, they pretty much finished the job they started. The KGB doesn't like loose ends."

"What are you talking about?" I asked her, switching languages in an instant.

"Your grandfather—they finished him off in the hospital. Didn't you know?"

"Everyone said he died of a heart attack—you and Mom always said he died of a heart attack."

"Oh, no," Grandmother muttered ruefully, "that's what we told you children. We didn't want to scare you."

"But why—what was Grandfather involved with?"

"Oh *Bozhenka, prosti menya*, you were always the curious one, Lenochka."

With that, Grandmother began to tell a story I had never heard.

"No one knows the truth, Lenochka, that's the curse of Russia. What did the KGB have against your grandfather, that old goat, cheating on me left and right? With ugly ones especially, made him feel like a prince. But then one day he picked himself a real beauty, with breasts up to her nose. Except that she was also the wife of a KGB officer. Did that goon find out and try to kill your grandfather with a good beating and a metal knuckle in the jaw in our elevator? Maybe.

"There's another theory too, a terrible one, Yakov—that snake—said it once at dinner—no one wanted to believe it: what if he was an informant for the KGB and things got sticky? But then why kill him?

"Then of course there's your mother, and she fancied your grandfather a hero. She believed he was involved in strategic anti-Soviet activities—part of the dissident movement in Russia!"

"Wait—the Hijack Plot Affair—The Leningrad Trials—the sixteen dissidents—my grandfather?"

"Yes, that's what your mother believes. Don't look at me. She knew him better. She told your father some story about a dissident cousin, but your mother believes *your* grandfather was an operator in his own right. A big shot! He knew all of them—the pilots, Dymshits and Kuznetsov and all the others who plotted Operation Wedding. He studied Hebrew with them in the secret underground, and your mother believes he became a messenger, just like he had been in the War, passing information to Western journalists in Moscow. *Bozhe moy*, we could have all been arrested! Oh, I knew he missed the war, missed being the hero, my Grisha. He needed to do something with his life other than cheating and drinking with Russia's eternal sufferers. But to go so far—to take such risk—*uzhas*—*koshmar*—hard to imagine! And yet I could see him volunteering, mapping Moscow, passing notes on benches, while the KGB watched. The KGB would have killed him regardless; he was a walking dead man."

"But I don't understand—how would we have gotten out in that case? I mean, they didn't need us for anything then; we should have ended up *refuseniks* for years and years on end."

Grandmother's eyes glided over my face in silence as if she were balancing some weighty equation in her head. Then she uttered the following words: "I might as well tell you, this is where your mother's theory gets real crazy—even Bella herself does not know."

"What does Bella have to do with it?"

"Everything," Grandmother declared. "Do you remember how she had fallen in love with that *urod*, Nicholai, and swore that she wouldn't leave him?"

"Of course!"

"Your mother believes—*Bozhe moy, Bozhenka*—to think that we got out on account of Bella. You see, that Nicholai was a KGB infiltrator. We were certain he was sent to us to watch Grisha and his activities. The goal was to infiltrate Operation Wedding. Our whole house was tapped. Your father was terrified but what to do! None of us lived in those years, just fear—*strakh*—you can't imagine the fear! You and Bella were just children.

"When Nicholai came we knew instantly: he just didn't look like normal people, smell like them. He smelled nice . . . Oh, the gifts he brought us, the gifts alone were enough to make a grown man swoon."

Grandmother remembered with a smile. "Of course, what he hadn't counted on was Bella arrayed in all her glory. *Oy nasha krasavitsa* dancing for Lenny Avenbuch. Lenny didn't stand a chance. He fell in love and the next morning, *bah*! He was arrested for speculation, with two years in jail.

"In the KGB the more arrests you made the more money you got, the higher your status, and that Nicholai was ambitious. What delicacies he brought, and American turtlenecks and Levi's jeans for everyone. Even me—imagine me in jeans, *smeshno*! Oh, the way he strutted in his leather jacket and fine slacks the likes of which we had never seen. And Bella, no matter what we said—oh, she was so young and idealistic about love then—became so infatuated with him. Oh, she lost her virginity to him that very first night they met, and my mother theorized that it was this gift of her golden innocence that stumbled Nicholai in his plans for our Grisha, even for the rest of us.

"You were in Kiev with your father when the two officers dragged my Grisha into our elevator and beat him in the jaws with a metal knuckle. *Oy Bozhenka*, how horrible he looked, full of blood, the teeth just hanging out of his mouth." Tears fell out of her eyes, but she soldiered on. "Someone dragged his bloodied unconscious body to our doorstep but no one, no one dared to call the police. Why call the police when it's the police who commit the crimes! Your mother found him at ten in the evening— seven hours had passed—seven hours he lay unconscious, bleeding, with his broken jaws. It was a favor to grandfather from Nicholai—a warning to stop his activities. But my husband was so stubborn! He believed in the cause, our cause, the Jewish cause—how exactly did they kill him?

"A few months after Grandfather died, when no one was being let out of Moscow, our permission letter came in the mail. It was 1982 and the doors had already slammed shut. Your mother believes if it wasn't for Nicholai, we would have become *refuseniks* for years to come. That's how much Bella affected him!

"So many secrets, so many secrets between all of us," Grandmother cried, throwing her hands up in the air. "Your mother would never admit it, but I believe it was your mother who paid his wife an afternoon visit. I imagine they drank tea and nibbled on fancy chocolates your mother bought especially for her, and laughed for hours. Oh, your mother was very smart and she had such guts, your mother; my Sonichka was a warrior, never afraid of anything, *bez strashnaya*! When Nicholai came home and saw Bella's mother in his house, he understood at once what cards lay on the table—he understood the threat. Not simply to his wife, but possibly even to his career in the KGB—getting involved with a Jew *v podache*—with a traitor—would destroy his reputation, put a cloud of suspicion on his head."

"My God," I sighed, "that seems impossible."

"More impossible things have happened in that country," Grandmother muttered. I saw in her eyes that this wasn't merely a theory; Grandmother had put the pieces of a puzzle together, she had been putting it together for the last fifteen years.

"Does Bella know or suspect?"

"Of course not, *ni v koyem sluchaye*," Grandmother said. "And we can never tell her. It's a terrible thing to bear for a young woman. No doubt about it: whatever she had with Nicholai made her lose faith in love altogether—in men."

"Yes." I nodded.

"But we'll never know the real truth . . . so many things we'll never know, oy *Bozhenka*," Grandmother announced with a dismissive wave of her hand. "And memory is a faulty mechanism, feeding us truths one minute, inventing lies the next. *Oy ve iz mir*, Lenochka, how my heart hurts from all these memories. There's no justice in the world, as there's no justice in one's life—only suffering—*odni stradaniya*."

The same hand suddenly grabbed mine, her old fierceness crackling in her eyes again, and she said, "In our world there were no good choices, Lenochka, people *had* to compromise themselves. But it's different for you now. You're free to make the right decision! Do you see? *Otkroy svoi glaza*!"

I turned away from her, my attention at once on Eddie. "My grandmother just told me that my grandfather was murdered by the KGB."

"How terrible—why—what did he do?" Eddie's voice wobbled, his eyelids kept closing. He appeared drained of the energy necessary to keep up with Grandmother's inexhaustible Russian tongue.

"That's just it—Grandmother isn't sure but she thinks that maybe he was involved in—"

"Don't tell him," Grandmother interrupted, "it's not safe."

"Don't be ridiculous, we're in America now," I said, but I didn't feel secure. Like Grandmother I battled an irrational fear that the KGB could rise like the undead from the Soviet-era graveyard and yank us back into their black void.

"Oh, America, we thank America! Tell Eddik we're very happy to be in America," Grandma sang and tears sprang to her eyes.

"Grandma says she's happy to be in America."

"I bet," Eddie shot back, and somehow the moment ended; the romance between my grandmother and me and our beloved tango with the past snuffed out by that one pithy line. "I bet."

"Well," Grandmother croaked, "I better go upstairs to bed before I tire you two out." She rose from her chair and smiled kindly at Eddie. And I prayed that he had made his first inroads into her heart, by simply being there, by listening, by looking into her old anguished face. He beamed his genial smile at her, and managed to belt out, "*Ochen priyatno*," and Grandmother murmured, "*Spokoynoy nochi*." Then, glancing at me with her clever, inscrutable eyes, she added as an afterthought, "I'll look terrible tomorrow with so little sleep."

Appealing to the Higher Powers, i.e., Mom and Grandma

The next morning, with my lids half-opened and my heart chirping, I flew down the staircase and into the kitchen, a sprightly kite suspended indefinitely in the sky.

"So what do you think of him—what do you think of Eddie?" I said to Mom and Grandma upon first entering the breakfast area, certain that he had won them over. The sun was blazing though the transparent cream blinds and their eyes were fixed on the turquoise placemats on the kitchen table. It was only when I stopped speaking that I noticed the tapping fingertips, the dour expressions, the pursed lips, the bunched foreheads on their practically identical faces. "Isn't he amazing—that story about Alex and the Russian businessman—unbelievable—and last night, last night, Eddie listened to you with such, such intensity—"

"Eddie's gone to the grocery store with your father—we needed vegetables," my mother said ominously.

"I see—Dad's kidnapped him?"

"Listen, Lena, I won't deny that he's a very unusual American but on this point, your grandmother and I are firm: you can't marry him."

My heart came to a standstill; the sprightly kite lay battered on the kitchen floor. No comeback, no good old-fashioned "Fuck off" came out of my mouth. I stared at them in silent disbelief. In my head, I could only lament the sorry state of our culture, our distinctly Russian lack of the American happy-go-lucky-parenting technique—of letting one's children "live out their own lives" and declaring a moratorium on one's *actual* feelings. What relief, I thought, it must be to have fake, insincere, cautious, civilized parents, those stately beings who surreptitiously jab but never offer their true opinions! Here, here, at this kitchen table, disagreements were waged like battles with tongues surpassing

AK47s. Get ready, set, shoot—*action*! I was being reprimanded, deprogrammed, morally, courageously improved.

"Marriage is serious business," my mother began diplomatically, "and your grandmother and I feel that he is *not* for us—"

"You're such a liar—you liked him!" I yelled. "That's the worst part—you liked him more than Alex, far more. Out of everyone, *you* out of everyone, I thought, would understand—"

"I've never said I didn't like him. But the moral stakes were set in place long before you brought him to this house. You knew, you knew our objections—always, and yet you insisted! Meeting him has changed nothing."

"Why is Grandmother so silent suddenly—what does she have to say?" I cried. "How long are you going to be her mouthpiece—always obeying your mother, always the perfect daughter!"

"This has nothing to do with your grandmother. This is my decision." Her voice was calm, yet firm—a terrifying ordeal for anyone but I was, after all, *her* daughter.

"Listen to me, Lena." My mother seemed to be trying a new tack, her voice weaving a string of rhythmical cadences. "I know you think you're in love, but love fades; love can survive tornadoes but not hardwired differences. How close is he to his mother? For the closer he is to his mother, the more—the more likely he'll listen to her, perhaps not now when he's so madly in love with you, but later when you have children, when the first flush of mad passion has worn off, and all that's left between you are these differences. Differences, you see, my Lenochka, can grow into thorns, then bushes, then forests you can't penetrate—these differences will tear you apart. Don't you think I want you to be happy—if only I thought you found him: your fount of happiness! But I—I and your grandmother—we see things you cannot possibly see."

"Didn't you hear him—he's willing to convert for you!" I felt desperation lodging in my throat.

"He's a cunning operator," Grandmother observed.

"I love him—can you both understand this concept?"

"Love—what's love!" Grandmother jumped on her favorite topic. "Love was invented by the goyim to seduce the Jews and throw stardust in their eyes. But being a good mother, a good person—that—that is a far greater, nobler cause than the love of a man. Who is a man anyhow—a dick in dirty socks?"

"What are you saying? Is that how you think I should treat my husband—with contempt?"

"Contempt is inevitable," Grandmother said. "Look at marriage from today to antiquity! If only young people knew that love is like having a noose around your neck—you suffocate, see stars all around you, feel like you're dying, can't breathe—am I right or am I right?" She looked at me with a clever grin. "But then the grip loosens—and reality hits you *Bach! Vot i vse!* Like a brick to the head, back in the real world—washing, cooking, cleaning, wiping noses and asses—the real stuff of marriage. Biggest problem if you ask me: women's expectations! We want too much out of men, believe in men as if they're gods but they're just shmucks who lie, cheat, and shit all over your new bed sheets and they never put the toilet seat down."

"Eddie puts the toilet seat down," I quipped.

"It's a metaphor, Lenochka," Grandmother assured me, "the toilet is a metaphor for marriage."

"I hope you realize, Lenochka, that I was once madly in love with your father," my mother joined in. "After six dates, ten bouquets of chrysanthemums, and an assistant professorship at Moscow State University in mathematics, I knew your father was a spectacular catch. Here was a man with a brilliant future, a man who was not afraid to speak of Solzhenitsyn and Bulgakov, and who could crack out in-depth analyses of obscure paintings at the Hermitage as if he were spitting cherry pits into a bowl. Oh, make no mistake, Lenochka, *I* chose *him!*"

"Then why did you have an affair?"

Grandmother declared like Moses on Mount Sinai, "Because when a man wants, a woman can't say no, and Fedya—oh, did he want your mother. Like a bat, he flew in every night to play *durak.* I was a fool—I didn't see it. I couldn't imagine that Sonya would fall for him—with his red face and his lisp—"

"What lisp, *maman*, what lisp?"

"If I had only stopped you—I knew everything but I thought, let her, she's having a hard time—it was my fault, I allowed you too much!"

"You knew nothing, nothing about me—you're still blind," my mother cried.

"Shock me please—what didn't I know?" Grandmother mocked.

"What happened, *mamulya*," I whispered, "how did you and Fedya first—begin?" I knew that secretly my mother was sympathetic to my longings. She lacked Grandmother's absolutism— the stern cage of her reproof and outrage. There were moments when I could feel my mother relent, venture into the forbidden unknown, but these forays always ended in Grandmother's decrees, with my mother becoming more ferocious, more puritanical than Grandmother, as though to compensate for her own fear of uncertainty. My very predicament of loving Eddie—of choosing Eddie—had only been possible because my mother allowed it; *she* let me flutter and re-interpret their admonitions— to discover my own take on the world. And although I myself suffered from an inability to separate prudery from goodness, sexual license from evil, mother offered me a release from the rigidity of time and traditional views. She whirled around me, flapping her golden wings like *Zhar-ptitsa*, whispering, "Run, child, be free— drink, eat, love—free yourself from us!" Or was it just a dream, a memory of a magical bird that grants Ivan his wishes, and turns imagination on its head, with *me* trying to free my mother as well as myself? For wasn't she hobbling behind Grandmother, as much in her keeping as I was, as haunted by her commands as I?

"The night I came back from," my mother admitted at last, "the night I was sick—you remember that night, *maman*?"

"What night?"

"The night I came back from the hospital in July of 1980—during the Olympics."

"Oh, no, don't," Grandmother groaned, "don't tell this to your child."

My mother ignored her. Her mouth quavered as she spoke. "Did you know that I was pregnant then, Lenochka?"

"I remember you once asked me if I wanted another sister—"

"Yes, we were already *v podache*. But the wait was agonizing, we had so little money, and your father and I fought all the time. He refused, categorically refused, to do anything to help. I had to get myself out of the Komsomol, and your father out of the Communist Party—I went in his stead and stood there, took all their horrible insults. So much bureaucracy, so many documents to hand in—I was the only woman standing in line with all the other men. I went to the KGB offices to figure out where we stood on the list; I was willing to do anything to get out. Nothing distracted me until the pregnancy. Oh, the relentless vomiting—no one thought I should have it, not your father, not your grandmother, not my mother-in-law. Only I thought about it, perhaps in the back of my mind I even wanted it. But our world made decisions for us. Abortions were standard, our only method of birth control. Like a frozen pork chop in a meat factory, you stood in line until it was your chance to be cut up."

"The doctor didn't use an anesthetic. They cut the fetus out raw, raw out of my flesh. I was five months pregnant. The pain was excruciating, impossible to bear. When my screaming turned into a wail—I couldn't keep it in, Lenochka—the nurse barked, "You keep your trap shut, you dirty Yid, or we'll cut your whole vagina out.""

"When I came home, still bleeding, keeling over in pain, no one looked my way or noticed me. Fedya was over at our house, playing *durak*, and your father said to me, 'You better clean your face and put some makeup on. You look awful, and there are people here.' Your father was in the first flush of his affair, and I became a nobody for him. If I screamed, he ignored me. And I never let him see me weep. It wasn't only about vengeance, as you always thought, *maman*. I could have taken anything, even that cheap whore—but to be ignored—to be ignored—that I *refused* to bear.

"It was Fedya who noticed my pain. One look in my face, and he knew instantaneously what had happened to me. He left the game and took me to the kitchen, and held me. He kissed my face, my eyes, my neck, real kisses with feeling in them. In front of him I cried.

"He wasn't much of a lover but what a soul he had. It was he, not your father, who shared my anti-Soviet feelings and wanted so desperately to flee."

My mother looked at me, her eyes moist, and then she smiled. "But that's the ancient past."

"What if Fedya came to America—I mean if you saw him now, would you leave Father?"

"Oh, Lenochka, life is so very difficult. Being here in this country, isolated from the outside world and alone—it's changed your father and me, made us strangely dependent upon one another. There we existed as separate beings; we each had our own circle of friends, our interests, our summers apart, our lovers. We were bound together only by you and Bella, but here, here we've been forced into each other's company and I've grown attached to your father."

"Do you hear yourself?" I exclaimed. "'Attached, attached,' but where's love? You loved Fedya but because of grandma, because of—oh I don't know why—weakness, fear, you couldn't do anything—you couldn't act! Imagine a lifetime of being in love, of being understood! Dear God, your lives are study charts in human suffering and paralysis—why should I—why should I follow in your footsteps, tell me?"

"Because of goodness, because there *are* things that are higher than human pleasure. I'm proud of my life. I've done right by my children, by my mother, my father, my husband; I'm not ashamed to look you in the eye." She spoke with conviction and strength, and yet her eyes betrayed a shift that only I could see. My words had momentarily transported her to him, to a feeling she'd only known briefly, to the bliss of feeling perfectly understood.

"*Yerunda*, nonsense!" Grandmother shouted. "Love is nonsense—stop torturing your mother."

"It's a good thing your father and I stayed together." Mother perked up, retrieving her pragmatic Mother-Hen persona. "How many children of Russian immigrants are pursuing an advanced degree in statistics while secretly painting works of art?"

"How do you know about that?"

I stared intently at my mother, recalling that special gift she possessed for peering into people's souls. Did she see Eddie too?

"Don't think I don't understand you," she said. "I may not agree with everything you do, but I understand you."

"I don't want to end up like Bella," I cried. "You pushed her into marrying Igor: she could have had anyone."

"Oh, but she couldn't!" Grandmother spat. "She only attracted hoodlums and rich assholes. At least Igor loves her—he respects her."

"She could have waited, searched more—she needed time and practice," I insisted.

"No, what she needed was a bucket of cold water on her head to wake her up from delusions of grandeur on the stage," Grandmother said.

"*You* pushed and pushed," my mother shouted, suddenly turning on her mother, "even when she returned from New York dejected and helpless, all her curves had disappeared and that short awful hair, dear God, she would have said yes to a branch if it asked. You handed her Igor on a silver platter."

"I won't be blamed for Bella's chronic unhappiness—"

"You take too much upon your old shoulders—let people live, *maman*, let them live!"

"Ahhh, do you even know what you're saying, you fool! 'Let people live!' Hah—how modern of you, dear daughter! You think it is of no consequence that Lyuba Tourkman's son is on drugs, or that Felix Gourevich doesn't have any identifiable profession and now his Korean girlfriend's pregnant and his parents are paying for the hospital bills. Or that Lana Shtein's daughter is marrying a goy from such a simpleton family that he's demanding a stripping contest for the bridesmaids and hotdogs for hors d'oeuvres? That's what it means to let your children live—to not ever tell anyone what to do—to leave fate in the hands of stupidity and lust—"

I couldn't hear Grandmother after a while, her words lost their grip, their meaning, just sounds weaving a familiar drone. My mind drifted to the cottage in Maine, to that moment I ran back to Eddie, wrapped in my towel, and jumped in the hot tub, splashing water to the floor, speaking so strangely, so freely: "Yes, yes, Eddie, I'll marry you." He had intended to ask me formally over dinner, but he confessed that he couldn't wait. He ran out of the cabin, soaked and naked, to ferret the ring out of the Jeep's glove compartment, and returned with a silver box embroidered in amethyst stones and Latin engravings, which he had some difficulty prying open. The ring itself startled me. The shape and texture of the silver band resembled a panther whose head came to rest at the joint, and from its parted mouth a purple diamond flared, its smooth surface pricked by the predator's miniature silver teeth.

"This ring, I've never seen anything quite like it," I told Eddie, unable to tear my gaze away from the lilac and indigo hues emanating from the diamond's center.

"It's one of a kind," he said, "now don't get a big head, but I—I bought it at an auction. It once belonged to the Duchess Du Barry."

"Duchess Du Barry? The courtesan you believe I resemble?"

"Yes, I saw her portrait—"

"You told me once, at the National Portrait Gallery in London."

"I stood there for hours in front of her. They were having a retrospective on eighteenth-century female artists. On my favorite, Vigee-Lebrun."

"A retrospective on female artists in the eighteenth century? I think you and the curator of the National Portrait Gallery are the only two men in the world who know Vigee-Lebrun! I mean, really! Name anyone who can speak of Mary Cassatt and Monet in the same breath!"

"I am trying to seduce you," he said, "for one moment, could you let me seduce you?"

"Please go on."

"I had seen the portrait a few weeks before the fateful client meeting in La Cote Basque, and for some reason, it struck me. I was so bored during that meeting—same old jokes, same tap dance to say the right things; I turned my head to look around and there you were, like an apparition—so beautiful and angry and you wore red."

"Yes, I remember you looking."

"I remember you catching me. Our eyes met, and I felt transported. You reminded me of the painting, of the Duchess. I knew instantly you were from another world. When you got up to go to the bathroom, I got up as well. I had to get there first. I kept thinking—if I could just touch her."

"I had no idea, I always assumed I wanted you first."

"No, no, *I* wanted *you* first." He paused. "When I heard about the auction, you and I were in the first flush. I didn't know if you'd ever be with me, but I took that chance."

"How crazy of you! Our first flush was just sex!" I exclaimed incredulously.

"Never underestimate the power of 'just' sex," he said, laughing.

"And here I thought you were a committed playboy."

"I was," he returned, smiling, meeting my gaze boldly, "but for me, you were never 'just' sex. I fell in love with you that night, the night of La Cote Basque, before I knew anything about you. I thought, I must see her again. I thought, why didn't *I* get her number! So when I saw you again at the gallery, when I saw you in that turtleneck and skirt. Your body, your body owned space, and you—and your eyes: there was so much power and magnetism in your eyes—I swore at that moment . . ." He paused; his hands seemed to be shaking. "I was instantly in love with you. I *am* in love with you."

"Are you listening to me, Lena—where's your brain?" Grandmother broke through my reverie like a hammer. "What are we going to do—what are people going to say about us—us who are such devoted Jews?"

"What do you mean 'devoted,'" I sneered, "we don't even know where the closest synagogue is!"

"Devoted in our hearts, in the way we defend Jews, in our fight against anti-Semitism," my mother exclaimed.

"And the way he touches you," Grandmother put in, as if she could envision him lying naked across my forehead, "why, it's outright pornography! Did he touch you like that when you met his mother? You think all Americans are liberated, but I'm telling you this mother of his probably doesn't subscribe to your feminism."

"Oh, dear God," I groaned, "not my feminism again, Grandmother. If there's any feminist among us, it's you. You! You don't like men, and you don't like sex—and you're never willing to compromise or listen to any man or to any woman, for that matter."

"Now that you have fancy degrees, you think you can talk your way out of everything. Besides, who said I don't like men and sex—just because my standards were always very high does not mean I was happy that your grandfather was *shtupping* half of Moscow. Was I supposed to swallow my pride and let him *shtup* me as well and become the laughingstock on our block? If there was one power I held over him, it was not giving in! What—you think I'm not a normal woman—you think I wasn't interested? Sure, sometimes I thought about IT"—Grandmother's face and neck were suffused in hues of burgundy and red—"but the thought of IT with him made me nauseous. Once in a while I'd give in, on days when he wept and begged my forgiveness. *Staryj kozel!*"

"Then why did you marry him?"

"Oh, Lenochka, I've already told you many times: it was the war, there were few men left, and you grabbed whatever you could," Grandmother said, "or you ended up with the crumbs: the red-faced drunks. Everyone said, 'how, Zinayida, how did you manage to snatch *him* up,' as if he was made of *gelt*. As soon as I saw your grandfather, I thought *Tsuris*! He's too good looking to be faithful—he'll cheat on me. But did I listen to my instincts? I was like you, always misguided by illusions of love and passion. And where did my passion get me—walking in on your grandfather and our neighbor from downstairs, Nina Pavlovivna, in my very bed. He's got one hand on her breast and the other on her *tuchus* and she's smiling wildly, like she's just bought herself Italian leather boots. So I ran in and smacked him across his head. Nina started crying, apologizing. I couldn't care less what she said; I just kept slapping him till he went red in the face. That was the last time your grandfather used our bed for his habit. You know what the old ladies on benches used to whisper when they'd see us pass by: 'oh there they go—the blond fool and her sly cat.'"

"Sounds to me like you loved him, Grandma," I said with a smile.

"*Tfu*! I spit on love!" Grandmother threw back, actually spitting on the turquoise placemat on the table, "I never loved any man!"

"I'm going to marry Eddie," I cried. "He's going to be my husband so you better start thinking of him as your grandson."

"Over my dead body," Grandmother screamed.

"Then so be it—I declare war!"

I jumped from the table and, to my shock, saw Eddie in the doorway, carrying two heavy grocery bags in each hand. Long-stem carrots and potatoes and parsley root and green onion and beets mingled together in anticipation of Grandmother's war-weathered borscht. My father carried nothing; Russians loved to test the mettle and health of a new man entering their clan.

"I like him," my father suddenly announced, to my shock, in Russian. "He's a good guy."

"Traitor!" my grandmother screamed, glaring at Father.

"Is anything the matter?" Eddie asked.

"Don't worry—Grandma is just angry because my father forgot to buy butter," I offered.

"Oh."

"Why do you always side against us?" My mother tried to be calm, but her anger at Father was already beginning to pulsate at her temples, because as usual this incident was not just about this incident but every other incident where he had sided against her.

"I didn't know we had already made a decision," my father remarked cheerfully. "I thought we were still deciding." I looked into my father's face but I couldn't read him; I didn't know whether he was more interested in opposing my mother and grandmother, or genuinely supporting me.

"We already decided," my grandmother announced, "and you need to support us—we need to present a united front." She said this even though I was standing in front of them. The united front was a concept I was familiar with since childbirth: parents squabbling and pretending to be a united front but never actually uniting.

"I'm really excited to try your borscht," Eddie said to my grandmother. "I hear it's incredible!"

"Always be careful wiz women—you tink it's borscht but maybe it poison? Ha, ha!" my father exclaimed, laughing.

"To show you just how much they *really* love you," Eddie chipped in.

My father smiled at Eddie. "I like him—a very unusual American."

My father put his arm around Eddie and said, "You chave sense of humor—I like zhat—a man who understands me."

"You like everyone," my mother snapped in Russian, then she turned to Eddie. "Forgive us Eddie, ve're being rude. Ve're very happy to make borscht for you."

A pang went through my stomach. I came closer to Eddie, cutting the distance between us, leaving only breathing space, suddenly afraid that their words mattered, that words could kill feelings, that it was dangerous to be around their bare tongues. The fear bent me in half. I leaned toward him, my body in his orbit, and whispered to myself what he told me on the plane: *It's about us, not them, remember that, Emma, about us, not them.*

He stood, bound by heavy bags, breathing on me, imprisoned by our Russian language, disparate sounds swirling, flying around him like the grating notes of a malfunctioning instrument he couldn't quite tune. Mutely, he bore his need for me. My lips landed on his mouth—hard, harder, harder, I whispered to myself, and pressed my chest against him. How impertinently I stuck my tongue in! I grabbed his neck and pulled his hair with fingers lithe and quick. I even considered pawing his buttocks but this was plenty: this was enough to dazzle them, to stun them with my fearless silent snarl: *you cannot break my will.*

"Look at that insolence!" my grandmother said, "again all this pornography in my house."

"Enough!" my father said, "let them be. Why do you always stick your nose where it doesn't belong?"

"Don't speak that way to my mother!" my mother chimed in.

"He's a great guy," my father reiterated, then he added in a strange voice, "She's in love with him, can't you see that? And we're in America now—if there's one thing she should be able to do in America it's marry for love."

"We're Jews," my grandmother retorted, "first and foremost, that's why we're in America—not for love!"

"Why is everything black and white for you?" my father exclaimed. "Can't you see how unpredictable the world is?"

"Oh I see." My mother's face suddenly exploded in red hues and in a span of a second, she looked twenty years younger, the way she looked in Russia. "You're thinking of her! Of your love! The one you had to abandon. I see: we couldn't love in Russia but we can love here—in America! I hear she's in New Jersey, your love! You're free to go visit her. No one is holding you down, no one has you in chains, Semeyon!"

"Have you lost your mind? Or maybe you want me to bring up Fedya, my student, my math student? How could you? Or have you forgotten? Do you think I didn't know? You think you hid your secret well? Did you know that I once walked in on you two kissing—and I didn't say anything—I kept it to myself because I thought: she'll come to her senses eventually! She'll forget him. Do you know where your precious Fedya is now? In Boston with his young wife and two children. He wrote to me, that bastard, do you know why—he needed a reference for a university position, as if I was some kind of fool!"

"You said nothing?" my mother muttered, her forehead perspiring. "Why didn't you reproach me?"

"How could *I* possibly reproach you—what right did I have?"

The rest of us had disappeared. My parents looked at each other as if they had seen each other for the first time.

"I said nothing," my father went on, "because I loved you—I loved you madly!"

"You loved her!" my mother blurted out through tears.

"A momentary lapse in judgment," he returned gently. "When I saw you with him, when I saw the two of you, I thought my stomach was being ripped in half. That's when I knew."

"What did you know?"

"That I couldn't bear it: you being with another man." He reached toward her with his hand and caressed her cheeks, her hair, and the moment hung like a miracle between them. "So I waited for you. Do you remember that—how you couldn't look at me, all that time, you couldn't look at me."

"I was repulsed."

"I know."

"And then I was lost, Semeyon, lost . . . and ashamed."

"So let her be!"

"Who?

"Our daughter—let her be."

"But what if she's making a mistake?"

"Let her make it . . . we made ours."

I smiled at Eddie. We're going to be all right, I whispered to myself, imagining my father's support wrap around my shoulders like a protective wool coat, like the oversized *shubas* I had worn as a child.

"Not sure if I should ask what's going on or if I should—just wait," Eddie wondered out loud.

"You should always wait, Eddik, patience is very positive for women!" my father exclaimed cheerfully. "But let me give you zhis hair of advice: if you want to marry into zhis family, you better learn some Russian and fast! Ha! Or my vomen vill eat you up."

Eddie laughed as if he understood what my father intimated, but his laughter was carefree and flat and somehow to my ear quintessentially American, unaware of the nuanced layers of meaning and duplicity that permeated our Russian world, unaware of the warnings hidden in my father's jolly face.

Americans are Invading

Out of love for my father, my mother relented, allowing me to make "her mistake." Both of my parents receded into the familiar background, the landscape behind my grandmother's front lines, behind her war. Unmoved by my parents' sudden softening and gazes at one another, and losing my mother as her ally, Grandmother escalated her offensive. She greeted me in the morning on our way to the bathroom with stories of American anti-Semitism. She recited at will the indeterminate future of Jewish children, and my hybrid children in particular. And she foretold horror stories of Eddie's Catholic mother, the woman she had never met but whom she anticipated with great relish and enthusiasm, and celebratory vengeance, which culminated in the ominous statement: "YOU WILL SEE!" On my end, it was important to show similar warrior-like resolve, and to periodically fan my heavy artillery, which included such statements as "you know nothing," "you live in a dream world," and "you've never truly been in love." Grandmother laughed at me, but it didn't matter: as long as I fought, I still had a chance. Submission was out of the question; this too pumped through our Russian blood—this implacable proclivity for war—which could only end when the weaker one lays down her weapon. Perhaps I always knew it would have to be me, but in the meantime, it was important to keep fighting, to soldier on. I simply moved forward, toward a future she refused me.

I called Mrs. Beltrafio in the presence of my grandmother, and announced in clearly articulated English: "My parents are dying to meet you!" I knew that Grandmother would submit out of social pressure because Grandmother was a social bee, a queen in her own right, a charming exuberant hostess with meticulous cooking skills and a love of vodka. She wisely calculated that if she couldn't kill this relationship now (we were deep into September), then surely she would have to endure Thanksgiving staring across the table at the mysterious goyim. Mrs. Beltrafio in turn squealed that she was "supremely delighted" and bade me to assure my mother that she has always "*loved*" the Russian people. Cynthia and Hal purchased tickets to Chicago the same day, lest they, God forbid, appear hesitant or nonplussed about our engagement. My family, upon learning of the Americans' impending arrival two weeks hence, had no choice but to begin preparing themselves in the proper fashions, as well as swathing their brains in nerve-soothing epigrams.

Grandmother's brain was particularly afflicted. Days before the visit she broke into rapturous shrieks: "*Amerikantzy* are coming, *Amerikantzy* are coming!" On the eve of their arrival, as she prepared the food and reapplied the lipstick for the fiftieth time, she posed hypothetical questions to the stove: "Where are the *Amerikantzy* going to sleep?" (In a hotel, not in our bedrooms!) "What do they like to eat?" (*Lasbanya*, (more commonly known as lasagna), Saltless Rubber (more commonly known as grilled chicken), Raw *Uzhas* (more commonly known as steak au poivre) and Turkey on a Bed of Sugar (more commonly known as Thanksgiving). "What do they like to talk about?" (Weather, real estate, and Bill Climpton's sex life.) "Are we going to like them?" (Not one iota.)

My father went from anxiety to ecstasy within the span of a minute, for the mere arrival of guests (of any nationality or political persuasion) offered us a chance to stun them with our musical talents. My mother was a weeping soprano, my father a lugubrious tenor, Grandmother a masterful alto, and Bella that rarity of voices—a coloratura. I inherited the dramatic mezzo-soprano from my grandmother, Liza, my father's mother. When we sang together we sounded like a band of starving opera singers, voices leaping one over another, never exactly in tune, deafening our adoring audiences. The living room was our communal stage and the embarrassment we sometimes felt at our exhibitionism was quickly squashed by the exquisite pleasure of performing and the customary compliments from our guests: "You're all so talented!" or better yet, "you should be performing at the Metropolitan Opera!" A collection of Broadway's greatest hits rested on the Steinway, and my father soaked his fingers in warm water and soap to groom them for his virtuoso stunts on the mandolin.

Mr. and Mrs. Beltrafio arrived on a hot September afternoon, tired and sweaty from the plane ride. They looked wet and peevish, like neglected children. Neither was hungry, or so they said. Grandmother stared at her table overflowing with food, and one got the sense that she loathed them already. She and my mother had slaved over meat and potato pierogies, garlic-laced cow's tongue, sour-creamed tomatoes, an eggplant salad, a meat stew that contained to my and Bella's delight a cow's brain, a liver pâté, and the ever-present Beluga caviar, which Sirofima eyed with passion and to which, at five years old, she was already addicted.

Mrs. Beltrafio immediately complimented us. "Everything looks so good, Mrs. Kabelmacher," but we could see that she had no idea what that "everything" was.

"Thank you," my mother said, "my mother cooked most of it."

Mrs. Beltrafio shot a glance in my grandmother's direction and nodded.

"EVERRRRYTHING LOOOOOOKS DELICIOUS!" she exclaimed in a ringing voice, enunciating every word with visible care, so that Grandmother, who was far shorter, had a perfect view of Mrs. Beltrafio's well-cared-for gums.

"Why is she yelling?" my grandmother asked me in Russian.

"Americans often make the mistake of thinking we immigrants are deaf," Igor pointed out in his usual caustic manner.

"She's trying to be polite—she says your food looks delicious," I said.

"Ask her if she likes a cow's brain in a bone?"

"My grandmother wants to know," I said, turning to Eddie's mother, "if you like meat stews—she cooked one especially for you."

"Oh, she didn't have to go all-out on my account," Mrs. Beltrafio demurred.

"Vy of course, you our guests," my mother exclaimed wildly, and then offered, "why won't you sit down, why won't all of you sit down." But no one sat down. Mrs. Beltrafio was wearing a long silk brown dress, and an expensive cream on her face that she either forgot to dab with powder or purposefully left shiny with grease to display her smooth, wrinkle-free skin. She kept staring at the cathedral ceiling, which stretched nearly thirty feet into the air, and at the carved wooden staircase that seemed to coil into the very sky.

"You have a beautiful house," Mrs. Beltrafio offered after another silent pause.

"Sank you," my father said, who felt that his success could be measured by the height of our ceilings.

"She's not very good looking," my grandmother said in Russian to Bella, while smiling at Mrs. Beltrafio.

"But she has excellent skin," Bella observed.

"Eventually, Sonichka," Grandmother addressed my mother, "you should ask what she uses." Then Grandmother shot a wry glance at my mother's slightly wrinkled neck, an act that always provoked defiance in my mother.

"I think it's surgery," my mother snipped. "Besides, she doesn't seem to like us."

"Offer her vodka," Grandmother suggested.

"Would you like vine, Cyntia?" my mother asked, fearing that vodka had become too much of a cliché.

"Yes, I'd love some," she replied.

"What kind of a name is Sisiya?" Grandmother wondered.

"I think it's German," my mother said.

"And Billfarto?" Grandmother asked.

"Italian for sure," said Bella, cackling as she winked at me.

"Did Grandmother just say 'Bill farted?'" I whispered into Bella's ear, and we laughed the way we used to laugh as children whenever anyone said "*ya puknul.*"

"My daughters are halways laughing at somesing stupid," my mother explained to Mrs.

Beltrafio, but when she barked, "*perestantye!*" at us, she was not able to control her own exploding grin.

Cynthia gulped the wine as though it were beer, and then excused herself to search for her husband. I followed Mrs. Beltrafio through another passageway, knowing that Mr. Beltrafio was in the living room, supposedly admiring our bird paintings.

Our house had many secret passageways because, at the back of their minds, my parents feared a KGB invasion in some unforeseeable future. For instance, in our magnificent mahogany library, behind the bookcase devoted to Russian texts, specifically behind a thick tome entitled *Stalin's Evil Genius: Schizophrenic Paranoia or the Accident of Historical Convenience*, there was a gold button that transformed the bookcase into a revolving door and ushered one into an entirely different section of the house. This superbly insulated, win-dowless, concrete space contained three rooms we called the Triangle, stocked with canned and dry foods in case of a third world war or a shattering family quarrel that God forbid involved Russian swear words. Here we kept our most precious books and notebooks, my father's poetry, letters from lovers, Bella's diaries, and my sketches of every family member, starting from the time I was seven (when my father gave me the art jour-nal and my first grade teacher, Ludmila Vasilievna, anointed me an art prodigy). On the right, a staircase hid behind a lustrous gold velvet curtain and connected to an underground beneath our basement. The underground was equipped with conven-iently placed maps and embossed directions that led one out into the front yard, the highway, or the Winnetka shopping mall (though the walking distance in this case was only advisable if you were consciously trying to lose weight).

I tried to imagine what Mrs. Beltrafio might say if she learned about our secret *mishugas* as I hid in the library, which was demar-cated from the living room by French doors. They were opaque but had zero insulation, and so I leaned my ear against the door, truncating my breaths.

I couldn't see them, but I could hear them bickering quietly with each other and settling into our triangular purple couch.

"Don't do anything Cynthia, I beg you, please."

"When have I ever *done* anything?" she admonished, "I only observe human nature.

"Their taste is despicable—I mean, Good Lord, this sofa should have been on *Star Trek*," she snorted, "and they butcher the English language to such an extent I feel like I'm at a steel factory and I've forgotten my earplugs. I know this isn't kind of me, darling Harold, but for a scholar like myself, well, you can hardly blame me for feeling put out. How can I possibly be expected to get along with her mother or God forbid that other woman—her grandmother? She's got the eyes of a witch! She wants to swallow me whole, can't you see that, Hal? To be in this country for how many years—fifteen, sixteen—and still remain so ignorant—why, it's shameful!"

"He doesn't expect you to get along with anyone—he just wants you to be civil to them." "Oh, I'm perfectly civil."

"He's in love with her, Cynthia."

"Oh, he's always in love with the Jews, our son."

"Oh, dear God, not that again," he moaned.

"Can you honestly tell me that you've forgiven Russell for stealing all our money? Have you forgotten his Jewish origins?"

"He was half-Jewish, the half that didn't matter to him. We met him in the Catholic Church, Cynthia, for Christ's sake! You can't think every Jew is like Russell—you can't blame our situation on these folks—" he whispered rather loudly.

"Honestly, Hal, I can't stand the way these upstarts come to our country and get rich, while you and I can barely keep our heads above water."

"These are nice people," he said. "They don't know about our troubles. It's not their fault."

"You don't seem to understand me, Harold—I don't want Jewish grandchildren!" Her whisper became a hiss. I wanted to rush in and staple her mouth shut—I didn't want to know or hear anymore but I was mesmerized by her hatred. My blood curdled again, the way it did when I was a child, indignation jolting me awake in the morning and indignation lulling me to sleep. How invigorating it might be, I thought grimly, bitterly, to battle life's grand injustices again with my own mother-in-law!

"I don't want to stare into the eyes of little babies," she spat, "and think to myself, 'now there go *our* little Jews!' They may have blond hair and blue eyes and they may be beautiful but that's how people will see us from now on. We'll be the grandparents of Jews. Of course not all of them are the same, I'm not disputing the existence of outliers—but their people have been so marred by common greed and mendacity that it's impossible to have an open mind. To think that other people will associate *me*—with *them*—what purgatory!"

The word "purgatory" grew louder and louder in my head, and I pulled myself away from the door. That's when I saw it: her eyes catching mine through the French doors. Was she staring back at me? Did she realize that I was hiding, listening to her—was she doing this for my benefit?

"Cynthia, my love—you've got to let go of your parents' antiquated views," Hal said beseechingly. "Don't you remember, your father hated me too?"

"It has nothing to do with my father, dear," she trilled, her gaze quickly returning to her husband. "Until now all the Jews I've dealt with were acquaintances, neighbors, accountants, nobodies, but we're talking about family—"

"Remember us when we were in love—"

"Don't confuse apples with potato chips, Harold, we were perfectly matched." Cynthia's whisper grew louder. "Besides, I think she's loose—like Eddie's other one. A common whore."

"Where do you get 'whore'?"

"Call it a woman's intuition—"

"At this rate he'll be alone and buried in work for the rest of his life!"

"What are you proposing—to siphon him off to these people?"

"What are you plotting, Cynthia?" Hal spoke in an almost inaudible tone, leaning fearfully into his wife.

"I don't plot, my darling Hal—I await opportunities. Besides, these people are very smart—they don't want us as much as we don't want them."

"Lenochka, *gde ty, my sadimsya*," My grandmother's voice rang through the library.

"They're yelling again," Mrs. Beltrafio noted.

"It's rude of us to stay away." Hal rose from the purple couch, but Cynthia remained in her seat, still and defiant.

"Mother, Hal"—Eddie ran into the living room—"dinner is served."

I opened the door slightly and saw Mrs. Beltrafio beaming at her son, her eyes evaluating his face, shoulders, jacket, shoes. "You look wonderful, Ignatius," she said softly, brushing her fingers along his forearm.

"Mother, get up, we shouldn't be rude."

"Give your mother a hand, I barely see you anymore."

She moved one shoulder toward him, but her arms stayed at her sides. He grabbed her arm and pulled her from the couch, his face cringing from irritation.

"Be gentle with your mother, Ignatius, haven't I taught you to be a gentleman?"

"Mother, please don't." But he bowed his head and his body slumped into a subjugated curve.

He held her tenderly this time, his arm guiding her forward as though she were blind. With his other arm, he held his father's elbow, and the three of them moved in one synchronized uniform motion into the entrance hall. I froze, unable to feel my legs, my mind crashing into the same nagging, repetitive thought: he was their seed.

During the initial stages of dinner, the Beltrafios looked like parrots pacing in a cage. They smiled, nodded, prodded each other under the table, and sought in our faces branches to hold on to before they drowned in our loud, boisterous laughter and melodious tongue. For Russian reigned over the appetizers like a necessity, like vodka, before English came wobbling in. I did nothing to remedy the situation; in those first couple of minutes, the Beltrafios had become one, and as one, they were my enemy. I refused to translate, to look at Eddie, to smile politely at his mother, to nod at his father. I wanted to starve them of language, to make theirs fade away; I wanted the engagement off and my life rewound to the moment I had first laid eyes on Alex. I regretted everything. Everything until Eddie said: "Did you know, Mr. and Mrs. Kabelmacher, that Emma is an incredible painter?" Until he touched my thigh under the table with the feverish urgency that sometimes gripped his entire body in my presence. And I felt his urgency within me, pulling me out of the fury I felt only seconds before. I felt myself being torn between two forces, or was it two selves? Who was whispering in my ear: *you cannot wish this away, cannot snap your fingers and undo the damage of her tirade; you are in the thick of it, in the swamp of it, tasting the acid on your tongue—if you are indeed an individual, then you will choose— and each choice will be a compromise of your constitution, your principles, your will.*

"Of course ve know." My mother looked at him, as if she was seeing him for the first time. "Our Elena is talent at many, many vonderful hobbies."

"This is not a hobby," Eddie said bitterly.

"So what does everyone think of Russia's new democracy?" Hal appealed to my mother.

"Many people zere are not happy," my father declared like an expert. "Zey want tings to go back to ze way it vas. Democracy is chaos. Still, I wish my mozer was alive to see it all."

"What happened to your mother?" Mrs. Beltrafio inquired with interest.

"Tree years after we left her, she need gall stone operation but in hospital, she got infection and died."

"That's terrible!" Mrs. Beltrafio exclaimed, leaning across the table toward my father.

My father's countenance lost its social ease and camaraderie, and was replaced by a debilitating gray frown that immersed us all in the guilt he carried so ostentatiously on his sleeve. As he succinctly put it for my mother during their fights, "My mother's blood is on my hands—not Yakov's—it is *I* who left her."

My mother gave my father the usual two minutes of silence to demonstrate her respect for his feelings and then announced: "Well, in Russian hospitals, only strong survive. And zis so-announced democracy will not last. I give it ten, fifteen years at most and watch—some *tiran*—excuse me, I mean tyrrrant vill take control and it vill be back to dictatorrrsheep. Maybe not Communism zhis time, not like it was, but ze same prison."

"My wife is verrry pessimistic," my father countered, retrieving his jolly persona. "I believe tings will improve. Look at America: it vas chaos when America vas young democracy—mafias and vild cowboys, and look at America now. All anyone talks about is Monica and Clinton entertaining oral sex!" My father erupted in laughter, then added, "Soon Russia vill follow example but zere no one cares about oral sex or any sex for zhat matter!"

Hal merrily joined my father with his own nasal chortle, and Mrs. Beltrafio stiffly grinned.

"Always kissing ass to Americans," Grandmother snapped at my father in Russian.

"I wasn't kissing ass—" my father meagerly defended himself. "I was making intelligent prognostications about the future of Russia."

"The future of Russia! Hah!" Grandmother grumbled, cackling, "Going to the dogs, that's where it's going—like it always was! There's no justice, no justice in the world, as there's no justice in one's life. What can Yeltsin, that red-nosed drunk, do for the people now—steal more of their money to build himself more mansions? The KGB are the new mafia and that's what they always were!"

"What's your grandmother saying?" Mrs. Beltrafio addressed me without looking at Grandmother.

"She's saying that Russia is going to hell," Igor suddenly joined us in English. "And that we should stop listening to Russian radio, stop reading Russian newspapers, stop enjoying Tolstoy, Dostoyevsky, and Pushkin, and to irrefutably seal our separation we might as well cut out our Russian tongues!"

"I vill toast to zhat," my mother declared as if to signal this new era. "Let's stop being Russian togezher!"

"Well, I remember Russia being glorious," Mrs. Beltrafio intervened. "The Hermitage was perhaps the most astounding museum I had ever set my eyes upon, and the golden-domed churches took my breath away."

"Vhen were you in Russia?" my mother asked.

"I was a student in the late 1960s—I was doing a year abroad and in those years everyone wanted to see how the other side lived—"

"Yes, I was student then too," my mother murmured, "zhat was when Semeyon and I met."

My father looked at me and said, "Your mozer was most beautiful woman I ever met!"

"Still is!" my mother corrected him.

"Still are!" my father in turn corrected her.

"My parents met at Moscow State University," I told Eddie, "at a Komsomol meeting held for the whole university. They were sitting next to each other and my mother had a copy of Chekhov's short stories in her lap."

"*Dama s sobachkoy*" my mother said.

"*Lady with a Lapdog,*" I translated.

My father jumped in. "I said to your mozer, 'If you marry me, I'll buy you whole collection.' And you know vhat she reply? 'Get in line! I already chave three suitors buying me Chekhov and all ze others are sworn to Pushkin. Vhat makes you different?' So wizout blinking one eye, I said: 'I don't drink, smoke, swear or chave big ears.' Your mozer look at my ears and say, 'Zhat's rare trait for a man.' 'Perfect ears?' I ask. 'No,' she says, 'understanding zhat women always want perfection.' And zhat was zhat, as zhey say in fairy tales."

"We had to sell that *kollektsiya,*" my mother said wistfully.

"Yeah, but you still chave my perfect ears!" My father laughed so hard tears sprang from his eyes. Then he swung his head from side to side to present the bewildered Beltrafios with two perfectly proportioned, miniature ears that lay snugly against his head.

"So, Emma, how come you changed your name? Elena sounds very beautiful," Mrs. Beltrafio inquired with aplomb.

"I—I didn't want—" I could barely remember why it was that I had changed my name; all that drummed in my mind were her perfidious remarks about Jews.

"It was the Cold War and Reagan called Russia the Evil Empire," I droned on with my stock response, when Igor suddenly stepped in. "Don't you know, Mrs. Beltrafio, that Russian Jews are the most beleaguered people in the world?" He addressed her with a look of jaunty disdain. "The American Orthodox Jews hate us because we're not religious. The American secular Jews hate us because we've managed, despite our jarring accents, to make more money than them. The American gentiles see us as relics of the Cold War, whom they still fear, and to be sure view us as inferior to themselves because we are not only Jewish but immigrants polluting their evolved nativism. But in general I find that American individuality is an illusion Americans feed themselves to feel at ease with their own prejudices. They prefer conformity over individuality. And while they like to 'feel' multicultural, in reality their cultures don't mix at all. Look at the current state of black and white relations, for starters!

"Except of course our Lena—she's that perfect amalgam of two cultures, the Yin and Yang of Russia and America. Unfortunately that's an illusion too, you see, created by die-hard assimilationists who believe immigrants can be neatly brought into the fold—folded into identical squares, stripped of their languages and everything else. If we completely negate who we *were*, only then can we change who we *are* and be accepted."

"Oh, I think Emma is doing a wonderful job," Mrs. Beltrafio swooped in. "Why, I would never have suspected her of being an immigrant had Ignatius not alerted us to the fact! Her accent is downright Midwestern—you have to be extraordinarily talented to be able to pick up local dialect."

"No one can be both," Igor protested. "For an individual can no sooner cut himself in half than he can change the color of his skin."

"Surely, you can be both," Mrs. Beltrafio insisted. "Look at me—I'm a Catholic and an American."

This announcement sent shivers across the spines of all my family members, and a quiet gurgle of Russian spilled from their lips, culminating in the word "Catolik," which now hung over the dinner table like an ear-splitting military helicopter.

"There is a price to pay for wanting everything, Lena," Igor continued with even greater determination. "No one can have everything in life, or you might lose your head—"

"That's the Russian ideologue in you talking," I said. "In America, wanting is the only way to exist."

"Here, here!" Mrs. Beltrafio cried supportively, downing her wine glass, "that's what I always tell my other son, Augustine, you must fight for what you want, not let life pass you by."

"You have other son?" my mother inquired. Then in Russian, she berated me: "What's going on—why didn't you tell us this?"

"Told us what?" Grandmother asked.

"Eddik has a brother," my father explained.

"Where is he? That's very suspicious," Grandmother noted.

But Mrs. Beltrafio, to my utter shock, seemed intent on saving me. "Oh, this is our fault, Sonya—we wanted to surprise you. Andy was going to come with his wife and twin boys, but then our manager fell ill and Andy felt he absolutely *had* to stay. He heads my husband's business, you see—I'm not sure Emma told you but we're in the transportation industry."

"They're small-time merchants," my mother told Grandmother in Russian, while smiling at Cynthia, "not intellectuals!"

"I knew it," Grandmother countered in Russian, "but she acts like she's some sort of aristocrat!"

"Did you know, Mr. and Mrs. Beltrafio"—Igor addressed Eddie's parents in a glowingly acerbic tone—"we used to war in this house over who Lena should marry—an American or Russian. The case against Russian men is that—"

"They are shovitin pigs," Sirofima cried in delight.

"Chauvinist—chauvinist pigs," Bella corrected her daughter.

"Yes," Igor said, nodding, "I plead guilty to that pleasure myself."

"And the case against American men?" Eddie asked, facing Igor like an adversary.

"Oh, don't you know—hasn't our American ambassador informed you—they are stupid."

The table quieted down, and my parents in a unified gasp fixed their eyes on Eddie.

"Thank you, Igor"—Eddie came back with a splendid, genial laugh—"for brilliantly alerting me to a major national epidemic. But if we wipe out male stupidity, right up there with teenage pregnancy and drug abuse, the country will be overrun with pompous *mudaks*!"

A quiet laugh percolated from Bella to my parents to my grandmother until it met Igor's grim countenance, where it died.

"What's a *mudak*?" Mrs. Beltrafio wanted to know, but none of us answered.

Only my father offered a way out. "Let's make toast—to ourrrrr new family! To new beginning!"

"I'll drink to that!" Hal Beltrafio lifted his arm in the air as if to break free from his wife, and shouted, "To my wonderful new family!" My father extended his wine glass so far across the table to reach him that we felt his unwavering spirit of harmony and camaraderie soothe our aggravated throats.

Grandmother brought out the stew and placed it directly under Mrs. Beltrafio's pointy chin. A big white bone containing the cow's brain sat in the middle of the platter.

"What's that?" Mrs. Beltrafio inquired with a gracious smile.

"Stew with a cow's brain," Sirofima declared.

"Be quiet, Sirofima," Grandmother commanded in Russian, "let them eat it first. Haven't we taught you yet to keep your mouth shut?"

"Grandmother doesn't want me to tell you," Sirofima explained to Cynthia, unaffected by Grandmother's escalating wrath, "but you should eat it. Grandmother says it has more vitamins than all the Total cereals combined." Sirofima had her father's dark, brooding brown eyes that seemed already vexed at the ignorance in the world.

"Is that kosher?" Mrs. Beltrafio asked to avert attention from her injured sense of propriety.

"I told you already—they don't keep kosher," Eddie said.

"Well, surely I can try new things," Mrs. Beltrafio announced with enthusiasm, but neither of her hands moved to partake of the cow's brain.

An unendurable silence set in, and my father quickly ended it with his favorite tension breaker: "Vould you like some vodka?"

"Yes," Mr. Beltrafio cheered, "vodka on the rocks."

My father laughed as though Mr. Beltrafio had just tickled his armpits and poured vodka into our gold-rimmed Russian shot glasses. My parents at last seemed to settle into themselves. The shot glasses glistened like old ribald friends from the motherland, murmuring of upcoming festivities. My father churned out another abbreviated toast: "To new love, to our children, to zeir happiness and healths!" We clinked our glasses together, but Mr. and Mrs. Beltrafio retained their stifling nervous calm; only their polite smiles zigzagged frenetically at the edges of their chins.

"Um, do you have any ice—" Mr. Beltrafio attempted his request again.

"They drink it straight, Hal," Eddie said, blushing from his father's insistence.

"But I don't," Mr. Beltrafio snapped at his son. Mrs. Beltrafio's mouth involuntarily curled into a grin.

"Of course, we have ice," my mother sang and ran to the ice box.

"Why aren't they drinking?" Grandmother cried out in Russian, "what more do they want from us?"

"Ice," Bella snickered.

"You shouldn't have brought out the vodka," my mother said to my father in Russian, "it's not their thing."

"What, I can't drink vodka in my own home, when my child is about to get married again?" my father exclaimed.

"Please, already, can we please switch to English," I begged.

But no one seemed to hear me. Eddie gulped down his shot in seconds and, following Igor's lead, took a spoonful of the cow's brain stew. My mother cried out, "Whoooh" and Grandmother emptied her glass with heroic speed. My father was already pouring us seconds, while the Beltrafios were slowly sipping their vodkas on the rocks, still making no movements toward the stew. My mother rose and miraculously returned with a new dinner for them, consisting of sandwiches of Russian bologna and salami, which they found "charming and delicious."

The Pagan Dance

But it was after dinner that the Beltrafios were truly overexposed to our culture.

At first we behaved ourselves. Bella and I performed our favorite classical pieces on the piano, holding ourselves hostage to what we felt was the American reserve. Then Bella and I performed a duet of "Sunrise, Sunset" (everyone in the family felt that God had personally summoned them to submerge the gentiles in our Jewish identity, and no album, besides perhaps *The Jazz Singer* by Neil Diamond, was as fitting for our current predicament as *Fiddler on the Roof*). And although Grandmother and Mother acted as background hummers (because they only knew the melody), their voices occasionally outgrew ours, enhancing the chorus with Soviet-era Yiddish ballads. But when Sirofima began to tap dance, my father, overtaken by the child's enthusiasm, broke into a gypsy song on his mandolin. I endured a few seconds of reserve while my legs trembled and the music invaded my ribcage—*podayte mne bokalo, naleyti mne vina, i dayte mne malchonku v kovo ya v lublina* . . . I only managed to translate to Eddie, "give me a glass, pour me some wine, and give me the boy I'm in love with," when Bella pulled me into a circle forming in the center of the room. Together with Mother, Grandmother, and Sirofima, we stomped our feet and shook our breasts and shoulders, howling, "*na, nee, na, nee, na, nee, na,*" arching our backs toward the floor, each trying to outdo the other. Grandmother couldn't go down as far but she mimicked our movements with her head and arms, so that she appeared to the uninitiated observer as though she were participating in a pagan worshiping ritual. Bella and I smashed our hips together, our legs and arms intertwining, our hair flying helter-skelter, our bodies dropping into full back-bends midair. Sweat poured down our foreheads, washing the mascara, the lipstick, the foundation off our faces, allowing our true skins to emerge.

I felt myself growing aroused from my sudden exposure. My white cotton shirt clung to my breasts and untucked from my jeans revealing my midriff. Bella was in her customary figure-fitting red dress that barely covered her knees and revealed an impressive cleavage.

We imagined ourselves on the Broadway stage—believing momentarily that this was where the Kabelmacher sisters truly belonged—but that by some accident of our fortunes, some beguiling factor relating to our foreignness, our lengthy immigration, our Jewishness, our Russianness, we ended up resigning ourselves to sedentary careers, fated to be stars only in this mammoth house, in front of family and friends. Only intermittently did I catch glimpses of Mr. and Mrs. Beltrafio's faces. They sat in an unconscious stupor, frozen, yet fascinated by what we would do next, swallowing bricks as they attempted to smile.

At some point, my mother, drunk on her beauty and voluptuousness, climbed on top of my father's shoulders while he played "Kalinka Malinka" and planted a moist, ardent kiss on his grinning mouth, climbing over him like a plump caterpillar. My mother's breasts, which were housed in a tightly knit blue sweater, pressed into my father's cheeks and eyes, and seemed to have a most profound effect on Mr. Beltrafio. The glances he shot at my mother after that incident appeared to reflect a new admiration for her, one that he was not skilled enough to conceal from his frightened wife.

It was not long after that kiss that Mrs. Beltrafio announced that she was ready to go to their hotel, because "a violent migraine has suddenly overtaken me." In parting, Bella asked her if she wouldn't perhaps like to hear a repeat of Beethoven's "Moonlight Sonata" to soothe her. But Mrs. Beltrafio smiled, massaging her own temples, and said, "that's very kind of you, Bella, but I'm afraid that if I don't lie down soon, I'll collapse. It was *lovely* to meet all of you." And with that emphatic "lovely" the Beltrafios rose from the couch.

As everyone gathered in the hallway, and Igor was ascending the staircase, carrying a sleeping Sirofima in his arms, and my father was handing jackets to the Americans, the doorbell rang. "Who could that be?" my mother asked and everyone froze like characters on a TV screen that's been set to "pause" by the VCR. Everyone except for Grandmother, who swiftly and cheerfully unlocked the door. There, shrouded in black gauze, stood an exact replica of Mrs. Bagdanovich.

"May I come in?" Mrs. Bagdanovich in the flesh announced, and without waiting for an answer, she marched into the living room, where her excavating gaze landed on Mrs. Beltrafio.

"Come in, come in," my grandmother murmured sweetly, "just yesterday natural Valium came in from Russia, just as I promised, but we're still waiting for powdered vitamin C extracted from natural cranberries." Grandmother was running a small business venture as a middleman, ordering minerals, medicinal herbs, and other favorite Soviet remedies from the new Russia, and distributing them to Russian émigrés in the Chicago's suburbs.

"So that's them—the Americans you've traded us in for," Alla declared in an accusatory tone.

"I thought you weren't speaking to her anymore!" I stared at Grandmother, while my brain thawed from the initial panic freeze.

"Why wouldn't I speak to Allochka?" Grandmother replied. "Just because you're no longer dating Alex doesn't mean I have to cut off ties with my friends."

"Are you trying to ruin my life?" I asked, trying to mentally ward off a scorching itch on my lower back and the quick deadening of English-speaking neurons.

"Oh, you'll do that on your own without my help," Grandmother said with astonishing composure, "I was merely trying to get Alla her Valium." It dawned on me that at some point during our pagan dance Grandmother had disappeared from the living room, only to reappear when the Beltrafios rose to leave. She must have stolen away to make a phone call. And she had nudged Bella to perform another round of the "Moonlight Sonata" to buy herself time.

"Who is this woman—why is she here?" The alien language seemed to come out of nowhere, and it belonged to the irked Mrs. Beltrafio, who now clutched the lapels of her beige jacket like a woman confronted with a rapist.

"A friend of my mozer's," my mother said. "She stop by to get Valium."

"Valium is highly addictive," Mrs. Beltrafio noted in a nervous voice.

"No, it better for who zhan if you take sleep Tehelenol," Mrs. Bagdanovich angrily spat (her English was intimately connected to her nervous system). "Did who know people die from Tehelenol?"

"Allochka, please, this is Eddie and his parents, Cyntia and Hall," my mother went on.

As they shook hands, Alla Bagdanovich grimaced at my mother and murmured through her fake smile, "You aren't going to tell them who I am, are you? Coward!" Yet despite her threatening demeanor, I swiftly understood that Alla would never reveal herself. Having escaped Russia in its first flushes of Jewish emigration in 1978, Alla knew the importance of silence better than anyone. We had all come from a world where betrayal was the true mark of evil, where ratting out your friends, neighbors, even your enemies could only be done by reptiles who scurried at the edges of society and drained humanity of spirit.

"There's something I must say," I suddenly cried out. "This woman, this woman is Alex's mother."

"Alex Bagen?" Eddie mumbled.

"My son is Alex Bagen?" Alla inquired in disbelief, forgetting momentarily that her son had chopped down his Russian name.

"Don't be a fool!" my mother gasped in Russian, "he doesn't have to know. If you tell him the truth now, it will ruin it. I know, I know, your grandmother and I have been pushing but I'm proud of you—"

"What are you saying to her?" Grandmother screamed.

"I'm proud of you for standing your ground, for fighting us," my mother said, "so why retreat now—this is only the beginning!"

"The truth has been forced out—Grandmother made sure of that," I whimpered.

"Don't you throw stones at me—no one's going to rat you out," Grandmother put in.

"That's true," Alla averred with a dollop of Russian pride, "I'm not an evil person. Whatever happened between you and my son I have to accept it. I may not like it but I have to accept it. And if you left my son for this—this"—she pointed with disgust at the Americans—"then what can I say—it's your life."

"Tell him the truth," Grandmother shouted. "I want to see what he does. He'll run from you like a cheetah, I assure you, and Godspeed! I don't want them—these anti-Semites in my house! Remember, when you marry him, you marry her too. You think your children will be Jewish? You think they won't step foot in a Catolik church?"

"My children, my children," I burst out, "they'll have my— *my*—my blood running through their veins."

"Marriage is bigger than you, than love, than sex—marriage is the future, it's your children, and they're your destiny! You can never escape your destiny—don't you understand what I'm saying? I've seen it all—women ruined by the choices they've made; Jewish men alienated from their own children, children who spit in their father's face and scream, 'Yid, get your dirty physiognomy out of my face!' Intermarriage will kill you—and us! Look at his mother—don't you feel her hateful glare burning your skin? Don't you feel it? I feel it—I can spot an anti-Semite from a hundred kilometers away—"

"You can spot a KGB agent on Deerfield Road too, so what! So what!" my mother shouted, intervening on my behalf. "Where are you getting your evidence from? You're a deaf mute in this country—you understand nothing, *nothing*! I see no evidence of your anti-Semitism—she's been perfectly civil to all of us—she's been trying so hard—"

"I can put burning coal on your skin and hold it there, and still you won't cry." Grandmother spoke strangely now, her voice seemed ancient, centuries old. "That's how you always were as a child: smiling at pain, smiling and holding it all in. You're the deaf mute, my daughter, you're the deaf mute."

The chandelier began to twirl and faces fused together in a rainbow of lights across the ceiling. Old thoughts broke into old words, old words into disparate sounds, disjointed from meaning, falling, falling—*splat!*—across a silent canvas aglow in lucent white, erasing cultures and points of view, each individual drawn indistinguishable in my abyss.

Nothing, no one mattered—least of all me. No matter what I said now, I knew he was vanishing. "I've been lying to you," I said at last—in English. "I've been lying! Right up until Maine I was still with Alex. This is his mother and we were engaged—do you understand, until about two months ago we were still engaged."

I repeated the word "engaged" as if it were a hammer, but he appeared inexplicably unperturbed, except for the fact that he didn't speak.

"What kind of show are you people running here?" Hal Beltrafio exclaimed.

"Fascinating—how did you ever manage it, my dear?" Mrs. Beltrafio remarked with a befuddling grin. "Why, Emma, my dear, it's a dangerous thing, you know, confusing life with art!"

My family stared at me without comprehension.

"What did she say? What did Lena say?" Grandmother demanded in Russian. "Someone translate for me!"

Eddie looked wildly around the room—at my mother and father and grandmother and Bella and then his eyes shone upon me.

"Is that all—is that all, Emma, is that all you've been lying about?"

"Yes," I replied, stunned.

"Don't be a fool, Ignatius, she's just admitted who she is—"

"I know who she is," he said, giving his mother a quick abrasive glance, "and her lies don't scare me." Then he looked at me again, kindly, with such forgiveness in his eyes I thought my heart would burst from pain. "I don't care—I don't care about the past. It was difficult for you to get here, but now we've arrived: we're together. Do you hear me, Emma? You're with me, fully, I know that. I don't care about any of them. Or whatever nonsense you had with him. I know who you are." His hands waved the room away and pulled me in, bringing my face close to his. "Do you understand what I am saying to you?" He kissed my mouth in front of them but there was a quivering in his lips, panic in his eyes.

"I—I don't understand—why—why are you doing this—"

"Because I love you—I love you and I know what this is—what all of them are doing. You have to be strong, Emma, you hear me? This is the moment to be strong, to remember who you are, what we have, to remember the 'us' in this chaos." He paused, looking at me intensely. "You have to be honest now."

"I am honest. I am finally honest. I was with him—engaged to him—I led a double life. I was indecisive. I told you I'd be honest with you when I came to you in my burgundy dress and I went on lying. I just went on. I told you I loved you, and I went back to Alex when I went to Chicago. I got into the habit, the habit of lying, of bifurcating my identity."

"But did you lie in Maine? Were you fully with me in Maine?"

"Yes, in Maine, I was yours. I had broken everything off by then—I broke it off for Maine, for you."

"You took her to Maine—to your house in Maine? That was supposed to be our house!" his mother whined. "How dare you? You promised me, Ignatius, you'd keep it as it was—"

"As it was?" I was suddenly confused. "I thought it was your house, Eddie."

"Emma's my life now, Mother, you have to accept that, and the cottage is going to be ours, hers and mine—it belongs to us."

"I don't have to accept anything—I don't have to accept her or them," his mother announced definitely. "You are my life, and I'm here to tell you that these are not people I want to be connected to in any way. They are not like us, Ignatius, they're not to be trusted—she's not to be trusted—can't you see that?"

"Mother, you need to leave now—you need to leave me alone!"

"Why don't we go to our hotel now, Cynthia, we really should let Eddie work out his own issues." His father spoke so meekly his voice fell into a whisper.

"Shut up, Hal, you stupid fool!" she snapped. "Can't you see, Eddie, can't you see it—they don't want us either!" She was screaming now, her controlled features seeming to melt into her face.

I backed away from him, after catching sight of her rage.

"Emma, please, please I'm begging you—don't let *her* come between us—try to remember what I told you in Maine—Emma—"

"What's happening? Someone translate!" my grandmother screamed. But no one did.

"Why haven't you asked your fiancée the most critical question?" Mrs. Beltrafio was suddenly calm, her features sewn back into her skin, her jaws hardened, her eyes releasing a malicious smile. "Why don't you ask her if she slept with Alex, if she was sleeping with the two of you at the same time?" The room glared at her at once, as if she had punctured a vein in the collective flesh of our entire community. "What—why are you all looking at me like that? It's a legitimate question—the question of betrayal! Don't you think my son deserves to know to what extent—to what depths these lies reach?"

"I tink you should leave," my mother said. "Take your son and leave."

"No, I refuse!" Eddie didn't look at anyone but me.

Then with a sudden, violent leap forward, he grabbed my arm. "Let's get out of here, somewhere, anywhere away from them—all of them!" He pulled me into the library, to the same room where I hid, listening to his mother speak.

I looked at him for some time before he lifted his gaze to me and said, "Did you sleep with him?"

"You would think *that*, wouldn't you, together with your mother?"

"Forget her. Just tell me the truth!"

"I've lost all track of time and space and definitions. I don't know what anything means anymore, Eddie—"

"Don't pretend to be crazy—grow up, Emma, for once in your life, grow up!"

"How was I supposed to decide between two different worlds? Between you and them, but don't you see—I chose you—I—" I flung my hands through the air and my mind involuntarily recalled the image of Mrs. Beltrafio's purgatory.

"Tell me the truth, why can't you just answer me—"

"I don't want to—"

"Why?"

"Because don't you see—it's your mother's question."

"It's still a legitimate one—"

"Then you understand nothing. You still know as little about me as you did when we first started—"

"You're a fool—I was willing to do anything for you, anything. I would have converted if you had asked, never spoken to my mother if you had asked. *I* wanted to know everything about you but you're always one step forward and ten steps back, always concealing. How could you lie in my bed, fuck me, and not tell me what bothered you—not tell me the truth! We lived together, for Christ's sake, looked into each other's eyes—and you were planning to marry him? Were you fucking him as well? It's unbelievable, like some daytime soap except the cuckold is me!"

"I tried to tell you—you can't imagine how many times I tried but I kept thinking I'll end it with Alex soon enough, when he calls . . . Then I thought—no, it's better to say it in person, but I didn't want to see him in person. When I was with you, I forgot about him, forgot about everything, the wedding, my grandmother; I forgot they all exist. You were the only reality I had, the only reality I wanted."

"So what made you break up with him at long last?"

"Because the thought of losing you was unbearable, the thought of losing you made breathing an ordeal, made living an ordeal, made, made everything else irrelevant—" Tears rose to my throat and then burst from my eyes in torrents. But he didn't seem to see them.

"Why would you tell me this ugly truth now? Why not tell me before when I was at peace and in control of my faculties? When we were alone? But here I've been railroaded—why here—in front of your parents and my mother—why this humiliation now?"

I should have told him about his mother at that moment; I should have told him what I heard. But my memory was slipping so that I could no longer recall with indubitable confidence the extent of her venom.

And why would he believe me anyhow—me—a veteran liar with no excuses save for the country where she was born? For lying was our daily sustenance there, our breathing tube. There was no reprieve from lying—it was the simplest, most expedient way to survive, a self-protective layer against cruelty and torture, ridicule and exile.

Yet what irony it was that my own women, like oracles of ancient Greece, always spoke the truth! They harangued and tormented you with the truth: how you looked, how stupid you sounded, how you shouldn't do that, how and what you should eat and drink, and whom you should fuck; you knew their opinion on everything. When you were on your own, you were still entangled in their cobwebs: you knew exactly where "you" stood.

Yet here in America, in the country where honesty was so highly prized that when you cheated on a test in high school, you got an F; a test in college, you were expelled; a test in law school, you could never practice law; and if God forbid you lied on the witness stand, you went to jail. And if you were the President of the United States, you were going to be impeached for lying—not for the screwing in itself—but for lying to the American people. But when you got together with well-meaning friends at a barbecue and saw someone in an ugly dress, you lied, lied to preserve civility at all cost, lied to preserve the status quo.

I opened my mouth to say, *Because of your mother! Because I don't know if it's possible for me to love you . . .* But instead, rage greeted me like an old friend.

"All you care about are the petty aspects of life: the little lies," I shouted, "why I said something or when, or why didn't I say it at the right time. You're so outraged by your little sense of justice that you can't see the real truth, the big truth. You want to rewrite the past because you've discovered something ugly in me, and you can't handle that—you can't handle any ugliness in life. Your unhealthy idealism doesn't allow for any glitches in the road—"

"'Glitches in the road,' 'glitches in the road'—is that what you call *this, this*?" he cried. "If only the problem was your family's disapproval of me! Your family would have accepted me eventually, even your grandmother! But the truth is that it was always about you: you couldn't decide, in spite of everything we had, you couldn't decide on me. You still can't!"

"No, that's not true. I did decide. I loved you—from the start—it's always been you. There was no decision to make. I was late in acting on it but inside I always knew, always!" I looked at him now, fearlessly, and added, "That's not what this is about. This is about more."

"What more could there be, tell me?"

"It's about *them*."

"*No*, no, I don't believe that! Maybe you enjoyed it: me and Alex together, the juggle, the double life, the lies—I get it! I've dated, I've been the player, I know the thrill of two lovers. Maybe this was your experiment of two men—your feminist theories set into motion—just to see if you could pull it off—to see if you could avenge centuries of male oppression on us—do you feel liberated now? How does it feel to be a man at last?"

"Ah, that's where you're wrong—you assume desire belongs only to you, to you, the men! You assume desire is the male province, but I'm here to tell you that it's mine too, that it's as much a woman's sphere as yours, if not more so! Playing you and Alex *was* a thrill! Loving you did not detract me from wanting both of you!" I screamed, and I wanted to scream more: I wish I had slept with Alex, I wish I had slept with Eric, I wish I had it in me to sleep with everyone I longed for and everyone I loathed, without fearing the stamp of "slut" and "whore," without dreading my family's judgment, his mother's reproof, without needing or wanting his fake forgiveness. *I don't need it! I don't need any of you!*

"I've told you—I don't care about that—I forgive you—all I want to know is if you slept with him after Maine? That's all I want to know."

"No—that's not what you want to know—you want to know if your mother is right about me! If I'm her—the girl from your past, the betrayer, the whore!" It came to me in that instant that he had never mentioned the girl's name.

"I don't understand—what was this supposed 'love' of yours? I still don't know why you even use the word! Was it all just within the context of inaccessibility, of that edge you like so much?" He breathed in, then let it out. "In telling me the truth you meant to end it!"

"That's not true—I meant to come clean—"

"If only that were true—if only there were such a thing for you as coming clean. But you didn't come clean—you were forced into it by your grandmother."

"They weren't going to reveal anything—I—it was I who wanted you to know the truth!"

How desperately I wanted to say yes, yes, it was *I* who *never* wanted him to know the truth. *I* would have kept it hidden, through the arduous year leading up to our wedding, zipping my lips at the altar before God, and then with each year of marriage, I'd forget to tell him. The memory of my engagement to Alex would fade—a mere blip on the rich quilt we'd weave together—and with time, I'd dismiss it as that thing, that thing you do when you're young and reckless with other people, and with time I'd free myself of its parasitic guilt. And one day when we were old, decrepit, barely breathing, I would tell him and he would laugh. Laugh without bitterness or vengeance—laugh out of love.

"What is the fucking truth? Tell me! Don't be a coward now—not now after everything we've been through! Don't be a coward without guts!"

Isn't that redundant, "a coward without guts," I wondered? Did he love me *that* much? Or did this question in itself mean that he had stopped loving me? I couldn't see clearly; his expression blackened, the room swam in bleak brown blobs, the bookcases floated through the air. I felt as if I were going temporarily blind. I tried to think of what to say next. Would it have been "guts" to prostrate myself on the floor and beg his forgiveness and speak *a* truth: *I do love you—I have always loved you, I am so madly in love with you I can die.* Or would it have been "guts" to straighten my back and indignantly state, *no I did not sleep with Alex—ever—is that the truth you're seeking, will that mollify you?* No, "guts" was something else entirely. For these words would never be uttered inside my family's home: here, my love and loyalty swung heavily to their side. How could he ever match up to *them*? What I did next took guts.

"I slept with Alex," I lied calmly. "I slept with Alex—after Maine—because he asked me for a favor. He was a virgin!"

"You what? He was a what? After Maine?" He stuttered, seeming at once struck and lost like a child. I wanted to reach out and hold him and seal the wound I had just opened, but he went on incomprehensibly, bleeding. "But—but—I don't—I don't quite understand, but before you said—that you—you said that you broke it off before, before Maine?"

"I lied."

"You lied—again. Just now. You lied again?"

"I didn't want to hurt your feelings again," I went on, not comprehending my own self.

"You're not making any sense. At all. Nothing is making sense."

"Maybe this will make sense: I slept with him to compare the two of you—and yes, I stayed with you because you turned out to be a better fuck."

He stared at me with such hatred his arm twitched at his side, as if itching to hit me. Hit me, I pleaded in silence, then out loud. "Hit me, why don't you hit me? You'll feel a lot better!" And then, shockingly, I smiled.

Bitterness glowed like oil on his face, and he quickly came back at me. "I am not interested in your games, Emma. Nor am I interested in being a truck stop for you—a service boy for your personal refueling."

"Exactly what I was for you," I swung back.

"Don't confuse us, Emma. When I met you, all the women I had known before you disappeared—no one could compare. I couldn't be with Sylvia after I saw you again—couldn't stand the sight of her—because I fell in love with—with—you—"

"Because I was a good fuck," I came riding in, to save him from further humiliation.

"No, no—because you were complicated and beautiful, because you were Russian and Jewish—"

"Because I was different—because I was your rebellion as well—still am—because you thought you couldn't have me—"

"I could have you. I can still have you. I just don't want you anymore," he retorted, smashing each word through the wall I had built around myself.

He stormed past me into the living room like a tornado that raised me up and hurled me down against the earth. *No, no, don't leave,* the impotent voice inside me screamed, but I couldn't move a finger or toe, much less my mouth. I heard hangers clanging, his blazer rustling, arms reaching into sleeves and heels clicking, Hal Beltrafio saying, "It was very nice to meet all of you. Thank you for dinner," and Mrs. Beltrafio's voice singing triumphantly, "thank you for the *lovely* evening," and the door slamming shut.

"Well, that requires a drink," my father swooped in, with his booming voice, as though here, finally, was his chance to save the family.

"I must get going," I heard Mrs. Bagdanovich say. "I'd love to stay and drink but Fima is threatening to buy another car if I don't cook him dinner every day." After throwing her black shawl over her shoulders, she lingered on the doorstep. "Don't let it get to you, Lena," she called out from the living room. "Marrying for love is a luxury most women can't afford. We settle on the middle ground, not to be terribly happy but to live normal decent lives. All right, I've said my piece, now I must go."

My mother and father and grandmother and Bella filed into the library like a procession of confused psychologists, preparing their incoherent speeches. Igor showed up a few minutes later, and the five of them fixated on my blank stare. There was no concept of privacy in our world. Pain was a collective experience, and talk wiped tears out. I wanted to scream GET OUT, but I looked at them helplessly from the floor as my father prodded, "Come, Lena, have a drink with us! You'll feel better."

"Are you all right?" my mother asked. "You look a little swollen and red —are you having an allergic reaction?"

"I'm sorry—so sorry about the way I acted," Igor mumbled.

"Well, good riddance," Grandmother muttered. "I could tell his mother was a bitch from her stinking perfume!"

"Be quiet!" my father yelled. "You've done enough!"

"I—I—what have I done?" Grandmother shot back. "She didn't have to tell him anything—we would have all kept our mouths shut."

"Don't worry," my father said, leaning toward me, "he'll come back to you, I promise. Love, real love is difficult to shake off."

I looked at him helplessly, thankfully, but somehow his words induced even more pain.

"Oh God, she's losing breath—give her some Benadryl! She can't breathe! Get a brown paper bag!" Bella cried. They looked at me, awaiting a word, some response, a twitch on my face, but I couldn't speak. I was flat matter, devoid of self, only my mouth was open, ready to swallow death. But Bella stuck two pink tablets on my tongue and held cold water to my lips, then held a paper bag to my face. "Breathe, Lena, breathe! Now!" I closed my eyes, put my mouth inside the bag, and swallowed gulps of air, forcing it through the closed passages of my lungs. I don't remember time moving, only my eyes opening and seeing my mother, her blue moist eyes, her soft arms cradling me, her fingers running through my hair.

In the Warm Pouch of Failure

I lay on my bed with the windows flung wide and warm fall air gushing in. Every once in a while a cool gust would intercept and seep inside my ribs—whispering of October, November, December, of the impending winter hurrying to rob us of this deceptive heat.

I felt a freezing wind rattle in my lungs. Intermittently the tears would return and I'd let out a muffled wail. A blanket sat in a heap on the edge of the bed, and I crawled inside, compressing my body into a tight ball like a snail burying itself in her shell. My mind whirred around one thought: could it be possible that all my suffering in Russia signified nothing? How did I let it come to this gridlocked silence, to this abysmal lie, to this anticlimactic, thoroughly unsatisfying end? I'd changed nothing, fought for nothing, my paralysis taking root, invading every cell in my detestable organism. I repulsed myself.

"What have you done?" A figure appeared in the doorway. "You've ruined everything!" It was Bella. Her blistering red dress swam inside my head, and for a moment, I imagined she was a Communist flag swaying over the horizon.

"So I have," I said after a long silence.

"Why?"

"Because there was no other place left to go. I couldn't stand her—"

"His mother?" Bella seemed surprised.

"She's a rabid anti-Semite," I said.

"That's Grandma talk," she admonished. "I think she did her best, given the situation—I just thought she was a weird cookie, that's all, kind of charming even—"

"I overheard her; I went to the library and listened—she said things about Jews." I wanted to give evidence but I couldn't remember a single sentence Mrs. Beltrafio had uttered.

"But maybe, Lenochka, you're just being overly sensitive—I mean, it can't be easy with what you went through, but you must remember, this isn't Russia."

That's when I realized that I had kept the truth from him *not* out of fear but out of shame; *I* was so ashamed for Mrs. Beltrafio that I began to feel her heinous blunder to be *mine*, to be *his*—I needed to wipe it clean.

"Oh, it doesn't matter anymore," I whispered, half-dead.

"You're too far gone—that's the real problem."

"Gone?"

"In love," she offered.

"Yes, in love," I echoed, emptiness stretching before me.

"You're so stupid," she said.

"Yes, I am, aren't I?" I looked up at her, and through tears, I smiled.

"I'm going to tell you something right now, something I've never told anyone. Not because I have an overwhelming need to reveal the truth, it doesn't really matter, but because you—you need to hear it. That year I spent in New York auditioning—"

"That mysterious year you never talk about?"

"So everyone—you, Mom, Dad, Grandma, you all thought I failed, right?"

"We just assumed."

"Wrong. Yes, it was very hard at first, there were plenty of rejections, but there were also acceptances—you know, little roles here and there in small theaters. I took acting and singing classes, met people, networked at parties. I created a portfolio of songs, Broadway and pop, became proficient in jazz and modern dance, and had all my monologues memorized like a good little Russian soldier, sad ones, funny ones, emotionally stunted ones. And then there were the endless open calls where I'd sit in a room with hundreds of other beautiful struggling actresses and I'd have two minutes in front of the casting directors to sing and do my monologue, and like clockwork, the words, 'Thank you, next!' would ring in my head for days afterward. I always had to recover after those, but I went back again and again. I wasn't sure how much stamina I had in me, how much longer I would last, but I thought *maybe it'll happen this time*. Except that I knew nothing! It wasn't until I started dating this guy in one of my acting classes, not just some guy, but someone whose uncle was a talent agent and who had connections. I didn't know any of that when I slept with him, but after sex, he said to me, 'you're really very talented and you have an excellent voice.'" She laughed uproariously but it was tinged with an implacable bitterness.

"He took me to something called a 'closed audition.' It was for a little Broadway musical, perhaps you've heard of it: *Les Misérables*!"

"Bellochka, I—I had no idea—"

"Wait, let me finish. They had already filled out the chorus, but there were small roles, small singing solos they still needed people for. I got a good night sleep. God, I looked beautiful that day. I wore all black. I was in a room with seven people staring at me from behind their casting table, one of them was the director, and I knew at once who he was: I could see his eyes light up when he looked at me, like he was in love. And it gave me confidence, the way he looked at me, I felt as if I already owned him, owned the room; it was exhilarating!" She laughed again, strangely. "So they asked me to come back again and again, and they asked me to sing 'I Dreamed a Dream.' I had that song down cold. Still, you can't imagine how nervous I was—but my voice didn't fail me. I was perfect, better than I had ever been in front of the mirror or with my voice teacher, and I knew in that instant I had captured them, captured the director, all of them. They said it right on the spot: you have the role. 'Which one am I—in the chorus?' I asked. 'No,' the director said, 'we want you to play Fantine.'"

"My God, Bella, why didn't you tell anyone?"

"It happened so quickly—I was in the city for only nine or ten months and in the acting world, it's nothing, really. Nothing! It was practically overnight. I did the right thing, I told myself. How smart I was not to listen to Mom and Grandma and you! Here I am—cast in a major role on the biggest stage in the world, and what are they offering me: the world, really, not just prestige, not just my own money, but freedom, superb freedom! I felt such acute happiness!

"I didn't want to call home right away—I wanted to absorb it first, keep it to myself for a bit, like a secret that only belonged to me. Rehearsals were supposed to start the following week. So I said to my roommate, let's celebrate. You never, never, ever drink before you plan to sing! But I—I was Russian, wild, invincible!

What did I care! So my roommate and I went to bars each night and met men. Every place I stepped into, the men came at me, one more handsome, more successful than the next. I felt like a Goddess. I'm a Broadway actress, I'd say with pride. I forgot the family, forgot even to boast—oh, how miserably I wanted to boast to Grandma. And I drank, dear God, how much I drank.

"Then suddenly my voice gave out—kaput, nothing. I woke up one morning the day before the Monday of rehearsals next to some dark-haired model. I don't remember anything about him except for the tattoo on his navel of a tiny butterfly, and I remember wanting it to come to life, to flutter between us. I don't remember the sex: nothing, all a blur.

"The whole day—that whole day I ran around frantically drinking tea with honey, and eating garlic. I thought I had the flu but it was just my voice and it became more hoarse. The day of rehearsals I arrived: I got up on that stage, opened my mouth but instead of a sound, a croak came out like an old staircase about to split in half. Here and there my old smooth voice would peek through but it was sporadic and broken by static. The director and producers were horrified. The other actors, especially the women, stood in silence, trying to hide their grins. They knew what this meant: it was their turn soon.

"I was a nobody. I had no clout, and they certainly weren't going to wait for me. A few days maybe, but my voice was gone—it was totally gone! I thought I'd never sing again. I went to the doctor and he said I had damaged my larynx slightly, that it would heal eventually—in a few months. But I didn't have a few months!

"Who knows what stunts I pulled in my drunken stupor. My roommate says it was at Lime, where they had this huge fantastic stage. I got up and danced and sang 'I Will Survive' so loudly that the whole audience went wild. But when I got off the stage, I couldn't speak—it must have been then.

"How could I have been so stupid? And how could I tell our family the truth, that I ruined everything for myself? The director asked the understudy to replace me, and said if you ever recover come back to us. I never recovered, not emotionally at least." She looked out the window at the trees swaying idly on our lawn. Nature didn't care about our mangled destinies, our self-destructive feats . . . nature remained unperturbed, I thought.

"I've spent years trying to figure it out, Lenochka—why? Why, why? After that, I auditioned for a few movie roles, and was asked to show my breasts for a horror film. I thought to myself, why should I degrade myself like this when I know what I *can* have?

"The only thing I ever wanted in life—the Broadway stage—I destroyed. It was time to go home."

"But I don't understand," I murmured, "how could you hold this in your palms and let it go? You must have realized it, you must have not really wanted it . . . were you afraid?"

"Maybe. Maybe I was a broken vessel and a broken vessel needs to heal first. Because the truth was that I didn't believe I deserved it—this wonder, this success, this miracle only God could have put into my very palms, and you know, I have lots of quarrels with God, but still . . . if there was a God, why would He let me self-destruct? I want you to understand something: you are not me! I know it was partly fear, and I know you suffer from it too, but don't for one second confuse us: you changed your name, you went to New York, you brought Eddie home to Mom and Grandma—you're far more courageous than I could ever be. I married Igor, enough said."

"But why don't you leave him? Divorce him, Bella!"

"Leave him? No—I can't! How can I raise Sirofima as a single mom? No, that's not my lot in life. Let the American women be feminists; let them be brave. I'm of the old country; I know that now. The tradition of living out your misery is deeply entrenched in me."

"I know he follows you. He has people follow you. He controls the money, your bank account, your credit card, your every move . . . Bella, please, I know you know this. He's paranoid and controlling, a quiet snickering tyrant is what he is! You can't even have a fucking affair," I cried out feverishly. But Bella only laughed, her ringing operatic voice devoid of any bitterness or sarcasm.

"You, Lenochka, are always seeking doorways, escape routes, holes through which sunlight might burst through and melt your chains. But not me—I know my prison! This is the prison I've chosen for myself, that I've watched being built around me. Don't for one second mistake me for some unconscious fool—I know who I am. And maybe there were openings but I never pried them open. I stayed. He's my gatekeeper; he's also the rock that keeps me tethered to the ground—"

"You mean chained?"

"No, don't, don't do that! He keeps me sane. He reminds me that I should keep my expectations reasonable, modest."

"Like a good little Communist—reasonable, modest . . . oh, Bellochka!"

"Because if I let myself dream for one moment—I would die."

"It's not too late, Bellochka," I whimpered. "You can go back to New York. You look young and beautiful and you sing, you sing even better now. It's never too late."

"No, it is," she said resolutely, pushing back the tears that sprang involuntarily into the corners of her eyes. "After all, being here is in a way what I need. I need *them*: Mom, Dad, Grandma." Her eyes appeared in the evening light to resemble two turquoise stones that had grown more transparent with age.

"I was afraid. I'm still afraid! This—this"—she pointed at the parquet floor—"is the only life I can accept in peace. But this is not *your* life—this is no life for *you*!"

"What am I supposed to do—go back to him? Beg his forgiveness? I don't want him anymore."

"Do you love him still?"

"Of course, can't you see?"

"Everyone can see," she said, "but you know how I feel about men! We, strong Kabelmacher women, we can live without them. But we can't live without our passions and I know you want to paint, that you *have* been painting."

"So?"

"Listen to me, Lena—go back—quit the program. Go back for your art. Stop taking money from Dad. Do it on your own, without any crutches, without anyone, without Eddie. Don't get lost in other people's opinions, or in things that offend you. If there's one thing that Yakov's right about—we're always getting offended. You have to take it, be strong. Look at me, Lena, take a good look at me: is this what you want for yourself? Mother sees through me, you know, she sees how much I suffer. And she's always suspected something."

"Who doesn't Mom suspect, who doesn't she see through?"

"So she sees through you; she'll understand."

"And what about Grandma?"

"Grandma will be in hysterics but I'll be here to comfort her like you did when I left."

"We had to put the pieces together—you were her golden pony—her pride and joy."

"And you're not?"

"Not in the same way," I said.

"Maybe that's why you feel freer . . ."

"Maybe," I whispered, tears cascading down my cheeks. "I'm so, so sorry for what happened to you. So sorry you have to live with him . . . in this prison."

She stared out the window without wincing, without any display of pain or regret. Then she turned toward me, smiled gently as if I were an awkward child, and ran her fingers through my tangled hair. "Not a day goes by that I don't wish I could take back those days of revelry. Not a day goes by that I don't wonder what my life might have been if I had had the courage back then to claim what belonged to me—because that stage belonged to me, Lenochka, because I knew how to live on it, and make it come alive."

"It still does, Bellochka, it still comes alive—even in Yakov's restaurant—those people have never seen anything like you!"

"I know it's ridiculous," she said, "me on Yakov's neon pink stage. I'm the Belle of Moscow Nights, Lenochka, laughable, me with my aspirations and yet it's brought me back to life." She looked out the window at the trees bending from the rising wind and said, "But I have no regrets—I have Sirofima now and all roads lead to her, her future. I'm done for."

"My God Bella, you're only thirty-one—you're so young!"

"As I said, done for. It doesn't hurt anymore. It's a memory the way Russia is a memory—there are no time machines, no way to reach back and change the facts—what's done is done, as they say. But *you*, Lenochka, you have no children, no husband, nothing to hold you back. *Carpe Diem! Derzhis!* There's something in you, something fearless and real and different from all of us: all you need to do is hold on and ride your *Zhar-ptitsa*." My *Zhar-ptitsa*, my Bella, myself, we were all of us, firebirds with magic in our feathers and flames in our souls.

Old watercolors and acrylics were hidden under my bed and I took them out after Bella left the room, and set three empty canvases side by side, as if something were unfolding in front of me, a saga dissected in three parts. I filled empty cans with water, extracted battered sable brushes and an old crenulated palette, used a scissor to poke holes in the green and blue and yellow acrylic tubes, whose original openings had dried shut from lack of use, and began to work.

Paintings #4, #5, #6

I'm on the train platform in Kiev holding my father's hand. Metal beams arch over our heads like prison bars across the sky and a giant clock carved in steel glares from a slab of concrete, mimicking the bleak white sun. Trains screech and huff like humans carrying bricks upon their heads and we stare into their puffing mouths, spewing fumes into the sky. The sky lives here, inside the station, among the passengers below, and rain and lightning and snow, all grimaces of nature, pass through here on a sour day. It is a sour day today; we've come to tell my other grandmother, Grandmother Liza I call her, that we're leaving for America. My father's face is roped in guilt, his cheeks are limp, as though they're hanging from his brows. He takes me out for walks, for movies, runs from his mother's bleeding eyes. She's said her piece, she's wept for us, she'll never come with us. I will die here, my son, this is my soil, Grandmother Liza smiles, a gray smile on a plump soft face with wrinkles hanging from her neck, death whispering in her ear. She brings out the sour cream and farmer's cheese, fresh and aromatic, just whipped and sieved, squeezed from a local cow. Eat, she tells me, eat! You're too skinny—they don't feed you anything in Moscow. I put a spoon against my gums and lick the fat with my long tongue. I close my eyes and feel this rich, smooth, sour-sweet mass glide inside my mouth like frozen snow and gently thaw. The taste remains, engraved in memory, a single moment stretched into a longing that will follow me into my other, my English-speaking life.

Stay here, Grandmother says, why can't you all stay here, what's wrong with Russia, what's the rush? She places black tea under our noses and the aroma fills our mouths with nostalgia as though we're already in a foreign land. My father doesn't budge: we're going for a better life, but he doesn't define what that is. There's horror here, he tells her with defiance, we're suffocating, we're going for the children, for a freer life. He's reciting my mother's words, my mother's feelings. She is speaking for him, through him. Grandmother Liza stares in disbelief. I don't see it, she says, I don't see what you mean. That's because you've never known anything but this provincial town, you've never wanted anything but this . . . this—he points at the sour cream. You don't know, my father stumbles, what's happened to the children, to Lenochka, his voice gaining conviction. I feel invisible under their adult fury and plug my ears with my invisible hands. I see my father's mouth moving, lips trembling, eyes becoming moist. I know the story he's retelling—the year that I was five—the first "incident" to light the fire of leaving, the first trigger to father's indecisiveness, his inner tension: how do I balance Lenochka against my own interests, against my own life? He cannot mention the Camp for Intellectuals—too fantastical, too horrific—the real reason he's agreed and we've applied.

Nothing burns the way humiliation burns—a tumor growing in you, on you.

How many of us on that day—thirty, twenty, fifty—laid out like sardines on silver cots during our mandatory nap, pretending to be asleep? But I and Alla Feldman, or was it Feldshtein, Ferber, Fishbein, I can't remember which, another Jew like me, and four other rabble-rousers are giggling, tickling one another's toes, making farting noises with our lips upon our arms, riling the others from their supposed slumber. And suddenly the room is full of mirth, sardines have turned into sprites, and forearms, thighs, and elbows serve as instruments in a symphony of farts. No one hears the heavy breath behind the door, her thickset arms and barrel legs tensing in an awkward stillness, gulping time; no one feels her scorching eyes surveying, seizing who to punish. She has hair like viscous tar wrapped round her head and she wears white—a nurse's sacred garb, caretaker of our bodies, our stomachs, our health. Though the teachers theoretically wield more power, we fear only Her. Kabelmacher, you and Feldman get *up*! Get up! She appears out of nowhere, black pupils glinting, lips curving upward as though from some internal hilarity of hatred. You are punished, she yells. What are we punished for? I have the courage, the chutzpah, the *hrabrost* to ask. For disturbing all the other children from their naps, she screams. *But I*—One more sound out of you, Kabelmacher—she waves her mammoth palm close to my cheek to blot out my outrage, my spirit. You and Feldman in the closet, *now*, she roars—a roar inside my spine. Only the dark and hunger will cure you of your obstinacy, your arrogance, your affected manners. She speaks in doublespeak, in adult-speak, and pulls us by our shirt sleeves, our necks, our hair. You stay here, she commands, throwing us in the closet of mattresses and cots, until you understand who you are—peons, pawns, *peshki*!

Inside the closet, foul-smelling mattresses are folded and stacked on wooden shelves. Only silver cots protrude from corners, from the dark. Before the door slams shut, I catch the other children squinting, eyeing us in a guilty—or is it a giddy—silence, running for their cookies, tea, and milk. How long, I want to ask, are we to bear your nonsense, you fat, foul-mouthed *Baba Yaga*. But my throat is parched and Alla's sobbing, laying her head upon my arm. And though Alla's taller, stronger, three months older, *I, I* keep my head up high—no dragon will make me cry.

The mattresses are cumbersome and stained, yellowing from piss. Food rises to my throat but I push it back, I put my tough face forward. My legs untangle and I swing open the closet door, I look beseechingly at the two teachers fussing with the dishes, but neither looks my way. You're punishing us for nothing, nothing, at last I scream. We were all, all of us making mischief. Thick brown fingers grip my collar, and at once she's upon me, in my ear: *your punishment has not been terminated.* Vomit shoots out of my mouth—I cannot hold it back! The undigested porridge spurts from my nose, my throat, acid trickles down my neck and shirt, seeping into my underwear, my shoes, my stockings. You filthy Yid, the monster yells, flinging her filthy hands before my eyes. You made the mess, now you clean it up! The puddle of my vomit spawns tiny rivers that cross the threshold of the closet's door and stream under the cots and mattresses arrayed along the floor. The odor overtakes the air, and children screech in bliss and in disgust. The monster brings gray rags and two buckets of soapy water and sets them under our kneeling forms. Alla wrings my vomit from putrid rags, coughing from nausea, from weeping. And after we have finished, Alla crouches in a corner, away from me, because I'm wet and reek of acid, clumps of porridge still cling to my skin.

The children laugh, yet all I hear is a cacophony of nervous shrills and broken echoes, and in a blur I see them in their *shubas* running out, out, out into the freedom of the yard, shouting into the cloudless winter day. The monster now appears, grotesquely grinning, having grown larger in the interim of time. She commands Alla to rise: *you* are being released. And I catch shame spread on Alla's face, the shame of wanting to abandon me, to be like them, to be of them. You go, the monster tells her, Kabelmacher still has work to do!

The door slams shut. I am now alone, alone and hungry. I see shapes from corners forming, silver eyes flickering, watching me—predators gathering for a human feast. And suddenly I see entire walls collapse into black rivers that spawn black silk that thicken into fur: they're panthers now with cobalt diamond eyes—scraping walls, floors, slashing mattresses, etching blood-vines along my skin, and still I am alive. I'm breathing. I spot a panther perched upon the upper shelf, but as I stare, it changes, its physiognomy transmogrifies into a human face. The lines draw human features but instead of skin it sprouts black-green seaweed and claws appear instead of hands and feet, and snakes instead of limbs, a monster whose breath can kill—*Babushka, dorogaya, Zinadiya*, where are you, why have you forsaken me? The clock is ticking, ushering more monsters in, until my mind fills to the brim; I pull my legs in closer to my torso and feel them coming, in large wet spots around my eyes, my ill-begotten tears of cowardice and petrifaction, burning up my skin.

Then through my hiccups, I hear a voice, a teacher speaking: It's enough, Darya Ivanovna, let Lena out, she's learned her lesson. Always pitying the Yids, the monster barks. Enough, the teacher says, her grandmother will be here soon. What can *she* do to me? the monster says, laughing. They're speaking things I know. I know that Yid's a Jew, and Jews are bad but who's the Yid? Not *I*! The door is thrown ajar, light gushes in, and there the teacher stands with arms like white wings flapping. She cradles me and whispers: wipe your eyes, Lena, get yourself in order, wash your face, straighten up, don't feel sorry for yourself. She strips me of my soiled shirt. Naked, I'm fitted in my *shuba* and pushed into the freezing January gale under the red-rimmed sun. By the time Grandmother Zinayida comes to pick me up, my face is clean and white again, stripped of trauma, compressed into a small hard ball. And when Zinayida asks me how my day went, I say, fine, fine, I played in the snow today with Alla Feldman, we made a snowman with our frozen hands. But then her face transforms, her features wilt, her veiny hand is on my naked chest, her lips press on my burning forehead. My pants are full of vomit, piss, and shit. The fever's risen to 104 degrees, I'm shaking, smiling, nodding, coughing—the winter gale has come in—see, here, it's whirring in my lungs. Zinayida grips her skull with fingers stiff from horror, cheeks palpitate from scarlet rage. She yells at everyone, the teachers, monster, children, and seeks a sign, some hint of shame, to trickle out of their unified apathetic gaze. An accident, they say, an unfortunate coincidence.

She was her kindergarten nurse, I hear my father saying to his mother, she had pneumonia for a month. We wrote a letter to the director of the kindergarten, demanded that the nurse be fired, but she's still there, working unpunished and unperturbed. Terrible, Grandmother Liza murmurs, terrible, but that is not all of Russia, not all Russians. I plug my ears now harder, a fist inside each hole, and through a distant echo hear the door slam.

My father grabs my hand and into the rain he takes me, a black gargantuan umbrella opening in his other hand. We're running to a movie about dinosaurs and earthquakes, an import from Japan. Rain fills our shoes, beats against our legs, washes our faces. Wind pulls our bodies forward, jerking the umbrella from side to side. Try to stay under it, my father says, hide from the rain. But my father is tall and wide like a giant, and I feel like a Lilliputian from the story grandma Zinayida reads to me at night. Swaying, I tilt away from father and gulp the water tumbling from the sky. Hold the umbrella, he says, hold on or you'll keep getting wet. I clasp the slimy handle in my fingers and squeeze it hard. Wind rages at my back and creeps inside my coat, a serpent of cold air encircling my ribs and thighs. At first I think I'm dreaming, but no, I *feel* the wind unfurl the sidewalk underneath my feet and up, up, up into the angry air I rise, no longer bound by gravity to earth. I'm flying, look, *papochka*, I'm flying, I shout, delighted, in his ear. He doesn't hear me; his thoughts are tucked away in Grandmother's apartment. *Papochka, papochka*, I'm rising, climbing, disappearing in feathery black clouds. I'm Jack on the beanstalk. I'm the Snow Queen in the sky. He turns to me abruptly, a stricken twisted face, and at his shoulder, my green galoshes dangle like inverted cactuses suspended from the sky. Who's the giant now, I wonder, drunk from weightlessness, from power. He grabs my legs and pulls me down; my father's arms are stronger than the wind. He takes away the magical umbrella, untangling my fingers from its grip. Stay under it, he yells, irritable, scared. My feet are on the sidewalk now, treading the earth like all the other tiny people of the world. I feel sadness entwine my heart, the sadness of not being able to fly.

Back in our kitchen in Moscow, a red table and red chairs face a window without sun and Babushka Zinayida is fussing over me, beating eggs inside a silver bowl, her face zigzagging in blue-gray wrinkles, her alabaster skin's like mine, her emerald eyes look at me beneath two blonde brows. I have a surprise for you, your favorite, she mutters, relaxing the space between her brows. I wave my spoon in ecstasy, drooling as I catch Beluga in a pickle-sized jar—a sea of shimmering black pearls. I tear into it, ecstatic, ravenous. I am eight and queenly and special, imbibing a deficit from the black market, the same black market that got Bella her new expensive Levi's jeans. I purr with pleasure and my fingers work in competition with my tongue. But I am small and my stomach fills up quickly and I say full, I'm full, Grandmother, I don't want to eat any more. Grandmother's wide forehead crinkles, a frown gathers in the brows, and she shakes her blonde head at me, her hand at me: hear, stupid child, of a world that was mine:

It's 1941 and I'm an angel with golden flowing hair and green eyes and porcelain skin, colors so light, no one ever suspected me of being a Jew. The Russians said, "you're not a Jew! Tell us the truth: did you mother have a secret lover? Did she sin with a Slav?" I'm eighteen years old and I'm running barefoot in a blue sundress through alleys of pines and un-graveled earth. It's 1941 and the Nazis have invaded Ukraine and now they're entering the outskirts of Moscow, moving quickly through our forests and meadows and entering our dachas, looking for Jews, hounding Jews with their German shepherds and bayonets and idiotic ideology. Suddenly people are running, I'm running, everyone is running to the trains to evacuate to the South—to Uzbekistan. I see the Nazi pilot, I see his face. The plane is so low, so low, Lenochka, he can reach out and choke me in his hand, he can pull the trigger. But he only fired bullets at my bare feet. I was saving ten children, eight-year olds, five-year olds, three-year-olds, an infant in my arms. My grandmother, with her royal golden hair and brown eyes, like a queen she presided over her eighteen children, eighteen children, all of whom, except for three, will die by 1945. Out of the ten children in my care, only five will survive the war. The Nazi pilot laughed at me, at me and the children! Laughed like crazy. Laughed and fired bullets. Bullets at our bare feet. Bozhenka saved me, God saved me! My blonde hair saved me. All would have been different if he had seen a Jew. I see the Nazi pilot always—in my dreams, when I wake, when the door shakes. I see him now—shhhhhhhh, don't ever tell anyone what I tell you—you're too young to be burdened with my life, so eat, eat this precious food. Grandmother quiets down when my mother and father come in.

But they're too late: I heard everything and licked all the caviar away, leaving the buttered bread untouched upon my plate. Why do you spoil her like that, my mother laments, there won't be any left for Bella; she must learn to share with her sister. She needs the vitamins, Grandmother says, it's good for her, it's just for her. And my mother, frustrated, fatigued, plops down next to me. You're always spoiling them, she mumbles in defeat. I spoiled all of you, Grandmother bites back. My mother sighs, consigns herself to silence. Her face is luminescent white, an oval rising out of a dark red mane. She is in her new silk robe, a grandiose black canvas embroidered in wine-colored roses that stare like rejected lovers from her breasts. Her features soften and a smile blossoms, bathing her countenance in a godly glow. Her lucid eyes swim in blue twilight waters and settle from time to time on my mesmerized face. Will I ever be beautiful like you, I ask my mother. You're already more beautiful than me, she whispers and her long thin fingers wipe the envy off my face. I push the jar of caviar toward her; I want to share with *you*, I say. No, no, my mother murmurs, blushing, finish it, I'll get more from the black market soon.

How was Kiev, my mother asks my father, how was your mother? But he says nothing; his eyes strike venom at his egg-filled plate. She was sad, I speak for Father, sad to see us go. I feel my fingers numbing, I feel a fight is brewing, my father's anger growing in each unspoken word. She should come with us, Zinayida says. We don't know yet, my father snaps, if we'll even get out. Bella enters the kitchen in a blue silk robe, an imitation of my mother's. Have you told them yet, she asks. While you two were away—my mother turns to my father, voice like a bowstring breaking—Grisha was attacked. Your grandfather was attacked. Grandmother looks only at me. Behind her high demeanor and stoic face, she's weeping, just not for us to see. What, how, my father asks and jumps from fear out of his chair. The KGB, Grandmother whispers as though they're here in our kitchen, hiding like toy soldiers in our red cabinet drawers, they smashed his jaw with a metal knuckle bar. She forms a hard red fist.

When Grandfather returns from the hospital he looks pale and gaunt; deep creases cut his forehead into roads, distorting the outlines of his eyes. His mouth is toothless, formless, a pitch-black cave, and when he smiles at me, I stare from curiosity and disgust. He wears fake teeth, but only for an hour—for the guests. And when he pulls them out—this bleached white fence out of his mouth—he gags and starts to cough. He smokes three packs a day, as though he's still young and virile, hanging with his war buddies on the porch, whistling at my grandmother's undulating behind. He smokes each cigarette with love, bearing in each puff a dole of memory. I hide his cigarettes under my pillow. I hide them in the ground in our park. I send them off to garbage cans in alleys. Where are my cigarettes, he yells, accusing Grandmother, where have you taken my only pleasure in life. You can't smoke, Grandpa, I tell him, the doctors say you can't smoke. And so he knows it's me and ransacks my closets, drawers, and pillows, his porcelain teeth glistening at my dour face. He runs his fingers through my tangled hair, as if to say, that's sweet of you, child, but you're too young to understand the old.

Enraged and breathless, I run to find my parents to complain: he's ruining his lungs, his heart, his toothless smile. But my mother and my father bear his guilt upon their backs, for they too are smokers, elegant and regal, recent members in this club for shattered nerves. They're smoking more now that two years have passed and there's no permission slip in our mailbox, no word yet from the KGB. They have even acquired the physique of longtime smokers, their shakes and twitches calming as they puff. They're moving seamlessly from pack to pack each day now that the mailbox stays empty through New Years Eve, 1982. They're closing the gates, Grandfather says, hundreds are being refused. We're done for. We should have applied sooner, my mother says. Her eyes accuse my father. We can't become like the Goldmans and the Shapiros, my mother wails, they've lost everything—jobs, respect, friends, they're ghosts now with packed suitcases under their beds. What will become of the children, if the teachers—oh *Bozhenka* and the neighbors find out, what will Bellochka and Lenochka do? We should never have applied in the first place, my father whispers, but only I can hear him. But Isaac Goldman is a nuclear physicist, Grandmother points out, what are we—nothing—we're nothing to them! What do they need us for? Bella begins to whimper, tears drawing circles around her gray-blue eyes. We should have applied sooner, she cries, copying my mother, then runs to the middle bedroom where she sleeps alone like the princess on a pea.

Grandfather smokes as he dreams of America, watching rain turn into sheets of gray, reading newspapers full of lies in the green wallpapered room he shares with Grandmother and me. They sleep on a tall plush bed with lion feet and a metal fortress at their heads, their bodies rising and falling to the sound of their synchronized snoring. Now that Grandfather has a mangled jaw, air rattles on his gums and whistles like a dragonfly he's caught and caged. With each day he looks grimmer, grayer, his white skin turning a yellow-green, and a cough tears apart his lungs. In America, he tells me, you'll learn Hebrew and find out about Passover and Hanukkah. What's Hebrew, I ask. It's a language that Jewish people speak. Who's Jewish, I say angrily, we're Russian, everyone says so! Everyone, *everyone*, he says, inhaling smoke into his ailing lungs, is stupid! And until you see it for what it is—stupidity as the patriotic hymn of a Marxist Socialist Whoredom, you'll never be free of it yourself. I'm confused, I whisper.

Let me tell you a secret, Lenochka, lest you think I'm just an old fool, coughing and croaking like an invalid. I'm a big operator—shhhhhhhh, but you must not tell anyone for I speak now to strengthen you against the future, to give you pride in who you are: I'm fighting rats, you see, suffocating them slowly, dribs by drabs, the information leaks out, soaked up by the hungry on the other side. When you get to America, don't forget me. But you're coming with us, I cry. No, no, the rats will kill me soon, my sweet, but don't be afraid. I'm not afraid. Know that your grandfather did important things in his life, and I'm old now, old enough to die. You must listen to your grandmother, he tells me, for she's a very great woman and I fear I haven't been a very good husband at all. That's because you were fighting rats, I say. That's right, my sweet.

Two days later, at two o'clock in the afternoon as the sun seeps through our velvet curtains and dances on our parquet floors, two men appear at the door. They have human eyes and lips and noses, and they possess arms and legs, but I suspect they're *lyudoyedy*, blue-bearded ogres, with human blood drying in empty brown veins and green metallic stones inside their ribcages instead of hearts.

Gregory Abramovich Guildenshtein is having a heart attack, they announce in one voice.

Who said, Grandmother screams at them.

I said, my grandfather declares, stepping out of his room, a cigarette butt sitting stubbornly between his lips.

No, Grandmother begs, it's not your time yet—it's not your time. Where, where does it hurt? She's weeping, my grandmother is weeping and screaming all at once.

Let's not play charades! And let's not make this unpleasant, Comrade Guildenshtein—do not induce us to beat up an old man, one *lyudoyed* says, his gaze fixed on her.

You've already done that, Grandmother replies, then sputters words that sound like fragmented cries.

I'm ready, Grandfather says, already clad in his gray traveling suit, a black hat covering his balding head. But Grandmother lays her body down on the floor, a human beanbag, a human shield, and Grandfather leans down and lifts her from the ground and kisses her softly. I'm sorry for all the pain I've caused you, my dearest Zinochka, forgive me, Zinochka, forgive me, and she erupts in an earsplitting, heart-quaking, embattled cry. And in that instant, Grandfather disengages and spreads his arms out like a wartime jet. The men mangle his wings and take him away on a white sheet, on a white stretcher, in a white ambulance where he will die. The phone rings a week later and a voice in the receiver states: we are sorry to inform you that your husband, Citizen Gregory Abramovich Guildenshtein, died of a massive heart attack a few hours ago. Was it hours, minutes, days ago, we do not know, and the words, massive heart attack, like massive bullets, reverberate through our home. And when Grandmother hangs up the phone and tells Bella and me that our grandfather has passed away, I will smile. I will remember for a long time that I smiled, and feel horror and stupefaction for smiling. But with time I will forgive myself, for I was only a child and death seemed like a strange place where Grandfather had gone to smoke and dream of America in the rain.

PART IV

The Elusive One-Night Stand

I returned to New York in pieces, weak and depressed; only its vibrancy and anonymity and perennial crudeness gave me relief from my thoughts. There were multitudes of cranky cab drivers; gaseous exhausts from trucks and buses decreasing your lung capacity; vans and SUVs that almost ran you over as you crossed on green light; Fifth Avenue saleswomen who helped you find the exit; art gallery curators who stared you down till you were several inches shorter; outrageous fashions erupting on sidewalks on men and women, gay and straight and transgender, at whom you could gape without feeling self-conscious unless they were famous, in which case you had to jerk your head in the opposite direction to feign indifference; apartments the size of a kitchen sink in a Midwestern suburb with unobstructed views of other people's perverse habits; and, naturally, rude people who pushed, elbowed, cursed and glared at you in the subway, and for whom you prostrated yourself and murmured "I'm sorry" as they smacked your head with their briefcases (because of the still untainted Midwestern heart you hid in your chest).

Here where every waitress, doorman, banker, lawyer, house-keeper, taxi driver, doctor, butcher, and cashier was a closet writer, painter, dancer, singer, and musician—here *I* belonged, specifically on the corner of 44th Street and 7th Avenue, where a neon sign read FANTASY HOTEL and directed one to use the exit door to enter. On Bella's generous loan, I called this Broadway hole my home until I got a job and a more permanent hole for myself. Murals of jungle animals were etched into walls, and a leopard-print blanket straddled the king-sized bed. There was a coffin-like compression to the space that gave one the sensation of being interred in a cage for futuristic scientific observation. The amenities included Neutrogena soap, a sink large enough to wash one hand but not two at the same time, and cheap polyester linen masquerading (in the brochure) as "Egyptian silk" that enveloped the body like a heating pad. The heater raged incessantly, puffing my face into a fiery dragon. This was a "boutique hotel," New York's answer to the standardized and banal Radissons, Hyatts, and Holiday Inns.

I thought wistfully of the dungeon as I perused the *New York Times* real estate section in search of something that would not involve begging my father for money. But every dingy studio, every dilapidated loft, every ill-heated, mold-infested one-bedroom that faced brick walls required a salary that was forty-five times the rent, in some cases seventy-five times the rent, or a co-signer in the guise of a reliable, upper-middle-class parent.

But, as Bella kept reminding me over the phone, independence did not entail a "co-signer." She urged me to go back to NYU, to take art classes, to see someone, do something—but after the initial thrill of independence wore off (lasting approximately seven days), I descended into a terrifying depression. The memories had now pushed open a tiny porthole and spilled out, invading my mind, inhabiting public space: I saw him in coffee shops, waiting at ATMs, passing me on sidewalks, visiting random stores. Phantoms with his likeness. So I stayed in, ordered in, or failed to eat at all. I lay in my room, gazing at the neon ceiling, at lights flashing through cracks in the window, at the stiff air replete with the screams of ambulances and taxis and people clinging to each other in the morning crush. I thought of the morning he asked me, "What do you think our children would be like?" and answered himself, "I hope they'll have your brains and my resolve!" I shuddered: children? Was I supposed to bear them? Think about them? Perhaps I had never truly imagined that he and I could be a happily married, pregnant unit, not because he wasn't Jewish, but because it seemed like sacrilege to marry someone you loved.

Like a foot in my gut, the sensation of his touch would roll through me and I would hold the concave space that used to be a stomach in my arms. Nothing could cure this howling, breath-depriving pain—not of loneliness but of loss, not of love disappointed or foolishly imagined but of love prematurely severed.

I put Adrienne Rich between my naked thighs, Betty Friedan on my chest, Elizabeth Cady Stanton on my navel, Simone De Beauvoir on one shoulder, Virginia Woolf on another, and Judith Butler on my forehead, where veins and nerves converged. I read: He is the Absolute, the essential; she is the Other, the inessential, always defined in reference to HIM. I read: a woman has no space, no privacy to create. I read: women were hung from a tree or squeezed in tight clothes, or trampled by feet to speed up their labor. I read: there is a strain of homosexual women who are not attracted to other women but want to be the equals of men—to be recognized as men. I read about prisons and enslavement, about how the institution of marriage bound and tied us, threw away our wills, and felt the decompression of my body, the swift advance of hindsight and insight, the timely contextualization of my mind, breasts, hips, vagina, and thighs.

I saw him as my prisoner now: the enemy, the subjugator, the Man. In the pure realm of womanhood, in *this* unadulterated strain of feminism, love could not exist. There was only one struggle, the struggle against men, and it rejuvenated me like a shot of adrenaline administered to a still heart.

Look at my women, my strong, powerful, beautiful yellers—how they hollered their whole lives against injustice, only to dismiss their woes with a coarse rejoinder: "that's just the lot of being a woman—so why complain?" When my grandmother came home with two buckets of water after walking for sixty kilometers by foot through mud, Grandfather got angry because dinner wasn't ready and knocked the buckets down, spilling precious water across the floor. Grandmother screamed, "You spineless, hysterical pussy!" and then she lifted the empty buckets onto her sore back and began the trek again. *Blyat, whore,* they called any woman who slept around, flirted indiscriminately, performed fellatio, staked out her territory, verbalized her desire, divorced men and found other men, spat on society's double standards; *blyat, whore,* they called themselves. This moral language was tailored to describe women: sex conceived as a moral act, desire equated to bitchiness, unnaturalness, perversion. *Yeshche shto zahotela?* What else could she possibly want or rather how dare she want any more than *this, this* glorious life? These epithets were meant to implore us to lead the "good" life. Yet try applying them to men: consider for humor's sake the case of my own father. His transgression was an acceptable by-product of our Russian cultural mores, caused inevitably by my mother's wild, implacable nature. Hers was unacceptable, a threat to family and the state of marriage, inexplicable in the context of Father's mild temper. But if you really want to be confused ask my women who they are and, without flinching, they'll say, "*we* are the men."

I placed the feminist texts upon my body, to cure the wounds inflicted on my women, to cleanse my system of empathy, sentimentality, defeat, to channel Erica Jong and seek out sex as a refutation of love's entanglement with desire. A detangling, I called it. The very detangling I had intended that very night in La Cote Basque, as nothing but the act in itself. Grandmother won't appear on the wall, and there won't be any fluttering of possibility, of continuation, of emotion. The moment shall be circumscribed in space and time, restricted to my loins; I shall fuck for fuck's sake. A one-night stand, at last consummated and accomplished, will be my flag staff raised in times of war.

So it came to pass: I went on bar excursions—to seek them out—my death-defying, feminism-activating one-night stands. They were like a cold or flu or a venereal disease, I thought, all I have to do is stick my tongue out to get it. I wore the same thing: black leather pants, stretching like ready-to-snap gum across my buttocks, a woven Lycra shirt tied at the open back by a criss-crossing rope, which made the bra an impossibility, and wrathful burgundy lipstick. This was not romantic leather like the kind I wore to La Cote Basque—this was I-loathe-men, dominatrix whipping, frothing, I-don't-give-a-*fuck* leather. I made out indiscriminately with one man and another and yet another. I was a phantom following the instructions laid out in that ancient bible of seduction, watching myself from above: those pathetic hair flips and effortlessly winking eyes, sipping my chocolaty beer, pretending to be drunk, twisting my hips, arching my back, thrusting my breasts forward and up, up, up into the sky, to find the next man, the next escape. I danced everywhere: in hip discotheques in West Village and Chelsea, in run-down bars with dance floors somewhere between 10th Avenue and the river, in a seedy Irish pub in East Village with no dance floor where I squeezed in between chairs, between chests and backs, still dancing, still making music with my body out of a perennial internal beat. Can you see *my* admirers—smiling, hands clapping, eyes grasping, seizing, stroking my ego, egging me on. Some of the men took me to their places or I took them to mine. My oeuvre contained an intellectually riveting but sensually challenged lawyer; a happily married tourist lacking in irony; a self-adoring, gauche, cock-stuck-to-the-forehead banker; a long-haired, Jesus-look-alike, spewing-theories-about-existence-out-of-his-ass graduate student; and so it went. Their hands groping, tongues wagging, eyes admiring, wanting, none of them bathing me in pleasure—was I bathing them? Even in the actual world of rooms, where I would look up at the ceiling and a condom would pop out of a man's wallet and he would pull it upon his member, speaking in that alien language called "sexual talk," and I seemed "wet" and he would say, invariably, "you're so wet," as if to highlight his victory, even then, especially then, I felt lost, mentally removed. And when they moved, their faces interchangeable, inside me, I'd turn my head to the side, a patient on an operating table, anesthetized, told not to look, mining the memory vault for a moment of intimacy with Eddie. Against my will, he'd come to me, whispering, *why are you doing this to yourself?* And with my will, I'd kill him—blot out his image, his eyes, his warmth, his touch. All the men I slept with had one thing in common: they were all handsome, implacable in their physical perfection, and I adored the process of undressing them, of discovering their beauty fully, for I watched them as an artist. Not as a woman, never as a lover. One night I tap-danced on a bar table, not in drunken stupor but with a clear head, hitting my forehead on a low hanging chandelier; the bartender iced the bump in the backroom and stuck his tongue between my parted lips, sliding his fingers under the shirt's crisscrossed ropes to encircle my breasts, and then his penis suddenly parted my thighs, and that was that. Quick, visceral, inconsequential. Was this what women and men called "fun"? Was this the life of the eternal bachelors who renounced marriage and children and love? Or was this a glimpse of the undead, the vampires, the zombies, those heroes of American goth, descending on the night, offering their gift of the eternal casual-sex purgatory? With horror, I recalled my sister—did she too dance with the undead? Would I too end up home in black with my hair cropped and married to Alex?

I wanted to die, be done with myself. I wanted to get this life out—*out*—of me. None of it mattered. If I had sex it wouldn't matter. If I didn't it wouldn't matter either. I was alone. Without love, without Eddie, without wanting and feeling and yearning for this other soul, I felt broken, my limbs weakened, my face caught in a perpetual shadow. Whatever wars I had been waging—against chauvinism, anti-Semitism, anti-immigrantism, anti-humanism: all of them dead, all of them meaningless. The thought of going to my family for help was the un-thought; it made death seem like a salve. And the idea that I was depressed or that a therapist could offer a modicum of relief—a dissecting-pain-talk marathon with a stranger—was as foreign to me as the English language had once been. Some characteristics never penetrate, never assimilate. In some ways I was still as Russian as Grandmother's *vobla* . . . oh *vobla*, how I yearn for my briny *vobla* . . .

What does it really mean to survive this life? Where was one supposed to find the strength to lift one foot in front of the other and greet one's allotted slice of sunlight for that day? How was one supposed to seal the memory banks, the heart valves, the constant trickle of disappointment and meaninglessness, and say here begins another day—not as a shot at happiness or joy or inner peace but simply as an opportunity to not die—to not drown in your hotel's cracked bathtub, or "accidentally" leap toward the oncoming 1 or 9 train? To survive this life took guts, willpower, resilience, ingenuity; it took the abrupt, almost physical surrender to an old nagging desire: to paint!

The Androgynous Woman

The International Art Coalition of New York was an imperious school in midtown Manhattan. Instead of degrees at the end of its three-year apprenticeship program, the school produced showings—its focus was not simply to teach but to give birth to working artists. The place attracted corporate sponsors, gallery curators, private patrons, and ambitious youth. With its stellar reputation in the art world and promises of stardom, the Art Coalition was notoriously difficult to get into, and featured a fount of insane professors, stars in their own right. Professor Grayhart once mentioned it to me, and so I walked up to the front office, asked for an application, and was ushered into a studio. The lady at the front desk said, "We have an outreach program—you can paint in one of our public studios, as long as it doesn't interfere with the class schedule."

The elevator opened onto a massive room with fifteen-foot windows and aluminum pipes crisscrossing the ceiling. The stench of acrylic and turpentine stunted the air. Canvases shrouded in gray sheets and black garbage bags were piled against cement walls like priceless artifacts waiting to be unveiled. Active canvases in the throes of creation beamed from wooden stands, and the paintbrushes appeared to the unaccustomed eye like dancers who, independent of their masters, leapt from bottles into grotesque easels and settled with brilliant poise upon virgin canvases, erasing with one chassé, one pirouette, one grand jeté the chaos you felt upon entering the room.

Young-looking, disheveled countenances peered at me suspiciously. They sipped their coffees, edging away from their canvases intermittently to chat with each other. But for the most part, their socializing appeared guarded and stingy, their smiles carefully circumscribed in restraint, hiding from each other their fantasies, their grandiose ambitions, their already intoxicating stories of success.

I set a place for myself in a corner that was cut off from the rest of the room, shadowed by columns, illuminated only by elusive sunspots.

I didn't know how many hours passed or where the painters went, but when I stepped away from my canvas not a soul breathed around me. The other canvases were either shrouded or simply gone. The sky beamed New York's nocturnal pink light. Pain pulsed under my shoulder blades, my spine turned crooked, my fingers groaned from old age, swelling with arthritis, hardening into paintbrushes, as if they too were made from fine Italian wood. My torso was frozen at a sixty-degree angle, and to unglue it, I bent it in the opposite direction in vain. My eyes swam in red webs, and my stomach had contracted to the width of cardboard. Food had become a distant memory, though I vaguely recalled swallowing a blueberry muffin whole.

The image itself, an unfinished figure in a purple dress, had started out as a woman. But as the night progressed the body stiffened, the face grew into a square. Above its red-lined angry mouth, the eyes had become callous and the forehead protruded beneath a short black mane. The jaws cut out of brown shadows denoted a stubborn man. Yet the purple dress fell away to reveal a woman's breast. The androgynous figure teetered on the edge of a chair, tied and bound by purple ropes that resembled headless snakes, trapping her inside their own circular life.

I wrestled with the stubborn colors, ominous and bitter, a vision of an aging queen, a muse of wrath, a disillusioned woman so overcome with grief she has turned into a man. I swam invisible inside her mouth—I owned the muscles on her face, the stern reproof in her cat eyes that warned of bitch-fests, of diatribes, of war. I was speaking through her, at her, for her.

Stripped of this feminine body, I was a man. Inside that man, I was a woman. The soul was subdivided into a thousand *Matryoshkas*; inside each head the head of the opposite sex loomed, the characteristics through each unscrewing growing indistinguishable from each other.

I needed to lighten the purple ropes that had grown too dark but my fingers weakened and released the paintbrush. Flaws seemed to have multiplied from the will to perfect, and a wave of impotence washed over me. I crawled into the purple prison, pitying myself. A mass of translucent curtains fell over my soul, gaining whiteness and a presence. I could feel it shifting around me and then—I could barely breathe—something held me in a large warm palm. I was no longer afraid. I said, "Is that You, God?" but no one answered. "God, is that You, God, God . . ." I kept repeating until exhaustion overtook me and I laid my head gently on the cement floor and closed my eyes.

I awoke to the sound of a striking voice. "No, no, Mr. Kilburn, no, you're not early, we're late—we're late! If you don't take this class seriously or the work we do here seriously then you have no place behind a canvas. Because painting is serious business," the voice pursued. "It is as serious as law and medicine, as serious as saving another person's life, because the life you'll be saving is your own! The paintbrushes must become your friends, as dear to you as your ten fingers. So pick them well, treasure them, know their agility and limitations, because they will signal the limitations in yourselves.

"Now paint!" The woman appeared to be the commander of an army, and the students dropped their heads simultaneously, their collective gaze seizing the nude as if on cue. A model in her early fifties was sprawled on a leopard rug; her legs appeared to be attached to invisible stirrups, mimicking the act of labor. Behind her a cage contained a startling orange lizard, which, I later learned, was an import from the island of Tobago. The animal swished and hissed, staring occasionally at its own tail. One cloudy eye would widen under sharp scales and look at the students with human wonder. I missed my wounded blue-green iguana, my savior, my strange friend. When I stopped by Natasha's apartment the first week I arrived in the city, to get the last of my mail, she told me that the animal passed away the day after I moved out.

The students were told to paint the woman and the lizard superimposed upon each other; they were to paint the natural world in an unnatural setting, art superimposed upon the artifice of modern life.

I wanted to sprint from my concrete bed and join them—what wonder, what freedom—but I couldn't move a single joint. Pain gripped every bone, pinched every nerve. I groaned as quietly as I could but the lizard, as though on purpose, grew still and looked at me. And the students following her lead now shifted their gaze onto me.

"Let's see what the gods have dragged in this morning!?" the teacher cried, and the entire class burst into joyous laughter.

"An excellent case of androgyny, I'd say," she went on, focusing only on my painting, skimming over me as if I were a metal pole. "Add a touch of navy to the purple ropes to give her more definition and fix the fingernails—they look like dirty pancakes."

"Thank you," I said meekly.

She laughed. "Don't be afraid, speak up—what is your name, oh most dedicated of artists?"

"Emma Kaulfield," I whispered.

"Louder," she demanded.

"Emma, Emma Kaulfield—I don't belong—I'm not in the Coalition—I just wanted to use the studio—" I stammered.

"Well, that's just ridiculous," she said with a laugh. "Anyone who spends a few nights stinking of turpentine, rejects the comforts of her own bed, and who, I imagine, hasn't had a real meal in quite some time belongs here, among us, don't you all agree?" She seemed so beautiful and confident, despite the miniature size of her body and the delicate face, that in my sleepless daze I thought I glimpsed giant wings upon her back.

I knew who she was: the great Fredericka Unitcheska, known for the looseness and inventiveness of her classes and her bravura style of teaching with its hard, militant edge. She was the infamous 1960s French painter who was the only female member of the Imbolists, a movement that defied convention by exploring sexual content through rapid free-floating strokes as a conceptual representation of unremitting change. Imbolism had its etymological roots in nineteenth-century Immoralism, but had acquired political overtones, requiring its devotees to plant revolutionary seeds in society's fat conventional underbelly. Unitcheska first made her mark with her distinct study of reptiles on canvas, which she painted from memory (rumor had it) of her childhood in London brothels, where her mother belly-danced with a python. Her mother (it was said) was a descendent of Spanish gypsies and her father may have been an English lord, and her mother's most loyal customer.

In reality, of course, Fredericka Unitcheska was originally Ansel Bernstein, who grew up in Brooklyn and was the faithful daughter of Jewish German immigrants. She studied at the Sorbonne, spent a year painting in Florence, returned to the States satiated, and received a PhD in art history. The following year, after receiving a tenure-track position at Barnard at the unripe age of twenty-six, she lost her bearings. Painting, some believe, kidnapped her mind. She could no longer remember who she had once been. She renounced her family, laughed at their calls for propriety, and began to paint what she described as "a bubble in her stomach." Disembarking from her meltdown, Ansel Bernstein re-emerged as Unitcheska and rejected her hapless fiancé. "Until I find a man who understands my longings, my indisputable sexual equality to him, I will not subjugate myself to this ancient imprisonment known as marriage," she had written under a painting of a woman transmogrifying into a blue iguana beneath a pale yellow sky. Today, hailed as one of the most important living female artists and the Cleopatra of our time, Unitcheska enjoyed a plethora of lovers, beautiful young female and male models, and even husbands of important society women, many of whom were rumored to be so smitten with her that if she would only breathe in their direction, they would file for divorce. She never did; retaining her independence was the breathing mechanism of her work.

"So what do you call her?" Unitcheska asked, approaching me at the end of class.

"*The Androgynous Woman*," I replied, stunned at my own quick thinking, at this sudden unveiling of my explosive desire.

"Don't touch it anymore—don't detract from her maleness. Are you interested?"

"In what?" I murmured, sweating, half-understanding.

"We hold this seminar every Tuesday and Thursday—we would love to have you. You can start now, immediately."

"May I go and change though?" I asked, thinking desperately about a warm cup of tea.

She laughed. "I may be God but I'm not without human feeling! Sleep, eat, and come to my class this Thursday at noon. Don't be late."

In late October, Unitcheska single-handedly created a space for me within the Art Coalition's three-year apprenticeship program (a program that fielded close to ten thousand applicants and a hefty waiting list). The ripple effect of my unusual acceptance into the program was that I became a social pariah. People viewed me as an interloper or, worse, a thief, robbing them, the legitimate students, of their rightful access to the great Unitcheska, and thus I was quietly nicknamed "the Imposter." So competitive was the atmosphere in the school that to repeat my "stint" of success, students on the waiting list went so far as to sleep on the studio floor and awaken as I did—to Unitcheska's class streaming in—to demonstrate their inordinate commitment. But these hijinks only infuriated her and led the department to ban sleeping in studios.

Unitcheska's advanced seminar was tinged with subversion—a conscious revolt against convention, civilization, and imperious grandmothers. There was no discrimination in age or species. Human models included men and women in their sixties and early twenties, hermaphrodites, pregnant women, and the homeless in rags and broken shoes, still clutching brown bags over mysterious bottles. We were regaled with parrots, cages with lizards, snakes, aquariums filled with exotic fish, and rare African plants whose names we could never pronounce. She liked to see a human model against the backdrop of a cage—to imagine the human caged and the animal free. She would cry, "Models, imagine that you're the parrot or the toad, imagine that your mouth is a beak and your stomach is a green sphere—and now you, my painters, imagine that!" On days when Unitcheska wore red, she'd cry, "Remember, art is not about power structures, but the voluptuous human imagination."

Painting was no longer a guilty addiction for me but a way of life, my energy source, and Unitcheska was the magnificent human-shaped fire in the middle of the room. How my nervous system luxuriated in the new, the unseen, the hitherto unimaginable, how it understood before the brain that this joy was rooted in the act of self-embrace: in painting as a daily grind, in the notion that yes *I, I* possessed leafy-green courage, that my arms were the branches of an ancient oak and I could grab hold of what belonged to me all along—the will to create. For this inherent right had been stripped from my family tree and replaced by the overweening need to survive—so I painted for them as much as for myself.

That is why, after Bella's money ran out, I did not bury my head in a jar of viscous Soviet strawberry jam and return to Chicago, reeking of sweet failure. I was an immigrant after all, I told myself, a matter of great significance in an immigrant city, and I heard that a small international community in the West Village, a little sister of the Upper West Side's famed International House, or more aptly put, a sunless hole on Leonard Street, was still accepting applications. Despite the grime on windowsills, the bleak interiors, a squeaky twin bed, and a beaten desk, *Students United* required that I write an essay proving my international origins—a task I feverishly embraced, and within a week, I was accepted.

This room sat atop a charming Indian restaurant and shared a bathroom with another room. That's how I met Stone Hograth, the woman I credit with catapulting me to adulthood. She was one of Unitcheska's favorites, a strange blonde-haired creature who hailed from blue-collar parents, had Norwegian origins, wore military jackets and combat boots, and said "Fuck" a great deal. And perhaps, had we not shared a bathroom, she would have ignored me like the others. But I grew on her like fungus, she said, and she said other things too. "You're so fucking happy all the time, what are you so fucking happy for?" "I'm just polite," I'd reply, and she'd laugh and laugh. Laugh because she heard me weeping at night, heard me arguing with myself in Russian, heard me scream in my sleep. "You're pretty fucked up," she said one morning, "but you know what, Kaulfield, I like you—I like fucked up."

Stone didn't merely wish to help me; she saw herself as my savior, as my bridge to true Americanization. "You don't know the first thing about being on your own," she said. "Get a fucking waitressing job, for starters!" I admitted that I had never actually worked; I'd volunteered, interned, assisted professors, but I had never made a cent. We were passing Grizzly's Place during this conversation, a twenty-four-hour breakfast joint that had a neon flashing sign in the window: MULES WANTED, SIGN UP. Stone had to physically drag me inside to apply. To the manager, she said: "She's really upbeat—customers will *love her!*" It was only later that I wondered whether I resisted because I couldn't fathom myself as a waitress, or because the place was also coincidentally located five blocks from Eddie's apartment.

The Paintings I Left for Dead

After seeing my midterm, Unitcheska asked me the question that every aspiring art student hears in their tormented, acrylic-zonked dream: "Do you have anything else in this vein?" or, in Unitcheska's exact words, "So Ms. Kaulfield, what else have you broken your back for?" I stammered, "Nothing." "Nothing," she cried, "I don't believe you—you didn't start painting the day I saw you awaken on concrete!" "No, but it's not anything I meant for anyone to see." "Why, Ms. Kaulfield, those are the best kind.

Whatever it is you never meant for anyone to see—that is what I must see!"

Thus she sent me back to the underground, to the canvases I birthed while juggling Eddie and Alex and then left for dead in my NYU locker, number 38. I wanted them to rot there in the basement of the Art Building, my poor starved orphans, to never glimpse daylight again. They were painted with the express purpose of self-alleviation: painting as catharsis, painting for the therapeutic enterprise of recovering memory and rendering it powerless to infect. But when I opened the door with a glittering silver key, they were still breathing, still living, each canvas neatly leaning upon its neighbor, separated by black garbage bags: faces of children staring into unfathomable blackness.

I took out my camera, set them against the concrete wall, and snapped.

When I brought the slides to Unitcheska's office in a small blue container, it seemed incredible that human universes could shrink into inch-long squares, that Unitcheska could lift her head with a regal flip of her black mane and say, "Well, Ms. Kaulfield, place your babies here!" as if I were laying rags before her, and not my very limbs. I imagined the red scarf around her neck was an artery pulsing out of the open window, reaching for the landscape below—so that if she hated them, my children—my infants cut out of my flesh by an emergency C-section—I could grab hold of it, climb down without shame, and without shame disappear. Her fingers fumbled with an enormous gray projector, which in my nervousness I mistook for a bloodless heart.

She took a drag from a cigarette and exhaled upon them, murmuring, "mmmuhum"—an endless *mahaing* and *muhuing* that together with the twitches of her brow and the red twang of her mouth fried my nerves. Smoke coiled her head and emanated from my slides, and I breathed it in, an entire room of fire. A magnifying glass was attached to her right eye, and I felt her peering in, through these miniature portals, into my childhood, but if I remained nameless, if I eschewed vanity and memory and self-pride, they could be mistaken for a series of children at play. She didn't lift her head for over ten minutes, and I smiled meekly as I caught signs of her approval: the burning cigarette in the ashtray, the magnified eye aglow and widening, the cheeks slacking from surprise.

When she looked up, all she said was, "Do they have titles?"

"Some of them—I haven't been able to decide—"

"Well, get them all titled. And decide! You have something here, something extraordinary, I should say. It's as if I've entered another world—they are all very sad."

"They're of Russia," I told her, "of things I experienced in Russia." I wanted to say more, to reveal these truths, these boulders I carried on my back, but she waved her hand in the air as if to admonish me for trying to contextualize them—to ruin a universal truth with my private pain.

"So what were you doing with your life before you awakened in my studio that day?"

"I'm was in a master's program studying statistics at NYU."

"So you repressed it—your art? These paintings are like explosions from the center of your body! Out of all plausible repressions, why pick statistics—why graph yourself in?"

I wanted to say, "My parents, immigrant mentality, fear," but instead, I replied, "practical considerations—considerations of survival."

"And the survival of your soul—did you ever worry about that? You're a painter through and through. Paint one more—I need at least seven paintings to give you a show."

"A show—you mean like in a gallery?"

"Yes, like your own show in a real gallery, but don't get overly excited; it's early for you, the gallery is a small operation, and the owner will price your work very low. But it'll give you a chance to be seen."

I told myself the very same thing, *don't get overly excited*, but my lips distended, curling into my very eyes, and the eyes themselves seemed to sprout arms that enfolded Unitcheska in an invisible hug. Dear God, I certainly never expected this much so soon! I lunged for her wooden desk, knocked three times, and *tfu, tfu, tfued* myself under my breath as inconspicuously as I could, but she caught it. "Is that some kind of ancient ritual you're performing?"

"A Russian-Jewish superstition—our protection against total doom and fear!" I cried, and tears streamed from my eyes, but I smiled vigorously against them. "Thank you, Unitcheska, thank you."

The Waitress in Black

Winter came abruptly at the end of December when bounteous snow swallowed the city, and the missing seventh painting came with it, pouring out of me as though I were a mouth in the sky. I would spend fourteen uninterrupted hours battling my canvas like a man with an axe unable to cut down an ancient tree. During intense spurts of sleep I would see a child impaled on the tree, its face a replica of mine. I would reach toward it, wanting to save it, but when my fingers would touch its skin, the child would dissolve into rain, and I would crawl away, an injured wet dog, not wanting to save anything but itself. Upon awakening, my fingers would feel numb and a burning sensation would sting my tongue, and in the mirror I'd see Eddie, his easy countenance propping me up, firing my dead hands. I saw him in my dreams and when my eyes were open, I heard him say, "It's all right if you don't paint the whole truth—that's the way art is—it takes what it needs from your soul."

I wore red lipstick, a crimson red I'd never worn before, the day I saw Eddie again. I showed up at the restaurant at eight in the morning after painting through the night, my system subsisting on caffeine and the will to finish the painting when I got home. My expression would periodically freeze amid an order or at the cash register, seeking lost sleep in still moments. By three o'clock, sweat and exhaustion sat on my face like two fingerprints; only the lipstick pumped me with confidence. A MERRY CHRISTMAS sign hung over the entrance and greeted customers with giant electrical yellow letters that flickered and emitted muffled buzzing sounds. Table seven featured a teenage girl decked out in puffed army pants and a go-to-hell expression, which she directed at her plainly victimized parents. "They're from New Jersey," she said to me as if her parents were the site of a garbage dump. "She's always embarrassed of us," the mother put in meekly. "What's good here?" the father asked. "You should try the chicken gyro sandwich, it's very good," I said. The three of them nodded.

I made a mental note of three gyro sandwiches in my head (a head that never failed to screw up each order) and stumbled into a table of three men. "Hi I'm Emma and I'll be your waitress!" I chirped. The men's polished demeanor, starched shirts, college pinky rings, and smarmy glances gave me the sensation that I was serving advertising Lotharios. One of them even had an irreparable winking eye.

"So Emma, what do you do when you're not charming your customers?" he said as if on cue.

"Philosophizing—now, gentlemen, what will you be having?" I delivered this in a stern voice, scrambling to retrieve that critical mass of inaccessibility and disdain men long for in their ideal woman.

"I think therefore I am," the handsome one purred, "wasn't it Socrates who said that?"

"No, that was Descartes—and actually it was 'I think therefore I exist.' Socrates said an unexamined life isn't worth living," I said, correcting him with inexplicable contempt.

"So you want to play charades with us, don't you, Emma—you want us to *guess* what you do," the one called Frank taunted and scratched his shiny forehead.

I smiled, for I could weave a sweet fantasy—I would never see these men again—and my reply was not for them, but for Grandmother: "It's only because you're my most faithful customer that I'll let you in on a little secret—I'm studying to be an otolaryngologist."

"She specializes in tying up men's vocal cords," the quiet one suddenly joined in.

Frank put his arm around him and said, "Aaron here is practically your soul mate—he's studying to be a heart surgeon, but those chicks in residency programs—well, let's just momentarily suspend our politically correct persona—they look like dogs on sticks. Now you on the other hand—"

"Well, then you must be blind—last time I checked I was a Doberman pinscher and I bite." I could feel my anger roiling into hatred, flickering at the men.

"We don't mind a few bites in the right places—"

"Shut up, Frank—" the quiet man muttered.

"I'm getting hungry," the handsome one butted in. "Let's get the gyros already."

"The chicken gyro is very good," I offered happily. Because the chicken gyros were dried out, because they sometimes got stuck in one's throat, and because I loathed my inability to be disliked by men.

"You haven't answered our most important question," Frank said. "How about a date?"

"With all three of you?" I asked with an inviting smile, and the men let out a synchronized happy chortle.

"Sure, we'd be game." Frank, the winker, took me up. "Except that Doug and I are married—you'd have to make do with our man Aaron here."

I looked at Aaron anew; he sprouted curly brown hair atop pallid skin that appeared to have been dabbed with powder (a direct consequence of his lack of exposure to nature's elements), a rectangular forehead, and an intricately cut nose with two underdeveloped nostrils. He was not good looking, but he had intelligent black eyes that bespoke a satirical sense of humor and a small mouth that curled in disapproval at his friends.

"Hello, there, stranger." A familiar voice tapped at my back.

I stood still for a few seconds, unable to process the person whose voice I recognized. Behind me, I felt his face beaming, his hands at his sides, his tan skin, his blue eyes, his jeans crinkling as he walked, as he stepped closer. I heard myself say, Eddie, then "Eddie" out loud, my neck twisting to face him, my stomach in a vise, but I was an actress after all, and the old easy, flirtatious glance I had flashed at the three strangers I now directed at him. "What are you doing here?"

"No, better question is—what are you doing here?" he asked.

"Making a living," I retorted with pride.

"As a waitress? What—your parents finally disowned you for dating a goy?" He let out a compassionate laugh, marred by a faint note of ridicule. There was something remarkably spirited and loose in his expression. He moved like a stream around me, drowning out the excruciating memory of our breakup.

"Oh, no, I decided to cut myself off—I want to make it on my own."

"That's just where you were when I met you—living in the dungeon, wanting to be a starving artist and yet somehow you were never starving. Are you finally starving now?"

"And what happened to you—they finally let the prisoners out on a Saturday? Or is Norton Bank on a firing spree?" I inquired, consciously wanting to be cruel.

"Very funny! Actually, I've been promoted"—he paused, his face tilting humbly to the floor—"to managing director."

"So now they've given you carte blanche to fire anyone you want! Did you by any chance fire that *mudak* Eric?"

"Funny you should mention him—he just got promoted to senior analyst."

"Oh." I considered for a second telling him the truth about Eric, but my mouth wouldn't open.

"You look different," he said.

I wanted to ask "good or bad different?" to fall back into the safe zone of being evaluated by him, but I fought against this execrable weakness. "Yes, I've reinvented myself, you might say—painting full time now—that is, when I'm not serving."

"Or being picked up by your customers."

"Ah, good to know you still have all of your eavesdropping skills intact." We stared at one another with such intensity that there was no other alternative but to laugh. I wondered why we weren't more awkward together, why our tense banter was causing us such piquant euphoria.

"Waitress!" I heard the teenager cry out, "waitress, yoo-hoo, where are you?"

"Grant still talks about you," he said.

"I have to go." I looked at him with longing and my skin burned, my ruby cheeks giving me away. I wanted to ask—do you want to have coffee with me—but I caught his eyes traveling over several tables and landing on a striking, tall brunette. She was motioning to him with her hands, and her annoyed expression pierced my stomach with the force of a bullet.

"Hey, if you get a chance, give me a call sometime and we'll do coffee. We should stay friends," he offered, turning halfway toward her.

"Oh, Ignatius, don't you remember—I'm too sexual for friendship with men."

The smile vanished. His voice, hard and remote, said, "I remember you." I remembered him—the way he looked in the morning in a T-shirt and black boxer shorts, his muscular calves pressed against the leather couch, the *Wall Street Journal* rustling in his lap, a mug of black coffee in his hand, his gaze lost in small print, swimming past me and yet always, with the corner of one eye, reeling me back in. I used to wonder in secret: what alien textures, smells, sights are these—am I just a fly trapped in *your* world?

"Lady, I don't have all day," someone hollered from a table I forgot was mine.

"I have to go," he said after a long pause and then headed toward her—the immaculately pretty creature who reminded me of a fairy with her miniature lips and turned-up nose and wide-set quizzical eyes.

"Hey, Eddie," I called out. He twisted halfway toward me. "I'm having an exhibition of my work at this small gallery next week. It's really no big deal, really."

"Wow, an exhibition—congratulations! I'm impressed."

"I was wondering if you'd like to come—well, in either case, there'll be lots of people and you could bring your friend."

His expression went mute.

"I'd like that," he said after a long pause, starting to walk away. "I'm so glad you didn't give up on yourself—I mean on painting."

"January 15th at the Fern Gallery, eight o'clock," I called after him, "three blocks down from Nebu—"

"Where we met—"

"Yes, though you'd never think it's a gallery—"

"Hey, I'm happy for you," he said, turning away.

"Thanks. Merry Christmas!" My voice was loud, peppy.

He shifted halfway, and with an open generous smile, replied, "Happy Hanukkah!"

But somehow he sounded distant, and within seconds, his tall broad frame bent apologetically before her. I wanted to run after him, to remind him that January 15, 1998, exactly a year ago, was the day we saw each other for the second time and we began *this*—this *thing* I couldn't bring myself to call a relationship because the word was too prosaic to capture *what we had, what we still had*. But I remained in the same spot, my feet planted in imaginary sand that was rapidly disappearing. And in its wake, water spread and closed around me: an anthropomorphic ocean with a swaying torso and globular arms and a headless voice that roared—*I shall swallow you in my black foam*—until my head crashed against a reef, until my pain felt insurmountable, until the call, "Waitress, waitress, waitress!" struck my head like a singular shard of glass splitting my skull in half. Other waiters and busboys took over my tables. Ghigash, the manager, fumed behind his imperious host's podium. But I couldn't move; I saw him settle next to her, her mouth zigzagging in nervous strokes, wondering, asking what I would have asked had I been her: "Who is she?" He told her the truth, I was certain of that, because he didn't care for lies, because he laid himself bare like a jigsaw puzzle with every piece secured in its assigned place—and if she didn't like it, he would open the door and ask her to leave. I imagined he cared even less now because of what I had done to him.

At last I unlocked my face, my feet, my arms, and, shifting slowly toward the three men, said with some composure, "I'm sorry."

"An old boyfriend?" Frank, the psychic, noted.

"Yes." What did it matter if I was honest with these strangers? "An ancient one."

"So how about a new, modern one—our man Aaron here is a prime candidate!" Frank sounded wonderfully, oddly reassuring.

"I guess coffee never hurt anyone," I said with a wink at Aaron, and with the sudden ease and suavity of an old courtesan, I wrote my number on a napkin. Aaron's expression brightened and his small, pale mouth unwound into an eager smile.

As they left, Aaron sang out, "I'll call you, I'll definitely call you," forgetting the advice he had received from his advertising buddies: never seem too eager, too available, too desperate. But I wanted desperate—with the way I felt at that moment, only the desperate could heal me.

I watched the three men head toward the revolving door of the diner. I told myself to look away but it was too late: Eddie's hand was pressed into the girl's back as they pushed their way out the door. I felt something tear in my stomach and my legs weaken in preparation for a fall, but I stood where I was—Ghigash was eyeing me with contempt and the teenager was hollering at her parents. "Why do you always say these embarrassing things, like you're from the boonies? Wish I was dead!" The parents looked dumbstruck, or as they say in good Russian, "like folks who've been doused in buckets of shit." I gave the father the check and smiled reassuringly, as if he and I and his wife suffered from the same malaise. And the truth of it struck me: the three of us toiled under the same self-serving delusion—that what we love necessarily loves us back.

I ran outside into the merciless air. Ice-laden snow slapped my cheeks, whirred up my nostrils, pummeled my eyes. My austere black uniform became drenched in seconds. The cotton hardened into sheet metal. Still, I pushed ahead, fighting the wind and snow with my shivering arms and unseeing eyes, stumbling over the steps of some building, some bank whose neon lights flashed blue inside my head. I tumbled to the ground. It didn't seem real that he didn't love me anymore. Not love *me*—how is that possible—why *me*? And this thought pulled me down, taking with it my sense of self, my beauty, my confidence, even my art.

Then I saw it—a jittery shadow crept across the snow like a hallucination or a disjointed dream. I looked up and there he was, trying to out-scream the traffic: "What the hell are you doing to yourself?"

"Why are you here?"

"Have you lost your mind? Is this part of your artistic martyrdom?"

"Don't be such an ass, don't be such a conceited ass!" I spat under my breath, glaring at the snow.

"C'mon, get up and put something on—get your coat from the restaurant!"

"I'm not cold," I said. "Why did you come—did you forget something?"

"I wanted to see if—"

"Where is *she*?"

"In a taxi—going home."

The wind was howling at our backs, picking up speed, pushing us forward, then sideways. Wet frozen pants clung to my thighs and my tears formed a thin layer of ice on my cheeks. My chest felt bare, exposed to the cruelties of nature. Winter was repainting my blood in white. How my teeth chattered—in outrage.

"Is she your—are you together?"

"You must be freezing; come to my place," he said, taking off his jacket and throwing it over my shoulders.

"Take your jacket away," I said, throwing it back at him. "I'm going to catch a cab—what are you going to tell your girlfriend if she finds out I stopped by?"

"Why don't you come over to my apartment and dry off—I'm just a few blocks south of here."

"I know where you live, Eddie." There was viciousness and loathing in my voice I couldn't quite recognize. "Remember, I lived there once with you."

"Look, I can put your stuff in the dryer, and then you'll be on your way. If you get sick, how will you paint?"

"What do you care if I paint?" I flung back without noticing that he had wrapped his coat around me and held his hands there an instant longer than he should have, and that we had walked, one after the other, through the revolving door of his lobby.

"I care about talent, Emma, always have—"

"Eddie, stop—stop saying meaningless things—I didn't want things to be like this."

"What—our first meeting after the breakup to be awkward?"

"Awkward? You call this pain awkward?" I pointed at my heart.

"You never were much of a realist," he said, laughing cruelly.

I felt a knot in my stomach at the familiarity of the marbled foyer, at Clarence greeting people with his elastic smile, and I wanted to wind time back. I waved and nodded at him, but he didn't seem to recognize me. "Good evening, Mr. Beltrafio," he said mechanically, and I felt invisible, as though I had long ceased to exist.

His apartment was imbued with a new floral scent. At once, I saw her imprint everywhere: a bouquet of pansies rested in a vase that had remained empty while we dated, a pink embroidered pillow sat on his couch, fur-lined beige boots leaned against the closet door, purple heart-shaped Christmas cards were arranged neatly in front of pre-addressed pink stamped envelopes on his table, a pasta maker and a cappuccino machine loomed in the kitchen next to discarded ice cream cartons—it was a full-throttle invasion, and I saw her pretty fussy face worrying over thank-you cards and wedding invitations and time!

I trembled from the sudden memory of my own presence in his apartment: what had defined *me*, marked *me*, where were my pink envelopes and embroidered pillows and ice cream buckets? He used to say to me, you're not like other women—was I like other men? Sketches of my work used to congest his hallway corners and bedrooms. My notebooks, novels, philosophy, statistics, and probability texts grew like weeds from the floor, and *Crime and Punishment* in Russian lay in a perennial state of discontent on his nightstand—I read it three pages at a time in torment over this excruciatingly difficult language that I called my own. My unfinished paintings were piled against the walls of his second bedroom, and instead of ice cream cartons, empty jars of Osetra and Beluga caviar stood like testaments of his love for me in the recycling bin. The burgundy curtain that had split the living room in half was gone; only the rail on the ceiling remained, resembling an unprotected water pipe. A painting that used to hang in the living room had been taken down. In oil pastels a meticulously sculpted naked ice-blue man melted from a fire rising in the shape of a woman. I had spent days, as I had promised, painting Ignatius, forcing him to stand in the nude for hours while I struggled with color and depth and likeness. I had named it *Ignatius in Flames* and he had marveled at it for hours, saying it soothed his nerves.

"I thought your girlfriend looked very upset when she saw you with me," I said. "Did you tell her who I am?"

"Stop playing games. I don't want to regress. Stop with your idiotic jealousy—if you knew what it's been like for me, you'd know how stupid you sound."

"How do you want me to act—like it doesn't matter?" I retreated, submitting to the force in his face.

"I've taken up photography again," he said briskly. "I want a picture of you."

"A memento for your future grandchildren?"

"I want to see you naked," he said.

"What—have you lost your mind—what about her?" I pointed at the pink envelopes.

"I told you it's not serious!" He grabbed my arm.

"Does she know that?"

"I know that competition has always been one of your secret aphrodisiacs!" He laughed at first but then his jaws clicked and the pupils widened, an internal light flaring from hatred, and then the hatred grew. He appeared to turn into a beast, a demonic creature circling above me for the kill. He grabbed my wrists and pinned them belligerently against the wall, his breath streaming in hot swathes around my throat.

"Have you lost your mind?" I cried, struggling to wriggle myself free. But he held on and I didn't know what I feared more: what he would do to me or to himself.

"Take off your clothes—I want to watch you."

"Watch—watch me?"

"I don't have any respite from you," he replied, abruptly releasing me. "You're everywhere: in my apartment, in my cabin, even in restaurants. God, we must've sampled every goddamn restaurant in the city. I can't take these women anywhere without being reminded of you. It was such luck, I thought, to have run into you—now I can try to end it, end it in a way that ends it for *me*—for *me*, do you hear *me*? Because I don't want you back, Emma. I want a happy life, and—I can't have happiness with someone I can't trust."

"Your mother has never—now I know that for a fact—never wanted you to end up with me!"

"What does one have to do with the other?"

"I guess I never expected it. I was optimistic, you know. I was sure it couldn't be true. Not you, I thought, not your family."

"What are you talking about?"

"Oh, you can stop pretending now—don't tell me you haven't been apprised of your mother's anti-Semitic views—that she only verbalized them upon meeting me!"

"What are you talking about—what views?"

"I overheard her say things like: 'I never want my grandchildren to have Jewish blood! How will I be able to look into their eyes and not think they're the spawn of the Devil?'"

He laughed uproariously. "And you caught this illicit evidence—when—during dinner? When your family was skewering my family in Russian?"

"No, I overheard your mother speaking in the library with your father—I spied on them, through the door and I heard her, loud and clear—"

"You heard this? Is this a joke—you expect me to believe that you spied on my parents? Are you sure you understood her?"

"Are you questioning my English?"

"No, your sanity! After what happened in your childhood, don't you think you need to be more cautious when you accuse people? Maybe, just maybe, you've been so scarred that you see everything through this ugly lens? Wouldn't that make more sense?"

I closed my eyes to make him disappear, and recalled with unambiguous horror that moment—as it spilled from memory the pitch of her outrage. I rearranged her words and then I sewed the sentences back together, arriving at the same conclusion with which I began. Or did my English fail me? Did my mind? Could it be that she didn't use the word "Devil," that I merely imagined it? Perhaps I only witnessed their mouths moving, zigzagging, reproof marring their expressions, but their voices were muffled by the French doors? Perhaps I had only sensed the truth, circled *a* truth, but I didn't own it. Suddenly I didn't trust myself. Or was it possible that the mistrust of my own mind was an elaborate subterfuge knitted by an increasingly unbearable desire? This desire blindfolded me, blurring his motives into something vague and conveniently unimportant. What does it matter, I told myself, if he's ignorant of his mother's vileness? Even worse, what if he knows the truth but can't admit it? Why would he? I wouldn't if I were him—I'd deny it, the way I denied the existence of Alex, the way I denied what I saw that day in the woods, the way I stared into Sarah's eyes and said, "she's lying." Upon the final groping of my brain, I came back to the most terrifying possibility of all: I wanted him so dementedly I no longer cared. I was willing to mangle my own memory, assign insanity and auditory hallucinations to my psyche, playact at forgetfulness to do the very thing I swore to never do: pretend I don't mind—pretend anything for his love.

"You have to remember you're in America now," he went on, though I wasn't sure whether this speech was intended for me or for himself. "It's not like that here. Sure, there may be pockets of hatred here and there, in some bumble-fuck town in the middle of nowhere, but not here, not in New York, and certainly not in our home in Westchester. For all my mother's flaws, I never heard her speak that way." He looked at me with some strange culmination of kindness and anger in his eyes before adding, "Besides, what does it have to do with us? Her behavior in no way justifies your own—your betrayal of *me* was the issue at hand, still is!"

"I'm sorry, Eddie, I'm truly sorry for what I did to you," I muttered, recalling abstractly that I had entirely fabricated my "betrayal" of him.

But he didn't seem to hear me. He was looking past me into the enormous glass window at my back. "Look, Emma, we've crossed over some invisible line, from love into hatred—from hatred into hell—and we can't go back anymore. I can't even look at you."

"But you are looking at me," I broke out, beseeching him. "Perhaps you're even seeing me—seeing me at last—or for the first time . . ."

"You can take a towel and robe from the closet—you know where everything is." His face was now sheathed in his customary kindness, and his lips, as if to spite me, relaxed into their pleasant easy curve. "You can throw your stuff in the washer first, then you can put it in the dryer. After that, you can leave."

"I'll leave now!" I yelled, my pride swelling, aching from his mechanized, cruel rejection. I headed toward the door, but I could feel the grime caking on my pants and shirt, the freezing sensation on my back, and I stopped, wanting to be roped back in.

"Please, spare me the dramatics," he said, rolling his eyes. "Just take care of yourself."

"Eddie," I called out as he moved toward the bedroom. He turned halfway toward me to allow himself an escape route, and parts of his body visibly shuddered. I imagined his fingers and toes and even his heart springing out to touch me, but his head-center was commanding him: ABORT, ABORT! "Nothing, thank you, Eddie," I simply said. I too shall be a vision of stoicism and abnegation—I will not reach out and detach those parts of me that long for you—because *I am a boulder too.* Because there lie the pink envelopes on the kitchen table to remind me that *this— this I*—am an invasion of *their* home.

I moved knowingly toward the end of the hallway, where a spacious enclave, adjacent to the master bathroom, housed a giant washer and dryer. I peeled my clothes off my body, and at once the chill dissipated and warmth penetrated my skin. On the bathroom wall I caught sight of a photograph of my profile. A sliver of hope passed through my stomach—not hope for recon- ciliation, but hope that his feelings for me still rumbled beneath the jagged terrain that had now become his skin.

The black-and-white sly curve in my smile in the photograph brought back that weekend in Maine. Beneath the wild hair and the nose protruding into the black shadows, one could see the edge of a collarbone peeking, starkly white like a denuded bone that merged into the silver frame. Only he and I knew that we had been lounging naked on white fur, next to a crackling fireplace, and candles dripping wax brought out drastic oppositions of light and dark. That we were past an orgasm and en route to another one after he would snap forty more shots of me in different poses, that he would readjust my body, cut up my limbs with light, that he would reveal my exposed breasts, my thighs fusing together, the triangle of my navel crossing my pelvis into my pubic zone, that like my own paintings, his photographs would never draw a distinct line between my body parts and my face, granting me the gift of anonymity. He would disembody me as I had so often disembodied my subjects.

The moment stroked me again and again: the massive black concoction rising out of a duffel bag, his head leaning over my stomach, hands maneuvering the camera like a fragile infant, fingers nimbly straddling a thick long lens. "Let me do this," he whispered, "I haven't done this in years, but the way you look in this light . . . I want to capture your beauty." He dotted the space around my body with candles—a wizard casting a spell—and his compliments, like quiet incantations, healed my mind. He had built a fire in his imperious black marble fireplace, and we listened to it crackle, listened to the buzzing chatter of crickets in the air, seeming to mimic the conversation of the flames. He arranged the candles at my ribs to illuminate, sideways, my breasts, and spreading my legs apart he set the candles between my thighs to expose me to the encroaching lens. I struggled to free myself of my body, to release my spirit into the black hovering sky, so acute the pain of arousal had become.

It was *this* objectification of me, I understood only much later, the quick consecutive clicks, the knowledge that he was staring at me through a lens, which with every shot seemed like an organic outgrowth of his eye—that raised the debauched underground of my desire to the surface. In between shots, he would come closer and move my body around: "I want you to relax more, let it go." "Let what go?" I'd ask. "Fear," he'd say and place a warm hand on my stomach as if we both agreed it resided there. "Open your body more toward me. Open your legs. And breathe." "Breathe how?" "Breathe in and out. Normally." "Except that my heart is jumping, running somewhere . . ." He put his hand between my breasts and whispered, "Breathe as if your heart has only one purpose: desire. Imagine blood pumping into your heart, opening you up from within and then—breathe!" And so I did: I sighed, panted, breathed, with urgency, with a mouth full of steam and cravings. "Yes, like that, like that, yes with your back arched, God, you look stunning . . . your body like that . . . lift your chest higher and hold it there—beautiful, Emma." He whispered, "Keep it, keep your face still—don't move anymore. Quiet the desire." Quickly, he returned to the camera, as if the canvas lived inside that black mechanical concoction, and his fingers were the paintbrushes, swift and dexterous, clicking, seizing angles, shadows, translating the object into subject, cutting me up into fragments which then became images—works of art to be hung on walls of galleries, homes, museums—where eyes would greet my body and wonder curiously, how did these images get made? This process unspooled me: my legs spread, knees collapsed sideways, mouth parted, head fallen back. I felt more aroused, more stunned, more wet than I had ever felt from human touch, from any sexual encounter—this was the apotheosis of sensuality—the subversive pleasure in stillness, in being watched and devoured by a lens. He stepped away from the camera and looked at me in amazement, as if he suddenly didn't trust its mechanics, its ability to capture me. When he stood over me again, his hands fell between my thighs, his fingers grazing, circling, entering me, then traveling like feathers along my skin. He kissed my stomach and nipples and mouth and clitoris, and whispered, "I don't know if I can work anymore." "Oh, but you must finish," I urged him, laughing. "I'm in post-coital near-death bliss. Take advantage of it, and we'll call the image *The Quest for the Perfect Orgasm*." "Yes," he said, "you're such an acrobat with words.

"Lie still," he said, "so that I can finish. Let me finish you. Finish this post-coital, near-death version of you. Lie still. Stop breathing, stop wanting momentarily." He smiled. "Just momentarily." The clicking began again, quicker and quicker, and the pulse in my veins beat into my temples, and I forced desire down my throat through the intestines where it lingered, lighting fires in my kidneys and liver, in the nether regions of my pelvis, and then down it fell, down past the thighs into my feet. And it felt like death itself, as cumbersome and final and painful, this simultaneous outpouring and containment of desire. I found myself possessed, thrown into the impossible state of wanting and not knowing how to stop the wanting. I became a machine gone defunct, unable to experience true satiety. So that in the aftermath of being photographed, during our most dazzling sex, when he lifted my body off the floor and carried me to the dining table and, with one hand, removed the candles and the cups we had drunk from and the placemats we had laid out, and with the other hand, placed my entire body on top with my legs raised and my ankles in his grip, and my eyes upon him, I felt the quiet pang of dissatisfaction. Even after the excruciatingly spastic orgasm where my body convulsed, moaned, undulated like a ribbon in his hands, even after that—in light of all that—I longed for the stillness of the lens, and blamed it for the ensuing relentlessness of my desire, for longing to be objectified, again and again. In the shower, as I scrubbed and chafed my skin with hard, angry strokes, I blamed him for having corrupted me.

How miserably I wanted to confess to him! Two days after I accepted his proposal, we were driving back into the city under the arch of a charcoal sky. Stars peered through the front window like judges weighing in on my soul.

"Eddie," I started, "you've known me for such a short time. I mean everything, us, has happened so fast—"

"I know everything I need to know." He took one hand off the wheel and put it on my knee.

"You've corrupted me," I said at once. "I will never be the same person, the same girl. I will always want more."

"More than me?"

"I don't know," I returned, hesitating, tracing figures in the steam that had collected on the window. At last I said, "I guess I'm afraid I will never want anyone other than you."

"Well, then we're good to go—we're set for life." He beamed at me with such openness and wonder I should have kept quiet. But I was suspicious of happiness—itching to pry it open and dangle it under the elements to test its mettle.

"Are we—are we truly set, Eddie? You never mention your mother. Have you told her?"

He held one hand on the wheel as he turned to me with surprise. "I've been so worried about your family's disapproval of me that, honestly, I haven't given her a single thought."

"I mean when I met her I was just a girl—a girlfriend—and now, now things are different." I still couldn't bring myself to utter the word "fiancée," because Alex was too closely associated with it, because the word itself felt like a parasite I needed to expunge. "Do you think she'll want me? She seemed so particular."

"Everyone wants you, Emma," he cried enthusiastically, "tell me who doesn't want you? My brother will squirm from jealousy and my father thinks you're the most extraordinary and beautiful woman he's ever met! His words, not mine."

I recalled the sharp pinch of recognition, followed by a slow, dull nausea: he had conspicuously failed to mention his mother. My Russian instinct, my truth-telling, flag-waving, war-waging instinct, told me to confront him, and yet, yet, I felt secure enough, American enough to let it go—to keep it buried beneath the surface. He had already taught me to draw a line of distinction between a parent and a child, and now he wanted me to respect this distinction in him. Only it never occurred to me to wonder why he clung to it with such ferocity.

"You've awakened me," I announced with glee, backtracking to that mischievous, substantially less troublesome topic of desire. "Now I can bed any man!"

He smiled widely, taking both hands off the wheel as if to crash us into the black sky.

"Yes," he said ominously.

"Are you trying to kill us?"

"Desire has no limits," he snapped. "I know that better than anyone. Like all things of excess, it can turn into something ugly and banal into addiction. You end up worse off than before—who knows what our true motives are? Or at least I've never known or understood mine. Until you—until I fell for you. Now my motives are clear; I do things to be with you. Love creates its own moral universe, I believe that, and there are breaches that cannot be undone." He twisted his neck to face me and said, "If you ever cheat on me, Emma, I will never forgive you—do you hear me, no matter how I feel, I will not hesitate to leave."

I let out a rickety laugh. "Don't be melodramatic! I'm just playing with you!"

"Don't play! Don't play with this." He grabbed my hand and placed it on his heart.

We didn't speak for a while after that. I remembered my eyes closing involuntarily and sleep swallowing me as the car rocked from side to side. I awakened in the Lincoln Tunnel. "We're in New York," he said, and I feared suddenly that I had poisoned him with my mistrust.

"Are you all right in there? You're taking forever—" Now I heard him mumble through the door, and felt his breath intermingling with the steam from the shower, settling on me.

"I'll leave in ten minutes," I said, turning off the water. My feet had pruned—how long had I been there? Was he waiting for me?

I wrapped a towel around my torso and draped another one over my shoulders and chest, so that I was completely shrouded in white. Only my dark hair hung like a black curtain over my face.

"I just put your clothes in the dryer—it shouldn't take too long, another twenty minutes," he said, his body frozen at the other end of the hallway. "If you want, you could borrow Melanie's pants and sweater—I'm sure she wouldn't mind."

I couldn't speak; until that moment I hadn't connected a name to the pink envelopes.

"I'm sure she would," I said after an agonizing pause. "Look, if you can't stand to have me here a minute longer, I can put my wet clothes on and leave—I'll leave right now!"

"No, it's not that."

"What it is then?"

"You know perfectly well what it is. Don't look at me with those eyes—you forget how well I know you. I don't have to spell it out for you."

"Then don't!" I screamed and rushed toward the dryer. My clothes were roiling in an empty machine, smashing against the metal like the cry of someone drowning, gasping for air, gasping inside of me, and I thought quickly, consciously, that if I were to finish this great act of self-destruction, the minute I would step into the merciless wind and snow, my clothes would freeze on my skin and I would ride in the taxi half-dead, in the throes of pneumonia. But as he refused to move toward me, as that smug, scornful grin continued to crimple his face, I wanted to go on—to spite, to bite, to loathe. I was too vain, too proud, too confident to let pneumonia or death prevent me from declaring war. I yanked open the dryer and pulled the soaking clothes out.

One hand tightened the towel around my body, while the other hand tried to push one leg through a dripping, cold pant leg. I bent like an acrobat gone catatonic in the middle of an ambitious backward flip, all the while trying not to drop the towel. Still balancing on one leg, I managed at last to get the clinging pant leg up to one knee. My muscles stiffened from the wet cloth, both legs froze, and I teetered sideways like a dejected human triangle. He was watching me, his eyes fixed on the towel shifting over my thighs, riding up my hips, the edges coming apart as I struggled with the pant legs. He was closing in on me, exuding his familiar scent. *Let me not smile, dear Lord, or beam like an idiot or emit the shrieks of a fornicating baboon.* He slammed the lid of the machine shut with such vigor that I almost passed out from delight, and then he pulled the wet pants down my legs with enough force to peel away my skin. He rose back up, slowly, his eyes climbing up my calves, between my thighs, gliding over the towel, without touching me. From the waist down, I felt raw, skinless, and then a finger—a single index finger drew a line from my collarbone to the knot of the towel between my breasts.

"It was a mistake to come here," I murmured, shutting my eyes. I felt suffocated by the emptiness in my ribs, by the sharp ache of wanting and resisting. I clutched the towel with both hands.

"Don't touch me, don't look at me." I shivered.

"Why not?" he said, "why not? We're past everything, you and I."

"Why are you with someone else?"

"What did you expect—that I'd join the priesthood and wait for you?" He laughed, flaunting his pleasure.

"I had hoped that you'd at least mourn us—not jump right in—how long has it been, three months at most?"

"Ah, but now we're even."

"Is that what you've been doing all along—avenging me?"

"It doesn't feel good, does it—to know you're competing with someone else. Did you really think you're the only one who can play that game?"

"How did you know I'd be working at the restaurant—why did you come there?"

"It was a coincidence," he said.

"You're lying!"

"I called your sister."

"So you wanted me to see you with this other girl—you did this on purpose?"

"It wasn't a grand scheme, if that's what you're wondering. I didn't give it that much thought. But maybe it was a subconscious act—to give us both clarity."

"Clarity?" I laughed, full of bitterness. "Is that what we're after—does Melanie know that you're playing a game at her expense?"

"Don't play the considerate feminist with me, I beg you! I know you, remember!"

"I wasn't purposefully trying to hurt you! It's not just about you. I needed to decide the rest of my life!"

"How do you know it's any different for me? How do you know if the rest of my life isn't hanging in the balance?"

"What do you mean?"

He paused and turned from me. His eyes acquired a scorching cobalt hue in the gray afternoon sun. "This is *my* way of mourning." His voice trailed off.

"You're using her," I whispered.

"No, I'm using you," he said and with his index finger, I could see it through half-opened lids, he reached between my breasts and undid the towel, letting it drop to the floor. I stood naked before him as I had stood so many times before, only this time I felt the cruelty of exposure, the deprivation of privacy and power. He could see my heart as it was, extracted from my ribcage and perspiring on top of my chest. *Here, take it,* I wanted to shout, *you've taken away everything else.* Yet he seemed not to care; he could see it and still, he fingered it, mocked it—my poor dislodged heart.

When my body collided against his, his clothes seemed to transform into rough skin, hostile to my own, and even after he had torn off his jeans, shirt, and underwear, his skin still remained rough. Yet he clung to me as I did to him, with the same voraciousness and desperation. "I missed you," he mumbled, frantically kissing my eyes and cheeks and neck and breasts. We stood, entangled, transfixed in time. I had never seen him this naked before. The tenderness in his eyes was so peculiar, so aberrant on his thick masculine face, that for an instant I felt that I had glimpsed the countenance of a woman.

He bent between my feet and threw my wet clothes back in the dryer and pushed the start button, and that too aroused me—his nose grazing my calves and knees as he rose from the floor. The dryer rumbled in my head. He lifted my naked body onto the washer, pinning me against its cold metal surface, and it thawed between my parted thighs. I blinked from tears, from seeing his head burrow between my legs, his mouth kissing the insides of my thighs, devouring me there—the burning space in between—and then I screamed from the pleasurable torture of being tickled and then pried open, from inferno breaths unlocking a slick cool tongue. When at last I sang—a soprano's mournful treble—he stood up to face me, to lock me in his torrential gaze, to connect me to all my senses again, to my blurry eyes, wet with grief and pleasure, to my humming ears, to his fingers prying me open again, his mouth on my breasts, circling my face but never touching my lips. Why, why won't you kiss me? And yet I knew why. With his weight slamming against my pelvis, he entered me roughly, madness riling between us. And when his movement gained a beat in a staccato rhythm, and then grew into a long, ceaseless crescendo, my mind fell away and watermarks burgeoned on my chin and neck and stomach like time marking my descent to old age. Yet all I value now, the only thing that has escaped memory's cross oblivion, is the sensation of the moment when his index finger lingered near my sternum, when it invaded the space between wanting and resisting, when his clothes became grafted onto my skin, when my knees wobbled and then gave out from the pressure of wanting him so much.

In the aftermath, he turned away from me to look at the naked sun. His back glistened in the winter twilight.

"Eddie, Eddie—I want to tell you something—"

"I don't want to talk now," he said without looking at me. I was still seated where he left me, on top of the washer, no clothes or sheets to hide behind, only shadows dancing on my exposed skin.

"Please Eddie, if I don't talk now, I will never gather the courage to say it again."

He didn't answer. So I spoke into his back, into his silence.

"I want you to know—I returned to New York for you. Let me begin again. I mean for you and art. Eddie, I realized that more than anything else, more than anything—I—I want to be with you. I don't need to be with you; I'm not fragile, desperate, or lonely. What I feel—my love for you—comes from strength. Nothing else matters, everything else is meaningless. This—this"—I pointed at my heart—"will make us happy."

Abruptly, he turned to face me. He had a wild look in his eyes, the glare of ferocity.

"How do you know that?" he demanded. "Sure, in the abstract nothing matters, in fairy tales nothing but love matters, but not for us—not for you and me! In our case, everything matters and did matter. Our families would never get along. We'd drown in problems. You were right from the start: it wasn't realistic for us to be together. We were putting on Shakespeare—Romeo and Juliet, and now the curtain's dropped and it's time for us to go home to our respective, boring, conventional lives. Snap out of the fantasy, Emma, we're all just ordinary. There's no true authentic starving artist anymore, and there's certainly no forbidden love; there are just thrills and marriages of conveniences, and you and I—well, we were just a thrill."

I reeled from him, crossing my arms over my chest, wanting pitifully to wipe the traces of his saliva from my face and breasts and stomach, and there, there—between my thighs.

"Ohh, ohhh," I groaned as though he had smashed me in the stomach, "I—I see—you're planning a marriage of convenience for yourself."

"I am," he gloated. "Mother's hungry for another grandchild, and as she likes to put it, 'The great Beltrafios need another heir.'" Then he laughed uproariously. I understood at once: whether it was conscious or unconscious, his revulsion to me was real. The wall he had built around himself still had holes in it, and remnants of his desire still seeped through, but he intended to plug them all.

I retreated, bloodied, wounded, deserted, but still glad to be alive. Sadness seized me in its throat-clenching grip but I did not cry. A strange feeling of goodwill overtook me, ameliorating the pain of seeing his indifferent, haughty face. I did not regret telling him at this strange juncture how much I loved him, telling it without any reservation or engrained pride. I took my warm clothes from the dryer and dressed quietly in my plain black uniform. I remembered that the purple diamond ring was still lodged in the inner pocket of my purse, and I placed it gently on the kitchen table, against the backdrop of the pink envelopes. As I hurried down the hall, I called out, "The ring is next to your wedding invitations. Goodbye, Eddie." That was all I said, and he said nothing in return.

The Apology

The next morning I awoke to the deadening crush of rejection. I felt my body parts disengage, grow still, and refuse to cooperate. I forced clothes upon myself and, in a daze, with an asinine smile glued to my lips, I greeted customers and took orders, and nodded, yes, yes, thank you, and punched my hours in like a functioning individual when in fact I could feel my mind succumbing to the unremitting stillness of depression. How I needed— wanted—to anesthetize my cantankerous head! When drinking tea from a coffee mug, I heard Grandmother whisper, *see, see, I was right, you prideless fool, he's an alien virus, krovopijtza, merzkoye gavno!* Or while wiping my face with a cheap towel, I felt my mother chiding me for chafing my skin, for weakening, for parading my feelings with such cruel disregard for my own well-being. Or when I wept into a Tempur-pedic pillow, stifling my wails with hard yellow foam, I could hear Bella's resounding, sarcastic laugh at life's absurd injustices. Or while arranging tubes of paint,

I envisaged my father shaking his head at me, at the dilettante life I was leading, with no man to support my habits. Where is your 401 plan? he seemed to be tapping at my obstinate head. Will you have health insurance if you sell a painting? And when I sweated in the diner, returning home with my legs stiff and aching, when my arms fell to my sides like celery stalks, and when the stench of rotting lamb chops in a curry sauce emanating from the Indian restaurant became so endemic to my lungs that when I took a walk along the river I seemed to be polluting it with my own breath, I heard my dear ones, their hearts breaking into that old patriotic nag: *we didn't bring you to this country, didn't pay for University of Chicago, for NYU graduate school, didn't pamper you, feed you, love you so that you could end up here—torturing yourself for what? For whom? For this illusion of independence? The difference between you and every other struggling artist is that you still have a choice—you can come back to us!*

I had not spoken to Grandmother for three agonizing months—a time frame so unfathomable in our family that she was on the verge of declaring me dead or a crazy whore, the former clearly being the preferable condition of the two. I was certain she missed me, but her sense of injury was so finely honed that it rendered my suffering obsolete—and it became unconscionable to give in to me. The only cure to my suffering was to utter the dreadful apology—"*Ya izvinyayus ,*" and admit at last that the world ended and began in her, the one who metaphorically bore us all. *I would rather die a crazy whore.*

My mother understood us both, and brokered a peace treaty by sticking the receiver literally under Grandmother's loud mouth, into which the latter immediately yelled, "You wouldn't believe what people are saying about your mother—that she's lost her bearings! Your mother called Lyuba Berkovich 'a brainless, flat-assed viper' to her face because Lyuba accused your mother of not loving her younger daughter"—i.e., letting me go to New York by myself. "They're saying you've turned into a fancy feminist-spinster. 'Nonsense,' I told Lyuba, 'our Lenochka is a professor of feeeeemenist *teoriya!*'" These perky insults were Grandmother's roundabout method for teaching us moral lessons and so I sprinkled a little moral acid of my own. "They're all idiots, anyhow, your Russian friends, stuck in old paradigms from the old country."

"I couldn't agree with you more," she said, "jealous hags with enough evil eye to send a fly to the gulags! They can't stand the fact that you don't have to work because your father supports you."

"I have a job, *babushka*," I protested in a wounded voice, "he's not supporting me. I'm on my own."

"I hear he still sends you money because your fancy art school is very expensive. Your mother says it's impressive, this so-called art school."

"I'm going to be an artist, *babushka*—a painter, like Chagall," I said, swelling with sudden pride.

"Out of all your opportunities, all your talents, why, why would you choose to be an artist—it's a miserable profession, you'll never be happy!"

"Because this is my life, my life, don't you see it, my life to choose and screw up!" I cried.

"Yes, your life! Big words! What a fool I've been, thinking I can help you—save my Lenochka—for what? So much wasted breath!"

"That's not true!" Tears sprang from my eyes; how fortunate, I thought, that she couldn't see them. "I hear everything—I try to listen, I do, but I want to find my own path, be my own person."

"Funny word, 'own'—I, for one, don't know what it means," Grandmother said, "but you and your sister and your mother keep telling me about it, and I keep thinking to myself, if only I had had such a keen understanding of this word, 'own,' where would your lives be? Your mother was doing 'important' work with writers, and at night she went out with her 'high-culture' literary crowd. While I, while I raised all of you: bathed you, powdered your bottoms, fed you, clothed you, licked the floors practically with my tongue, cooked feasts from scratch, folded and ironed the laundry with my bare hands, cleaned up everyone's shit, and wiped everyone's and I mean everyone's asses—your father's and grandfather's included. I did it so that you could all study and develop your brains and succeed in your careers, while I worked as a maid for free. So I wonder now if only I had known such words as 'own,' 'free,' or '*my, my my* life,' where would you all be?"

We sat in silence, crushed by the weight of her perennial self-sacrifice as it hovered over our heads, over the telephone poles in New York and Chicago, over the entire Western hemisphere, and expanded like a behemoth hydrogen balloon across the sky. And for the first time, without seeing her proud face, I could hear bitterness in her voice: the bitterness of community, charity, devotion, and the worst, most insidious bitterness of all—family.

"You didn't have to do all that," I whispered. "You could have run."

"Oh, *dorogaya vnuchenka*, I could have done a lot of things, but one thing I couldn't do was run."

"Then why don't you let *me* run?"

"That's just it, that's what you don't see—I am letting you run. I've let you run very, very far. Don't you understand? You're a mouse in a maze; you think you're getting out by changing cities, careers, men, but you'll end up where I was, where your mother was, where your sister is—shackled just like the rest of us. There's nowhere else for us women to go."

When I hung up the phone, I laughed outright at my naïve old grandmother: what do you know, I screamed; shut your trap, I screamed; look at me, I screamed; I'm a hawk perched on a cliff ingesting the open sky.

The Long, Tortuous Trajectory of Great Art

The gallery was a dark cluttered basement of a three-story town house. Chintzy, bronze-encrusted chandeliers hung from the ceiling, and tall scented candles lit up cobwebbed corners. Incense burned on an altar table with a statue of a Hindu goddess, and a sweet odor of bark and ginger-root swirled in our nostrils. The gallery was owned by a woman named Linda Fern, who was decked out in a multicolored robe that clashed with her sallow skin and gave her a momentary lapse in coordination. She greeted the guests with an air of geniality and sweetness, and the usual array of characters who visit art galleries were reduced to their friendlier, kinder selves. By offering very low prices for the work she showed and talking up these artists as though they were the next Picasso, Dali, or Unitcheska, Linda would lure rich clients by convincing them that these paintings were "investments" that would eventually be worth thirty to sixty thousand dollars apiece, if not more.

Although it was not an established gallery, it was known among people in the art world as a "quiet swirl of activity," "a hidden gem," "a surprising mix of the traditional and the avant-garde." Once in a while a major critic would stop by and write a piece on some lucky bastard in a prominent art magazine. Even though I had to share wall space with two other students, my friend Stone and another woman from Unitcheska's class, Carol, I withheld this innocuous detail from my family when I announced the sensational news over the phone. At first, they didn't seem to understand me: was I buying art for myself? Did I need money? Did I want to come home now that someone was going to finally sell off my crazy paintings? Or was this just an educational event where I would get a simulation of what it must be like to be seen and sold without actually being seen or sold? When I told my father that Linda Fern took seventy percent of the profit from several hundred dollars, he let out a groan of pain. "Dear child, why, you're being robbed from your forehead to your toenails!"

Although Linda was mildly impressed with *The Mermaid-Child* and *Prehistoric Children*, commenting on their interesting suffusion of color and expressive eyes, she was mercilessly critical about the rest. For *The Girl Under a Green Umbrella,* she felt a kind of visceral disgust; the child suspended in the air appeared too skinny and pathetic looking under the massive umbrella, whose actual tint was not green at all, but "sewage-mustard gray." "Awful," she concluded. *My Secret Chanterelle* exposed the skin of a perforated orange mushroom, inside of which a pre-pubescent girl, in Carmen's red skirt and black blouse, showed her face and waved one plump thigh. "Are you trying to sexualize children like that pervert, Balthus?" Linda wanted to know. "With today's obsession over child molestation, do you think anyone is going to be bold enough to buy this?" Toward *Sprites in a Can* she expressed only intellectual dismay. "Now, here, I see you've moved on to torture?" The latter painting was my most ambitious undertaking, capturing eleven children lying side by side in a partially opened metal can, their bodies clad in silver gowns, irrespective of gender, their faces smiling and crackling with laughter. Yet underneath their mirth, you could see them squirming, pushing aside the arms of their neighbor to make breathing space for themselves, or perhaps even to escape. Toward *The First Cigarette*, which depicted my grandfather at the age of nine smoking a cigarette, his luxuriating face barely managing to fit inside the perfect square of the canvas, Linda summarized her feelings thus: "No one with children would ever want to buy *this*!"

But it was toward the last, the seventh painting that she directed all her acidity and motherly reproof: *The Monster*. A magnified oak trunk dominated the center of the canvas, its bark rotting and beset with gaping holes that resembled vacuous eyes. A cavernous mouth opened at the bottom of the tree, and from its protruding lip grew thick, snarling roots. Numerous eyes burned through the bark, red and glittery like rubies, and the torso was afflicted with thorns and sprouted sharp-toothed branches. A child was splayed across its width, its hands and feet bound to the trunk, a transparent child through whose diaphanous body one could make out teeth, eyes, claws. The roots that rose from the bottom of the canvas imitated human hands and tugged at the child's skinny, pale legs. It was, as I had often told myself, a scene of horror, and yet what joy, what satisfaction, what euphoria there had been in painting it—in watching the horror breathe with life. As I watched workers mount the canvas on a pallid wall, I breathed in long rapturous intervals, ballooning from pride, wondering, in secret, if I could possibly have it—that elusive quality that denotes true genius.

"Good Lord, child, what is this morass?" Linda exclaimed, glancing at it in clear physical dismay. "How am I ever going to sell this thing? No one but a freak would like it, and the people who buy art are as a general rule never freaks." She threw a leg up through the air for an exclamation mark, and her bright multi-colored skirt cascaded down her body like a parachute.

"I beg to differ!" Unitcheska appeared out of nowhere and gazed with tenderness at my work. "You should have placed Emma at least in the second room; it's a shame to exile her—"

"I took her in the first place out of a favor to you. This isn't a museum. Already they're cleaning out the warehouse next to me to build a new gallery. *I* toil in the real world—Oooooh, Samuel, how wonderful to see you!" And with that Linda was whisked away by the pitter-patter of money, for Samuel F. Levenson was an important patron of the arts.

"You'll be all right, Emma," Unitcheska assured me in a motherly tone. "You've got that rare quality that so few artists possess—a knack for making your audience suffer with you."

Even though *The Monster* would hang on the gallery's farthest wall, in a room that could only be accessed by a long winding corridor, I was elated. Consider that there was an invitation at all—a poster with tiny reprints of our paintings next to our names: *Reagan as a Cobra* next to Stone Hograth, *A Soup Medley* next to Carol Smith, and *Girl Under a Green Umbrella* next to Emma Kaulfield! I didn't care about the back wall or the exhausting staircase, or even the possibility that no one would buy my work—I was already envisioning myself as the next Unitcheska. Even the black velvet décolleté blouse I wore and the purple suede pants that hugged my behind and released torrents of sweat down my thighs made me feel magnificent, hip, accomplished, so quintessentially New York. Painting alone was not enough: it was the fusion of painting and showing, the process of seeing and being seen that so marvelously gratified me. Linda had arranged my paintings along two walls, creating a progression of themes and color from the olive-hued, muddied faces of *Prehistoric Children* to the surfeit of lime and verdant tones in *Girl Under the Green Umbrella* to the yellow-cobalt maze of *The Child-Mermaid* to the rust-colored mushroom in *My Secret Chanterelle*, culminating in the silver kaleidoscope of *Sprites in a Can*, which created a magical continuity between the paintings, imbuing them with a collective voice. But *The Monster*, ominous in its frenetic strokes and corrugated knife-like branches, stood apart on a separate wall.

On opening night, the guests passed from one painting to the next with a meticulous slowness, eyeing each canvas with the graveness I had only encountered in hospital waiting rooms. A woman and a gay couple froze in front of *The Child-Mermaid*, and I watched their heads bobbing up and down in assent to its free-form ambiguity. An intermingling of fear and joy charged through my veins: would they buy it? Occasionally my heart would squeeze from the sudden fear of seeing Eddie, and I'd scan the room in search of him. Confessing love was far worse than concealing it, I had realized in the bleak aftermath, so that upon discerning a suit, I would shudder and retreat into the deeper reaches of the gallery, scurrying into the corridor or hiding in the bathroom, giving the unidentified suit time to leave.

By nine o'clock, the place roared with excitement; people were streaming into the foyer in droves, piling their coats on hangers and counters, their faces red and pinched by the cold. We had no idea how Linda managed to greet four or five people at once, with her hands and eyes darting in opposite directions, and her face drenched in a constant oily glow of pleasure. But that's what she needed to do: for rather than pricing our paintings before the opening, the way established galleries did, Linda preferred the high-pitched frenzy of an auction. She felt that her method of smelling desire in the buyer—of gauging exactly how much they were willing to part with and asking for just a smidgen more—would yield the greatest profit. She was a natural saleswoman, she confided in us, she could have gone corporate if she didn't still have her ideals. I watched her sell Stone's *Boa Constrictor* with the rapidity of a train crash: "Sold!" she'd say out loud to spawn more desire, "Sold!" to prevent the interference of rational thought. "Don't you love this?" Linda murmured to me, "people are asking to meet you—someone wants to buy the *Prehistoric Children*," she said. "What are they offering?" I asked. "Three-hundred and fifty dollars." It took me five months to finish this painting, I lamented bitterly to myself, but out loud I asked to meet them. We pushed past a crowd gathered in front of *Nixon as a Rattlesnake,* down the corridor and into the back room where my paintings hung. There were noticeably fewer people here, but they appeared to my eager eye to be more engrossed in my paintings, to be—as I fantastically imagined it— embedding intricate parts of me in their languorous souls.

"Here's the artist," Linda exclaimed, situating me in front of a bald man and a handsome woman in a glittering yellow dress.

"We're so impressed," the woman murmured, "the colors are so understated, and yet the emotions are large and alive!"

"There's real passion in your work!" the bald man next to her said.

"My husband is already in love with you," the wife said. "If only we had more money, but living in the city—well I'm sure you know how hard it is—oh our daughter would love this painting!"

"I'm so happy you like it," I said, bowing my head to them.

"We're artists ourselves in a way," he said. "I'm a writer, and my wife is an actress; perhaps you've head of her newest production, *The Bird, The Cat, and the Everything.* It's playing at the Kraine, an excellent off-off-Broadway theater."

"Oh Clive, must you advertise my play to everyone?" She lowered her head bashfully and pulled a postcard from a crumbling leather purse. On skinny paper, a tiny reprint of her face accompanied a bold title: *The Cat, The Bird, and the Everything,* starring Bertha Fermish. I wondered vaguely if their only purpose at the gallery was to advertise her play, and the euphoria I felt seconds before in seeing my name in print vanished.

"Thank you, I'll try to see it," I said, taking the postcard.

"Linda says the price is 350 dollars—but would it be possible—I know this isn't customary—to give us a discount?" the woman said. "We'd be so happy!"

A tall, exquisitely groomed man in a shimmering black suit stomped in front of us, and after a perfunctory glance at *Prehistoric Children,* lasting a total of four seconds, demanded to know the price.

"Four hundred," Linda trilled.

"All right," the man said, "I'll take it."

"But you already gave it to these people—I want this couple to have it," I protested.

Linda smiled at the couple, and then pulled me to the side.

"This isn't a bazaar, Emma, this is a business. Highest bidder wins."

From the corner, I watched her scribble the word "sold" under my painting and usher the man into her office, his checkbook glued to the palm of his hand. The actress and her husband bowed their heads in humility and shuffled out the door.

After the initial sale, my paintings took on a sudden momentum. *My Secret Chanterelle* went to the gay couple who perceived the influence of Balthus in my work. *The Child-Mermaid* went to a fashionably attired lady in "finance" who declared it a "great bargain and a future masterpiece." *The First Cigarette* went to a wealthy, diamond-sprouting woman in her sixties, an old friend of Unitcheska and a patron of the Fern Gallery. She too had wanted *Prehistoric Children*, but settled on my grandfather, whom she felt perfectly captured her egotistical ex-husband. *Girl Under a Green Umbrella* went to a pregnant couple who felt that the verdant tones set against a gray sky would perfectly match their green-hued nursery.

But *The Monster*, as Lydia had predicted, appealed to no one. I clung to the hope that it would remain untouched, but an hour later I discerned a gathering of three people around it.

"Such interesting use of color," I heard a woman in white mink remark, "so much gray and then suddenly this outpouring of red."

"And the strokes here really evoke a sense of movement, of time, of continuity," an older gentleman in a tweed jacket noted.

"Yes," their companion agreed, "I think it's an excellent portrayal of a winter storm."

"What is that white thing in the center—is that a face?" the older man asked. "I think I see eyes."

"It looks like some kind of meditation on the elusiveness of existence," the woman observed.

"These artists nowadays—none of them have any serious training." An older woman in a blonde wig appeared out of nowhere. She could have put forth any idiotic theory and it would have sounded plausible on account of her age and sharp aristocratic features.

How I wanted to push them aside and tape their tongues to their noses! How many years had it taken me to gather the courage to bring color to canvas that was the exact replica of the color in my head, the color that was also voice, memory, confession. How many months of sketching and re-imagining it in its various disguises, in its palatable form!

It wasn't merely personal but political—outrage at the suffering of all children mapping the scars that Stalin's supreme manias left behind. The child's face was to contain universal sadness, and at its back, the trunk—the monster—was the ill-begotten offspring of human cruelty, capturing in its detailed claws and regimented bark scabs the way cruelty functioned, directing its bullets at the helpless and the weak, until the helpless and the weak rose in the social hierarchy to avenge their oppressors on the new crop of the helpless and the weak. This is not a meditation on the meaninglessness of existence, I wanted to scream, but on its painful and very present meaning—on the endless circle of vengeance, hatred, and rage.

There, in Russia, we were never alone. Even our thoughts hung like sheets in public space for inspection and approval. We were conditioned to exist without silence—to view silence as danger—to welcome interference, advice on how to live, what to say, who and what to believe, obedience as an incessant conversation. Disobedience could only live in silence, in the radical cessation of the collective voice. But here, here in America, I reveled in silence. I could shut the world out and it would let me breathe in solitude, indifferent to my miseries and pleasures. Happiness was within reach. Happiness as silence—as the impenetrable cocoon of one's own thoughts. I didn't have to be an artist; I could have been a statistician. I didn't have to be a statistician; I could have stayed at home with my parents. I could have married Alex or Eddie and stayed at home with them. I could go off to Montana, buy myself a cabin and paint, and that too would be a life—a perfectly respectable life. Even if the small town's people would gawk at me, an artist after forty, unmarried, they would leave me alone as the town's solipsistic freak. She don't bother me, they'd say, does she bother you? Even the prejudice I'd experience upon telling someone that I was Russian or Jewish would slide off of me, off of them over time, over my efforts, over the work I'd do. I was an individual, a separate entity from my mother and grandmother, from my father and sister, and from the men I loved or didn't love. If I uttered a peep against the chorus of peeps, no one would arrest me. If I wanted to fight, to carry slogans, to roar behind a podium, a road block would be set up to prevent cars from interfering with my speech.

Someone had left an umbrella on the floor next to my foot, and I picked it up—its sharp, almost knife-like edge glistened in the gallery's precise light. Holding it tightly between my fingers with its edge pointing down, I came between the older gentleman and the ginger-haired woman.

"Excuse me," I said, moving in front of them.

"You're blocking our view," they said, unaware.

"I'm the artist," I said.

"Oh," they murmured in a chorus, "there's so much we've wanted to ask you—what does it *really* mean?"

"Torture," I replied. And with a sudden violent jerk of my hand, I struck the sharp point of the umbrella into the center of the painting, piercing the canvas and the wall, and then, with a note of relief, pulled it out. A small hole now marked the body of the phantom-child. The hole seemed strangely congruous with the red ruby eyes scattered across the trunk, but the canvas was ostensibly ruined.

The room went aghast. The strangers' mouths were still open when I turned to face them. They staggered back in fear, for they suspected that if I could puncture a living painting, I could puncture their flesh as well. "No," I wanted to scream, "I'm sane—emotional but sane, broken hearted but sane, supremely depressed but perfectly sane!" But it was too late. Minds were fast at work. I could see their thoughts on their foreheads: *well for crying out loud—what in the world—who is this crazy fucking bitch?* Whenever civilization is interrupted by a socially inappropriate act, an act that has the potential to unravel it, human beings begin to feel as if they too could be infected by the "crazy" disease. It's important in such cases to promptly remove the threat. An ambulance will arrive any minute and carry me out on a white stretcher, I convinced myself, when suddenly out of the stultifying silence came this:

"Brilliant," a man exclaimed, "absolutely brilliant!"

"I see it too—" the mink-clad woman agreed enthusiastically, "the painting has gained a new meaning."

"So this is what they mean by performance art! How absolutely riveting and fresh!"

"Do you need serious training to do performance art?" a fortyish man asked, whom I recognized as a homeless man on my street.

"I want it," the gentleman in the tweed jacket announced, "it might be valuable one day."

"It's valuable already!" Linda descended on the crowd like a circus-trained tiger.

A man whose throat was wrapped in a pink scarf and whose head was pinched by a gray-checkered cap was taking copious notes. My recurring reverie whizzed by, and I deduced between ecstatic breaths that he was a critic from *ART* magazine. Things are happening, I serenaded myself, not in spite of the hole, but because of it! Other people were trickling in to investigate the source of the commotion.

"It must have been planned—the hole is dead center—pure genius!"

"But what does it mean?"

"It's an expression of the rupture of our society—of our morals and values—of the way the Internet will ruin all our lives—"

"Yes, I see what you mean."

"Someone mentioned that the artist is from Russia?"

"Perhaps it's a meditation on her double identity. There's a hole in all of us—and through it our many identities seep from one into the other—it's about the fluidity of identity."

"I hardly agree—there's something monstrous here, I just can't put my finger on it."

"Maybe you're referring to the fact that the painting is called *The Monster.*"

The admiration in people's voices and their conspiratorial laughter passed through my body like the pleasurable currents of a lethal drug, administered only to the incurably vain. How I beamed at all of them—how I marveled at my impulsive act!

"I'll take it for two thousand!" someone thundered from the back of the room, and in that instant all my pleasure turned to dread.

"I'll raise it to two thousand five hundred," someone else shouted and the auction went into full swing. Linda's face ignited, her voice rose. "Three thousand, do I hear three? Yes, we have three thousand from the gentleman in the back." More people streamed in; the room was engulfed in hysteria and commotion.

I felt it then—his eyes drilling into the back of my head. I shifted my body in a half-circle, cautiously, and then I saw him at the back of the room, gripped in an artificial stillness. He wore a sleek nocturnal suit with a crisp white shirt and yet another striped variation of his signature maroon tie. There, at the corners of his mouth, danced his easy habitual smile. The room vanished from my field of vision and only he remained, only his eyes beckoned to me, bringing me within inches of his face.

"You didn't think I'd miss your debut," he said, grinning. He examined my black décolleté blouse, taut pants, and the amethyst pendant drawing a triangle at the base of my neck, but his eyes never settled on my face.

"So you've come for advice on your upcoming nuptials?" I noted in my aloof, extraterrestrial voice.

"I don't understand you! Do you actually believe these pompous idiots, do you believe their praise? You ruined your best piece, right on time, as if to spite me—"

"Emma, I'm soooooo proud of you," Linda crooned, descending upon us. "I honestly have no idea how I'm going to part with this incredible painting! And who is this?" Her feverish eyes latched onto Eddie. "Perhaps you'd like to make your bid on *The Monster.*"

"I already did—I was the initial bid for two thousand," he replied with a polite nod.

"Oh, I wish I hadn't sold your others quite so early," Linda lamented to me.

"I hadn't meant to imply that I'm not in awe of Ms. Kaulfield's work," Eddie intervened.

"No, God forbid." Linda said. "Well, I must run! Do I hear five—the lady in the mink coat—yes, sold for five thousand dollars!" She had spotted an important-looking being in glitter and plowed a path through the crowd with her rakish arms and bulldozer heels. "Sold, sold!" she screamed in ecstasy.

"Is there any place we can speak in private?" he asked.

"We have nothing to say to each other," I threw back.

"Please, Emma—I won't take long."

I submitted out of a sudden hope and led him up a creaking staircase into Linda's den. *You poor abused heart, still so naïve, so opulently optimistic, imagining that he has come to apologize for the punctures he left in your four ventricles.*

But when I glanced at him, his face betrayed nothing: a polished mask.

The bedroom housed people's coats and purses, and the art world's salacious secrets. A stack of shrouded paintings leaned against a wall. Invitations to galleries, magazines, letters spilled from half-opened drawers, and slides of artwork were scattered on her oak desk. Candles burned in old wine bottles, illuminating the centerpiece: a mammoth scarlet bed.

We attempted with great difficulty to avoid eye contact with the lascivious silk bedding. There were rumors that Linda brought young male artists here after their shows and demanded gratitude for her labors. A draft blew in from a cracked windowpane and the candle flames, in a communal sigh, bent toward us.

He touched my arm and leaned chillingly close to my face, rendering me momentarily mute.

"What are you doing?"

"I came here tonight," he said, retreating, "to say something—I want to wash my hands of pretense—"

"You want to 'wash your hands of pretense'—let me try and decipher your meaning, my banker-poet!" I cried with an acrid shrill instead of the intended Zen laugh.

"Shut up—shut the fuck up and listen to me. I need for you to listen."

"You're too late—I don't want to hear anything from you—"

"I need to explain why I behaved the way I did—you must know the truth."

"The *truth*—the *truth*—when was there ever a more perfidious word!"

"It was never the way you said. I didn't grow up with a flag-waving racist."

"You've come to tell me your mother was, after all, or still is an anti-Semite—is that it?" I laughed hideously.

"Mother wanted to feel superior to everyone. She said things like: 'those people with their green pastures,' her favorite euphemism for Jewish money. My father used to argue with her at the beginning of the marriage, but I have few memories of that. The breakdown wiped everything out. The breakdown and the bankruptcy. My father's partner was half-Jewish and she clung to that. 'Do you think it's peculiar that Russell stole your father's money and professed to be Christian, despite his obvious Jewishness?' she'd ask Andy and me as if it was a riddle to be solved."

"Dear God—is this the world you grew up in?"

"Yes, everyone did. My mother wasn't unique."

"Are you excusing her? Am I supposed to be comforted by your bigoted environment?"

"I'm just trying to capture it for you. Prejudices were spewed about every religion and nationality: blacks, Asians, Indians, you name it, but the Jews, yes. You have to understand our neighborhood used to be all WASPs, people like my parents, people my parents were friends with—they considered themselves 'broad-minded' because they were friends with Jews or in business with Jews but in private, there was no restraint.

"My mother was better than most in keeping quiet. She'd even reprimand other mothers in our presence. She thought it was 'unsavory'—"

"I don't want to hear anymore. I've heard enough. I get it. You were raised as an anti-Semite and now—now—I don't even know what you want from me—"

"That's what I'm trying to tell you—what I've tried to tell you for so long. Just because she is my mother doesn't mean that's who *I* am. I was never, ever like my mother or my brother!" he insisted. "The girl I told you about—the dancer—I never told you her name."

He told me now, staring out the window at the street below. "Her name was Tziporah. Her father was Israeli, her mother an Orthodox Jew. That's why she couldn't date me or anyone, why she was so shy, why she—she—"

"My God—then all of this—us—you and me—you've just been trying to repent for her."

"I've spent my life—I've spent my life, Emma, trying—trying to—"

"Trying to atone for your mother's and brother's sins? You've spent your life seeking a way out, and hallelujah, you found me!" I dropped my face in my hands and leaned against the wall. "You—you—everything was calculated: that night the four of us went out—the night of the gallery? What luck that I was Jewish! Oh, you'd fight for me then. You had to. No one could stand in your way, not even a fiancé. It didn't really bother you that I was with someone else. You had to have me for *yourself*."

He let out an acrid laugh. "Are you crazy? Do you really think I fell in love with you for that?"

"God, I thought I had left it all behind. I thought: here's real freedom, freedom from being constantly differentiated and compared and judged on some invisible scale of a stereotype no one has yet been able to prove to have any connection to reality. I thought: no, no, there's no anti-Semitism here in this country I love so much. Grandmother can't be right on this one.

"And then I met you—ah, I'd be with you, the quintessential blond tan American." I laughed forcefully, the pain in my chest constricting my voice. "With you, I'd wipe it all away. You'd cure me with your optimism, your idealism, your marvelous manners, your very smile. You were my escape, my puerile happiness. I was ready to forget, to give it all up. With you, for weeks on end, I couldn't remember a thing—joyous amnesia. That's why I never brought up Alex. I was reborn, a new person who simply didn't know these ugly things exist, ugly things that could only happen *there*, only *there*, but here—here you are!"

He closed his eyes and stood there, a befuddling image swaying in the winter dusk. "Here I am," he murmured. "I'm still the same man."

"Did you ever consider the possibility that your mother influenced your brother's seduction of Tziporah—that she pushed him to steal her?"

"I don't know—that seems extreme. Whose mother hasn't interfered in their relationship? I mean, look at your parents!"

"Don't you dare compare us—in my family it's all out in the open—"

"Like Alex's mother showing up? Don't tell me that wasn't sabotage."

"My grandmother was merely trying to protect me from the likes of your mother. She saw right through her—she didn't need a single English word to crack her open!" I paused, glaring at him with impatience and a loathing all my own. "Think about it—all it would take is one carefully planned night—for you to walk in and find your brother and girlfriend compromised. I think it's totally within your mother's repertoire—I think she enjoyed it."

"What are you saying—what are you implying—that my mother is downright evil?"

"Why not? Why, when there's so much evil in the world, why should you or I be spared? People talk about evil as if it's out there, removed from them, in the news or fiction, or faraway lands, evil in the form of death or torture. But what about furtive evil that lacks color and stage presence, that doesn't announce itself when it walks in but sows its roots inside your own home? Imagine being so close that you can't see it."

"My mother is many things but she's not evil—she's just misguided, backward—"

"Maybe, just maybe, she used the rivalry between you and your brother to get what she wanted—to get rid of Tziporah. And maybe, just maybe, she used what you told her about me—my sensitivities, you might say—to fire directly into my wound. Maybe she meant for me to hear her just as she meant for you to walk in on Tziporah." I shuddered as I spoke.

"I don't believe it—"

"It's not just about anti-Semitism—it's about power," I kept blazing on. "She's always wanted power. And which anti-Semitic tyrant throughout history didn't?"

"Impossible—impossible—you—with your dark past, your life, your pessimism about human nature—only you could think such a thing!" There was such agony in his face that I wanted to soothe it with a tender stroke, but I felt beaten, my extremities in too much pain to help another being.

"I'm not afraid to face the truth."

"I don't care about my mother," he said. "I've come here tonight to tell you that I want you back—I want us back."

I laughed uproariously. "You must be joking—you must realize that whatever compromises I was willing to make for you—all peanuts in comparison to the compromise I'd have to make now to bear your mother—"

"If I understand you correctly, my only option is to cut myself entirely from my mother."

"Like all children of abuse, you must realize that it's not your fault. Your mother, Eddie—are you listening to me?—your mother is not your fault."

"And do you—do you believe that? Can *you* see that she and I are two separate beings? You're the one who's always conflating children with their parents—"

"I was wrong—now all I see is children trying to claw their way out—"

"But failing miserably. Look at you tonight: maybe that's why you ruined your own masterpiece—that took you how many months to complete, how many years to conceive? Yet I couldn't help but think there was greatness in your act. Just like you destroyed us, you destroyed your painting. I realized too late that you're even willing to destroy yourself."

"Are you saying what I think you're saying?"

"I finally got it, I finally understood—"

"That night, at my parents' house, I wanted to lie down on the ground and beg your forgiveness but instead—instead only venom and lies came out."

"Then let *me* lie down on the ground and beg your forgiveness now."

"For what—for what, Eddie?"

"Because I didn't see it then, at that moment I was blind, blinded by them, by my mother, by you."

"And what is it that you see now?"

"That you were willing to kill us off. I didn't have it in me to imagine anyone—any woman—going that far. You forced me into thinking—into imagining—a vision of you in bed with him! And here's the crazy thing: I was willing to forgive you—"

"I know—if only—"

"If only it was before Maine—before you and I shared everything—"

"That was the thing that seemed so unbelievable—that you were willing to forgive me so much!"

"How could you do such a monstrous thing? And I, I treated you monstrously in return." He grabbed my hand and kissed it suddenly without giving me time to rip it away. "I should have known, I should have figured it out right then, at that moment—why couldn't I see it? Why didn't you tell me that night that you listened to my mother's bile—I would have known instantly that your only way out was to break me, break free of me. I would have known, asked myself the right question: can our love survive her hatred? But you didn't tell me—why? Why?"

"Because I was loyal to them—in that house, my family owned me, in that house, after hearing your mother, I had to end it?"

"But here you are back in New York, away from them: you came back to me—"

"I did—and you didn't want me."

"I want you now!"

"I never slept with Alex."

"I know. I was a fool to ever think it: that night in your parents' house, in a split-minute decision, you felled us in one swoop, leaving no breathing organ to revive."

He caught my hand in his and said, "We can build ourselves up from nothing, from nothing, Emma, we can start anew on a clean slate."

"We're too attached to our little spheres of suffering, Eddie, to ever find a clean slate."

"I'm willing to erase mine—I am—"

"It's too late, Eddie, what you told me just now—the fact that it's real—that it isn't just a phantom in my mind—but that your mother's hatred is real! God, I kept thinking, hoping: I'm imagining this, I'm overly sensitive! Even my sister didn't believe me, but you—by telling me the truth tonight—you've made it real."

"You yourself said that my mother and I are separate beings—"

"I understand the theory, Eddie. I didn't say I could live with it. I didn't say I could ever look into your face and not see her in it. I didn't say that when the time came and my anger at you for something ridiculous like the dishwasher, or our child's misbehavior, or whatever else might happen in our future, wouldn't end up in me calling you an anti-Semite."

"You wouldn't," he said with confidence. "You're smarter than that."

"I wish you were right"—I felt my voice quaver—"but when you've been damaged like me, there is a price to pay. You'll be so much happier with Melanie. I'm sure of it now."

"Are you telling me that if I hadn't told you about my mother's real views, that you'd come back to me? Are you telling me that I ruined everything by telling you the truth?"

"Yes," I said.

"That's impossible. Completely unfair."

"Yes, but that is the way it is. You cannot unsay it. I cannot undo how I feel *now*."

"No, I refuse to believe that." He held his ground. "Just give it time. With time, you'll let go of the pain."

I thought about the dissidents, the Jewish fighters decaying in the gulags, dying for us, for me. I thought of my grandfather being carted off by the KGB. I thanked them all silently, as I often did, for this spirited voice I now possessed, for my dancing legs and strong arms, for the courageous stomach that lunged forward into the great solitary unknown, and in the distance I saw my heart hanging in the air, bright and red as a rotting cherry, and ventricle by ventricle, I shut it off.

"Time won't cure me. Can't you understand: this thing, this anti-Semitism business is the mainstay, the all-consuming trope of my life."

"Then you have not transcended anything at all," he returned, meeting my gaze with defiance, "not your past, not your circumstances—then what was all this art for?"

"For the children who cannot speak," I told him with sudden calm. "Now you must leave me, Eddie. You must leave me and never come back. Do you hear me: *never*."

He stood there, helpless, motionless, like a child lost, not knowing what to do. I wanted to say "goodbye," or to give him directions—to help him find the secret passage out of my life—but there wasn't a word available to me without the incumbent tears. I don't know how long it took him to shift his shoulders and then careen blindly toward the open door. An unfamiliar doom in his expression tilted his shoulders forward, making him hunch over, and I thought with bitter humor that I had finally done it: turned him into a depressed Russian soul. I heard his body hit the stairwell, his feet tapping, each tap growing fainter, disappearing from my life. I couldn't see anything after that. The candles had burned out and traffic screamed from below, and tears gathered in my throat like a noose that kept tightening until I let them surface. They had been there all along, and only now, in his absence, I could let them cut across my scarlet face—my lugubrious gray rivers swallowed up in all that red.

Painting #8 (For a Future Installment)

I'm in my thick black *shuba* with an ear-flapped hat and a verdant scarf to match my eyes, running through an arch toward the sound of children screaming. Screaming, I tumble into a mound of snow and lick it with my tongue, imagining white honey. Laughter escalates and grips me, at once a cackle and a ballad, an echo piercing a dazzling, phantasmagoric sky. Winter's mirth can never live in spring or fall or summer; see winter's merry tears harden on my cheeks and lashes and carve ice flowers on my skin. Into clear ice I turn—into *Snegurochka*—the fair snow princess can only breathe in winter air and so, like her, my *shuba* is an iridescent gown and my fingers are bluish-white like royal gloves. My toes are numb inside transparent slippers, my black felt *valenki* have holes and leak, and in my ear, my grandmother's dulcet voice beckons: *come, Lenochka, come home* . . . The other children laugh and tackle one another, and suddenly their *shubas* glisten—we're all transforming into fairies sculpted out of snow. We spread out our arms and legs and succulent white flakes paint patterns on our faces, and our frozen fingers burrow into diamond quilts beneath our backs. We stare up at the sky and speak to distant planets: oh capitalist universes where Levi's jeans and booming color televisions and shapely Coca-Cola bottles grow like oranges from trees—what dost thou think of us? Our cheeks grow hotter, redder, our hearts are beating wild, our eyes are rapt in stars. Our breath is glowing in ribbons of white fire, and as it intertwines, it dances and melts our differences in snow. *Come Lenochka come home* . . .

Epilogue

Grandmother is delighted because my fiancé, Aaron, is Jewish and a heart surgeon, and because I'll be twenty-nine in a month and my headlong plunge into the swamp of spinsterhood seems to have been timely aborted. Thank heaven for Aaron, she exclaims, even as she criticizes him. He is too gaunt, she quips, like a reed in the Siberian freeze. Still he must never gain weight, she points out faithfully, because fat men with such small nondescript features tend to lose their looks completely, not to mention the pitfall of no longer resembling real men. Yet she has solutions (as she does for everything): all his *mishugas* would be cured if he only took a bite of her Holodetz (a traditional Russian meat jelly held together by pure fat). She applies succinct axioms to describe his personality, the most noteworthy being: a starving British hound, a misguided interloper, and an American Neanderthal (i.e., a prehistoric man with American manners). The latter, in particular, stems directly from a breakfast confrontation in which Aaron lectured Grandmother on the perils of her yolk-rich omelets and liver pâtés for her aging seventy-three-year-old heart. "Did he just guess 'seventy-three'? If I was seventy-three right now, I'd be dead." No one knew Grandmother's exact age, but her green card said she was closing in on eighty, and so Aaron, by supposedly deducing it, committed two cardinal sins against Russian womanhood: first, mentioning a woman's age, and second, doing so without mentally subtracting forty years from that number.

"Only mannerless dolts throw calories and cholesterol diseases at your face while you're enjoying your egg," Grandmother told him, which I fortunately had enough *sechel* to mistranslate. Still, even as she dissects and upbraids, Grandmother repeats her favorite motto: "no man is perfect, and Aaron like your father is—*tfu, tfu, tfu*—very, very close!"

I nod my head three times and consider the facts: under Aaron's supervision, I've gained calm, muscle tone, improved reasoning skills. He is superbly disciplined in keeping me healthy and sane: garlic and tofu for my circulation, cucumbers and papaya for my boldly sprouting wrinkles and cuckoo digestive tract, and wheat germ and macadamia nuts for my—we won't mention it—brain. Although he can afford it and he is no cheapo, Aaron has been limiting my intake of steak au poivre, Hungarian salami, and Beluga caviar on thick layers of butter and French baguettes. Because of his initiative and perseverance, I'm finally contributing to my heart retirement fund.

Aaron believes genius is not an inborn trait but one that is cajoled into existence; case in point: he is God in open-heart surgery. I admire his confidence, attention to detail, thorough knowledge of all medical subspecialties, and lectures on topics ranging from the Himalayas and the benefits of yoga breath to the preposterousness of having robots replace humans in open- heart surgery. Although Aaron was raised in a conservative Jewish home, and although his father's parents came to America to escape the pogroms in 1914 under the Tsar, he does not like to dwell on *my* Russia—he believes it is "BAD" as in "BAAAHAAAD" for my nerves and digestion. For during those early years of our courtship (when I was still recovering from Eddie and could not hold a paint brush between my two fingers without succumbing to a hiccupping hysteria), he would inundate me with Post-its, announcing my deadlines, pushing me to complete one painting and move on to the next. Aaron was used to patients. He gave me valium and Ambien and melatonin to help me sleep but I was inconsolable. He didn't seem to mind that I sometimes lost track of days, forgot what he said, wept at inappropriate moments, or closed my eyes temporarily during his lectures. Aaron saved me. I was able to paint and produce, and despite that voice blaring in my ear—"you're producing shit, SHIT"—people seemed to be buying. I even gained a permanent spot at the Nebu gallery—until two years ago, that is, when Aaron proposed.

In my studio, on 27th Street, nestled between 7th and 6th Avenues, I climb to the seventh floor of a non-elevator building and "work" on my paintings, work and procrastinate, pace the narrow workspace, a rectangle of gray linoleum and red-brick walls. A torn, filthy sheet from *ART* magazine hangs from a nail, as a quasi-muse and personal torturer. I stare at it when I paint and when I can't, a steady reminder of that tumultuous year. My face is compressed into a tiny square, my smile wide and intact. Beneath it a caption reads: "Children at Play, Out of Soviet Russia." I'm quoted as saying, "My family and I came to America at the height of the Cold War when Reagan called Russia the Evil Empire. It was very hard in the beginning . . . I'm so thankful to my family for always being supportive of my endeavors. They have always believed in my art."

The Hudson River shimmers in deceptive charcoal hues and echoes to me like a handsome stranger with lithe arms. I've known for two days. I find it impossible to eat, sleep, speak, or make love to Aaron. I've been puffing on Albuterol and Flovent all day, the greatest intake since the first official diagnosis of my asthma four years ago, since the first emergency room visit and the shock of learning I am chronically out of breath. The water is a black soft quilt mottled in white lights under a murky moon—is he an artist now? Has the world turned upside down? Why am I still moving? I hold the invitation in my hand as though it's poison: a four by six reprint of a photograph reveals a man's face fused with a computer screen, and beneath it, the title reads *The Modern Corporation.* Why are my feet hurrying to the traffic light, clicking against cobblestones, crossing alleys into the heart of Soho, to see this exhibit? Over four years have passed between us, and I have not forgiven him; I have kept, nurtured, sustained my rancor. In a red satin V-neck blouse hanging loosely over taut dark jeans and red suede stilettos, thick black eyeliner magnifying my eyes and my hair clasped in a stern French twist high upon my head, I look exactly how I feel—ferocious. But as I approach the gallery—a stunning open space whose glass walls and doors give one the feeling of swimming and breathing in turquoise water—my knees wobble and the stiletto heels bend untowardly and threaten to send me, face-first, into a gray summer puddle.

I inhale, exhale, think of Aaron, brace myself with yoga breath, then I enter. My eyes settle on the black-and-white photographs, which even from afar strike one with their surfeit of gray, their mundane, muted expression of everyday life in the cubicle. People are sipping champagne in skinny postmodern flutes and tiny heart-shaped hors d'oeuvres pass from tray to mouth. Then I spot *him*: a tall statue in black. He does not move. He appears as if he's been stranded on an island naked and people have suddenly begun to materialize from the surrounding bushes. He does not seem to possess the same ease, smile, laugh I remember. The face is gaunt and pale, and a stubble sits in uneven crescents on square sharp jaws. His eyes appear to have been repainted in blue charcoal, grown inscrutable in a sudden dusk. A black T-shirt covers a narrower body. The muscles on his chest have shrunk; jeans hang from his hips. He appears to my great amazement to resemble the typical artist-type; the banker's polish has been effaced, except for the closely cropped brown hair. Two men and a dazzling woman, in a fuchsia-hued dress and hefty silver earrings, circle him like three giant wasps.

"Everything is moving along marvelously. I'm pretty sure I just spotted Frank Grovel, *the*—I mean *the* IMAGE critic," the woman chirps.

"I hear the upstairs hasn't had much action," the young prim-looking man declares, and the other nods. "We need to get them up there—I still don't understand why you didn't have the nudes on the first floor—they're by far your best."

Eddie remains silent.

Stay calm, smile, appear happy, it's been a century, act like you're completely indifferent. I approach them and meet his eyes.

"Eddie," I say, then with a grin, "Ignatius."

"Emma," he says with a kind smile, "Lena—Lenochka."

"So you're an artist now?"

"Oh, no, I'm still a banker at heart—I'm just a photographer on the side. The only real question is whether I have talent."

We laugh, and I note with the coolness and objectivity of a floating observer that the intimacy is instant between us.

"I hoped you'd come," he says. "You look—you look stunning!"

"It's the red satin," I mutter, glancing at my shirt.

"It's not the shirt." He comes closer and I stagger from him.

"Let me introduce you to Edith—she runs the gallery." But Edith and the two men have been swallowed by the throng.

"So how did you become a side-dish artist?" I ask with a pinch of envy.

"This almost didn't happen," he says, blushing. "I was this close to becoming the CEO of Beltrafio Movers and Shakers." A nervous laugh erupts from his mouth, then quickly subsides.

"Wow—that would have made your mother very happy!"

"After I lost you, I lost the desire, the drive to make money. I remember it clearly: the Triploch-Fennimore merger. The deal on the table was a mess, not good for anyone. But I was told to urge the client to take it. We were punching insane hours, operating on autopilot. Everyone was nervous, gulping caffeine by the gallon, popping amphetamines, snorting coke. That's when things got weird, you know. People just got weirder. I looked into one guy's cubicle and saw him surfing porn sites and laughing out loud. Sylvia was doing her nails at three in the morning. Next day I brought my camera to the office and after midnight I started snapping whatever I saw—nobody cared—haggard faces would smile at me and I thought: this could be interesting . . ." He points at the wall, and inside a thick black frame, a young man's enormous profile backlit by a computer screen reads, "Voluptuous Vixens in Threesomes." Another photograph reveals a magnified paper cup of Folgers coffee on a stack of copied documents, dripping brown on the word

URGENT. Next to it, a man is slumped over his chair, his slumbering face fused with the keyboard; the clock above him flashes 5:00 am, and drool trickles from his parted mouth. Another is a woman's half-turned face, invoking in my mind Sylvia's profile; it is juxtaposed against a pyramid of people's names, earmarked by the date when they'll be laid off. The photographs are intimate, precise; their derision of corporate life is coupled with a burning, gray-hued melancholy.

But instead of praising him, instead of saying what simmered on the tip of my tongue—*you're so talented, Eddie*—I ask, "Did you ever marry Melanie?"

"How can you ask me that? You know I never did—you knew the last time I saw you."

"I knew," I say, smiling, retrieving the buried feeling of being wanted by him.

"And you—are you with someone?"

"Me—with someone?"

"Don't tell me—engaged once again—the perennial fiancée?" he cries out, his voice reeking of cynicism, judgment.

I recall my short spurts of independence from Aaron, our fleeting breakups when I'd bury my head in my studio and deny myself a future comforted by another soul, when loneliness would claw inside my stomach and bleed through its walls. I was a speck in a sea of unremarkable souls, seeking a way out of the ordinariness of life only to sink back into its warm, dark pouch.

I want to tell him about this ugly loneliness but instead I say, "This one's definitely headed to the altar—definitely!"

"Were there any other fiancés along the way?"

"Aaron and I have been together for four loyal years now," I say sternly.

"Impressive!" he returns with irony and raised brows. "Are you still painting?"

Am I still painting, am I still living, breathing, thinking, am I still Emma?

I look at him with all the sorrow and blame I had amassed for the last four years and cut him down. "Let's talk more about you—about your artistic transformation! There you were, snapping pictures at work, so what? How did you go from Norton's resident photographer to this?" I point at the walls, wanting to scream: what kind of a strange, unkind life is this—where one's world can so easily be turned upside down? Why did it seem so proper for him to be a businessman and me to be the artist? Was it the female-male ratio of properly weighed monies and professions, whereas now, *now look at me*—a novice on a beam, legs in a quake, arms uneven, my art dried up and his just starting to sprout a lover's seeds?

But he picked it up without hesitation or acridity. "I was at a client's house for this lavish dinner at this ridiculously gaudy Fifth Avenue apartment. The evening was going well. Same old bullshit—we're talking about restructuring and the stock price when the conversation turns to art. The guy is a dilettante art collector, under the illusion that he's some kind of a cultural phenomenon, and after dinner, he takes us on a little tour to showcase his collection. Most of it is modern kitsch and commercial crap for which he paid astronomical sums, but here and there I'd see a gem.

"Anyhow, that's when I saw it—your painting hanging over his library desk. I felt you in the room suddenly, saw you there with us, laughing and flirting with your eyes. I ask him, 'how did you get this?' 'Oh, my wife,' he says, 'bought it years ago for pennies at this small gallery in Soho and now I hear it's worth serious money. I hear the artist was picked up by the Nebu gallery, but now they're threatening to cut her off. She's quit cold turkey—barricaded her studio with cardboard boxes—who knows why—it's been two years since she's produced anything. Of course, that makes her paintings all the more valuable. Now how outrageous is the art world—tell me!'

"'How can you stand to look at that scene of horror, of torture every day?' I ask.

"He laughs in my face. 'All I see is a winter storm.'

"'The white light is a child,' I tell him, 'dead center where the hole is—that's a child being tortured.'

"'The hole is great—everyone takes notice of it, and the white light'—he laughs again—'that's no child—that's the winter light blinding us all to what's directly in front of us.'

"'And what's in front of us?' I ask.

"'Sex and money,' he replies, 'the Devil's handiwork—just look at that rotting bark and the red eyes—and tell me you haven't tasted your share of hell! Pure catharsis!' That's when I knew—" Eddie stops talking.

"You knew?" I ask, blood flooding my temples.

"This dinner, this guy, the expensive china and chandeliers, his plastic wife, the work I was doing, the spreadsheet life, the endless analyses I'd been preparing for years for Grant—I was locked in some of kind of perverse universe. I couldn't see myself at all, or what I saw, I didn't recognize—*I* had disappeared. I had enough money, God knows, I had enough. I didn't know what to do so I showed this guy my very first image and he bought it. He introduced me to gallery owners, gave me a foot hold and then it just fed off itself—slowly, I guess it's still slow—"

"I wouldn't say it's slow."

"But the whole time, the whole time I couldn't stop thinking about what he said, that you had stopped painting. I didn't know if you had gotten married and had children. Or if you had become fed up with the art world."

"No, no, not that," I murmur.

"Why did you stop painting?"

"Something happened, something that took time—once I got everything I wanted, once I saw my work hanging from those very same walls I once envied, my fingers and my mind stopped communicating with each other. Do you understand how terrible that can be? What I saw in my head wouldn't come out. But my decline was gradual—I didn't see it until I found myself wanting to cover up my paintings with a sheet. They repulsed me. Sometimes I imagined that the faces inside them were alive, and speaking to me, but I'd turn away and close my ears."

I stopped to breathe, to remember, but the paintings had been sold and I couldn't recall a single distinct color. "They were nothing more than emotional diarrhea—no thought, no care was going into them, just a dumping ground. The reviewers were right. They were concoctions of moods—colors badly blended together—they were chaos—"

"You're wrong. They were some of the best work I'd seen you do. Yeah, it was dark, it was misery. People may not have wanted to chew a carrot stick looking at them, but that was always your strength. I bought two of those paintings."

"Throw them out," I retort.

I remember painting during those months following the night at the Fern Gallery, mired in nausea—what paroxysms of inspiration there were then! That was when a miraculous synchrony brewed between my fingers and my mind; I couldn't stop sketching, imagining, layering paint on every conceivable white hole, couldn't stop even when the stench of turpentine would clog my throat, and my intestines would compress, as if someone were squeezing them through my esophagus and out of my nose. Up and down, my stomach rode like a tractor mashing my nerves, never giving me a moment's rest. "You shouldn't paint anymore," the doctor said, "it's bad for the child." The child? What child, I wondered, you mean the embryo, the blood vessel, the cell growing on my stomach's wall? But I stopped painting anyhow; I scribbled with my black-ink pens and markers, with pencils and charcoal-stained hands. Anything that still made images, that captured my confusion, elation, anger, that made sense of this state of growing new life inside my body, like an exotic flower awakening in a petri dish, with beautiful spiderwebs and fins for hands and a tail instead of legs.

"After I left you that night at the gallery"—he seems hesitant—"I imagined you'd paint it again—paint it anew."

"You mean my war against anti-Semitism?" I laugh absently, loudly.

"The transparent child from your past—don't you want to redo her?"

"I don't paint *that* because there's no fight left in me. I paint new things now—new—"

"Oh, I was hoping to see that painting recreated somehow, you see, I thought . . ."

"I know what you thought."

"What do you paint now?" He trembles from the sense that something hidden and lurid is passing before him. But when he tries to grip it, I only make it slip away faster. I wait—let the dull, painful punch of ignorance form a crater in his head, then I point to a crowd and say, "Where's everyone going?"

People are ascending a white staircase that coils into the second floor, and I move catatonically toward them. He follows me. Our ascent is slow, ponderous, conversations shut down as we stare at each other's backs, and I feel him in my hair—his breath weaving around my neck. The second floor is rectangular and claustrophobic; the lights are dimmer, sharper like pencils pointing at haphazard angles at black-and-white images. There, hanging on every wall, are parts of me. My collarbone leading up to my profile stretches for close to six feet and is the centerpiece of his collection. Disheveled hair is arrayed across a naked back. A torso cut between breasts and pubic hairs lies on a black sheet, capturing a quiver in the navel. A profile of one breast dominates a wide expanse of wall, the nipple protruding into space, pointy, aglow. Legs are spread apart as two male hands reach seductively over bent knees. A view from above reveals a naked body arching on a wooden floor, candles between the legs, inside the armpits, lighting up the back of the head, which is tilted backward, revealing a set of parted hungry lips. He took these pictures of me in Maine, all shot in a matter of hours, but to me they're cryptograms of his nature, resurrections of his vindictiveness and cruelty the last night I laid in his bed. His anger fills every image: the black shadows, crisp silver lines, excesses of light delineating and dissecting my skin—how my body parts scowl at me like recriminations!

I want to bury myself inside an industrial-sized garbage bag but nothing big enough presents itself. I feel the onlookers staring, judging, connecting me to the images on walls, and yet my mind is lucid enough to see that the photographs are vague, even universal, that they can be said to comprise an exegesis of a woman. The visitors are unaware of me; their eyes scan over my body parts in wonderment and stupor, reminding me of the wonderment and stupor of my own shows. Unhurriedly, their collective gaze travels to the opposing wall where—I can barely look, barely breathe—grim images of Russia assail me from every corner. Stalin's shattered bronze head, a vandalized Jewish cemetery with Nazi swastikas emblazoned on my ancestors' headstones, the entrance door flung open to the Moscow synagogue where I had once danced "Hava Nagila" in a circle of ecstatic Jews, guarded by soldiers and the KGB. At its epicenter, I'm confronted by an image of a street: a narrow sidewalk luxuriates in poplars and lavender trees, marking a path between a dense nature park and a red-brick building cast against a cloudless white sky. An arch opens at the entrance and there, directly above, a child beams from a balcony where I had once stood, her right hand pinned diagonally across her face—the pioneer salute. I recognize her at once; the proud hopeful gaze is mine.

"How did you do this?" I ask. "That's my street—that's Usiyevicha—is that me?"

"The picture you gave me when you were eight—I inserted it into this photograph of your building.

"First thing I did after I left Norton was travel. There were so many places I wanted to see—China, India, Israel, Russia. But when I got to Russia—to Moscow, especially, I found myself only wanting to find you." He glances at the photograph of the child and murmurs, "but you weren't there."

"I'm confused. Why did you expose me like this?" I say and bite my tongue.

"I needed to understand you—to *feel*—to feel what you felt—to feel your powerlessness—to feel everything I couldn't," he says, smiling strangely. "I couldn't touch or see you but I could recreate you in my mind. That's what I did here—there's no proof these images are you. But to me—they probably capture you more than—"

"Than the real me—"

"Only in the sense of what it meant for me. These images are as much about me as you—my gaze into myself. God, this is such grandiose bullshit—the truth is—the thing is that I needed to find a way to see you again." He grows silent, his lower lip trembles, but when he speaks again, his voice exudes strength. "I went to the Moscow synagogue and prayed. I prayed with the Russian Jews. I couldn't understand a word, but I bowed my head out of respect. People cried. I—I've wanted to see you for the last four years so that I can finally tell you—I had so much to tell you.

"I tried to contact you. Three years ago I came to your building and waited on the steps till ten or eleven o'clock. But you never came out. I left messages with your family. They were very gracious, by the way—"

"I know."

"One of the paintings I bought—is of a pregnant woman, her stomach transparent. Inside a child smiles, playing with the cord wrapped around its neck, while the mother weeps—is this about us?"

I'm confronted with an image of four arms—*our* arms—how had he managed it?—entwined on the opposite wall. I catch sight of a small empty room beyond the one we're standing in and I grab Eddie's arm and pull him there and close the door. The room is entirely white and empty, nothing stands, hangs, lives on its walls.

"Your mother is our puppeteer—our invisible master of ceremonies!" I say, with a shrill sadistic laugh. The two of us face the pristine white surfaces in the enclosed square space. I think in wonderment of all the secret rooms and bathrooms and galleries Eddie and I have used as our battlegrounds in love and war. "My mother?"

I feel calm again, the inner deadness spreading through my center, cooling my blood. "I don't want to say anything now unless it's the truth. The night we were together—the night of the drying and washing machines—" My voice winds down and I look at him, wondering if I should go on. "I got pregnant."

"You got pregnant," he repeats mechanically, as if he somehow knew.

"Of course, it took me a while to figure it out. I'd start vomiting every time I'd take out a tube of acrylic paint. But I figured it was because I couldn't get you out of my system. Literally, of course. When I went to the doctor, I thought he'd say, you're dying, your asthma is acting up; instead he said, 'you're not ill, my dear, just pregnant.' There was no one else—it was yours. My family went haywire. They were ready for another grandchild, but for me to have the baby alone was outrageous—a sacrilege. What would people say?" I erupt with sudden joy at the thought of their simplicity.

"Grandmother said that if I still wanted Alex, he'd take me back. No one wanted to hear my proposal: that I have the baby on my own as a single mother. It was the ultimate expression of my feminist ideals. I'd deny myself men altogether, I'd become an ascetic. Pregnancy made me strong, invincible, gave me the courage that my stupid single life never could.

"There were other men, Grandmother insisted, that we could fool; if they fell in love very quickly, that is, we could fudge dates of my conception. It was December 24th, Christmas Eve that I got pregnant, it was surreal. I even went on two or three blind dates, but at the end of each evening I would announce, 'I had such a lovely time, and I want you to know—by no fault of your own, I'm pregnant.'

"By then I was sporadically dating Aaron. He was so in love with me he didn't care that I was pregnant. He wanted to take care of my baby, to marry me instantly. But part of me was terrified—part of me kept thinking, if I have this child with Aaron, I'll be locked in, forever locked in—" I stop myself, fearing I've said too much, then keep going.

"But instead of making a decision," I go on, "oh, you know how I am: I procrastinated, and with pregnancy that's as good as saying I do. So by virtue of doing nothing I reached five months. Five months, Eddie—by then I was so in love with the baby I talked to him every day, and that's when—" I pause, and Mrs. Beltrafio appears as she was then, her serene face superimposed upon Eddie's.

"That's when I saw your mother at the Calm, on the Upper East Side. I went to get a prenatal massage—my back was already killing me—and of course it turned out to be your mother's favorite spa." It was the best place in the city for microdermabrasion, glycolic resurfacing, Botox. "If you think about it, it was inevitable that out of the thousands of spas in Manhattan I would pick the one that was your mother's."

The moment rushes at me with sudden hysteria and grit. I see her again: naked, confident, unembarrassed by her small breasts and bulging manly thighs, but her body is taut, young, perfectly sustained like her face. An air of satisfaction emanates from her gaze, exposing her signature smugness. Lavender oil glows on her stomach and forehead, and I'm bewilderingly drawn to her polished surfaces, imagining that if I peel them away, I'll discover a magical cave containing all the secrets to my soul. Why, why, I wanted to ask her, why didn't you like me? It was so simple and childish, this desire of mine, that I felt my whole being perspire with the need to know, with the shame of having been rejected by her. I tried to recall what Eddie said that night when he came to offer me his truth and salvation: "she liked you, she just doesn't like Jews." But it made me feel the rejection even more strongly, like a spear rammed deeper in *my* stomach, a warning to *my* baby that the world is callous, and without heart. The child kicked me as if he already knew.

"I hid behind the locker like a guilty teenager," I say, turning to him after a long pause. "I in my underwear, and your mother—in all her naked glory."

He stares at me with open lips that fail to emit sound.

"Your mother dressed slowly, methodically; she seemed in no great hurry until she saw me. Our eyes met and then she caught it—my protruding belly. But she looked only for an instant—an instant of recognition between us—and then, with that kindly smile she wears, she turned her head away." I breathe, I remember. "'Mrs. Beltrafio,' I cried at last, 'Cynthia, Cynthia.' I ran after her, hugging my towel to my chest, but she had vanished into the incense-thick air and I wondered if I had merely imagined her.

"But I couldn't have, you see, I couldn't have!" I keep talking even though it's becoming more difficult to enunciate words, thoughts. "She was everywhere, you see, her scent, her face—I felt her on me—did we speak? I can't remember now. Did she say, 'Oh Emma, what a surprise to see you here. Congratulations are in order! How many months?' I could feel the baby grow so still as if he had already guessed his future. The pain of having lost you came back to me—and it stung again and again—how unfair life was, how stupid we were, how this baby was bigger than that, bigger than us. The magnitude of it all overcame me and I held my head in my hands with a full understanding of what I—then someone tapped my shoulder and asked if I needed a glass of water—I was dizzy—so dizzy with all these realizations—"

"But why didn't you come to me? Why did you let her in?" he cuts in, but I only see a stranger trying to cough my entire life out in one breath.

I begin to speak but my voice cracks and tears cloak my eyes. I want to tell him that this skin, my skin isn't skin but gauze—permeable silk that doesn't sheathe my body but acts as a conduit for the world outside, letting it stream in: there are no barriers or blockades here. There's fear too, my curse—my truest Russian emotion, palpitating in red, so grotesque and hidden, so deep-rooted that I don't recognize it anymore. Like a stingray, it sits dormant in my blood and when it strikes I'm unconscious, unable to intercept its deadly sting. Only later do I understand, only later do I imagine a different life.

But I suck my tears in and with sudden calm I explain away *this*, *this* unchangeable life: "What's done is done."

"Where's the child?" he asks.

"Child?" I tap my tongue on "d," hoarsely, barely. "Oh, Eddie. That night there was a terrible wind—a typhoon, really. It was June, a warm summer storm had descended on the city and I wanted to walk a little. I always loved rain, you know. But suddenly trees started to bend and trashcans flew through the air and the tiny drizzle turned into blinding rain. I couldn't see anything—a yellow cab came out of nowhere and I was lifted off the ground, I was flying . . . then I looked up and I was splayed on the ground in spectacular pain, bleeding. That night I lost the baby." I pause for a moment to let him absorb it, then without tears I sum it up. "Who knows why it happened! Was it my weakness—my weak fucking mind? Grandmother blames the cab driver, my mother your mother.

"I've gone over it a thousand times, but it doesn't change the fact—the pain—"

Pain contracts my stomach with the intensity and horror of that night, and I'm losing it again. The white walls of the hospital reappear and I'm there again in the emergency room, on the operating table, suspended in my comatose sleep. When I opened my eyes, they tell me it was a boy.

The wind blows at me now and the cab I never saw honks and Mrs. Beltrafio cradles my head in her immortal arms, and I blame them all for the cell, the embryo, the child I lost out of frailty and weakness, out of the powerlessness of youth. But most of all I blame us, him and me, for the pain we couldn't put aside. Hatred curdles upon my gauze-like skin. He meets my gaze without flinching, and only when I see *his* pain, crawling like black tar over his gleaming pupils, do I forgive him with a kindness and ease I've never known before.

"I'm so sorry," he whispers. His head hangs and his entire torso collapses, sliding against the wall. "I had no idea."

"I wanted it that way," I say. "I couldn't have borne it—first you returning to me out of guilt, then even worse, out of pity."

"Is that why you turned me away at your showing—because you thought I didn't truly love you?"

"Why couldn't you love me just for me, not the Russian-Jewish-me but for the Americanized-me—for the Emma-me, for what we alone had between us?"

"How can you say such a thing—I loved you for all of you—I still love you."

"It doesn't matter"—my voice splinters—"it doesn't matter now because I'm here—I'm here only because I know nothing of you remains." I point at my heart.

"Are you painting now?"

"In a sketchbook, I make notes, paintings I'm planning—planning as I plan the wedding."

"Back to your old cage?" he thunders. His eyes lift for an instant, then retreat to the floor. "Why are you marrying this person—this person who has zero insight into you?"

I clear my throat. "I came to you once—to *your* building. It was after you had come to me. I had a perverse curiosity."

I recall the whiff of the sultry spring air as I pried my window open and saw him approach. At first I imagined he was lost, but he sat down directly beneath my window, three floors up. He remained in a perfect stillness, as if gripped by some apocalyptic epiphany. Only minutes passed but they felt like hours before he rose and faced our buzzer. He pressed the button next to my last name, scrawled next to Aaron's. The sound rang through the apartment like an ambulance, its persistence smothering me. I couldn't move, couldn't lift my arms or legs, couldn't pick up the phone—Aaron was on call—I was alone and alone I neither ate nor drank; I sat at the window watching him till he left.

The next day I broke up with Aaron. "I'm too wild," I announced, "I can't commit—I can never be the wife you need or want." "You're being preposterous," Aaron repeated again and again as if my resolve had turned him into a drone. I packed my bags and went to stay with Stone, and during that week when my very breath seemed to have been allotted to my body in stingy rations, I went to Eddie's building to see him. I only managed to touch the glass door with my nose when I saw him with another woman in the lobby. She had brilliant, fiery red hair, the sort of red that appears flammable, that's all I remember of her. They were laughing and leaning coquettishly into each other, and he appeared to my stunned eye to be unapologetically happy—happier, I thought bitterly, than me. No, he had not come for me! He had come for more forgiveness, more truths, for yet another salve to lay across the ancient wound between us; only his was still festering and bloodied by guilt, the guilt his mother wrought and that he now bore on her behalf because she had none.

He was engaged again, or perhaps he was married, I berated myself, and ran from the lobby. I didn't want to ruin it for *her* the way I had ruined things for Melanie, ruined it for Sylvia, and within a few short hours, I had returned, breathless and contrite, to Aaron.

"Who was the redhead?" I reveal myself, wearing my jealousy like a turban on my head.

"What redhead?"

"I saw you with her in your lobby—after you had come to me, only a week later, only a week later you were with someone else," I accuse him now despite a renewed commitment to calm, "and you looked so happy!"

"Redhead, redhead—I can't even remember—I didn't date any-one for a while after that. I was happy—happy because I was finally free—free to be with you. I wanted to run and tell you everything. I finally confronted my mother and my brother—we fought and yelled and said all the things people never recover from. Then I left and haven't returned since. I've never breathed easier, never felt better. You were right—to liberate me." He steadies himself as anger overtakes him. "Did you ever consider the possibility that this redhead was just someone who lived in my building? Or someone else's guest? Why didn't you come up to me? Why didn't you ever trust me? For God's sake—your stupid pride!"

"Yes, I thought the worst—"

"Because you always think the worst—because—because—why couldn't you see that I loved you—why were you so blind?"

"Doesn't matter anymore, does it? None of it matters. I've come tonight to say goodbye."

"You've come because *you* want *me* to let you go," he says with sudden rage, "*you* want *me* to say *I* am moving on."

"You owe me that."

"For what—for having kept the most important fact away from me, for not giving me a chance to make a life with you—to have that child? I would have wanted our child!"

He's on the verge of something more, but nothing comes—nothing but a groan, some kind of strange animal sound that I can't name. I rush at him as he manages, "Why—I—I—" and pin his wrists against the wall. My mouth is on his lids and lashes. I drink his tears as they swim over my nose and cheeks and like transparent serpents run down his neck. I can't see him anymore; I only feel his moist breath permeate my skin. And our lips, from habit, from memory, from ancient longing, find each other with alacrity and ease. We cling to each other in agony. And as we sway in the airless white room, I see in my mind my own eyes glaring at me from the empty walls—accusatory pools of black—and pull away. "My sweet Ignatius," I say, pulling further and further away, "we'll be all right."

"We're past everything, you and I"—he speaks with urgency as if I might dissolve—"guilt, marriage, family, even—what did you once call it—our little spheres of suffering! We're past everything, Emma, and that's why we can do anything now—"

"You're free, but I'm not," I say quietly.

"Because you're engaged again," he reproaches me, laughing brokenly.

"I have to go," I say, my heart drumming. I open up the door of the small square room and burst out into the white purified space of the gallery, where my body parts—legs, breasts, pelvis, mouth, hair—stare at me from walls. I nod at myself and run out and down the corridor, down the winding staircase, I tip-tap-tip-tap-top down in my red stilettos, hoping not to tumble or fall. He runs after, his feet are tapping too, echoing my footsteps. We're downstairs where we began, in neutral corporate space, squashed between people.

He stares at me with defiance. "Can't you see that we're stuck in a circle—we keep repeating our mistakes—" He grabs my hand and, on the invitation that seems to have been welded into my palm, writes out an address. "After the show, meet me here—it's my new place. I don't live in the loft anymore. I'll be waiting."

"Waiting—how long is that?"

"We've been given another chance. It wasn't closure you sought, it was me. Tonight is our chance to rewrite the past."

"To rewrite it? No, that's not possible!" I protest. "Why would I even want to—these are my scars to wear upon my face—"

"You're even more beautiful now than I remember," he whispers.

But I'm immune to flattery now—it only glides on the surface but doesn't penetrate my heart. I take a breath and end it. "Nothing you say will make a difference. I will not hurt Aaron. I'm getting married in a matter of months." A debilitating melancholy cuts off my speech and the black-and-white images dissipate into a blinding grayness. I smile at him and shift unsteadily and click my heels with sudden resolve and walk across the wooden gallery floor and out the glass doors I run. I'm on the dusty street and trucks honk and cabs swerve maniacally and he is behind me, here, catching his breath.

I stop and turn to look at him and listen.

"It doesn't matter if you marry Aaron or anyone else because ultimately you will always be with me. The year we met something incredible happened and it has bound us for life—"

"Your mother would have sent me to the gas chambers if she had a chance! Can't you see how that makes everything *still* impossible?"

"Haven't I made it clear? I've cut my mother off. You will never need to see her again. I will always, always protect you!"

"You don't get it. I don't want your protection. Do you know what I didn't tell your mother at that lunch? My favorite Shakespearean play is actually *The Merchant of Venice*. 'Hath not a Jew hands, organs, dimensions, senses, affections, passions . . . If you prick us do we not bleed? And if you wrong us shall we not revenge?' What *babkus*! What about the end, the fact that Shylock's daughter is marrying the guy who wants to ruin him, and a gentile at that. As if Shylock would feel honored by such a match! What supercilious, superiority-ridden gentile bullshit! Shylock wants to be merely acknowledged as being human but by no means equal. That's not enough for me—that's a pittance if you ask me. I don't want these degrading sympathies! I want to be the one wearing the crown and the armor. I am the queen and the soldier all in one, choosing my life, my path—I am no one's servant girl in need of proving myself—"

"Are you sure about that? This new blissful domesticity you've mapped out for yourself—with this Aaron character—does he know any of this about you? You've withheld and manipulated and sugarcoated for him—you've told him nothing! What a fantastical creature you've given him! You're lying once again on a large scale—by omitting the truth."

"No, I've merely laid down my weapons. I've said yes to simplicity, contentment, to the normal life."

"Ah, again the fear of humanity—of trust—rears its ugly head! Is this your so-called reign? As far as I can see you've indentured yourself for life."

"At least it's an honorable prison."

"Imagine what I've imagined hundreds of times in my head: us five, ten, fifteen years into the future, and we're both married with children and we bump into each other accidentally or on purpose—doesn't matter—and the old spark returns. We'll have an affair or if we don't, we'll think about it—we'll want to—that's what matters. And we'll cause greater pain to more people—our spouses, even our children."

"Not if we never meet—not if we never, ever meet again."

"Listen to me, Emma, my mother's ruined lives.

"I told you about myself and my brother, but I didn't tell you the saddest story of them all—the story of Tziporah. After her parents found out about her 'sin' with Andy, they married her off to a Hasidic man thirty-two years her senior. She lives with him in New Jersey; she has six children. I wonder sometimes, does she still dance in her pajamas with her children or is that too painful . . ."

"Too painful," I reply.

"With me you'd still be painting."

"I don't need you to save me, Eddie—I am no Tziporah. I can save myself."

"Don't you hear what I'm asking for: I'm asking *you* to save *me*, Emma. Save me!"

He holds out his hand and I put mine in it and feel him pressing his heart into my palm—do you hear it, he seems to whisper—do you hear it bleating? We do not look at one another: our lips, our eyes are shut. It is only when I hear him say, "We can be happy, Emma, like we once were," that my hand breaks free and my feet carry me across the street, and I'm breathing the fire of possibility, and it stings and dances on my tongue. I don't feel my red heels click against the cold asphalt stone; I don't see the traffic lights before me. I run to the river with my eyes closed—to the house of white dresses and lost brides. I am among them. We're all Cinderellas at the royal ball—magicians, illusionists, dreamers. We don't see the prince, only ourselves, only the vision perfected over time: white lilies and orchids, white laced veils, white four-tiered cakes, white and luminescent like the silk that sheathes our expectant aroused bodies. I'm in the silk of crème, not white, not entirely virginal, but of the virgin's mind. A wreath of leafy vines and lush purple irises sits upon my russet head and sprouts teething branches from my hair. A rosy sheen of gloss sparkles on my lips and slippers shape my feet; they're made from stone or glass or flesh, I cannot tell, and I'm skipping on black waves, held up by other Cinderellas. The ghost brides are galloping like wild steeds, confused, disjointed, disconnected, and I'm among them.

We're here in the middle of the night, and yet it is *our* day— the day the sun is blistering and yellow-hot and summer calls all wild creatures out to marry! For solidarity, for strength, for will, for pleasure, for children, for the future, for sacrifice, for love—his address sticks to my wet palm and drips, imprinting ink onto my skin. And lest I lose it on this tumultuous, ink-blue day, I memorize the number, street, and corner: will I go there, tonight, I ask the pink industrial sky.

I start to walk, then run, my stilettos push into my toes, indent my tender skin. I take one shoe off, then the other, the pier's cold cement stings my bare feet . . . the river beckons to me. The winds and waves hold hands and sing and lure me under, under the surges. Water lashes out in spurts, in plumes of foam, crashing against cold cement, crashing against me. I'm soaked in the river's angry lashes, soaked in polluted water. I'm at last alone, naked, devoid of will, of ego, of preconceptions, freed from the claws of some primordial past that lived within me, the claws of morality and duty, those ancient schisms of good and evil that strove at will to vilify the nerve-endings of desire, to stamp out a woman's longing at her central spinal root! As if to surgery, I hand my body over, present it in blue cloth, under the general state of numbness, knocked out by the fist of anesthesia, lungs spastic, devoid of vitality, of lucid breath—is that what asthma is? Is that why I still have it, this disease of guilt, of obligation, of contrition? With each act of longing, with each paroxysm of desire, the fear sets in and swathes subversive words in spit, in mucus floods that permeate the nostrils, mouth, and throat, that occlude your vision. And if you dare to speak, instead of sound, a cough appears, a grating whirr, a barely audible orchestration of the larynx and vocal cords spewing from swollen lips, revealing your humiliation, your state of gutlessness, your courage stunted—was I ever breathing?

I see them: the faces of my women—Mother, Grandmother, Bella, great-grandmothers, great-great-grandmothers, my past and present—the living swimming with the dead. I see my blonde-haired great-great-grandmother who gave birth to eighteen children, who lived through Tsars and Cossacks, through pogroms and rapes and Stalin's collectivization of Ukraine, through starvation and oppression, through prison and gulags, through the loss of fifteen children, through the loss of husband and sons and daughters. I see her daughter, my direct lineage, my grandmother's beloved mother dying from diphtheria in the mansion Stalin's henchmen re-appropriated to the peasants, depriving my family of their dignity, their will. They now lie across the attic floor, how many of them in unwanted intimacy, their suffering I cannot fathom, and yet I am certain I was there among them. I see humiliation scattered across my soul like the infected molded bread crumbs in my great-grandmother's mouth and I see her, my eight-year-old grandmother weeping, feeding her mother poisonous bread crumbs, thinking she's saving her from hunger, hungry herself, not knowing that she's killing her mother, lying for days next to her mother's dead body, weeping, "Wake up, *mamochka*, wake up, why won't you wake up?" I see death fly in through half-open windows, through the cracks in the attic, in the hot starving summer of 1931, when people lived on ashes and there was no time to love, to write, to paint, to think of culture, to fantasize of riches, to dream: you barely existed—existence as survival. I see history, my history, coiled into the history of nations, stretching across the particular weave of my double-triple identity, from East to West to the Jewish Diaspora. And suddenly my pain seems innocuous, insignificant, inferior in this interminable web of suffering, of human wars. We are alone, abysmally alone. What is this being we call "myself" or, in my native tongue, "Ya"? What is "Ya"?

The river beckons to me now and I lean in, closer, closer, a blur of waves and memory and women, and I want to swim under the surges, swim among the dead. And Death appears like Beauty, a purple-blue-green goddess with perfect features in a swaying lilting shape, a thing of water seamless and seductive, smelling of algae and blue-green moss, perched at the mouth of the river. "Come in," she whispers, "come in, I'll soothe your pain, I'll plug the holes in your heart," and in that moment, she's the *relief* to my unexamined acts of living—for I was always in the act of dying! Paralyzed, plugged, asthmatic, stuck in cages of my own making or the cages built for me by others, always trapped, always yearning, never doing, never leaping, never living. Death as relief! Death as the river: tall, lithe, rising, defying gravity, facing me like a mother-mirror, a sinewy black reflection of the bridal dress. For this weave of pearl silk and lace, this symbol of purity, commitment, sanctified desire, entangled in one cloth, is a cage, my cage, the cage I had been put in, kept in, the cage I walked into and stayed . . . How long have I been here? How old was I when I first walked in? The river roars and spits upon the dress and turns the crème into rancid gray and putrid green, and colors bleed into each other, altering me from within. *I* will the dress to change—to wither—to succumb to mud! *I* mangle its static bodice, its voluptuous hoop skirt. *I* demand that the cloth is no longer silk but a mottled brown rag, devoid of luster, shine, color. *I* dissolve the glass slippers. And from my head, branches fall to earth and re-sow roots beneath my bare feet, feet bound by gravity, by dirt. I'm of the dirt. I unload all of me: my memories, my failures, my happiness, my love, my rage, my suffering, my implacable dancing heart—empty but I holler "free"—into the river's gurgling, snaking void. Until I'm just a sketch painted on an ashen sky, inviting image after image in, traversing empty plains of my mind, and there a paintbrush stands and paints me in, not as I've been, but as I dream: reborn upon the canvas, I am myself, the incarnation of my stubborn will.

"Emma." I hear a voice inside my head—it's him.

"Eddie," I say. "You're here?"

His laughter vanishes, his eyes grow cryptic, grim. "Why did you come tonight, tell me the truth—I mean, why did you come to my opening?"

"It's so simple, really. I simply wanted to see how you look, what you smell like, what you're wearing. I didn't want anything from you but simply to see you."

"What did you think?" he says, laughing. "How did I smell?"

"Like an artist, like you hadn't showered," I answer, laughing, pausing. "Like you weren't you."

"I was putting the images up on walls, I couldn't sleep. I must have switched the locations a thousand times. I thought you'd laugh at me—that I had suddenly become an artist, that you'd think I was a fraud."

"But still you wanted me to see you?"

"Yes, I wanted you to see me, see that I was more than what I once was, that I was more deeply connected to you than I had ever imagined—or you." He gazes at me strangely. "I saw it, saw you coming, envisioned your face, your clothes, the contours of your body. I watched the glass doors religiously all evening, but when you actually appeared—I gasped."

"You did? Why?" I smile casually, but his words clutch my heart.

"Because you were more beautiful than I had remembered you, but this new beauty was harder, somehow—oh, I don't know—there was new sadness in you."

"There is always sadness in me."

"Yes, but this new sadness and your beauty—your face—it was . . ."

"It aged, that's all."

"It cut across the room, your eyes cut across the room. Like you had suddenly become inaccessible. That's what I meant to say, your old sadness was kinder, approachable even. Sometimes your old sadness seemed to invite people in. Your new one encircled you like a wall."

"Because it is a wall."

"In the first few moments of seeing you I thought I'd never get the courage to speak to you, much less say what I had planned to say."

"So you planned to say all that in advance?"

"Yes, of course, I practiced." He pauses.

I laugh.

"I practiced how I'd win you back. I practiced what to say. But when I saw you—I wondered if it'd be better to say nothing. I wondered if I could just stand next to you in silence and we wouldn't speak, and you'd figure it all out."

"I did figure it all out, but I was engaged."

"You 'were'? As in past tense?"

"Yes," I say tentatively because even though I haven't called Aaron yet to break up with him, I know I will. I've memorized the words I'll utter in the breaking. I know I will never return to him, and Eddie knows this too: he reads *this* in my eyes.

I look at Eddie now, with full force, with my knotted throat, with tears swelling, bursting out of my gaze. "No marriage, Eddie, just us, from now on, just us—day by day—moment to moment."

"Moment to moment."

"You made me happy every day that we were together," I say. "Can you make me happy today and tomorrow and maybe the day after? That's all I ask."

Tears spring to his eyes but he holds them in.

"We've lost so much time," he murmurs and then lets go.

"Only four years, but look at what we found," I say.

"What?" He caresses my hair and pulls strands away from my face and runs his finger down my neck across my collarbone and lingers there, above my breasts. And then he kisses them, each breast, lightly, gently, with inexplicable tenderness, as if I might crumble if he exerts more force. I cup his face inside my palms but he can't look at me anymore; he buries his head in my chest and sobs. And I sob in return and he drinks my tears off my skin and clothes.

We stand in silence sobbing in each other's arms, mourning the loss of time, of tenderness, of fear and pain and pleasure—the loss of love's intricate joy.

I speak at last. "You were right about what you said in the gallery: no matter where we go, how far we run—we'd return here." Entwined in his body, I press him closer and closer to me till there's no space left between us. "Because we didn't understand then what we understand now . . . because this is all that matters, because I didn't understand, Eddie, it's me! I didn't realize I wouldn't be able to breathe . . ." And I can't breathe now because I'm buried in my tears, in my mucus, in my suffusions of feelings, my asthmatic lungs swelling and contracting to the silent beat of impatience burrowing through my blood. Through a blur I see my tears trickle down the pier's cold cement and into the mouth of the river, and quietly I say, "Everything I've said to you about myself, the things I said that matter so much to me: my family, my ancestry, my Jewishness, my Russianness, my suffering, this—this interwoven identity I have treasured and nurtured and kept, kept up—it will always stay with me no matter what."

"Yes," he whispers, kissing my wet eyes, face, mouth, "yes, stay no matter what."

"I said those things to you because there in the gallery I was breathing again: I was breathing again, living again, because I was with you again, and I didn't realize that, I didn't realize it until I ran out here, to this river and threw away my shoes and saw my past lives flash before me . . . I didn't realize that I can't breathe—can't live—can't survive this life if I don't have—if I don't have love—if I don't have you."

He simply nods.

And then he whispers, *"Ya lublyu tebya . . . Lena, Elena, Lenochka."*

I smile.

"You finally learned what it means."

"Yes," he mutters, "I finally learned—late, but I did finally learn."

"So am I, I am also very late!" I'm quick to reply, my heart is pumping faster, faster, my mouth goes dry, but I say it, I still say it with courage. "I love you, Eddie, Edward, Ignatius, I love you even more."

A cool breeze dances on my skin and on his skin and his breath slows down, and so does mine, and for an instant we stop breathing altogether. The air is humid and prickly and leaves rustle on bending croaking trees and the wind speaks in human monotones. And when we gulp it in, this unity of air and wind and water floating between us—we breathe more, live more, want more . . . and *there* on that river's edge where death meets life and ancestors swim on polluted streams and languages mingle and crisscross identities and open trapped doors and release imprisoned souls—*there*, he lifts me from the ground and holds me in his arms and beams his golden smile . . . I'm barefoot and wet and free. And he—*he* balances my body on his arms and carries me for seven city blocks and brings me to the footsteps of his brownstone and opens up the door and together we cross the threshold.